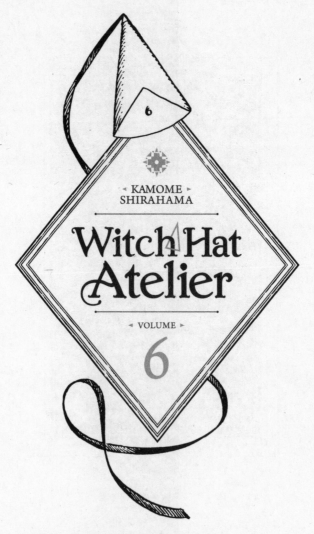

KAMOME
SHIRAHAMA

Witch Hat Atelier

VOLUME

6

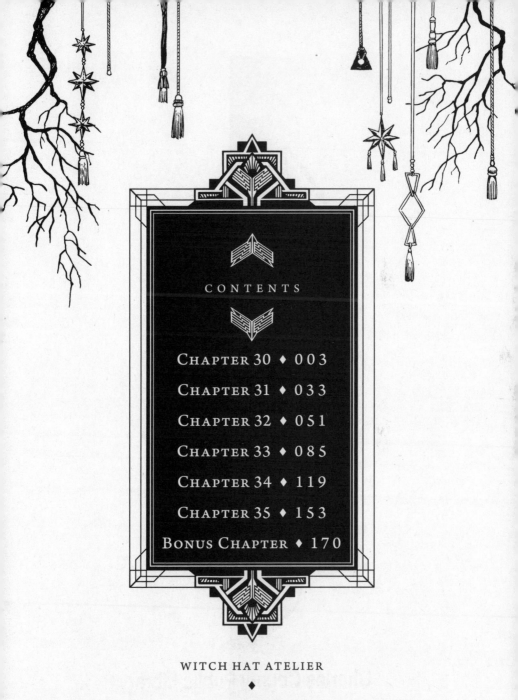

CONTENTS

WITCH HAT ATELIER

♦

KAMOME
SHIRAHAMA

CHAPTER 30

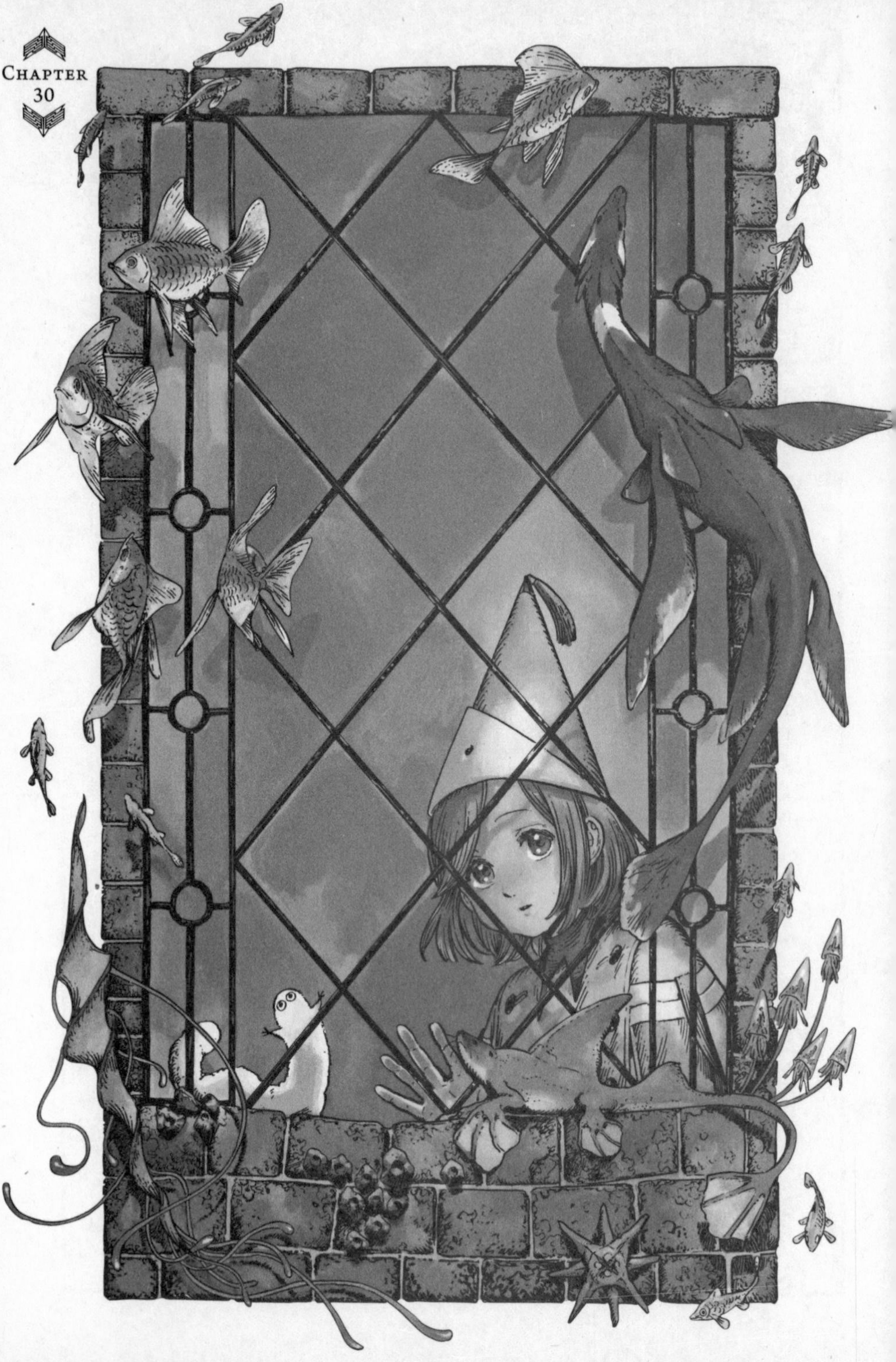

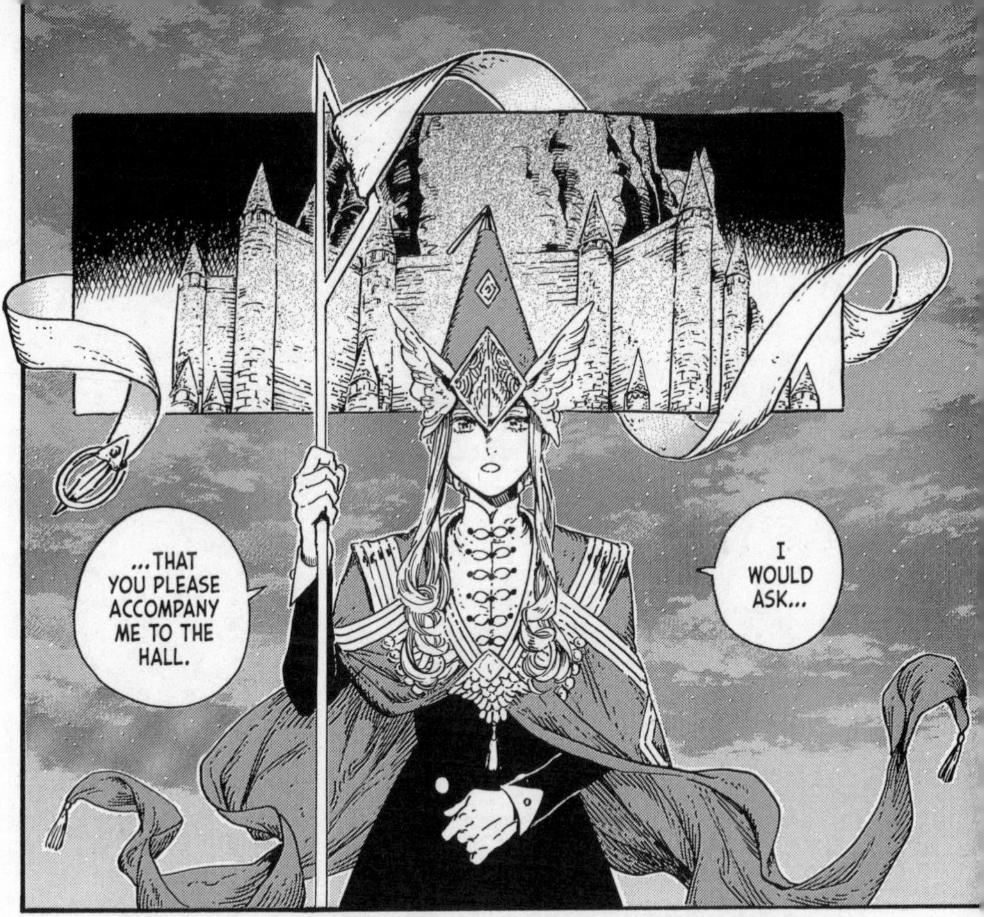
I WOULD ASK...
...THAT YOU PLEASE ACCOMPANY ME TO THE HALL.

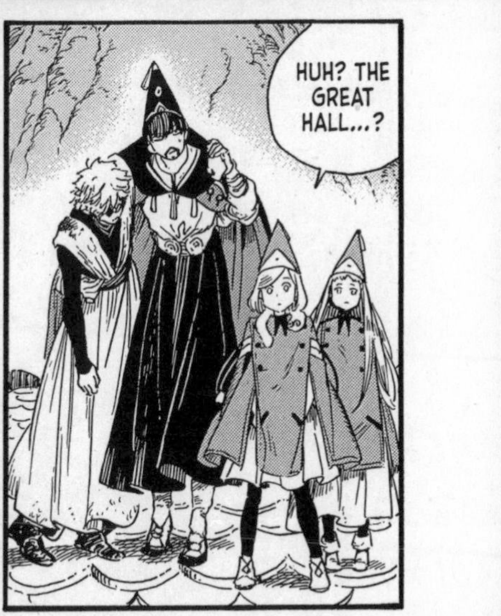
HUH? THE GREAT HALL...?

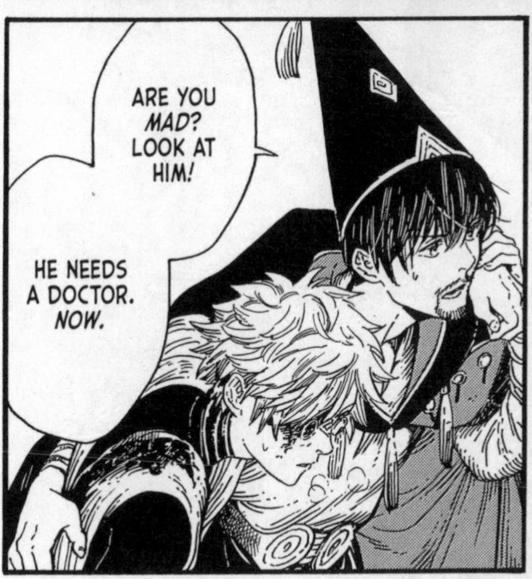
ARE YOU *MAD*? LOOK AT HIM!
HE NEEDS A DOCTOR. *NOW.*

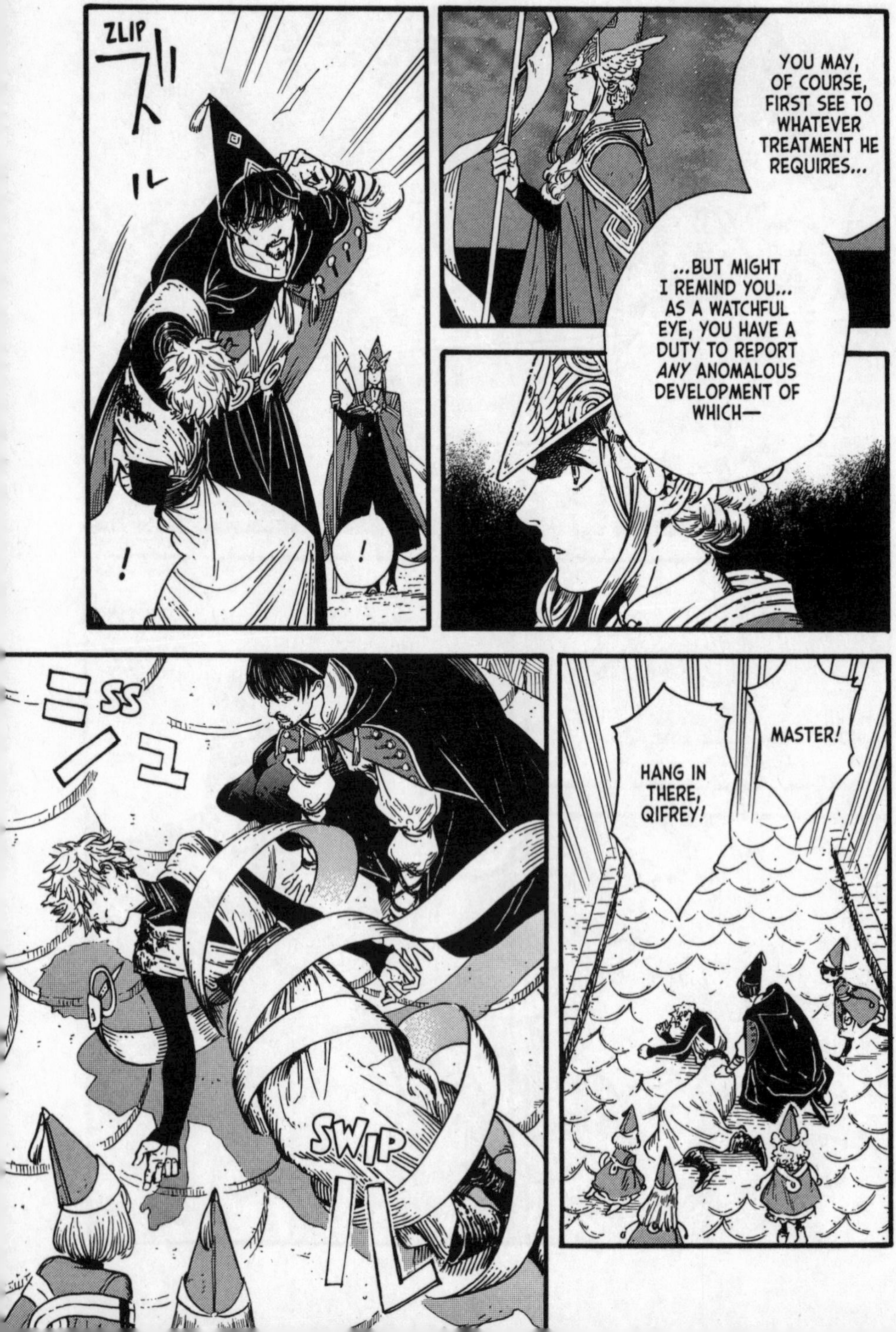
YOU MAY, OF COURSE, FIRST SEE TO WHATEVER TREATMENT HE REQUIRES...
...BUT MIGHT I REMIND YOU... AS A WATCHFUL EYE, YOU HAVE A DUTY TO REPORT *ANY* ANOMALOUS DEVELOPMENT OF WHICH—
ZLIP
ズル
!
!
MASTER!
HANG IN THERE, QIFREY!
SS
SWIP

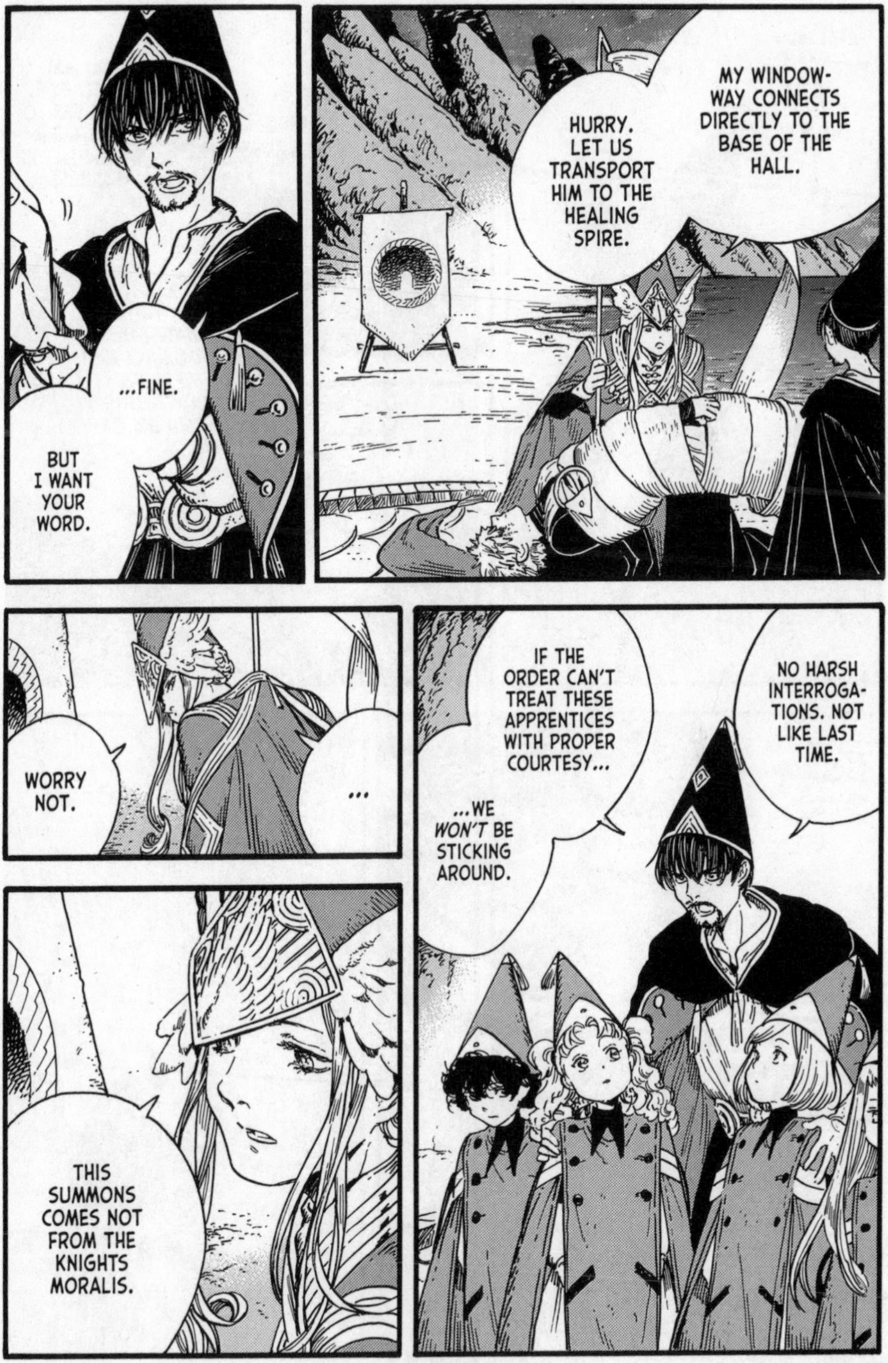
MY WINDOW-WAY CONNECTS DIRECTLY TO THE BASE OF THE HALL.
HURRY. LET US TRANSPORT HIM TO THE HEALING SPIRE.
...FINE.
BUT I WANT YOUR WORD.
NO HARSH INTERROGATIONS. NOT LIKE LAST TIME.
IF THE ORDER CAN'T TREAT THESE APPRENTICES WITH PROPER COURTESY...
...WE *WON'T* BE STICKING AROUND.
...
WORRY NOT.
THIS SUMMONS COMES NOT FROM THE KNIGHTS MORALIS.

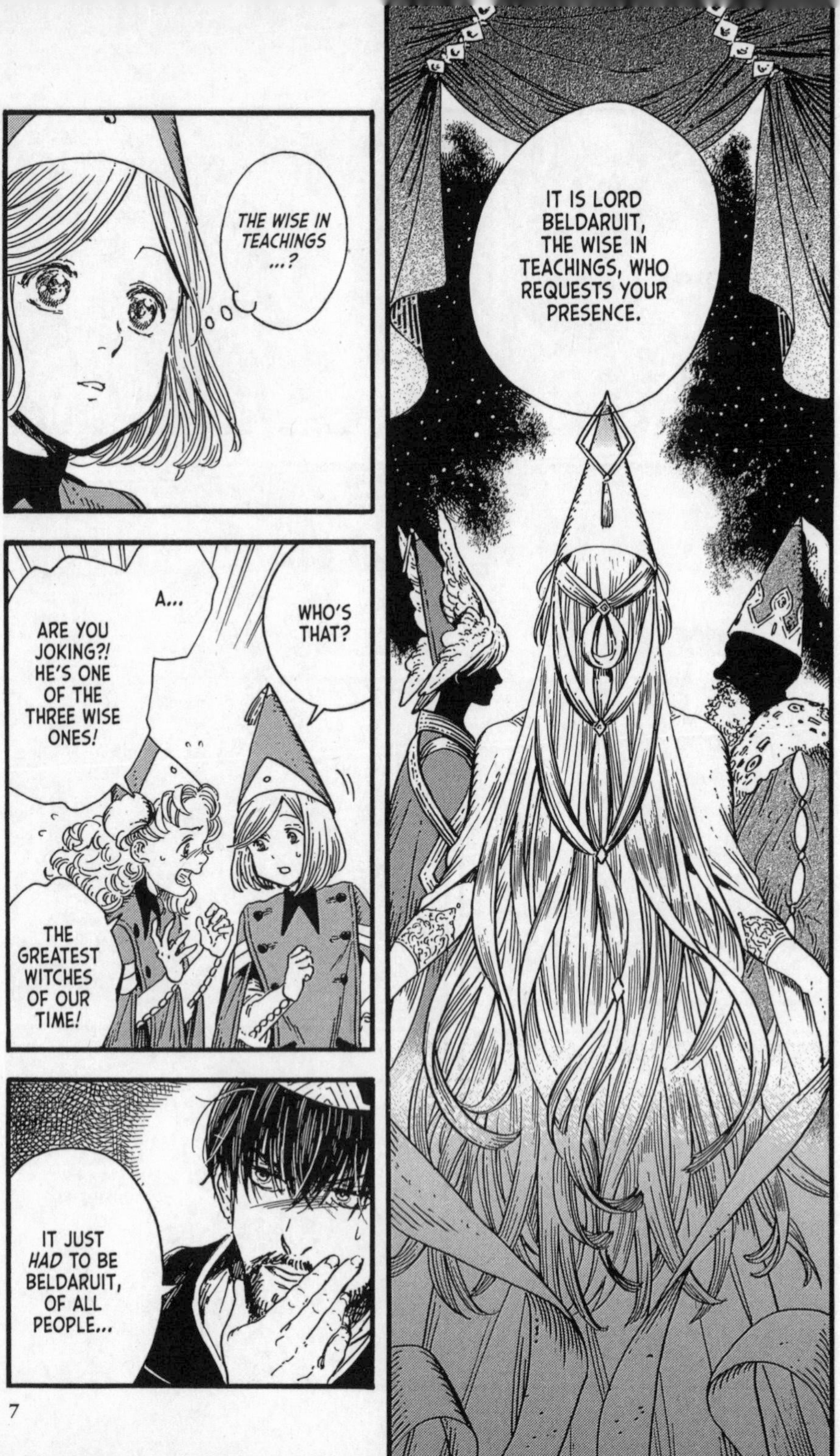
IT IS LORD BELDARUIT, THE WISE IN TEACHINGS, WHO REQUESTS YOUR PRESENCE.
THE WISE IN TEACHINGS ...?
WHO'S THAT?
A...
ARE YOU JOKING?! HE'S ONE OF THE THREE WISE ONES!
THE GREATEST WITCHES OF OUR TIME!
IT JUST HAD TO BE BELDARUIT, OF ALL PEOPLE...

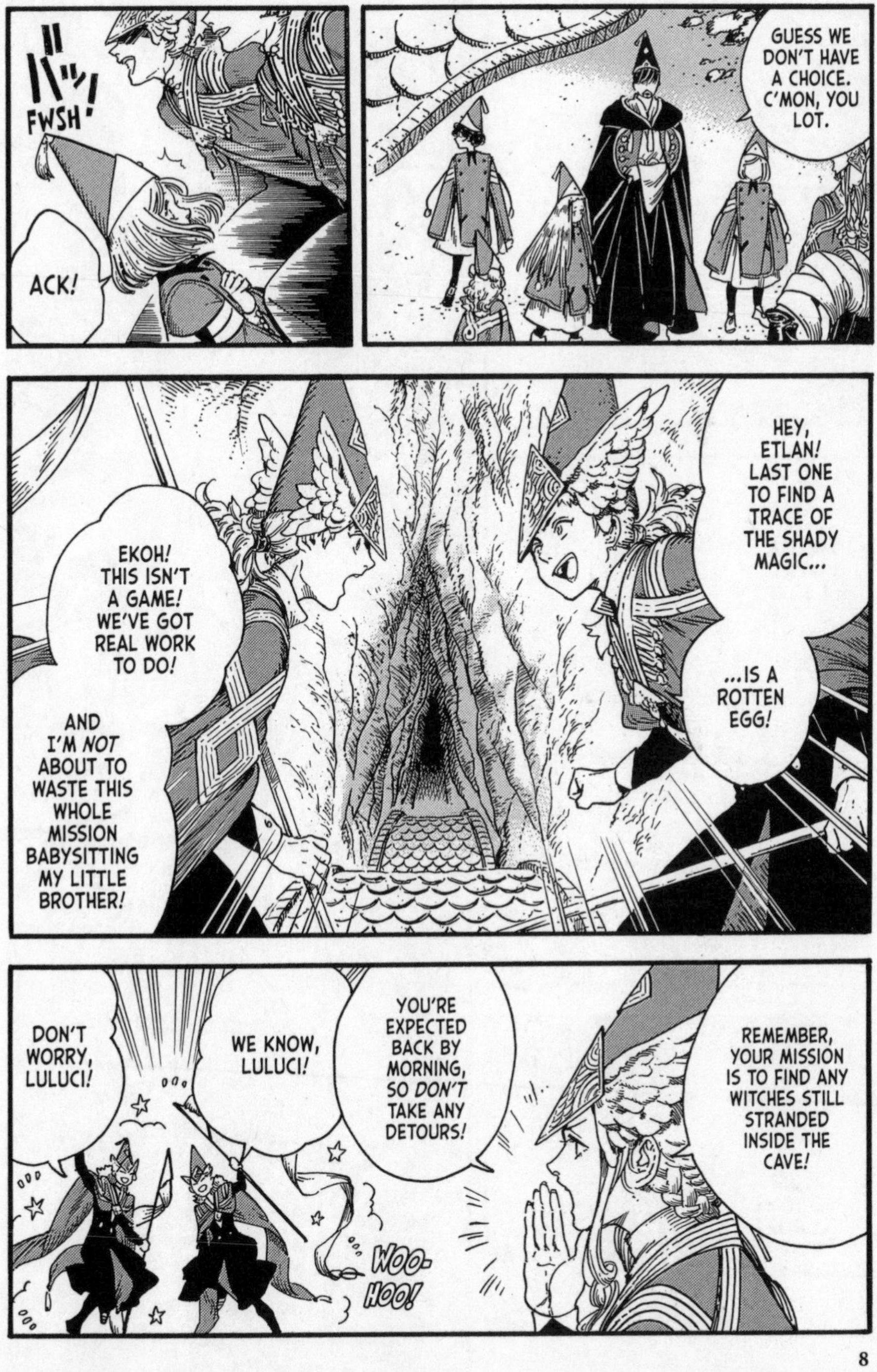
GUESS WE DON'T HAVE A CHOICE. C'MON, YOU LOT.
バッ!
FWSH!
ACK!
HEY, ETLAN! LAST ONE TO FIND A TRACE OF THE SHADY MAGIC...
...IS A ROTTEN EGG!
EKOH! THIS ISN'T A GAME! WE'VE GOT REAL WORK TO DO!
AND I'M *NOT* ABOUT TO WASTE THIS WHOLE MISSION BABYSITTING MY LITTLE BROTHER!
REMEMBER, YOUR MISSION IS TO FIND ANY WITCHES STILL STRANDED INSIDE THE CAVE!
YOU'RE EXPECTED BACK BY MORNING, SO *DON'T* TAKE ANY DETOURS!
WE KNOW, LULUCI!
DON'T WORRY, LULUCI!
WOO-HOO!

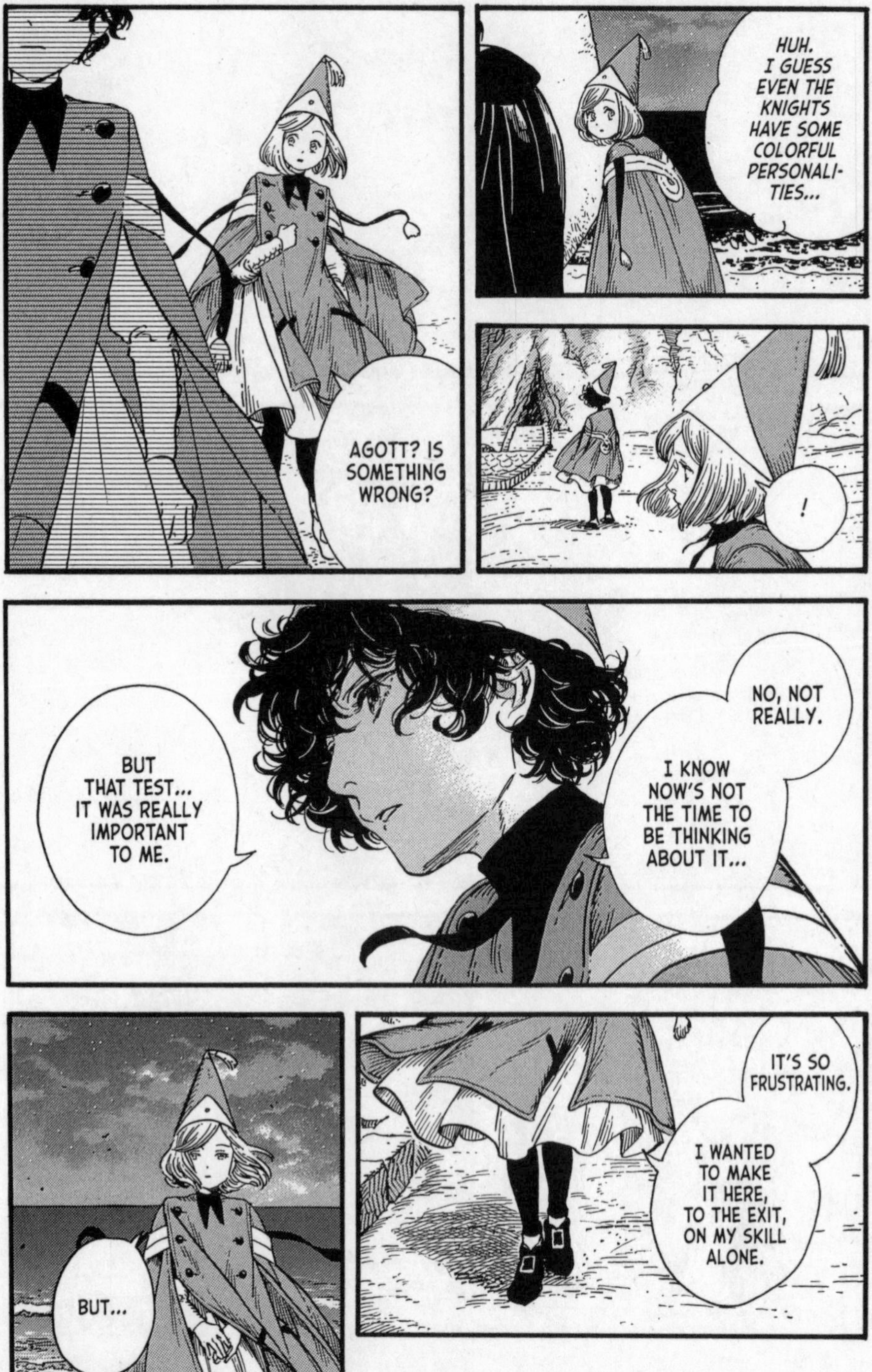
HUH. I GUESS EVEN THE KNIGHTS HAVE SOME COLORFUL PERSONALI-TIES...
!
AGOTT? IS SOMETHING WRONG?
NO, NOT REALLY.
I KNOW NOW'S NOT THE TIME TO BE THINKING ABOUT IT...
BUT THAT TEST... IT WAS REALLY IMPORTANT TO ME.
IT'S SO FRUSTRATING.
I WANTED TO MAKE IT HERE, TO THE EXIT, ON MY SKILL ALONE.
BUT...

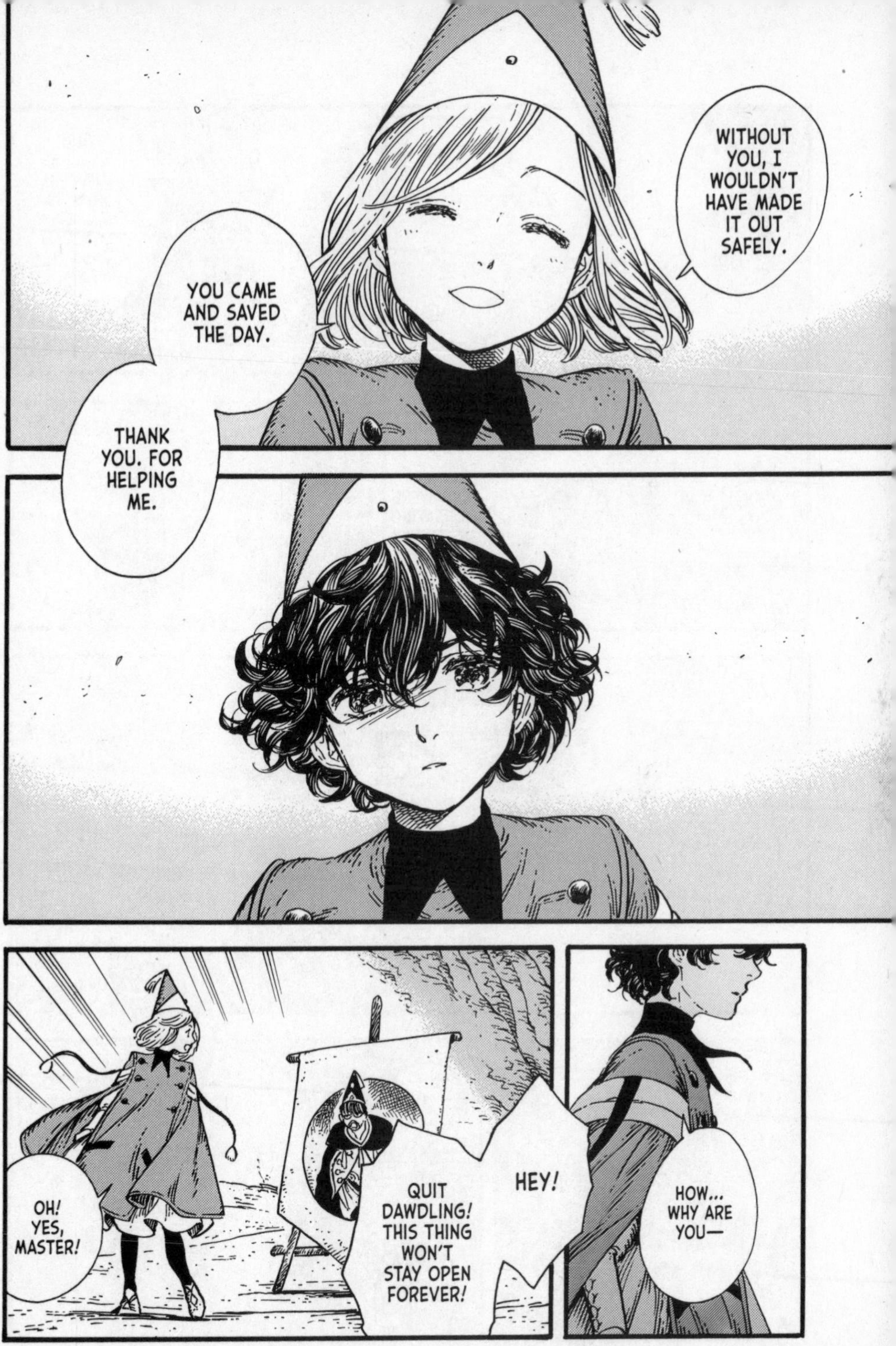
WITHOUT YOU, I WOULDN'T HAVE MADE IT OUT SAFELY.
YOU CAME AND SAVED THE DAY.
THANK YOU. FOR HELPING ME.
HOW... WHY ARE YOU—
HEY!
QUIT DAWDLING! THIS THING WON'T STAY OPEN FOREVER!
OH! YES, MASTER!

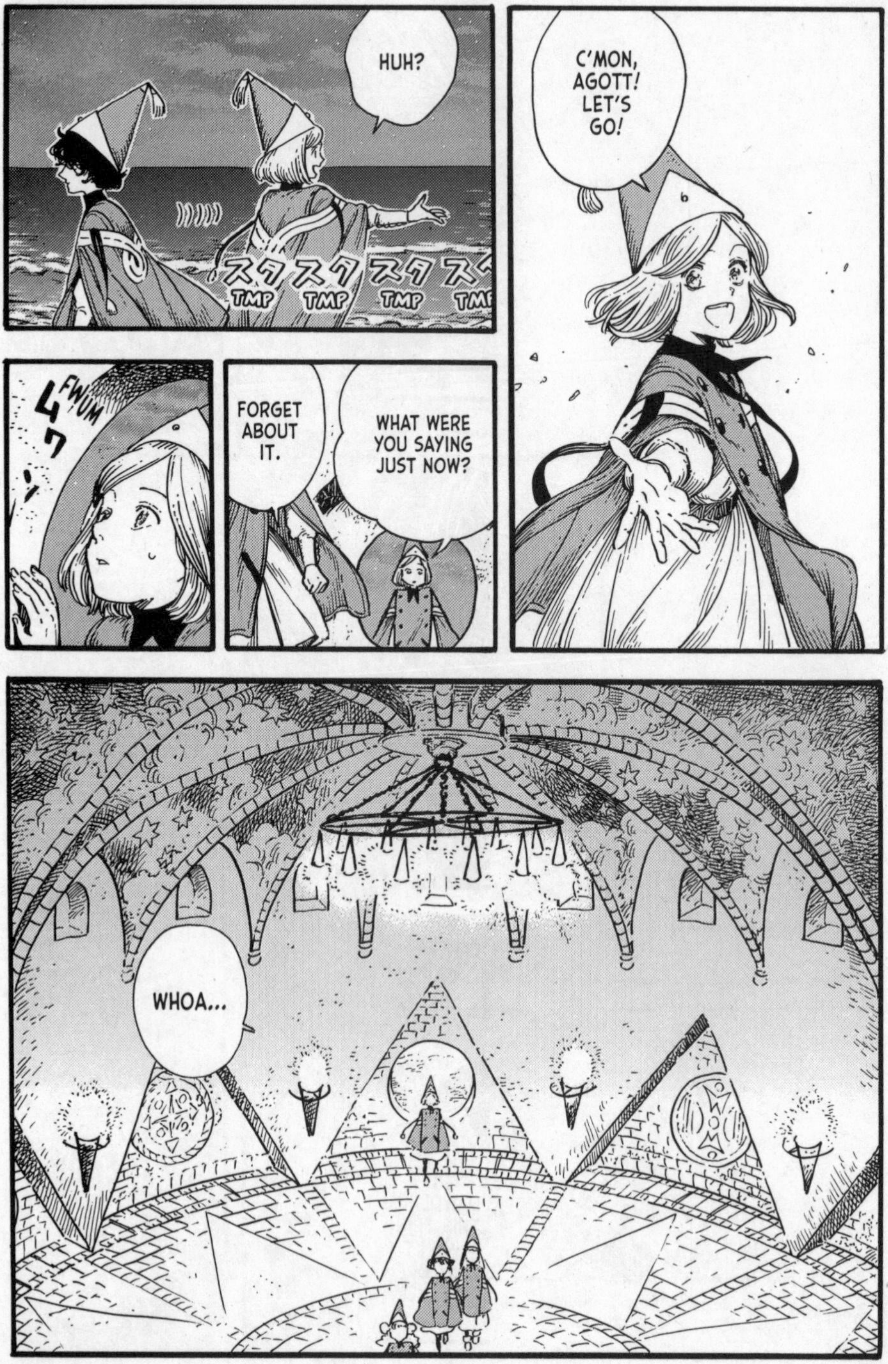
C'MON, AGOTT! LET'S GO!
HUH?
スタ TMP
スタ TMP
スタ TMP
WHAT WERE YOU SAYING JUST NOW?
FORGET ABOUT IT.
ムワン FWUM
WHOA...

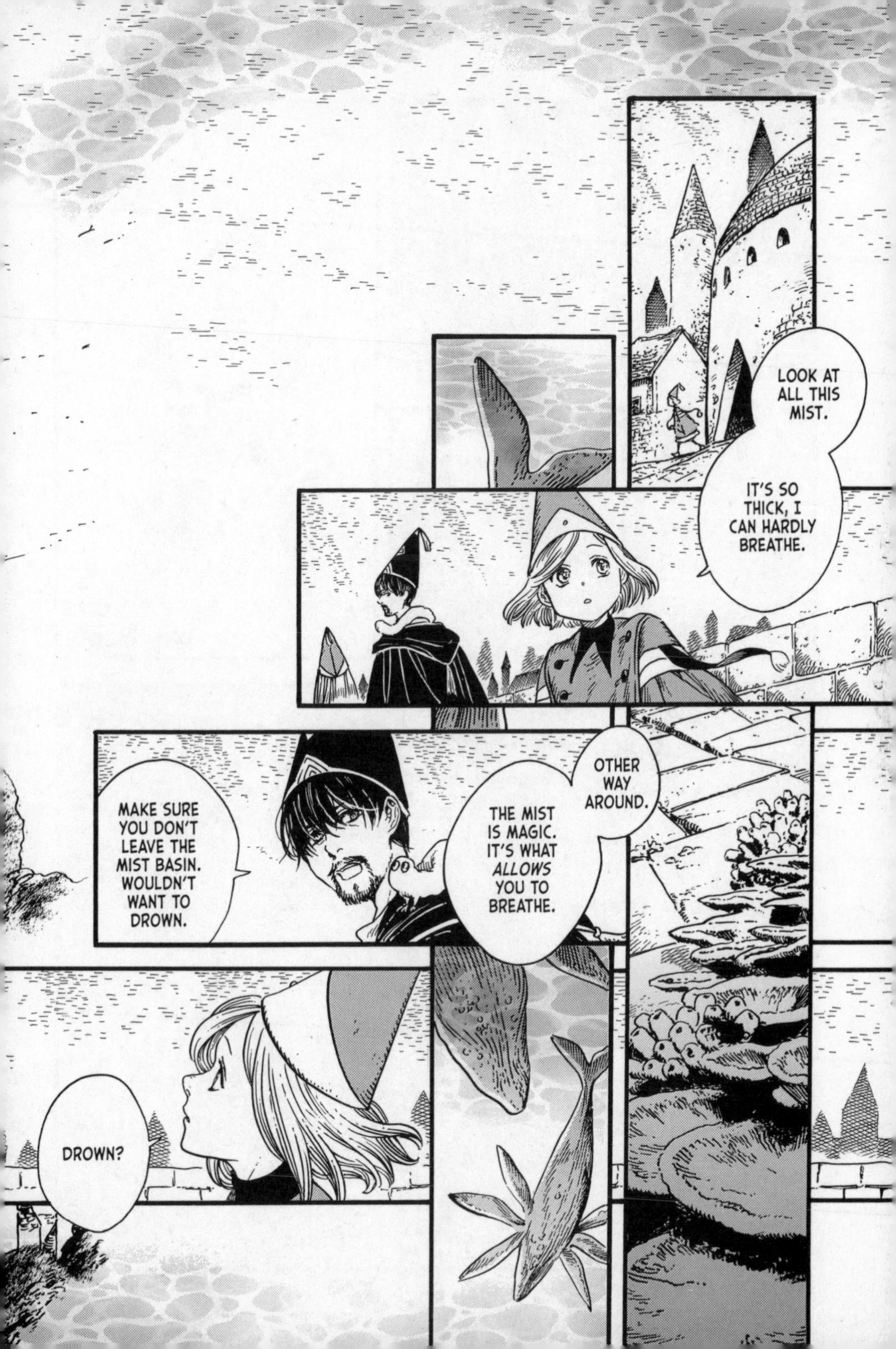
LOOK AT ALL THIS MIST.
IT'S SO THICK, I CAN HARDLY BREATHE.
OTHER WAY AROUND.
THE MIST IS MAGIC. IT'S WHAT *ALLOWS* YOU TO BREATHE.
MAKE SURE YOU DON'T LEAVE THE MIST BASIN. WOULDN'T WANT TO DROWN.
DROWN?

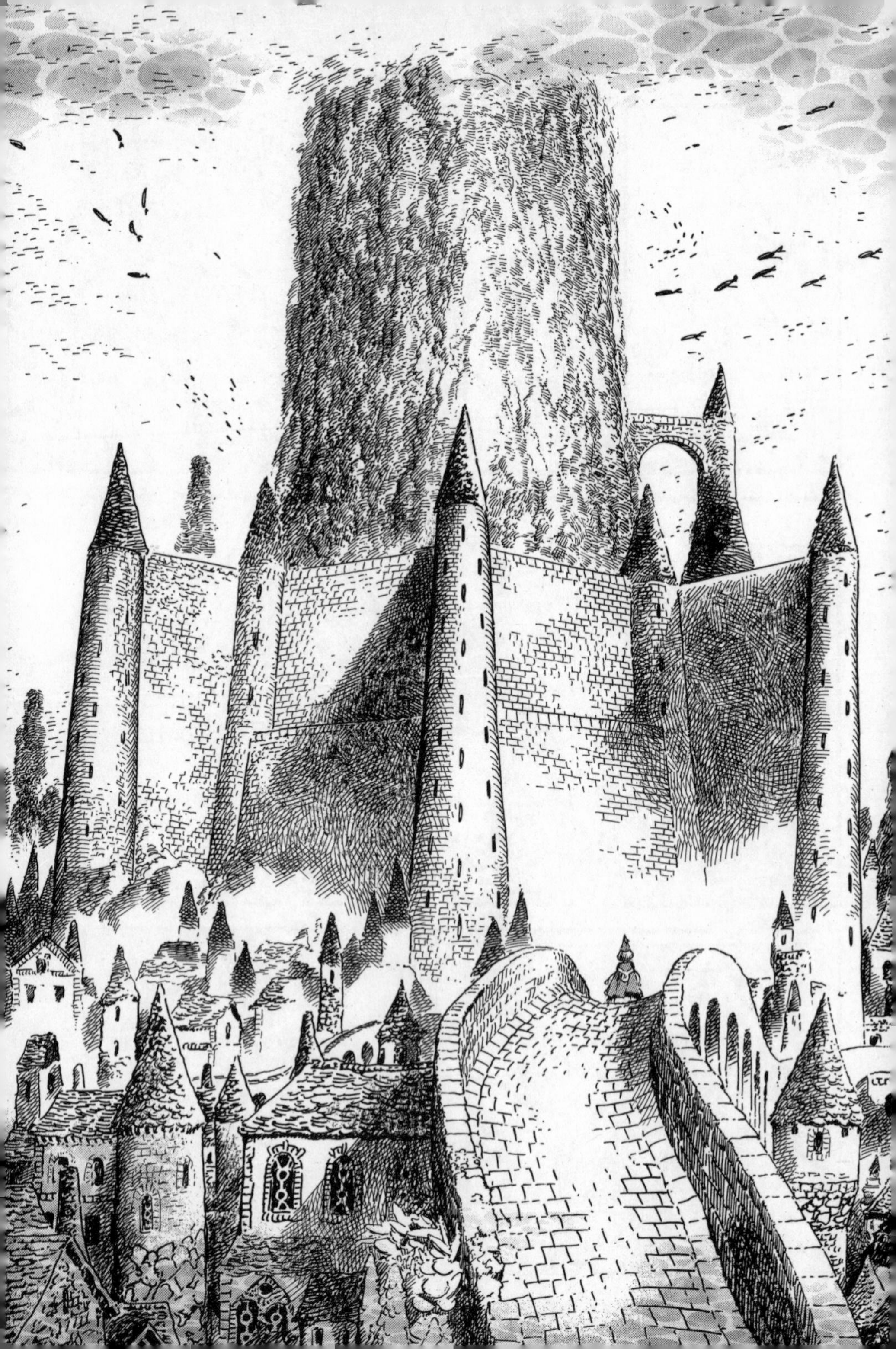

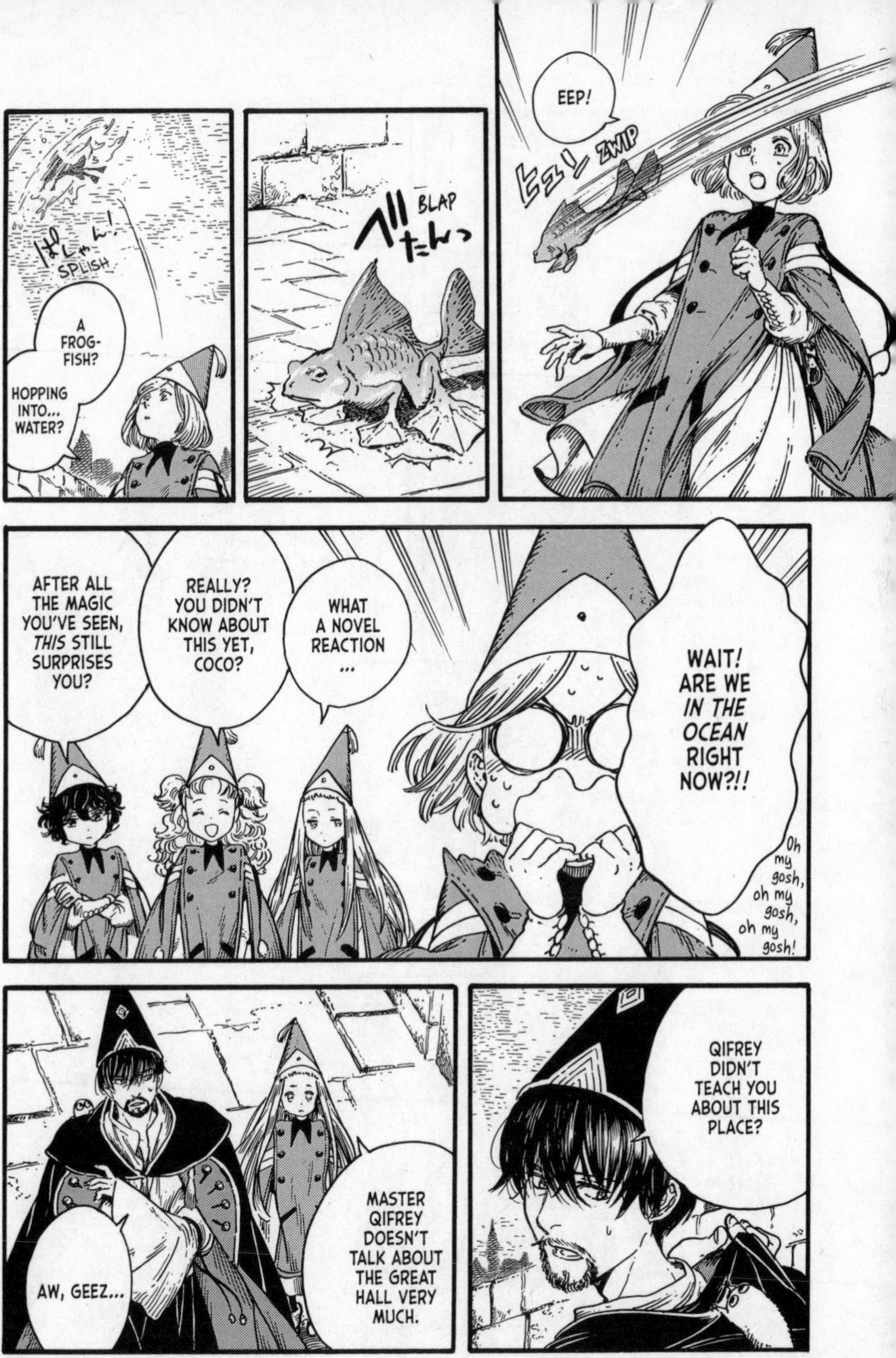
EEP!
ヒュン ZWIP
べたんっ BLAP
ぱしゃん! SPLISH
A FROG-FISH?
HOPPING INTO... WATER?
WAIT! ARE WE *IN THE OCEAN* RIGHT NOW?!!
Oh my gosh, oh my gosh, oh my gosh!
WHAT A NOVEL REACTION ...
REALLY? YOU DIDN'T KNOW ABOUT THIS YET, COCO?
AFTER ALL THE MAGIC YOU'VE SEEN, *THIS* STILL SURPRISES YOU?
QIFREY DIDN'T TEACH YOU ABOUT THIS PLACE?
MASTER QIFREY DOESN'T TALK ABOUT THE GREAT HALL VERY MUCH.
AW, GEEZ...

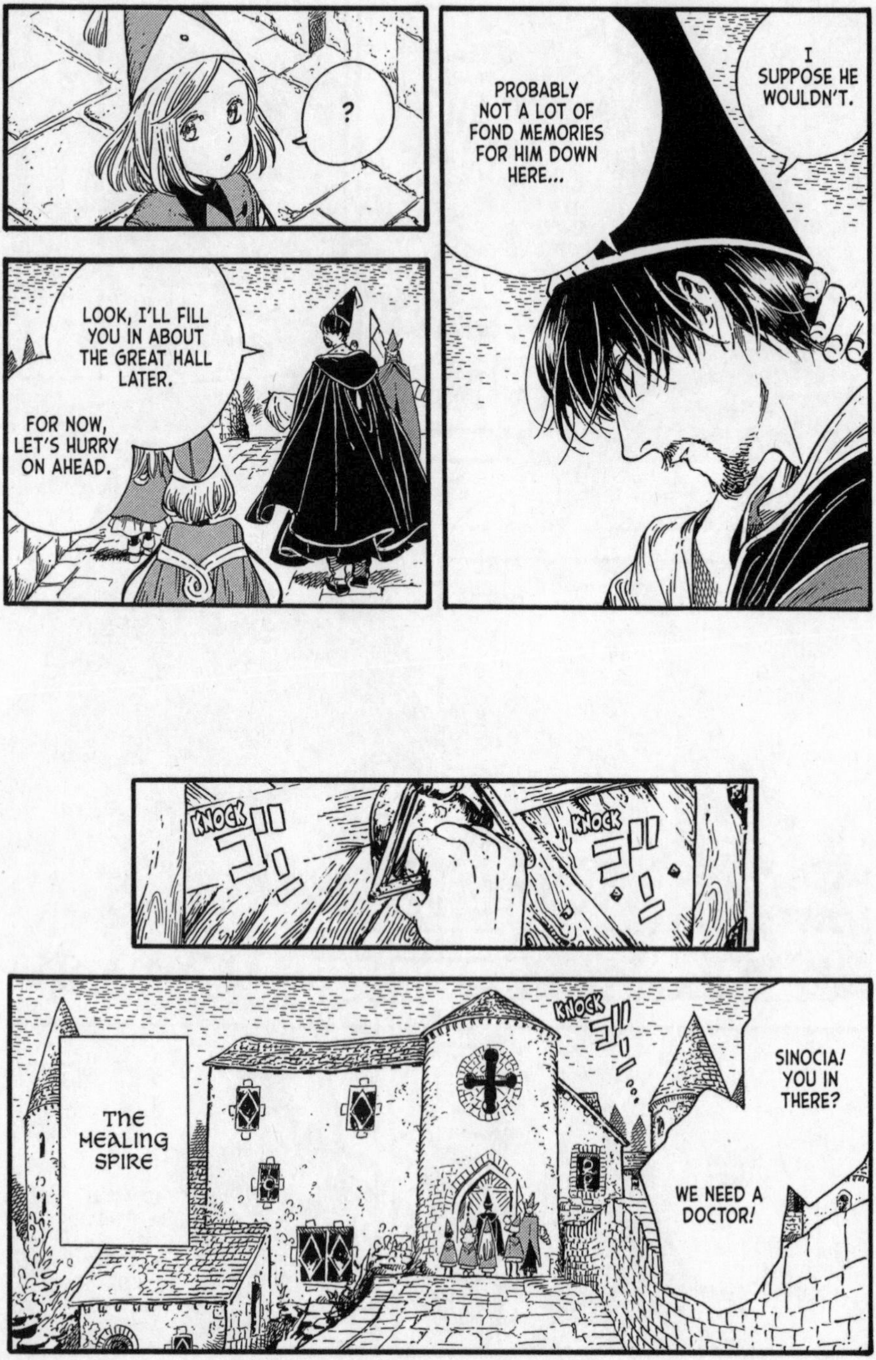
I SUPPOSE HE WOULDN'T.
PROBABLY NOT A LOT OF FOND MEMORIES FOR HIM DOWN HERE...
?
LOOK, I'LL FILL YOU IN ABOUT THE GREAT HALL LATER.
FOR NOW, LET'S HURRY ON AHEAD.
KNOCK
KNOCK
KNOCK
SINOCIA! YOU IN THERE?
WE NEED A DOCTOR!
THE HEALING SPIRE

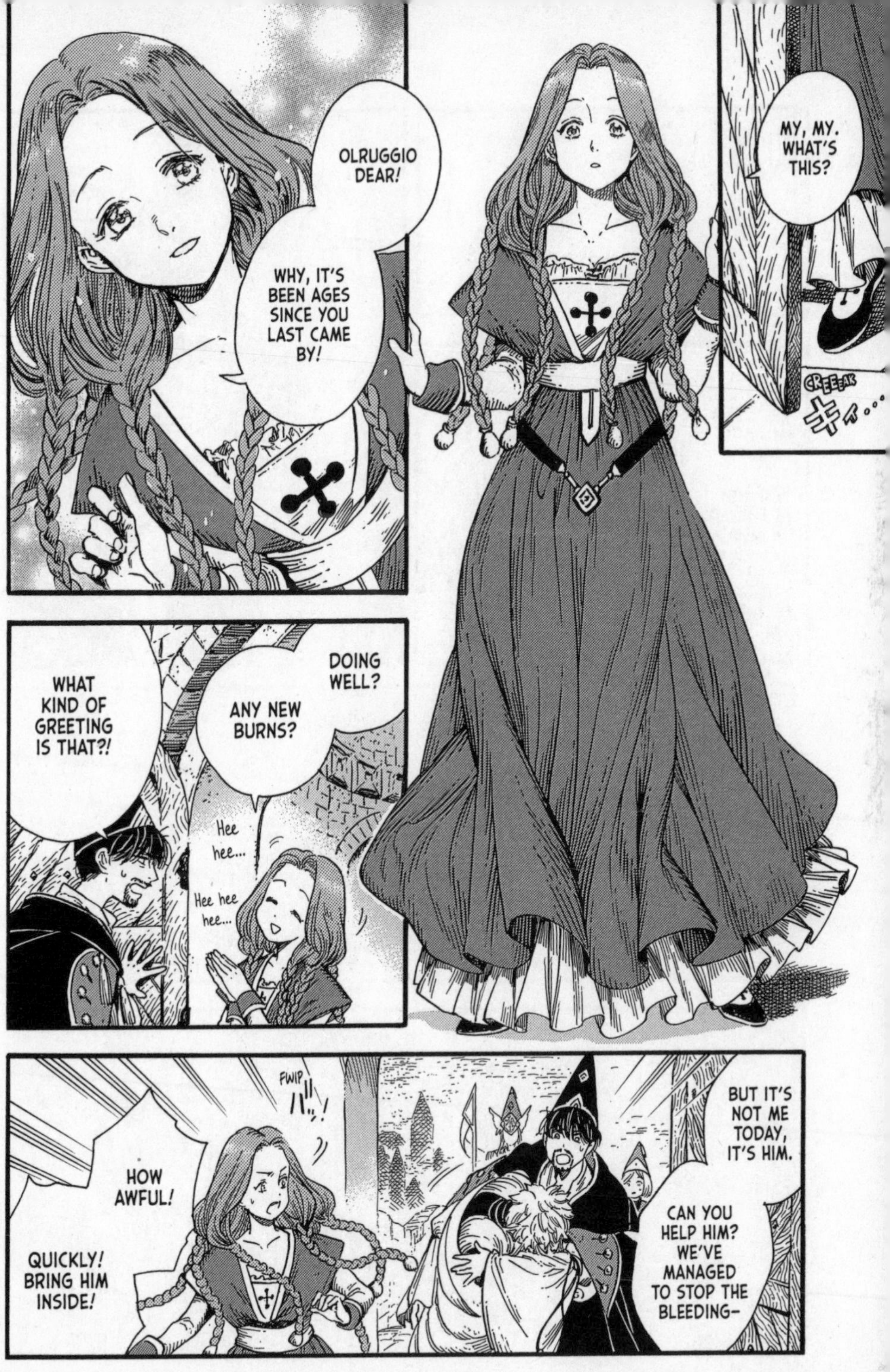
MY, MY. WHAT'S THIS?
CREEEAK
キィ…
OLRUGGIO DEAR!
WHY, IT'S BEEN AGES SINCE YOU LAST CAME BY!
DOING WELL?
ANY NEW BURNS?
Hee hee...
Hee hee hee...
WHAT KIND OF GREETING IS THAT?!
BUT IT'S NOT ME TODAY, IT'S HIM.
CAN YOU HELP HIM? WE'VE MANAGED TO STOP THE BLEEDING–
FWIP
ハッ!
HOW AWFUL!
QUICKLY! BRING HIM INSIDE!

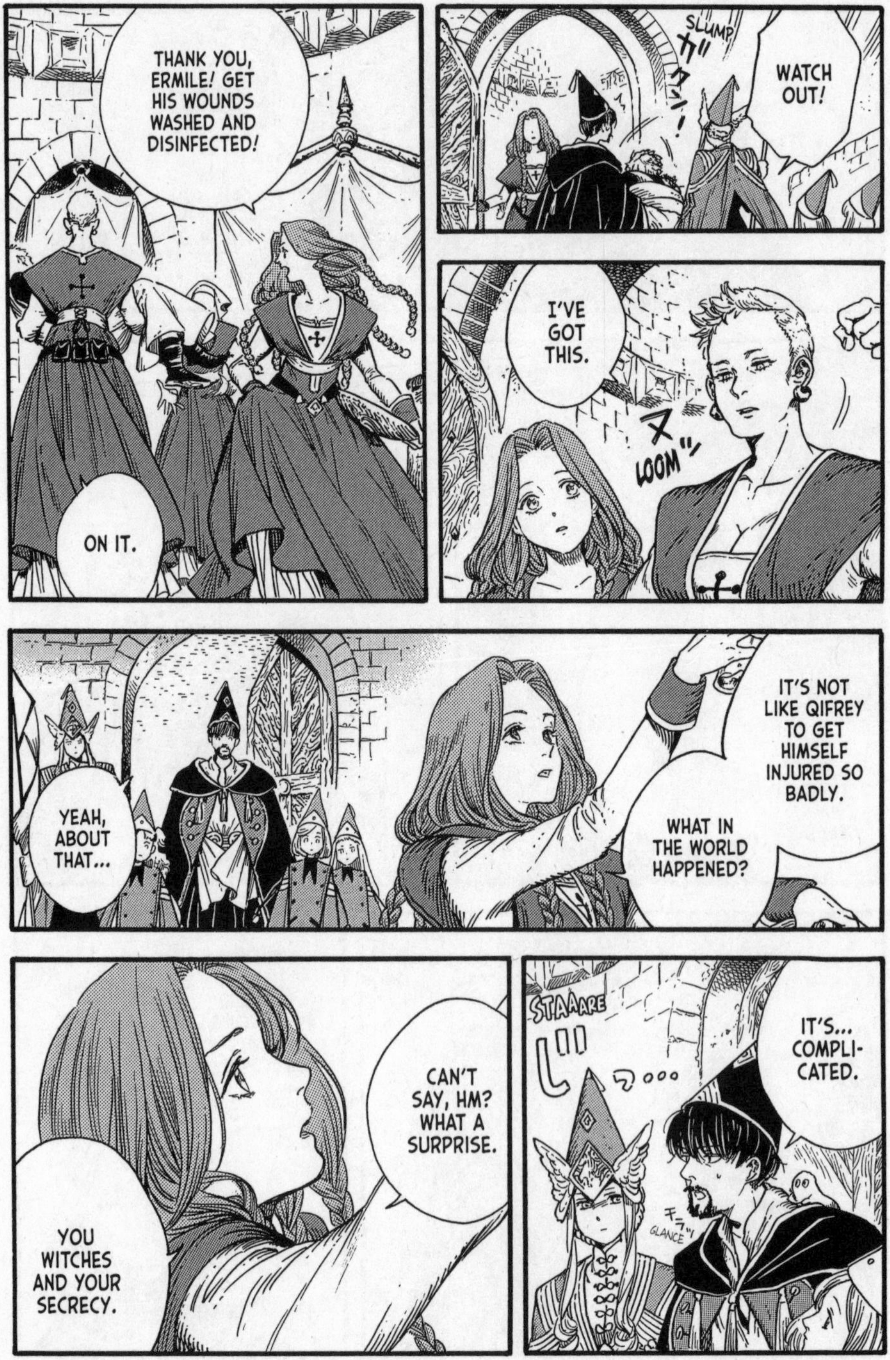
SLUMP
WATCH OUT!
I'VE GOT THIS.
LOOM
THANK YOU, ERMILE! GET HIS WOUNDS WASHED AND DISINFECTED!
ON IT.
IT'S NOT LIKE QIFREY TO GET HIMSELF INJURED SO BADLY.
WHAT IN THE WORLD HAPPENED?
YEAH, ABOUT THAT...
IT'S... COMPLICATED.
STAAARE
GLANCE
CAN'T SAY, HM? WHAT A SURPRISE.
YOU WITCHES AND YOUR SECRECY.

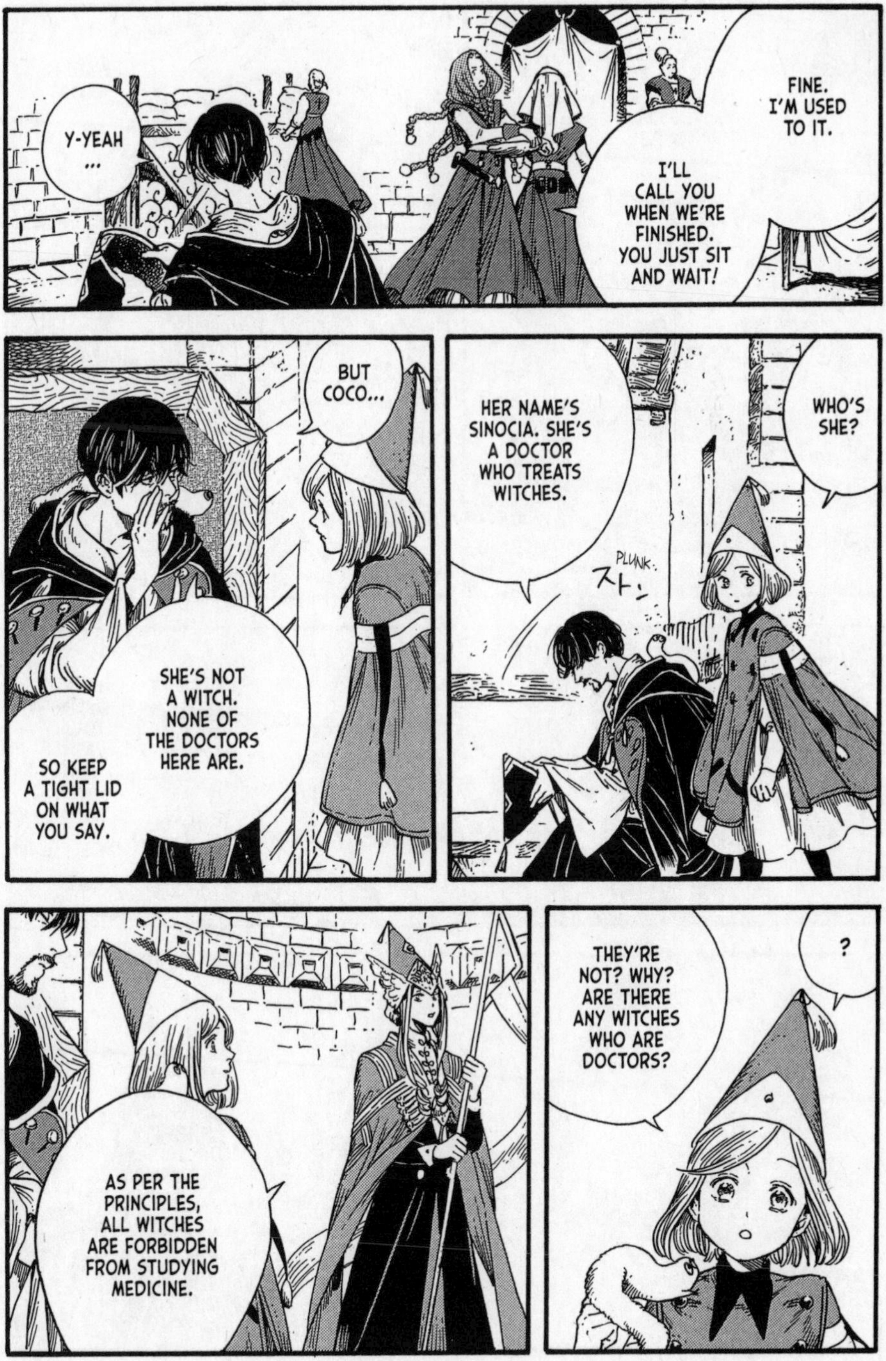
FINE. I'M USED TO IT.
I'LL CALL YOU WHEN WE'RE FINISHED. YOU JUST SIT AND WAIT!
Y-YEAH ...
WHO'S SHE?
HER NAME'S SINOCIA. SHE'S A DOCTOR WHO TREATS WITCHES.
PLUNK
ストン
BUT COCO...
SHE'S NOT A WITCH. NONE OF THE DOCTORS HERE ARE.
SO KEEP A TIGHT LID ON WHAT YOU SAY.
?
THEY'RE NOT? WHY? ARE THERE ANY WITCHES WHO ARE DOCTORS?
AS PER THE PRINCIPLES, ALL WITCHES ARE FORBIDDEN FROM STUDYING MEDICINE.

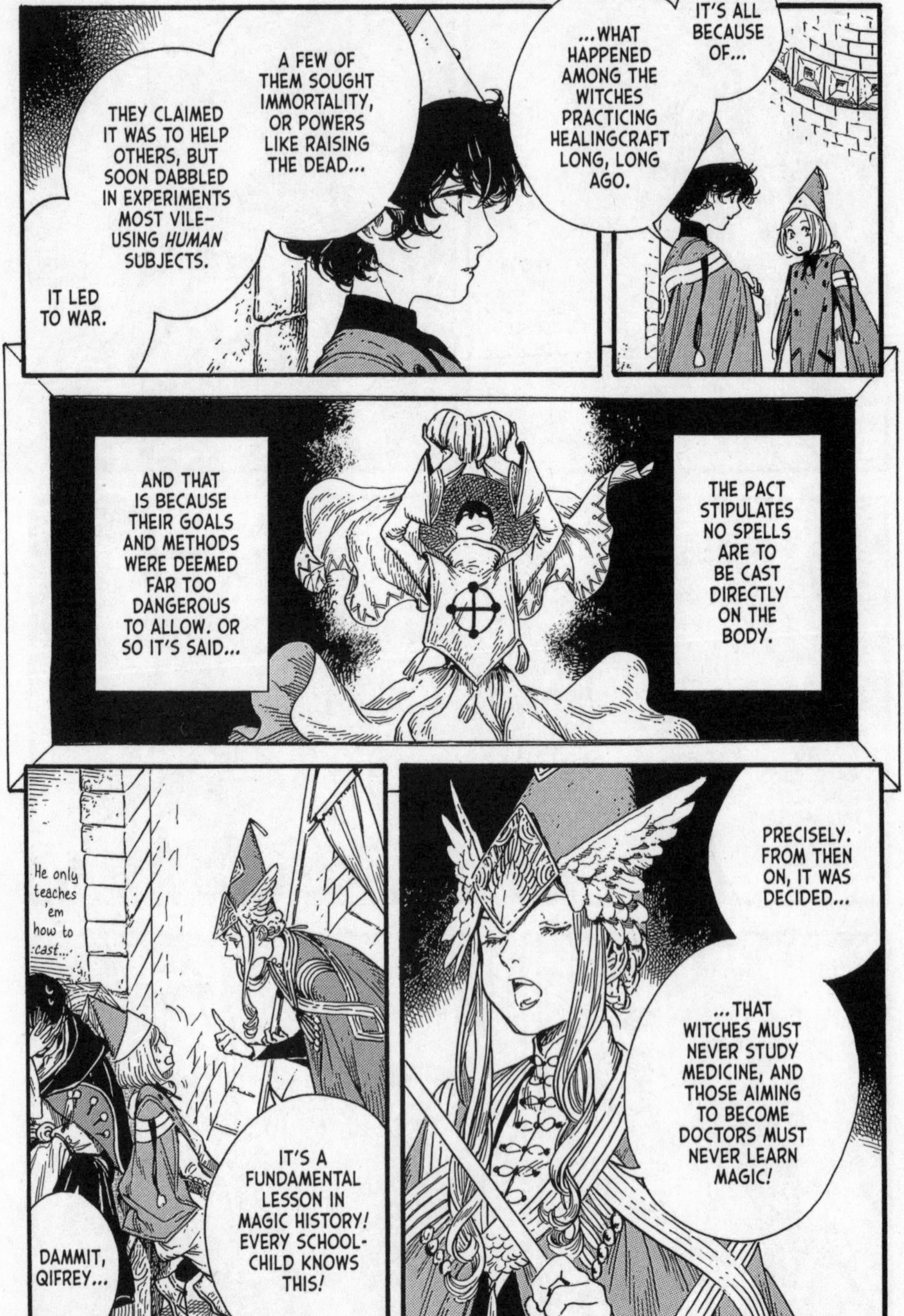
IT'S ALL BECAUSE OF...
...WHAT HAPPENED AMONG THE WITCHES PRACTICING HEALINGCRAFT LONG, LONG AGO.
A FEW OF THEM SOUGHT IMMORTALITY, OR POWERS LIKE RAISING THE DEAD...
THEY CLAIMED IT WAS TO HELP OTHERS, BUT SOON DABBLED IN EXPERIMENTS MOST VILE—USING *HUMAN* SUBJECTS.
IT LED TO WAR.
THE PACT STIPULATES NO SPELLS ARE TO BE CAST DIRECTLY ON THE BODY.
AND THAT IS BECAUSE THEIR GOALS AND METHODS WERE DEEMED FAR TOO DANGEROUS TO ALLOW. OR SO IT'S SAID...
PRECISELY. FROM THEN ON, IT WAS DECIDED...
...THAT WITCHES MUST NEVER STUDY MEDICINE, AND THOSE AIMING TO BECOME DOCTORS MUST NEVER LEARN MAGIC!
IT'S A FUNDAMENTAL LESSON IN MAGIC HISTORY! EVERY SCHOOL-CHILD KNOWS THIS!
He only teaches 'em how to cast...
DAMMIT, QIFREY...

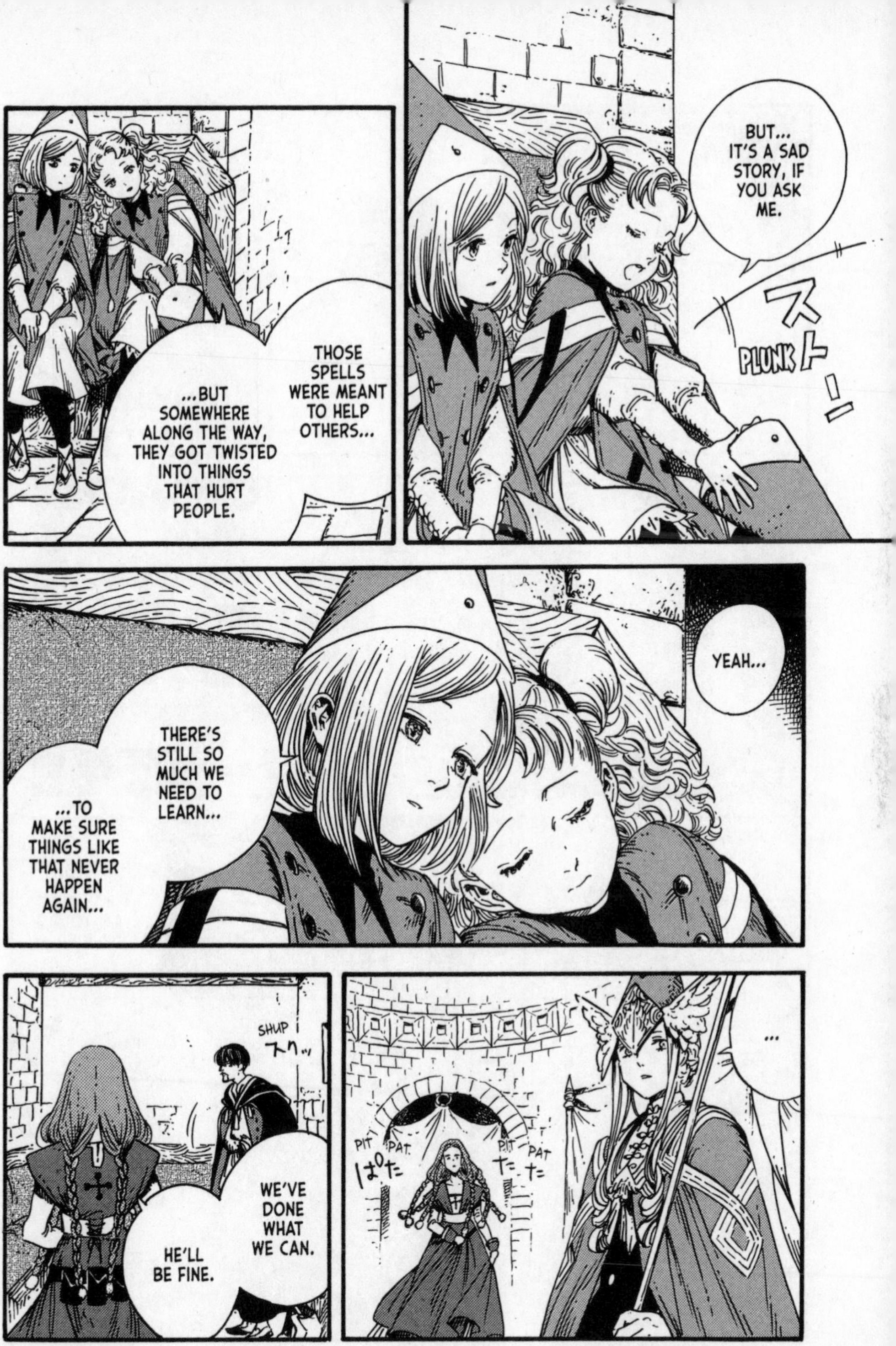
BUT... IT'S A SAD STORY, IF YOU ASK ME.
PLUNK
THOSE SPELLS WERE MEANT TO HELP OTHERS...
...BUT SOMEWHERE ALONG THE WAY, THEY GOT TWISTED INTO THINGS THAT HURT PEOPLE.
YEAH...
THERE'S STILL SO MUCH WE NEED TO LEARN...
...TO MAKE SURE THINGS LIKE THAT NEVER HAPPEN AGAIN...
...
PIT PAT. PIT PAT
SHUP
WE'VE DONE WHAT WE CAN.
HE'LL BE FINE.

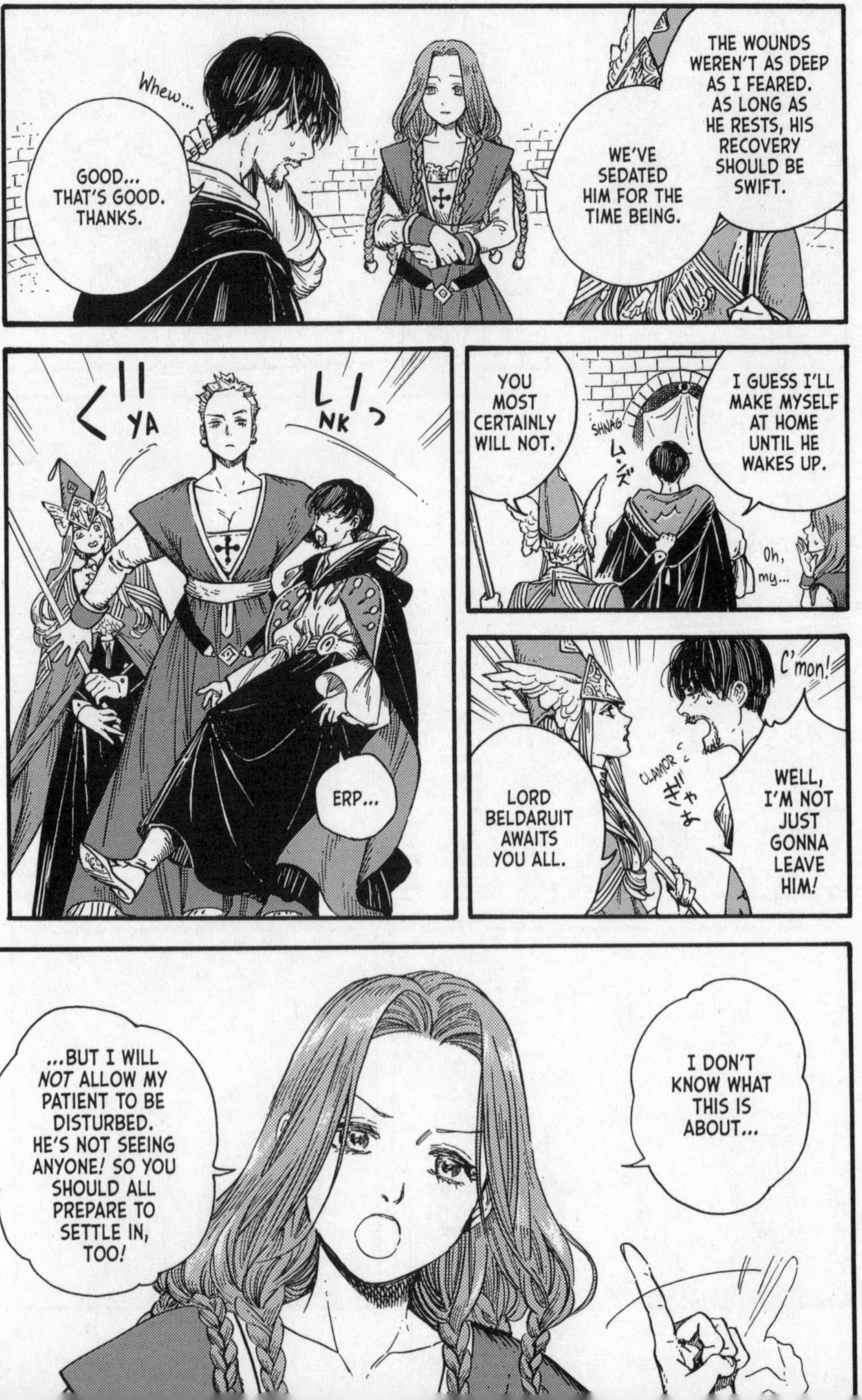
THE WOUNDS WEREN'T AS DEEP AS I FEARED. AS LONG AS HE RESTS, HIS RECOVERY SHOULD BE SWIFT.
WE'VE SEDATED HIM FOR THE TIME BEING.
Whew...
GOOD... THAT'S GOOD. THANKS.
I GUESS I'LL MAKE MYSELF AT HOME UNTIL HE WAKES UP.
Oh, my...
SHNAG ムンズ
YOU MOST CERTAINLY WILL NOT.
C'mon!
WELL, I'M NOT JUST GONNA LEAVE HIM!
CLAMOR ぎゃあ
LORD BELDARUIT AWAITS YOU ALL.
NK
YA
ERP...
I DON'T KNOW WHAT THIS IS ABOUT...
...BUT I WILL *NOT* ALLOW MY PATIENT TO BE DISTURBED. HE'S NOT SEEING ANYONE! SO YOU SHOULD ALL PREPARE TO SETTLE IN, TOO!

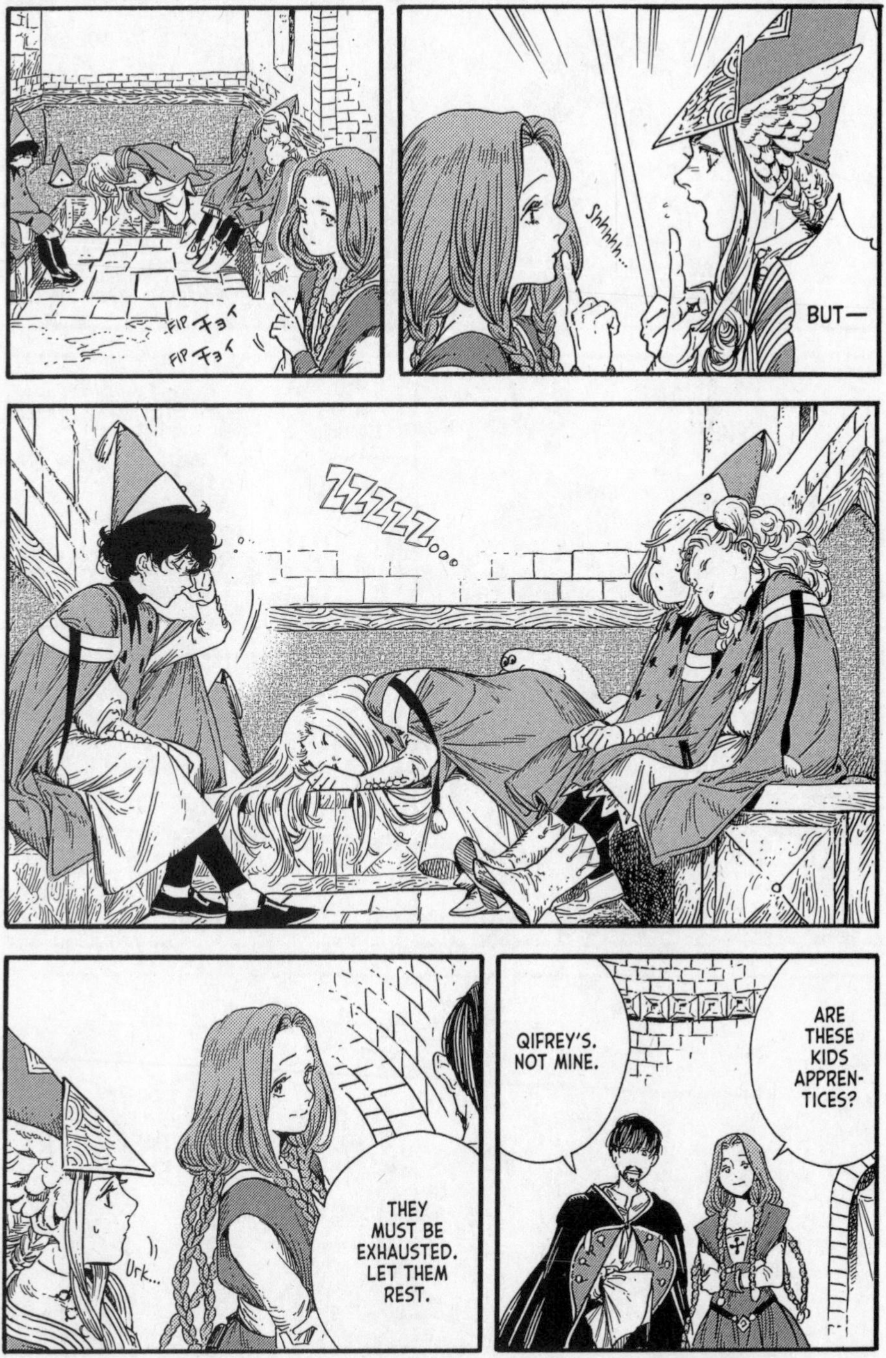
BUT—
Shhhh...
FIP チョイ
FIP チョイ
ZZZZZ...
ARE THESE KIDS APPRENTICES?
QIFREY'S. NOT MINE.
THEY MUST BE EXHAUSTED. LET THEM REST.
Urk...

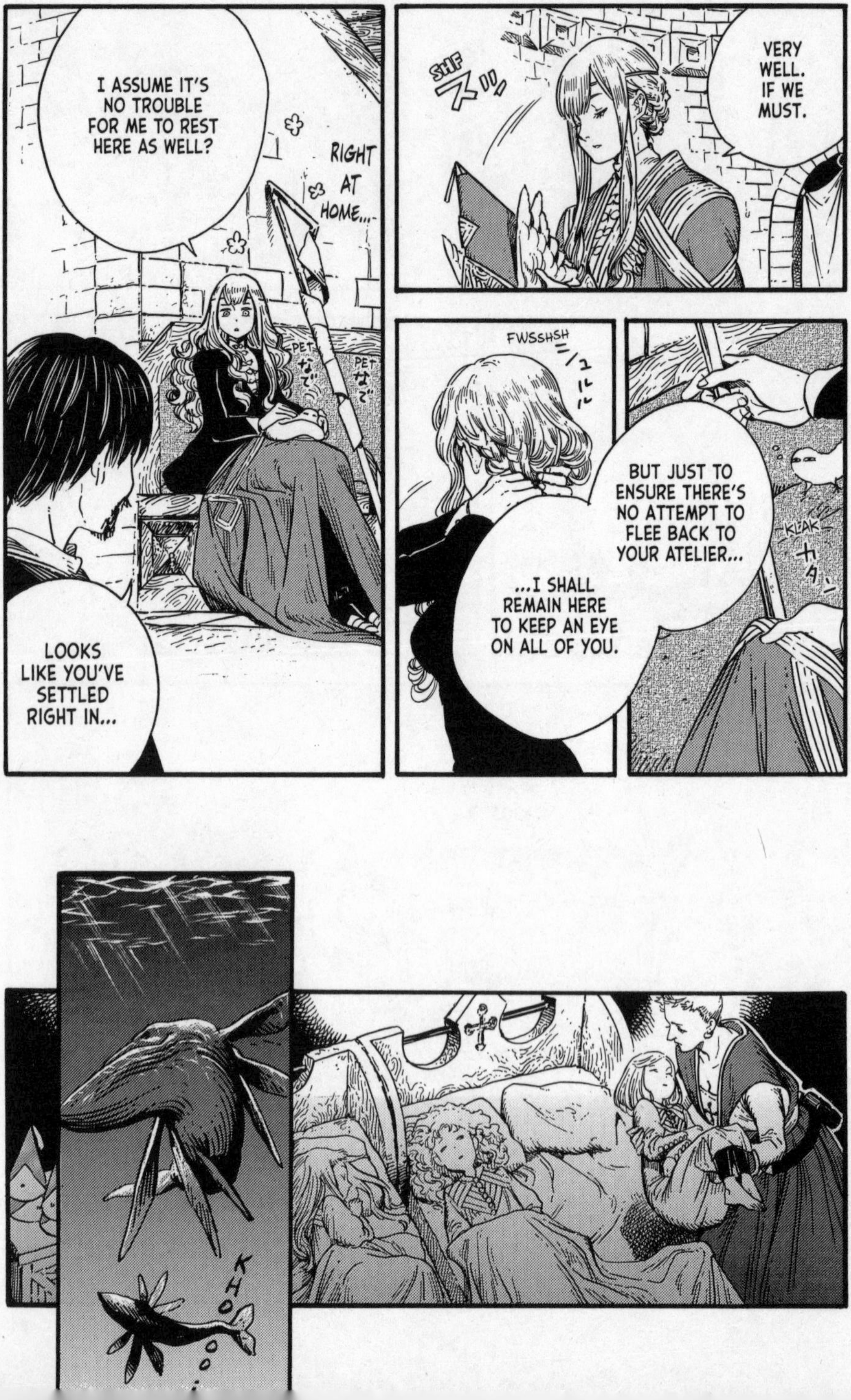
VERY WELL. IF WE MUST.
SHF
KLAK
BUT JUST TO ENSURE THERE'S NO ATTEMPT TO FLEE BACK TO YOUR ATELIER...
FWSSHSH
...I SHALL REMAIN HERE TO KEEP AN EYE ON ALL OF YOU.
RIGHT AT HOME...
I ASSUME IT'S NO TROUBLE FOR ME TO REST HERE AS WELL?
PET
PET
LOOKS LIKE YOU'VE SETTLED RIGHT IN...
KHO

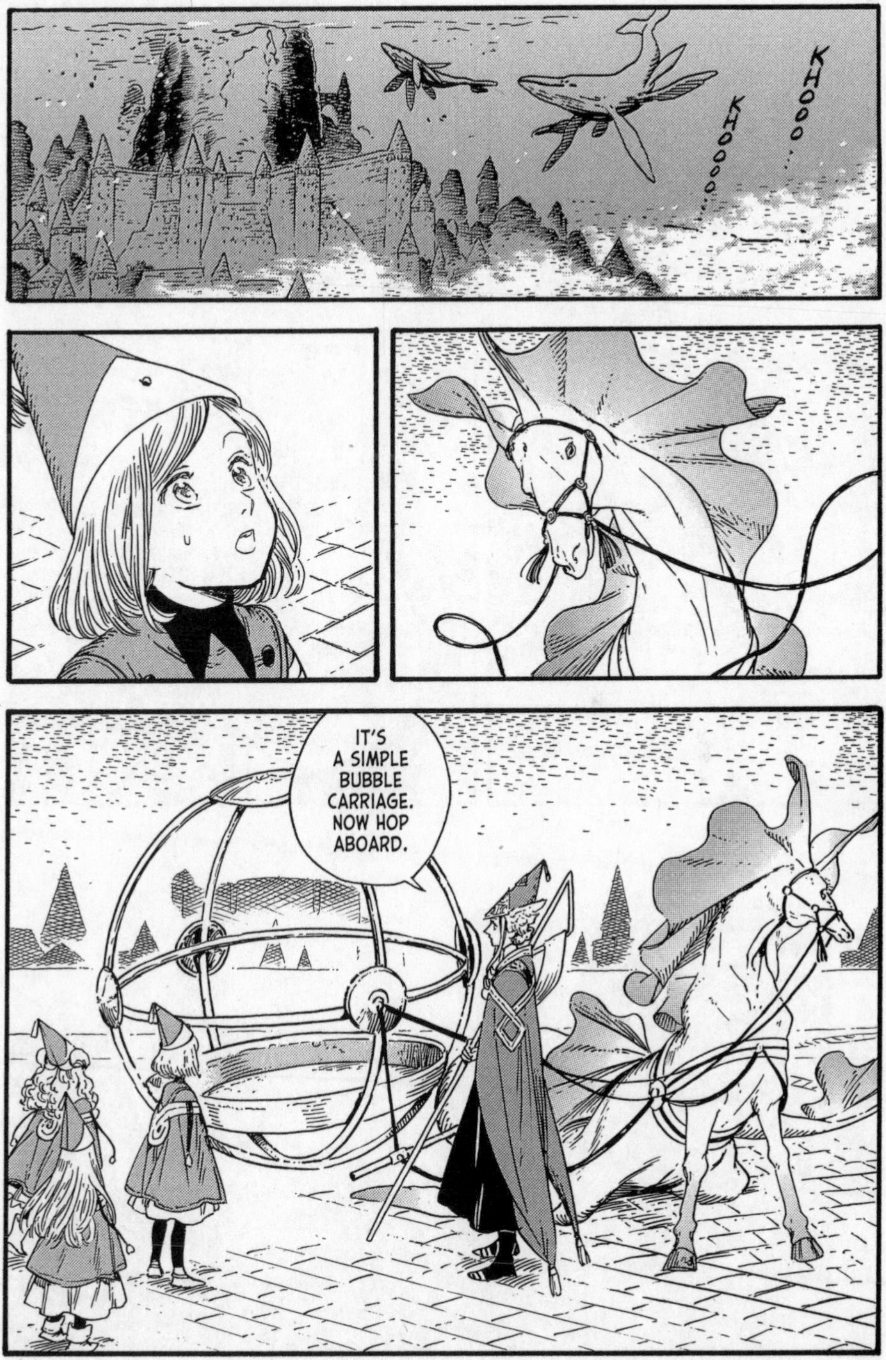
KHOOO...
KHOOOOO...
IT'S A SIMPLE BUBBLE CARRIAGE. NOW HOP ABOARD.

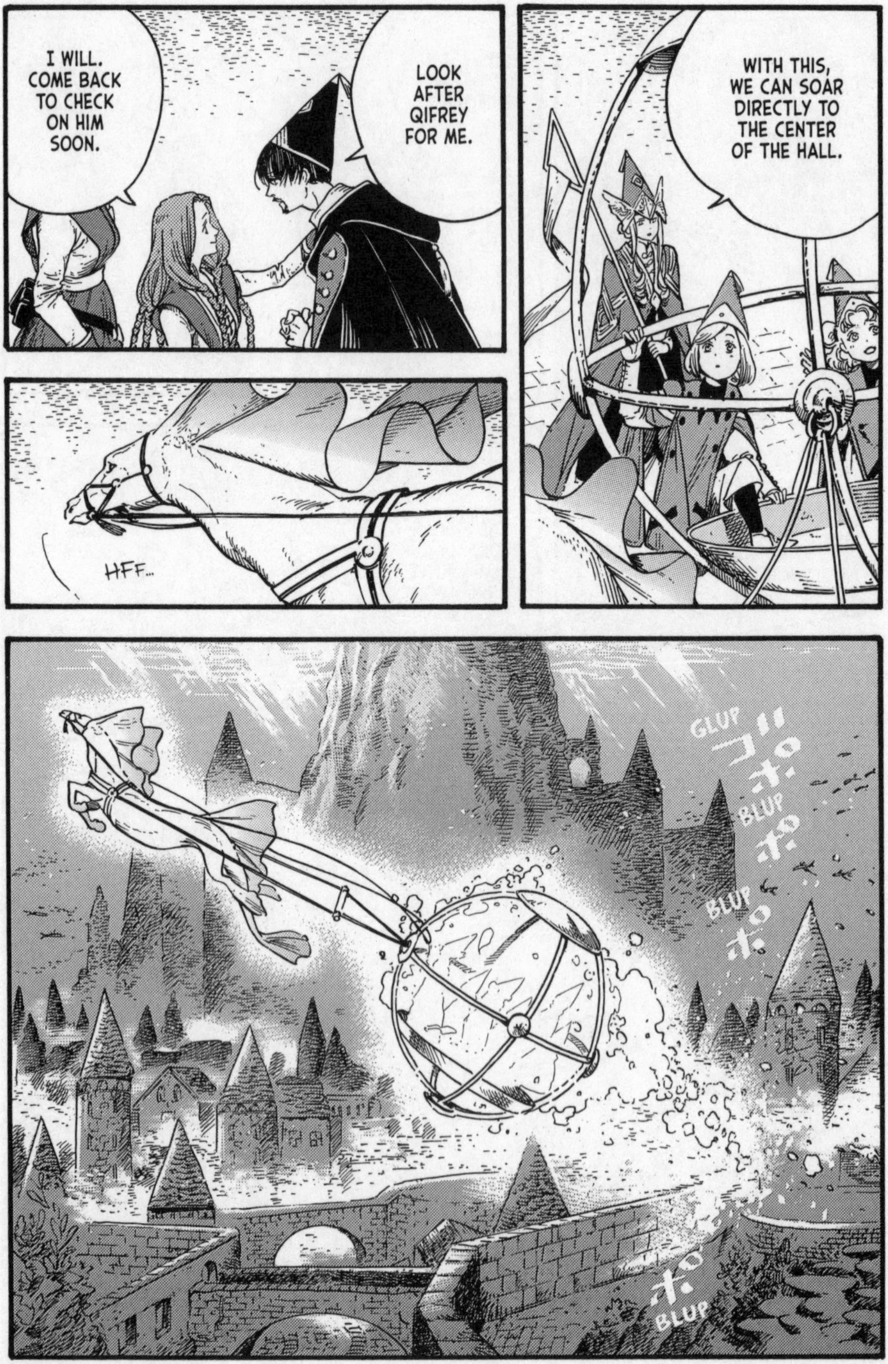
WITH THIS, WE CAN SOAR DIRECTLY TO THE CENTER OF THE HALL.
LOOK AFTER QIFREY FOR ME.
I WILL. COME BACK TO CHECK ON HIM SOON.
HFF...
GLUP
BLUP
BLUP
BLUP

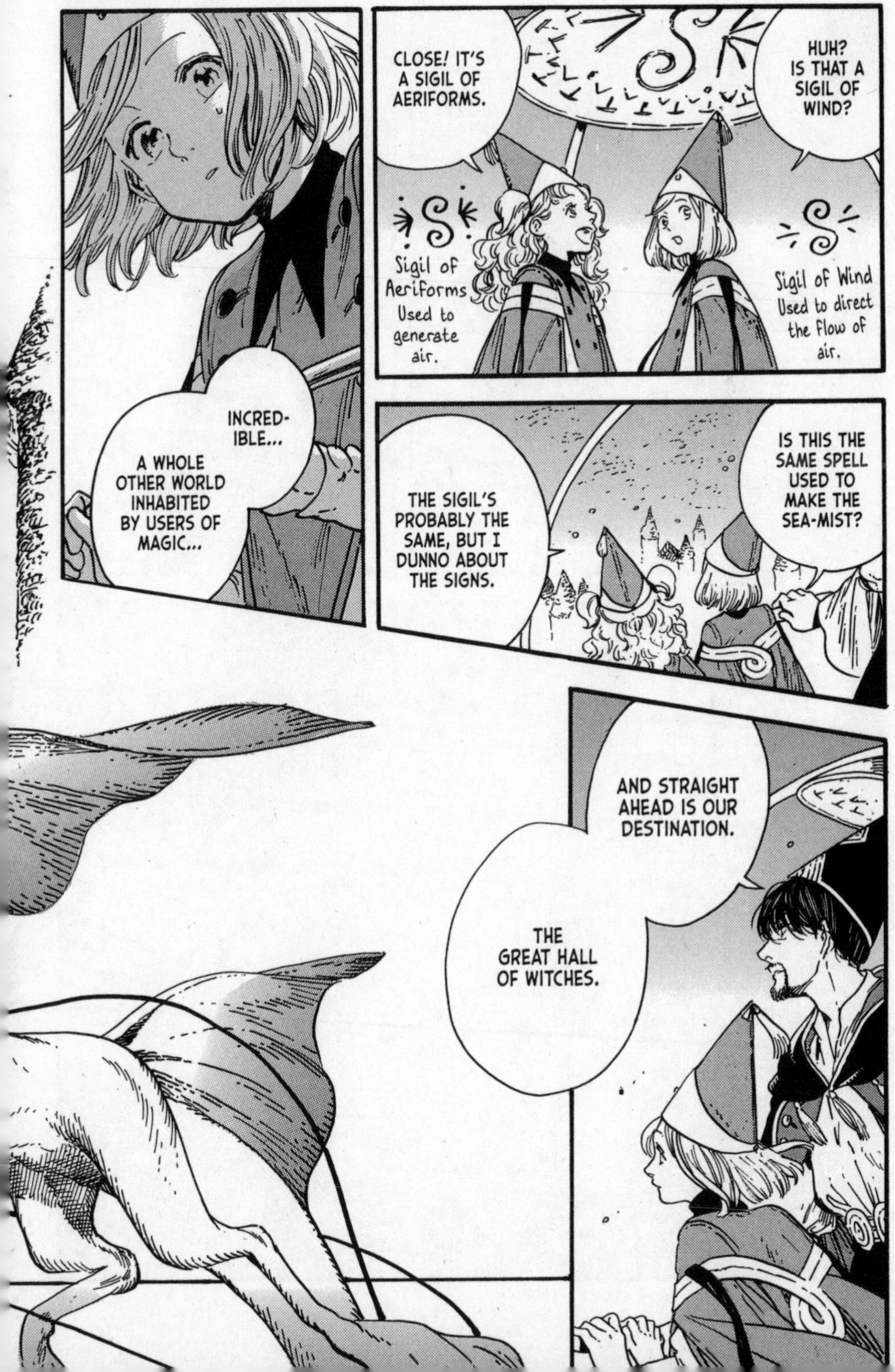
HUH? IS THAT A SIGIL OF WIND?
CLOSE! IT'S A SIGIL OF AERIFORMS.
Sigil of Wind Used to direct the flow of air.
Sigil of Aeriforms Used to generate air.
IS THIS THE SAME SPELL USED TO MAKE THE SEA-MIST?
THE SIGIL'S PROBABLY THE SAME, BUT I DUNNO ABOUT THE SIGNS.
INCREDIBLE... A WHOLE OTHER WORLD INHABITED BY USERS OF MAGIC...
AND STRAIGHT AHEAD IS OUR DESTINATION.
THE GREAT HALL OF WITCHES.

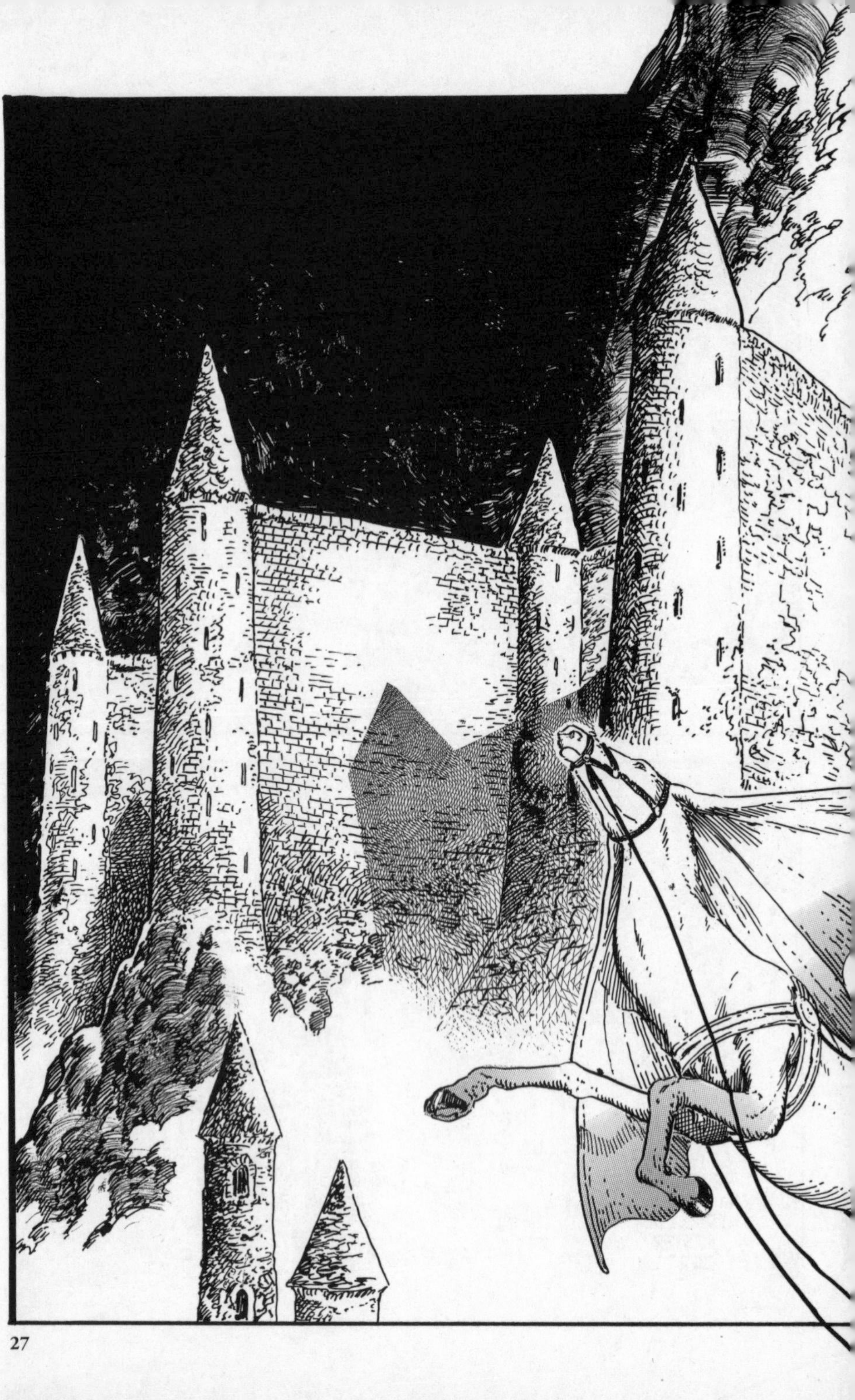

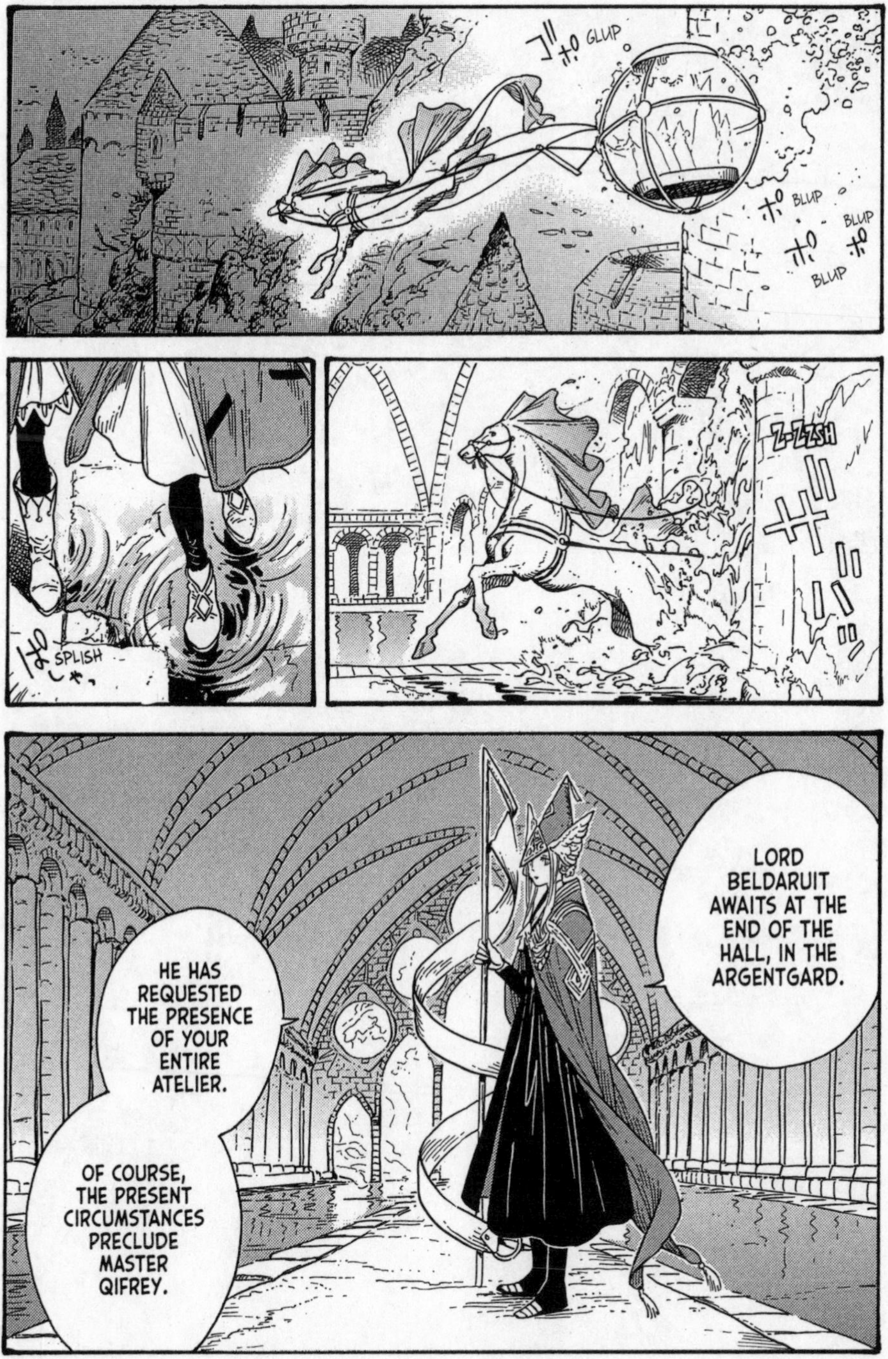
GLUP
BLUP
BLUP
BLUP
Z-ZZSH
SPLISH
LORD BELDARUIT AWAITS AT THE END OF THE HALL, IN THE ARGENTGARD.
HE HAS REQUESTED THE PRESENCE OF YOUR ENTIRE ATELIER.
OF COURSE, THE PRESENT CIRCUMSTANCES PRECLUDE MASTER QIFREY.

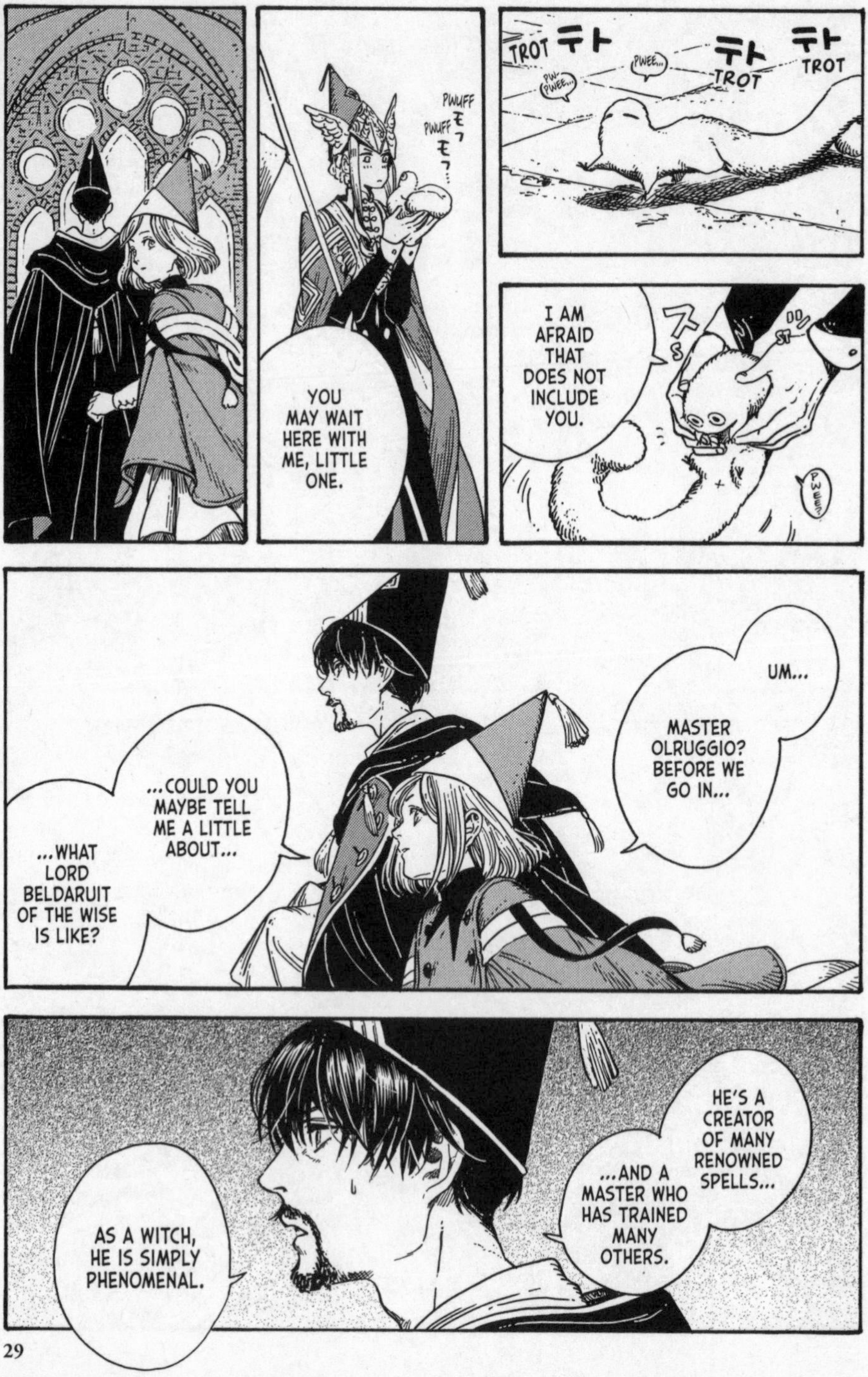
TROT テト
PWEE...
TROT テト
TROT テト
I AM AFRAID THAT DOES NOT INCLUDE YOU.
PWEE?
PWUFF モフ
PWUFF モフ
YOU MAY WAIT HERE WITH ME, LITTLE ONE.
UM...
MASTER OLRUGGIO? BEFORE WE GO IN...
...COULD YOU MAYBE TELL ME A LITTLE ABOUT...
...WHAT LORD BELDARUIT OF THE WISE IS LIKE?
HE'S A CREATOR OF MANY RENOWNED SPELLS...
...AND A MASTER WHO HAS TRAINED MANY OTHERS.
AS A WITCH, HE IS SIMPLY PHENOMENAL.

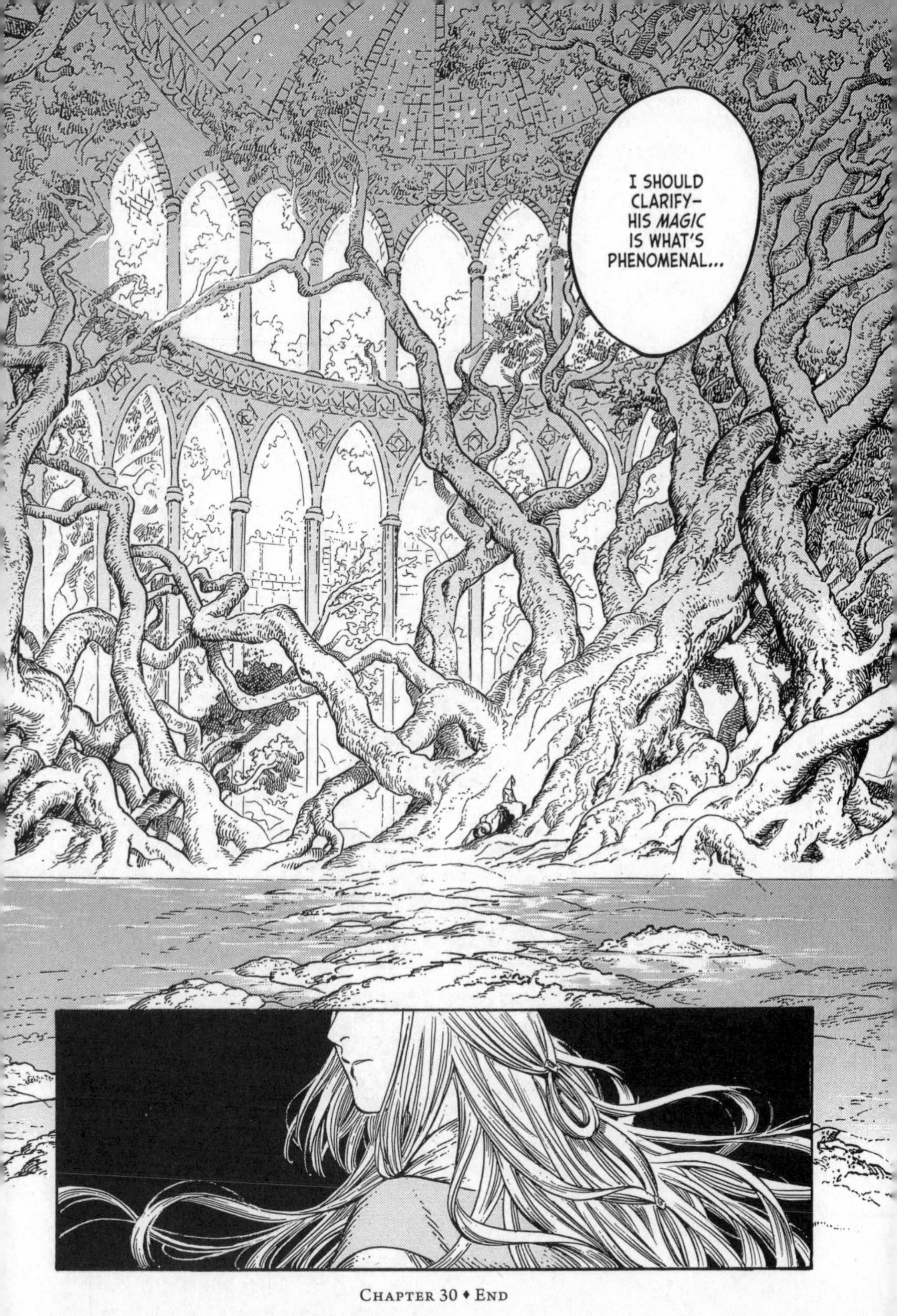
I SHOULD CLARIFY— HIS *MAGIC* IS WHAT'S PHENOMENAL...

Chapter 30 ♦ End

Witch Hat
Atelier

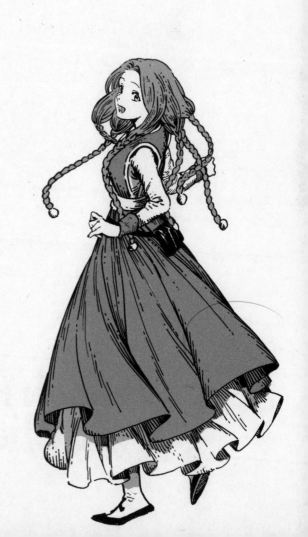

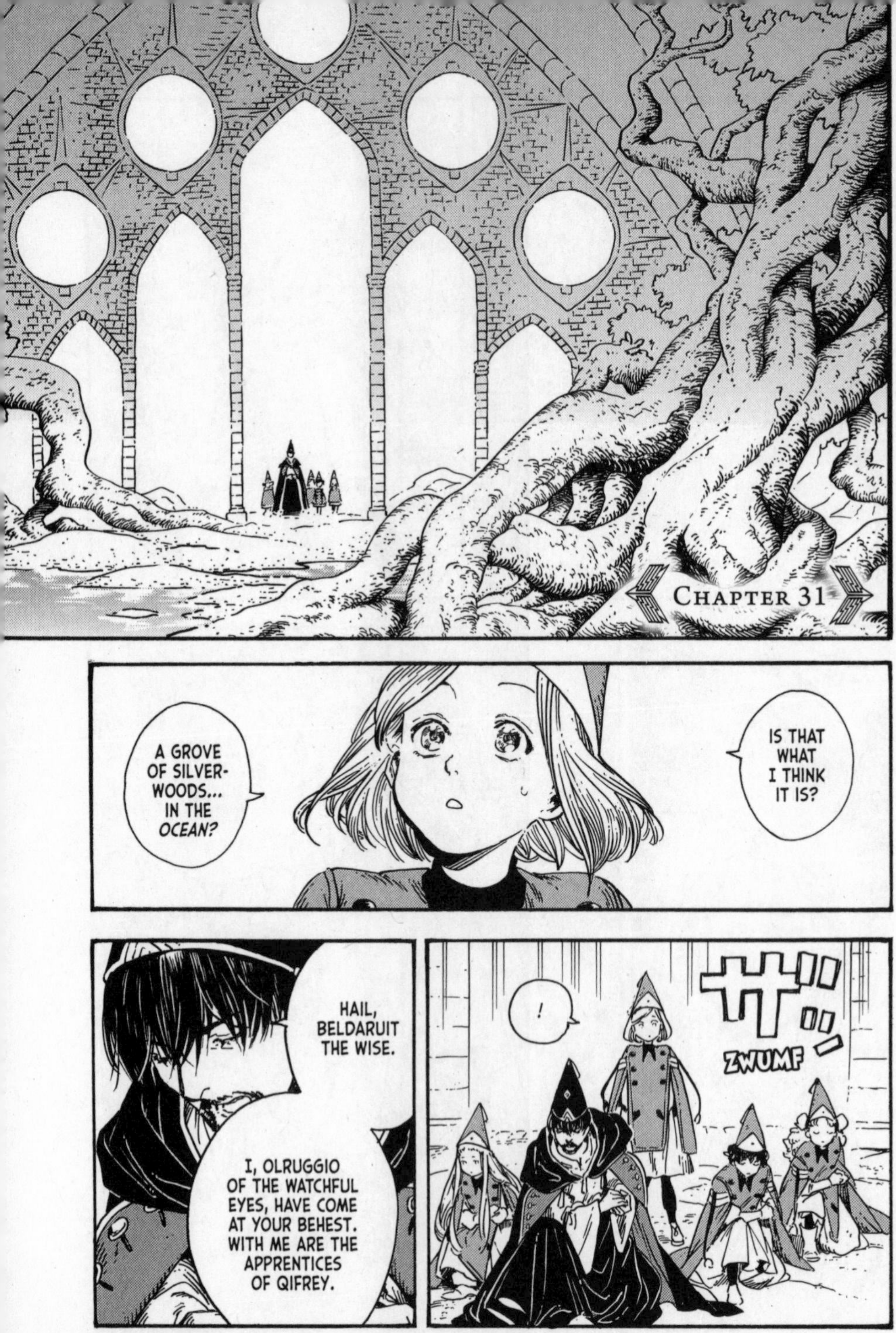
Chapter 31
IS THAT WHAT I THINK IT IS?
A GROVE OF SILVER-WOODS... IN THE *OCEAN?*
ZWUMF
!
HAIL, BELDARUIT THE WISE.
I, OLRUGGIO OF THE WATCHFUL EYES, HAVE COME AT YOUR BEHEST. WITH ME ARE THE APPRENTICES OF QIFREY.

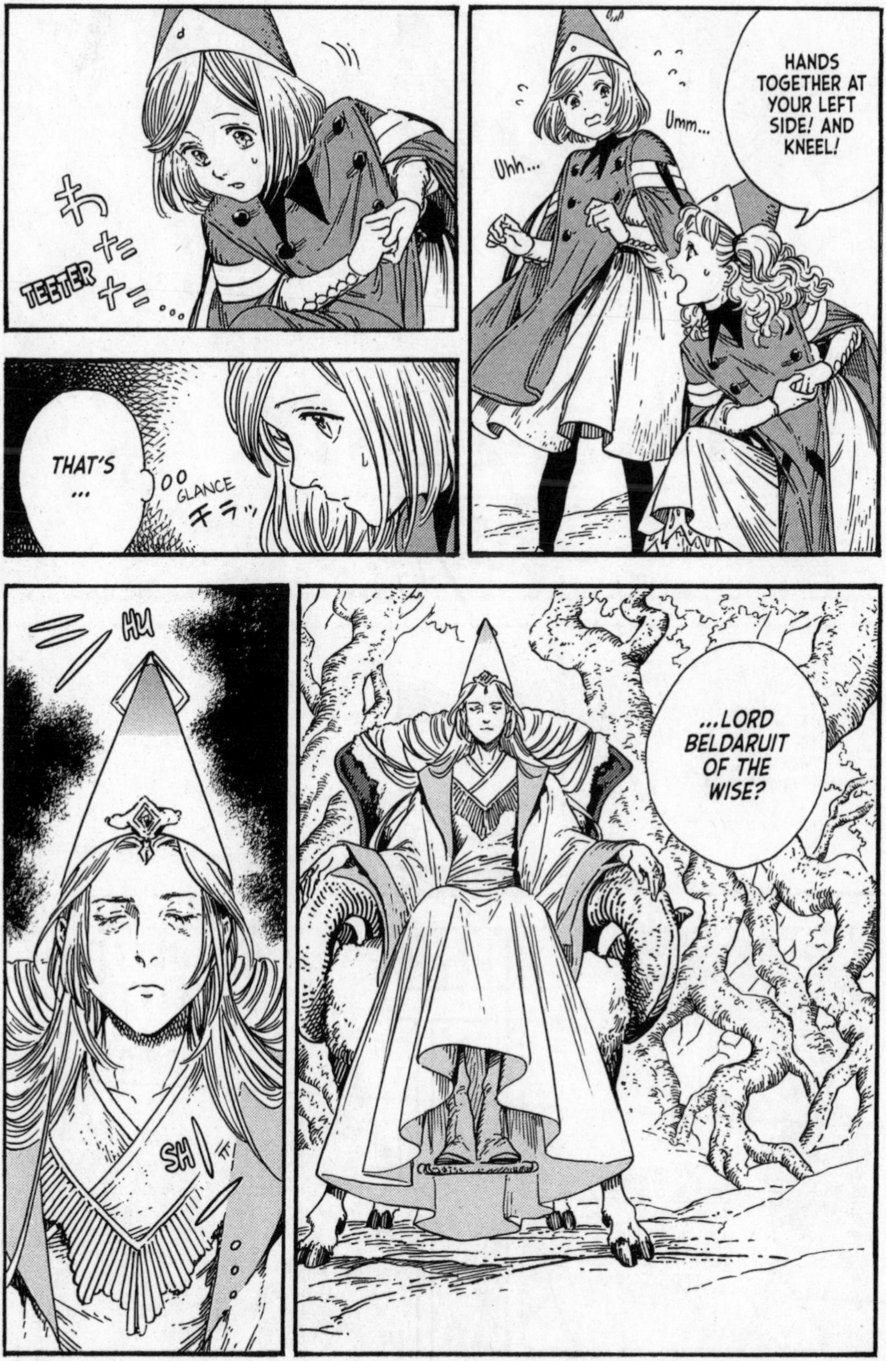
HANDS TOGETHER AT YOUR LEFT SIDE! AND KNEEL!
Umm...
Uhh...
TEETER
THAT'S ...
GLANCE
チラッ
...LORD BELDARUIT OF THE WISE?
HU
SH

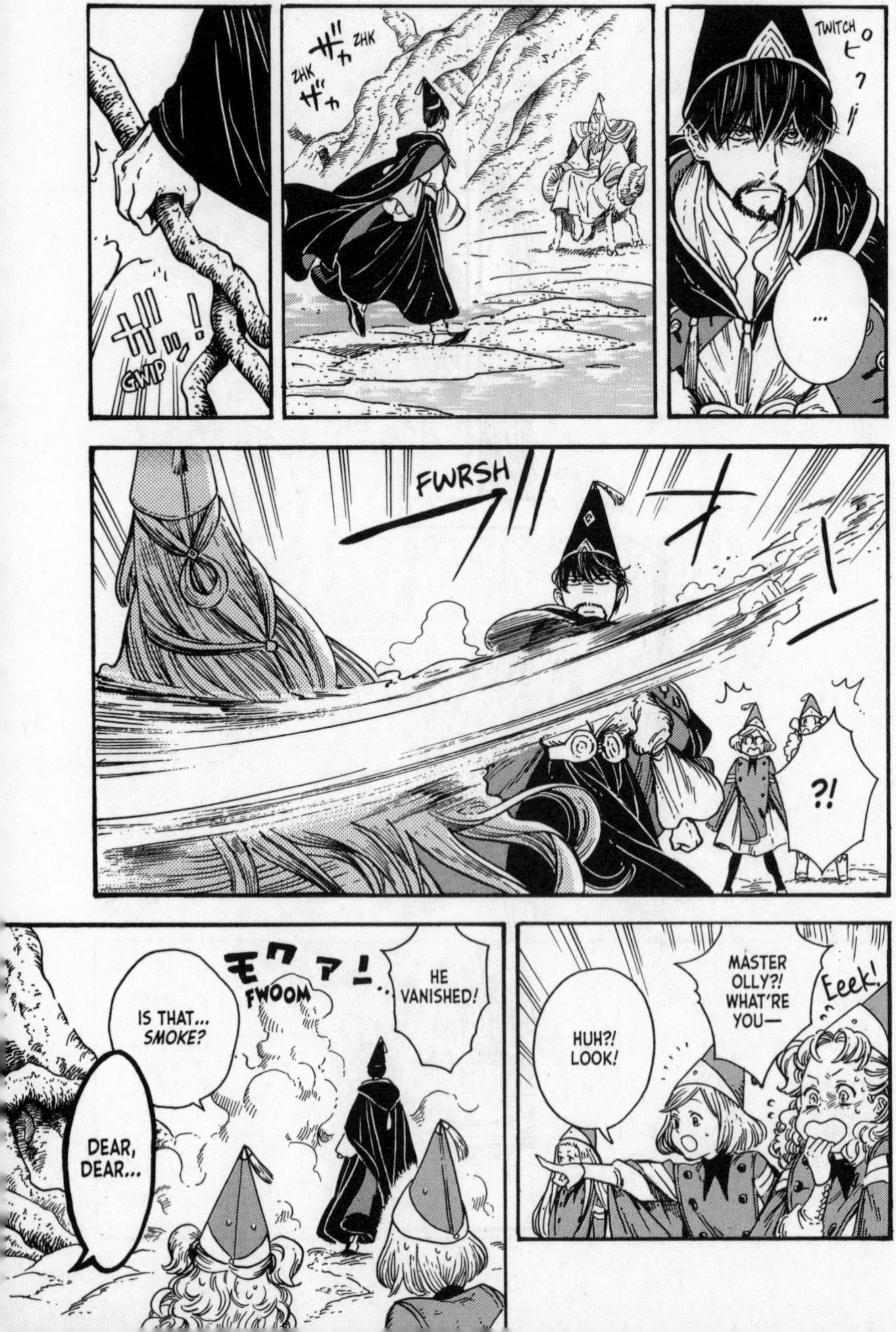
TWITCH
...
ZHK
ZHK
GWIP
FWRSH
?!
MASTER OLLY?! WHAT'RE YOU—
Eeek!
HUH?! LOOK!
HE VANISHED!
FWOOM
IS THAT... SMOKE?
DEAR, DEAR...

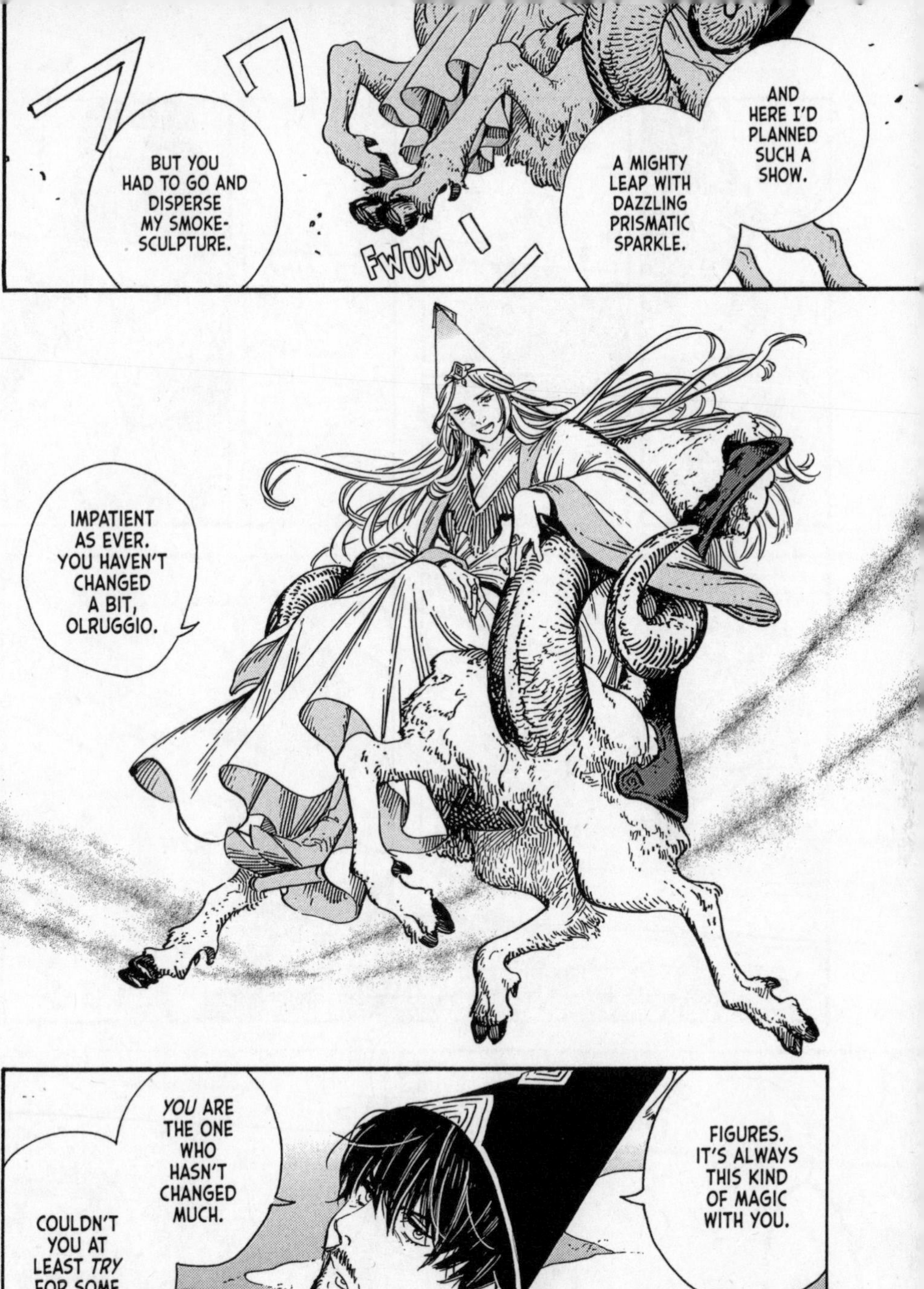
AND HERE I'D PLANNED SUCH A SHOW.
A MIGHTY LEAP WITH DAZZLING PRISMATIC SPARKLE.
FWUM
BUT YOU HAD TO GO AND DISPERSE MY SMOKE-SCULPTURE.
IMPATIENT AS EVER. YOU HAVEN'T CHANGED A BIT, OLRUGGIO.
FIGURES. IT'S ALWAYS THIS KIND OF MAGIC WITH YOU.
YOU ARE THE ONE WHO HASN'T CHANGED MUCH.
COULDN'T YOU AT LEAST *TRY* FOR SOME GRAVITAS?

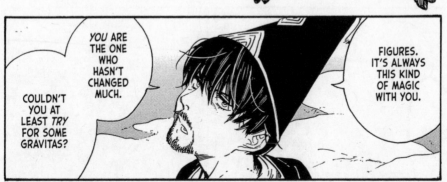

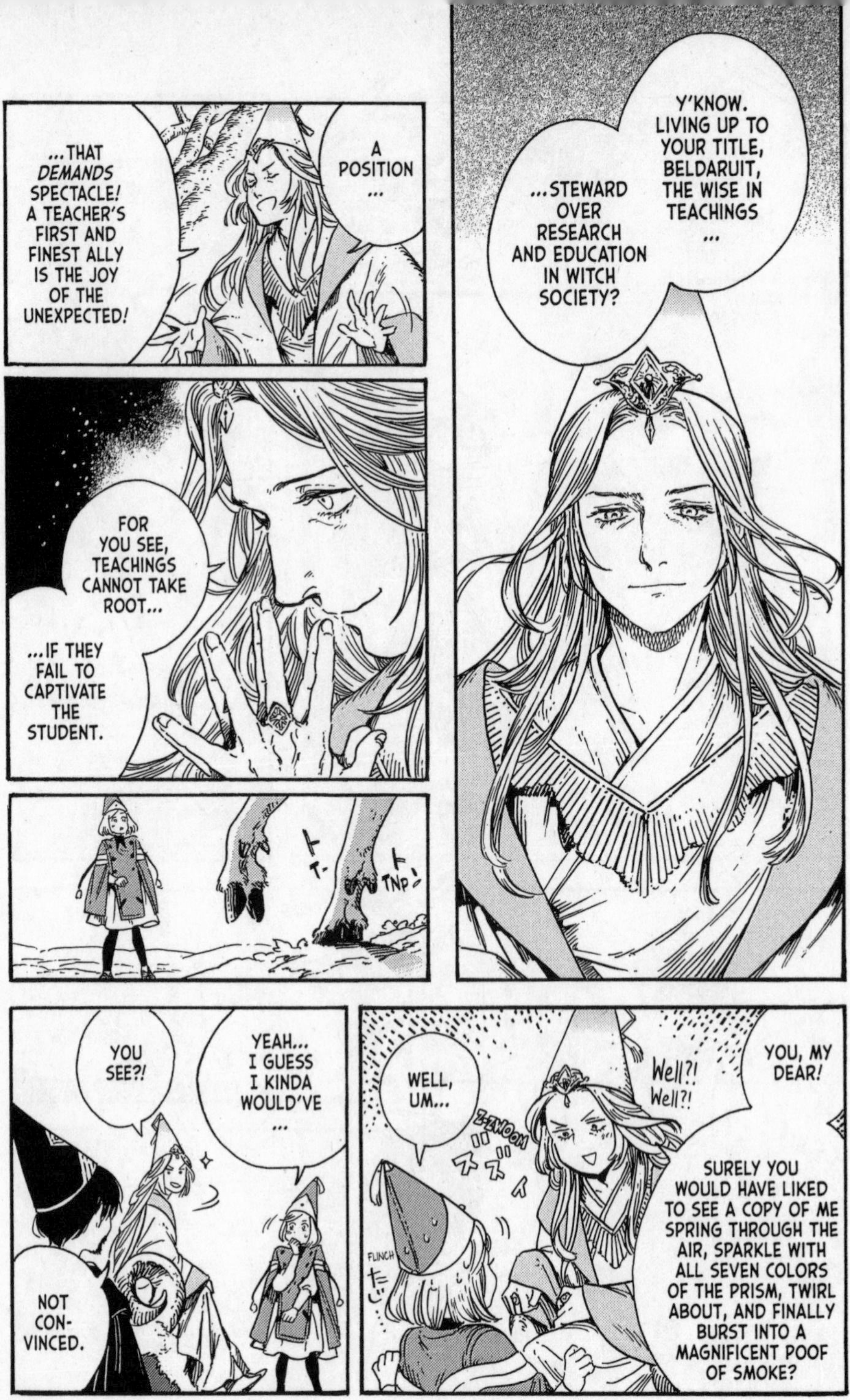
Y'KNOW. LIVING UP TO YOUR TITLE, BELDARUIT, THE WISE IN TEACHINGS ...
...STEWARD OVER RESEARCH AND EDUCATION IN WITCH SOCIETY?
A POSITION ...
...THAT *DEMANDS* SPECTACLE! A TEACHER'S FIRST AND FINEST ALLY IS THE JOY OF THE UNEXPECTED!
FOR YOU SEE, TEACHINGS CANNOT TAKE ROOT...
...IF THEY FAIL TO CAPTIVATE THE STUDENT.
TNP
YOU, MY DEAR!
Well?! Well?!
SURELY YOU WOULD HAVE LIKED TO SEE A COPY OF ME SPRING THROUGH THE AIR, SPARKLE WITH ALL SEVEN COLORS OF THE PRISM, TWIRL ABOUT, AND FINALLY BURST INTO A MAGNIFICENT POOF OF SMOKE?
Z-ZHOOM
WELL, UM...
FLINCH
YEAH... I GUESS I KINDA WOULD'VE ...
YOU SEE?!
NOT CON-VINCED.

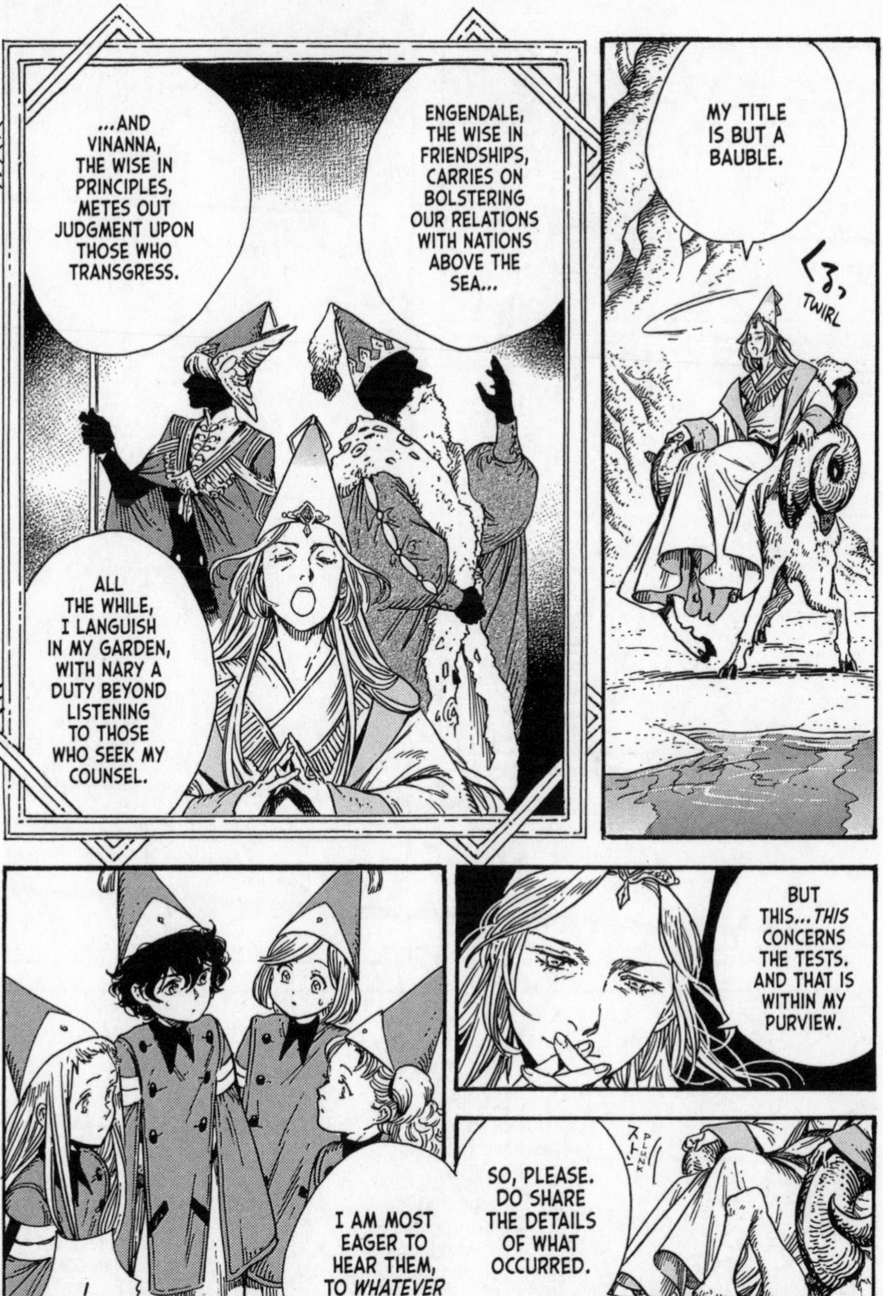

MY TITLE IS BUT A BAUBLE.
くるっ TWIRL
ENGENDALE, THE WISE IN FRIENDSHIPS, CARRIES ON BOLSTERING OUR RELATIONS WITH NATIONS ABOVE THE SEA...
...AND VINANNA, THE WISE IN PRINCIPLES, METES OUT JUDGMENT UPON THOSE WHO TRANSGRESS.
ALL THE WHILE, I LANGUISH IN MY GARDEN, WITH NARY A DUTY BEYOND LISTENING TO THOSE WHO SEEK MY COUNSEL.
BUT THIS...*THIS* CONCERNS THE TESTS. AND THAT IS WITHIN MY PURVIEW.
ストー PLUNK
SO, PLEASE. DO SHARE THE DETAILS OF WHAT OCCURRED.
I AM MOST EAGER TO HEAR THEM, TO *WHATEVER* EXTENT YOU REMEMBER.
!

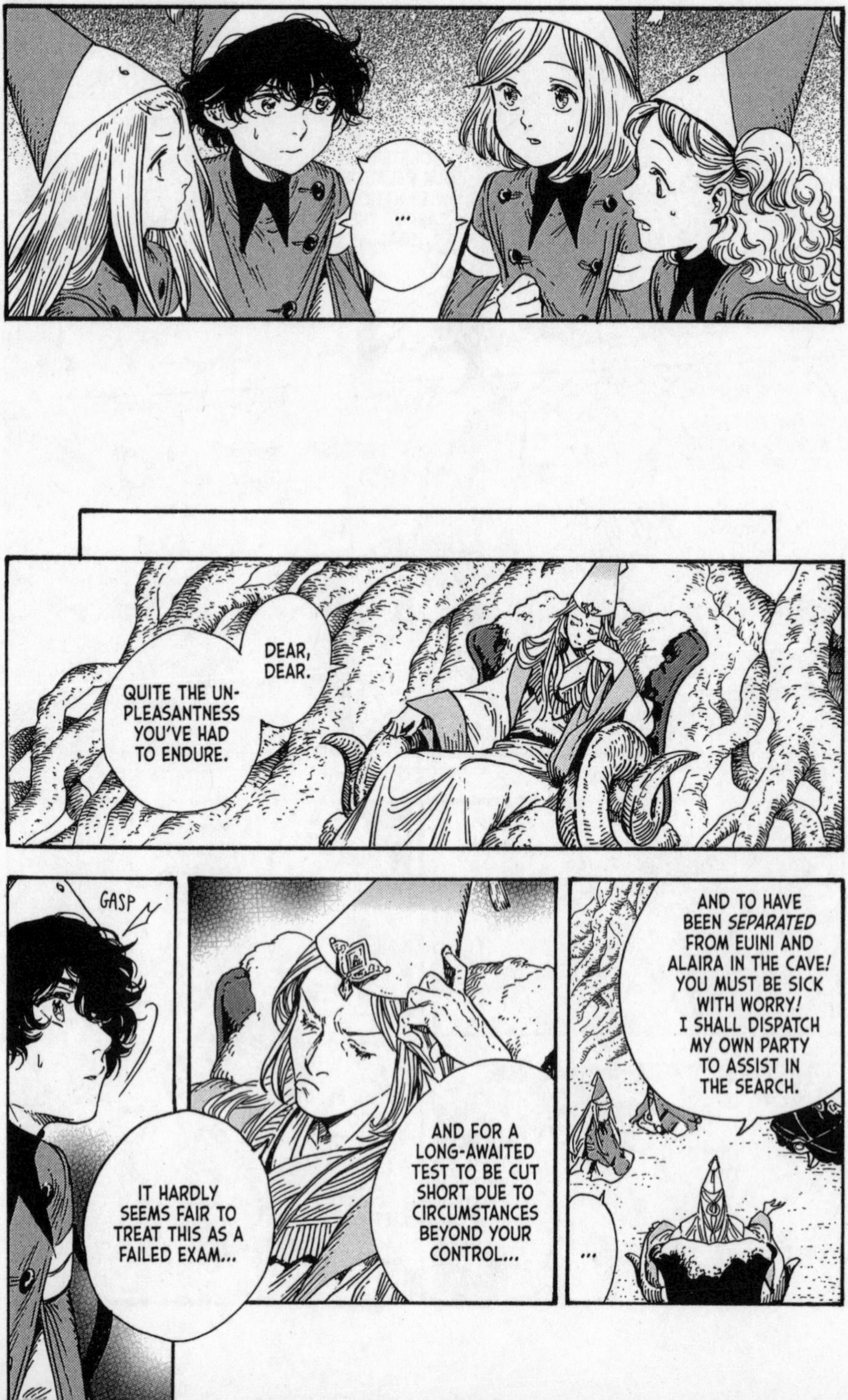
...
DEAR, DEAR.
QUITE THE UN-PLEASANTNESS YOU'VE HAD TO ENDURE.
AND TO HAVE BEEN *SEPARATED* FROM EUINI AND ALAIRA IN THE CAVE! YOU MUST BE SICK WITH WORRY! I SHALL DISPATCH MY OWN PARTY TO ASSIST IN THE SEARCH.
...
AND FOR A LONG-AWAITED TEST TO BE CUT SHORT DUE TO CIRCUMSTANCES BEYOND YOUR CONTROL...
GASP
IT HARDLY SEEMS FAIR TO TREAT THIS AS A FAILED EXAM...

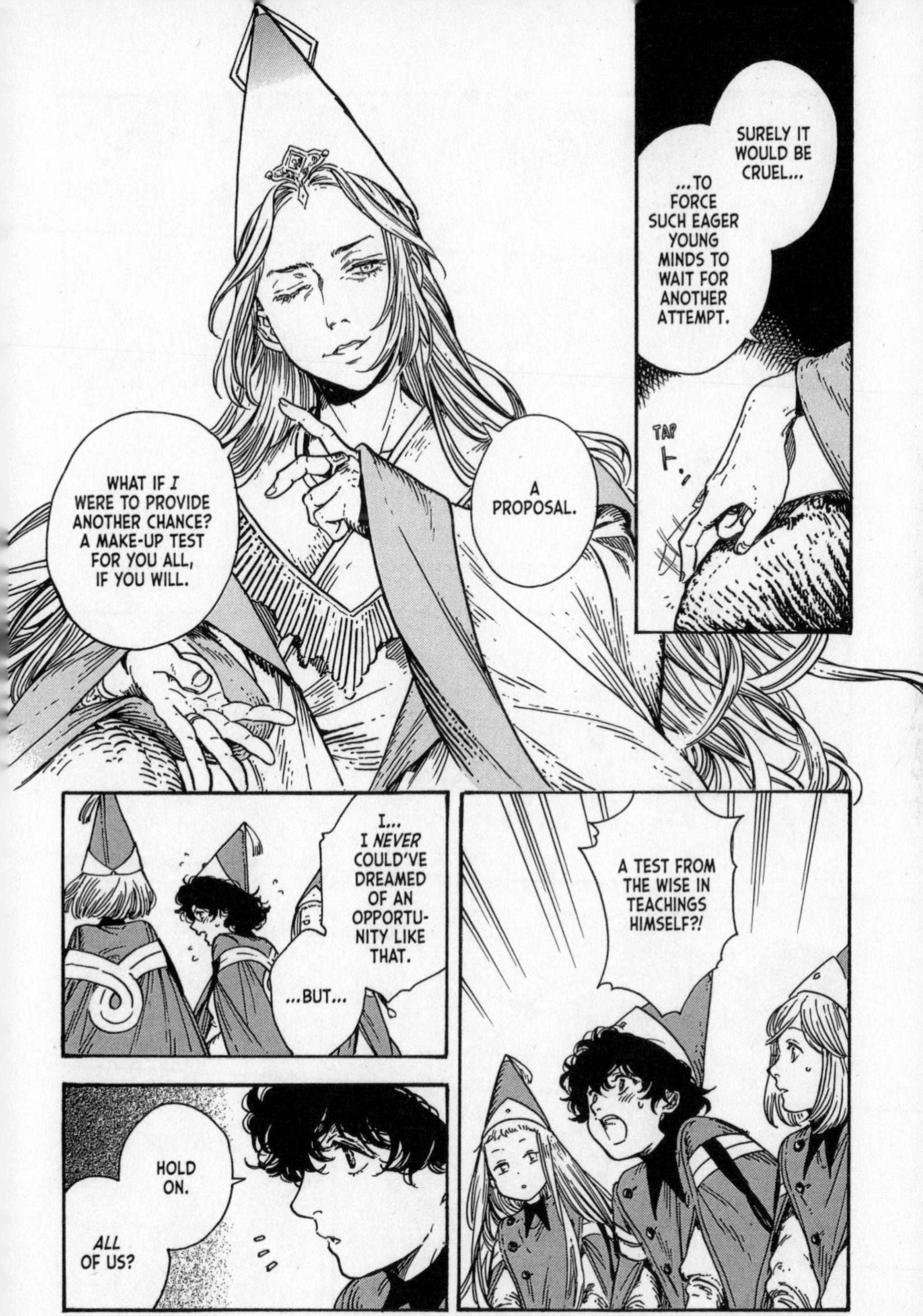
SURELY IT WOULD BE CRUEL...
...TO FORCE SUCH EAGER YOUNG MINDS TO WAIT FOR ANOTHER ATTEMPT.
TAP
A PROPOSAL.
WHAT IF *I* WERE TO PROVIDE ANOTHER CHANCE? A MAKE-UP TEST FOR YOU ALL, IF YOU WILL.
A TEST FROM THE WISE IN TEACHINGS HIMSELF?!
I... I *NEVER* COULD'VE DREAMED OF AN OPPORTUNITY LIKE THAT.
...BUT...
HOLD ON.
ALL OF US?

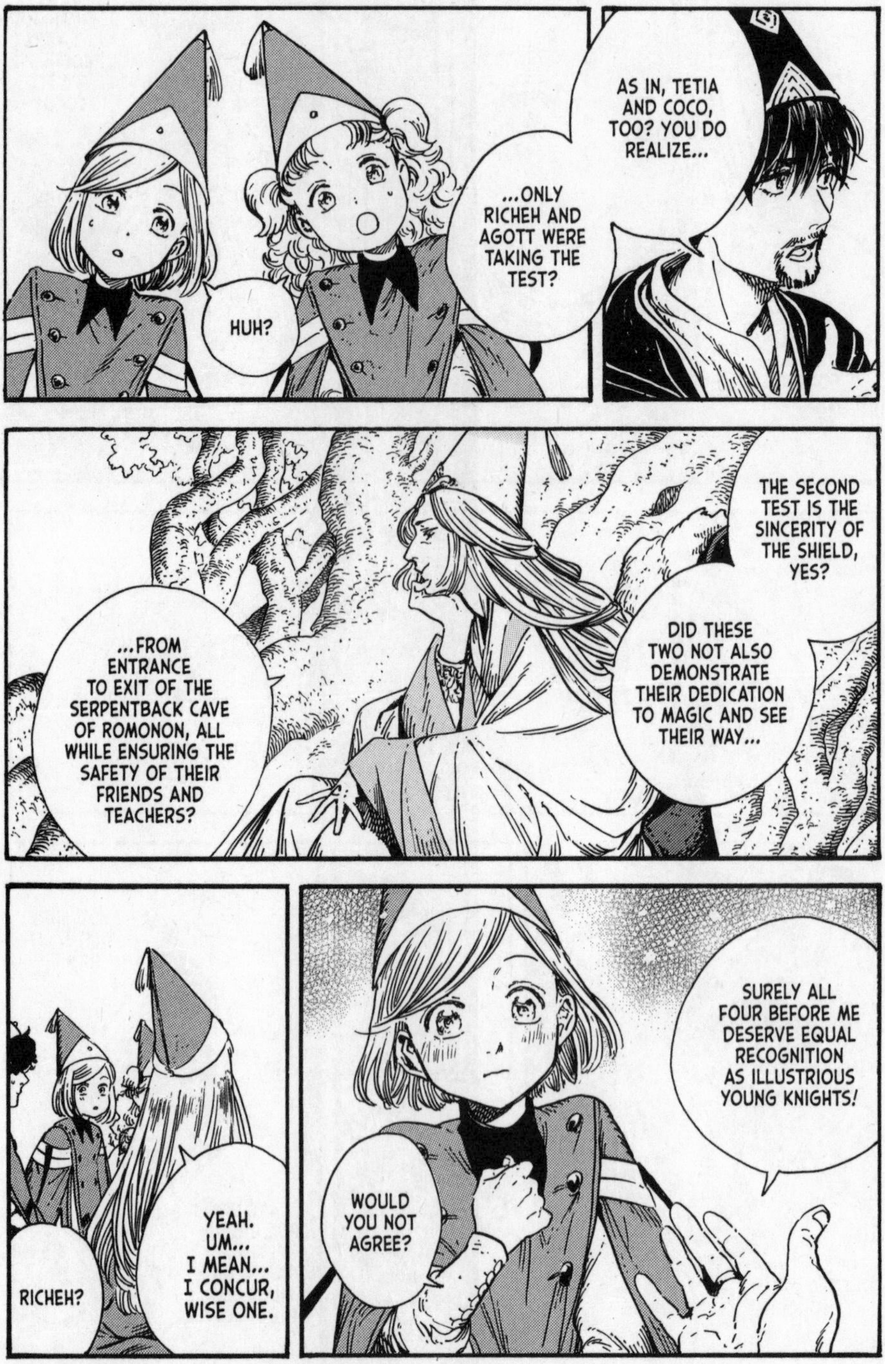
AS IN, TETIA AND COCO, TOO? YOU DO REALIZE...
...ONLY RICHEH AND AGOTT WERE TAKING THE TEST?
HUH?
THE SECOND TEST IS THE SINCERITY OF THE SHIELD, YES?
DID THESE TWO NOT ALSO DEMONSTRATE THEIR DEDICATION TO MAGIC AND SEE THEIR WAY...
...FROM ENTRANCE TO EXIT OF THE SERPENTBACK CAVE OF ROMONON, ALL WHILE ENSURING THE SAFETY OF THEIR FRIENDS AND TEACHERS?
SURELY ALL FOUR BEFORE ME DESERVE EQUAL RECOGNITION AS ILLUSTRIOUS YOUNG KNIGHTS!
WOULD YOU NOT AGREE?
YEAH. UM... I MEAN... I CONCUR, WISE ONE.
RICHEH?

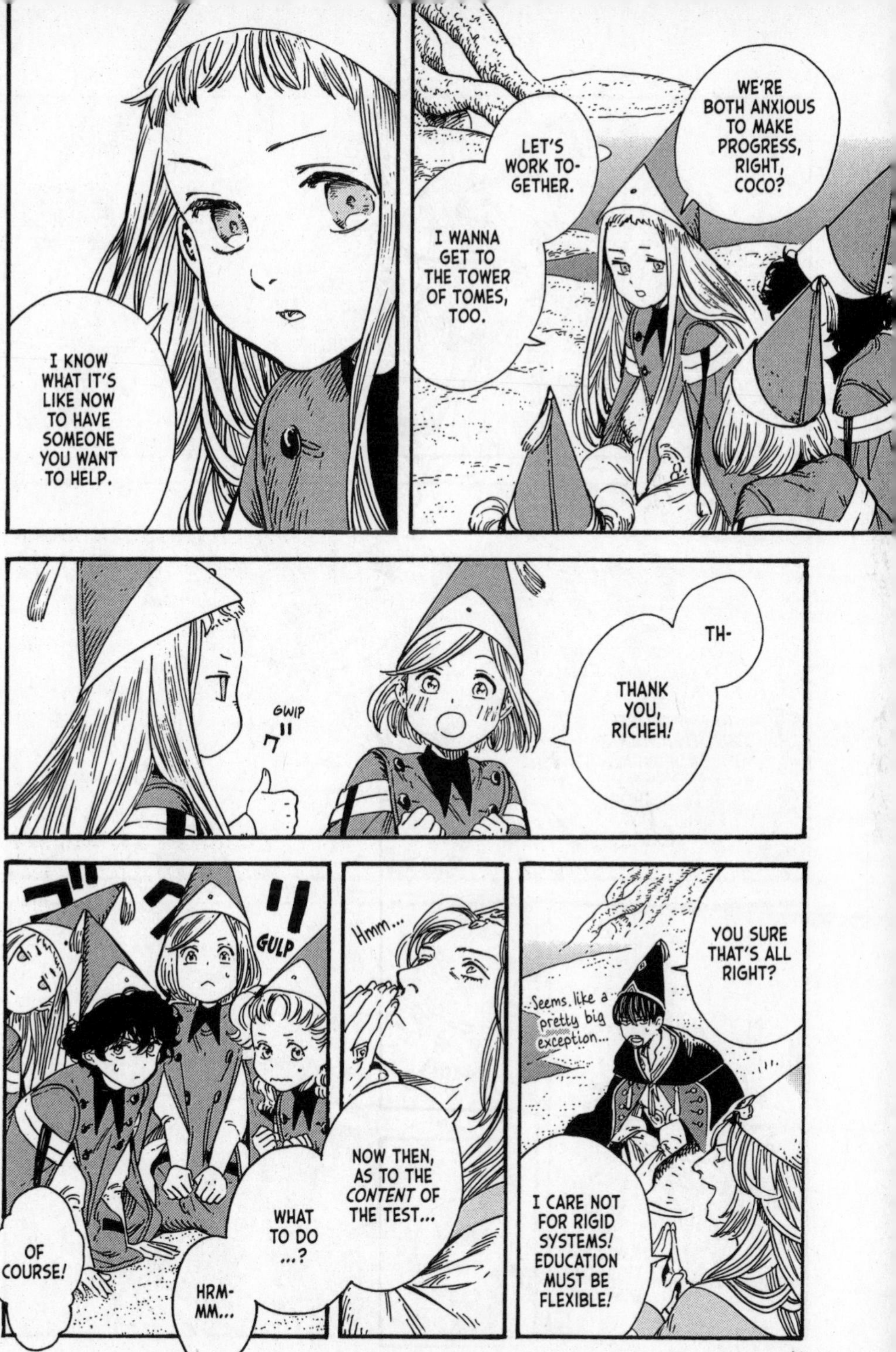
WE'RE BOTH ANXIOUS TO MAKE PROGRESS, RIGHT, COCO?
LET'S WORK TO-GETHER.
I WANNA GET TO THE TOWER OF TOMES, TOO.
I KNOW WHAT IT'S LIKE NOW TO HAVE SOMEONE YOU WANT TO HELP.
TH-
THANK YOU, RICHEH!
GWIP
YOU SURE THAT'S ALL RIGHT?
Seems like a pretty big exception...
I CARE NOT FOR RIGID SYSTEMS! EDUCATION MUST BE FLEXIBLE!
Hmm...
NOW THEN, AS TO THE *CONTENT* OF THE TEST...
WHAT TO DO ...?
HRM-MM...
ゴクリ
GULP
OF COURSE!

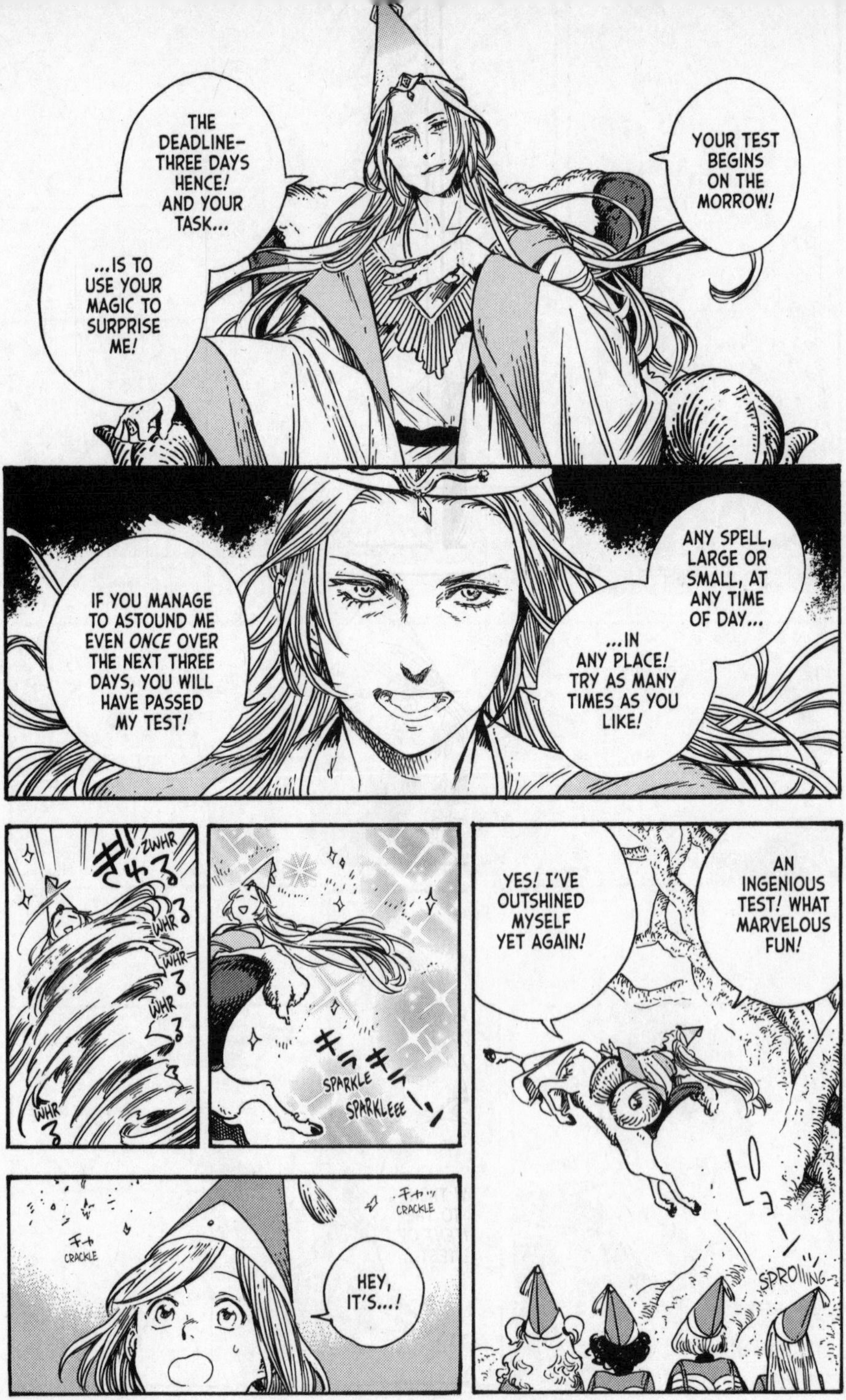
YOUR TEST BEGINS ON THE MORROW!
THE DEADLINE— THREE DAYS HENCE! AND YOUR TASK...
...IS TO USE YOUR MAGIC TO SURPRISE ME!
ANY SPELL, LARGE OR SMALL, AT ANY TIME OF DAY...
...IN ANY PLACE! TRY AS MANY TIMES AS YOU LIKE!
IF YOU MANAGE TO ASTOUND ME EVEN *ONCE* OVER THE NEXT THREE DAYS, YOU WILL HAVE PASSED MY TEST!
AN INGENIOUS TEST! WHAT MARVELOUS FUN!
YES! I'VE OUTSHINED MYSELF YET AGAIN!
SPROING
SPARKLE
SPARKLEEE
ZWHR
WHR
WHR
WHR
WHR
CRACKLE
HEY, IT'S...!
CRACKLE

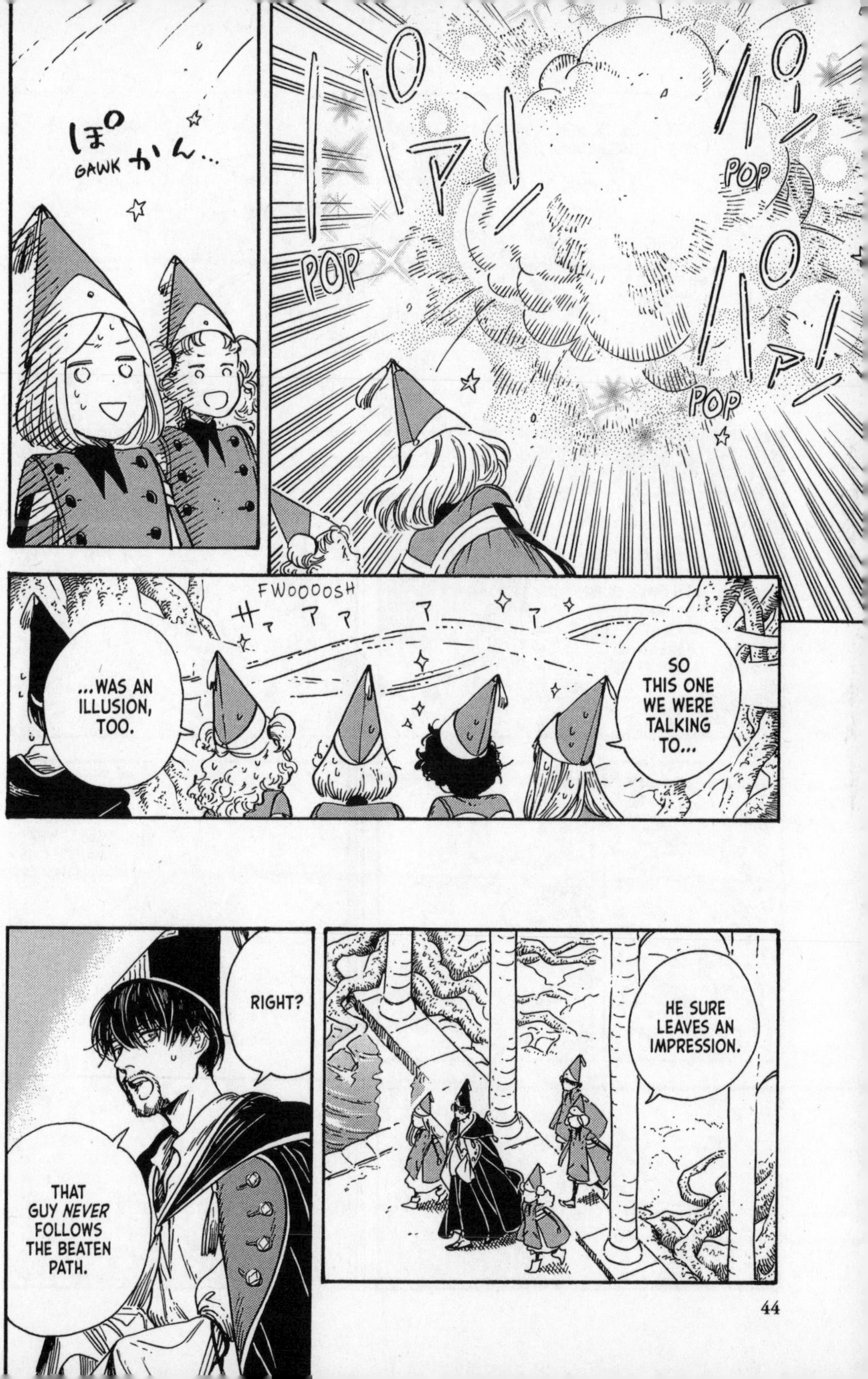
パーン
POP
パーン
POP
パァーン
POP
ぽかん…
GAWK
FWOOOOSH
サァァァーァ
SO THIS ONE WE WERE TALKING TO...
...WAS AN ILLUSION, TOO.
HE SURE LEAVES AN IMPRESSION.
RIGHT?
THAT GUY *NEVER* FOLLOWS THE BEATEN PATH.

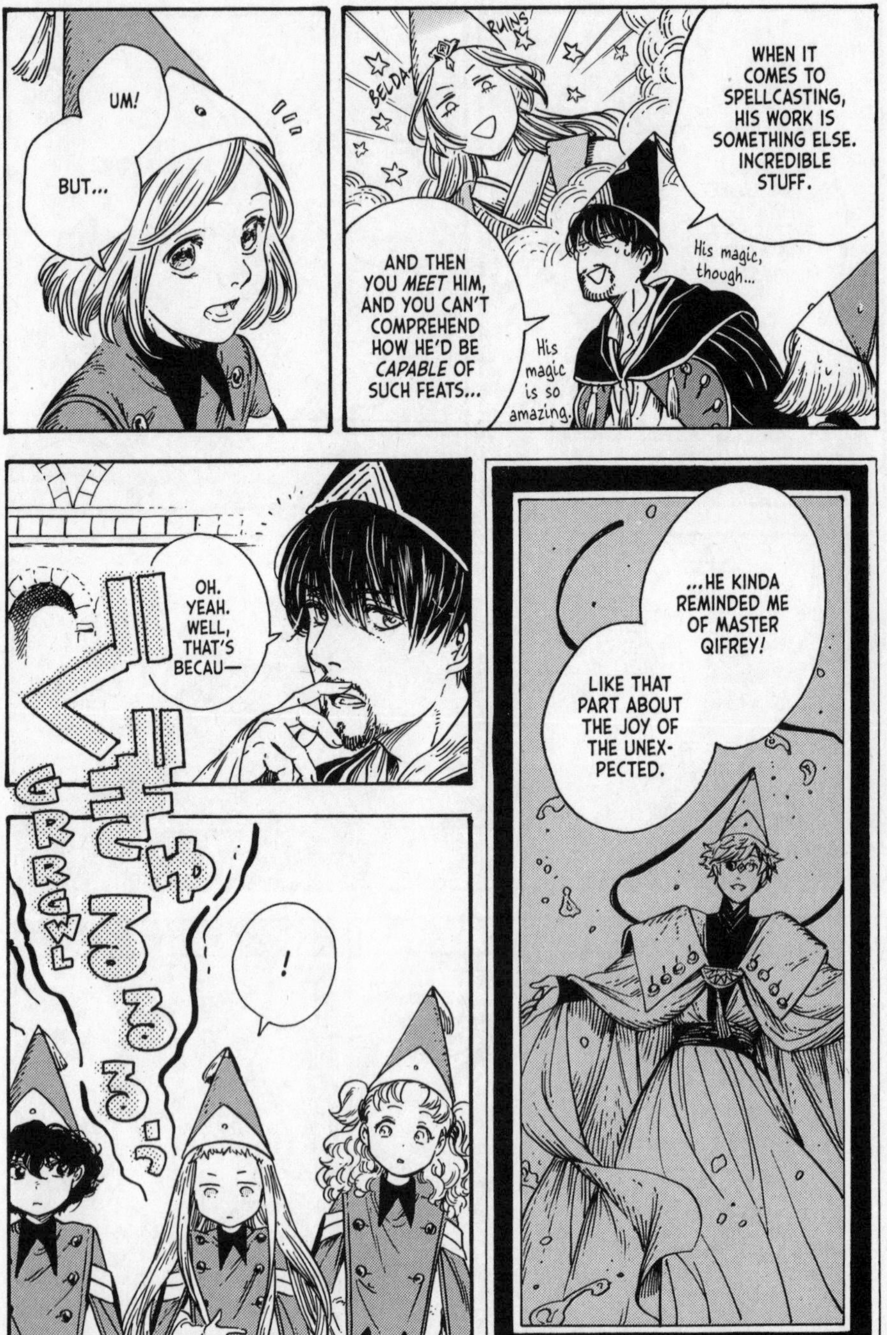
WHEN IT COMES TO SPELLCASTING, HIS WORK IS SOMETHING ELSE. INCREDIBLE STUFF.
BELDA RUINS
His magic, though...
AND THEN YOU MEET HIM, AND YOU CAN'T COMPREHEND HOW HE'D BE CAPABLE OF SUCH FEATS...
His magic is so amazing.
UM!
BUT...
...HE KINDA REMINDED ME OF MASTER QIFREY!
LIKE THAT PART ABOUT THE JOY OF THE UNEXPECTED.
OH. YEAH. WELL, THAT'S BECAU—
GRRGWL
!

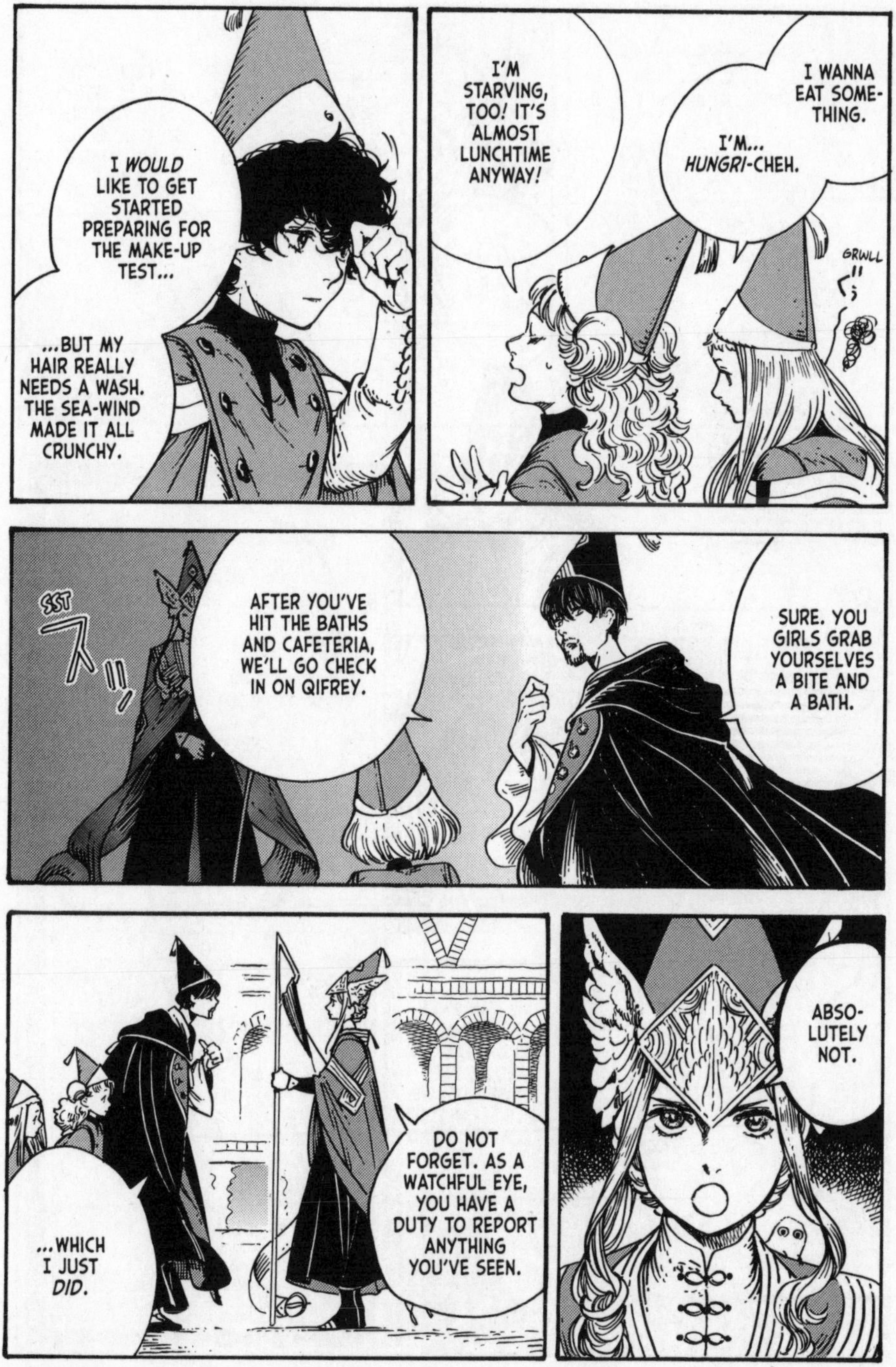
I WANNA EAT SOME-THING.
I'M... HUNGRI-CHEH.
I'M STARVING, TOO! IT'S ALMOST LUNCHTIME ANYWAY!
GRWLL
I WOULD LIKE TO GET STARTED PREPARING FOR THE MAKE-UP TEST...
...BUT MY HAIR REALLY NEEDS A WASH. THE SEA-WIND MADE IT ALL CRUNCHY.
SURE. YOU GIRLS GRAB YOURSELVES A BITE AND A BATH.
AFTER YOU'VE HIT THE BATHS AND CAFETERIA, WE'LL GO CHECK IN ON QIFREY.
SST
ABSO-LUTELY NOT.
DO NOT FORGET. AS A WATCHFUL EYE, YOU HAVE A DUTY TO REPORT ANYTHING YOU'VE SEEN.
...WHICH I JUST DID.

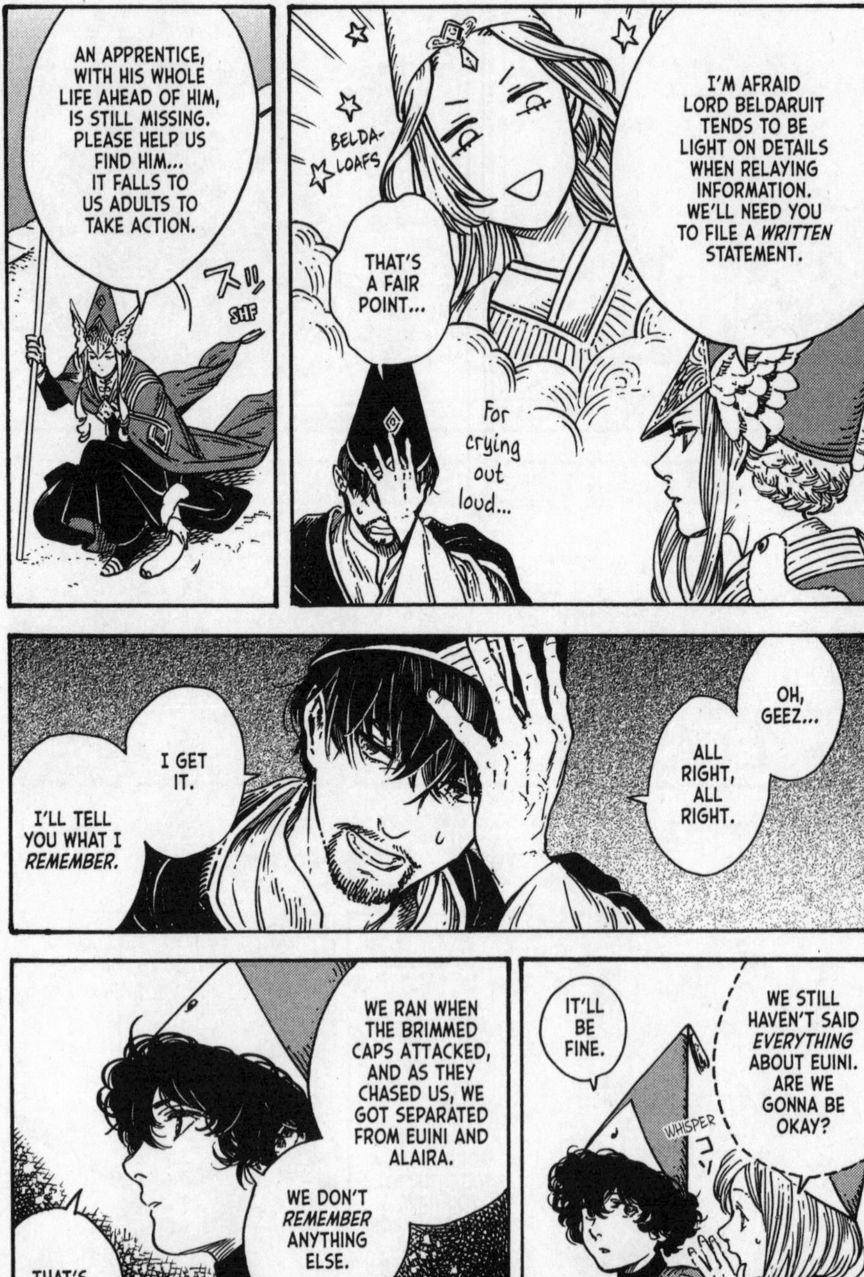
I'M AFRAID LORD BELDARUIT TENDS TO BE LIGHT ON DETAILS WHEN RELAYING INFORMATION. WE'LL NEED YOU TO FILE A *WRITTEN* STATEMENT.
BELDA-LOAFS
THAT'S A FAIR POINT...
For crying out loud...
AN APPRENTICE, WITH HIS WHOLE LIFE AHEAD OF HIM, IS STILL MISSING. PLEASE HELP US FIND HIM... IT FALLS TO US ADULTS TO TAKE ACTION.
SHF
OH, GEEZ...
ALL RIGHT, ALL RIGHT.
I GET IT.
I'LL TELL YOU WHAT I *REMEMBER.*
WE STILL HAVEN'T SAID *EVERYTHING* ABOUT EUINI. ARE WE GONNA BE OKAY?
WHISPER
IT'LL BE FINE.
WE RAN WHEN THE BRIMMED CAPS ATTACKED, AND AS THEY CHASED US, WE GOT SEPARATED FROM EUINI AND ALAIRA.
WE DON'T *REMEMBER* ANYTHING ELSE.
THAT'S ALL.

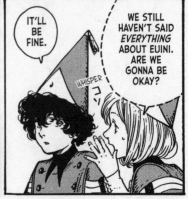

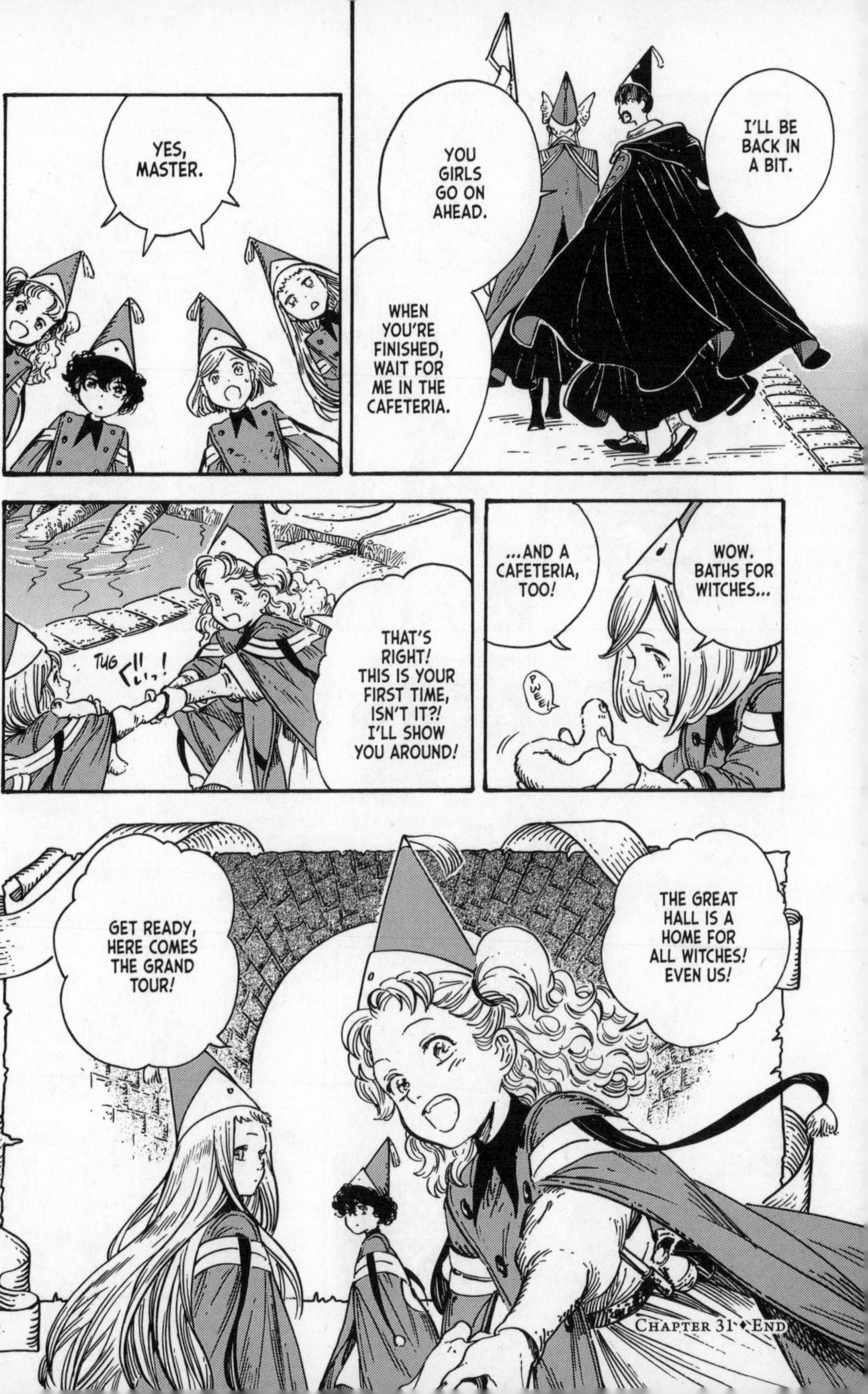
I'LL BE BACK IN A BIT.
YOU GIRLS GO ON AHEAD.
WHEN YOU'RE FINISHED, WAIT FOR ME IN THE CAFETERIA.
YES, MASTER.
WOW. BATHS FOR WITCHES...
...AND A CAFETERIA, TOO!
TUG
THAT'S RIGHT! THIS IS YOUR FIRST TIME, ISN'T IT?! I'LL SHOW YOU AROUND!
THE GREAT HALL IS A HOME FOR ALL WITCHES! EVEN US!
GET READY, HERE COMES THE GRAND TOUR!
CHAPTER 31 ♦ END

Witch Hat Atelier

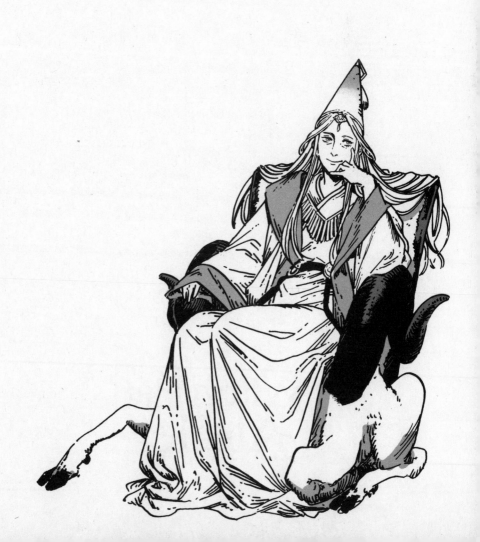

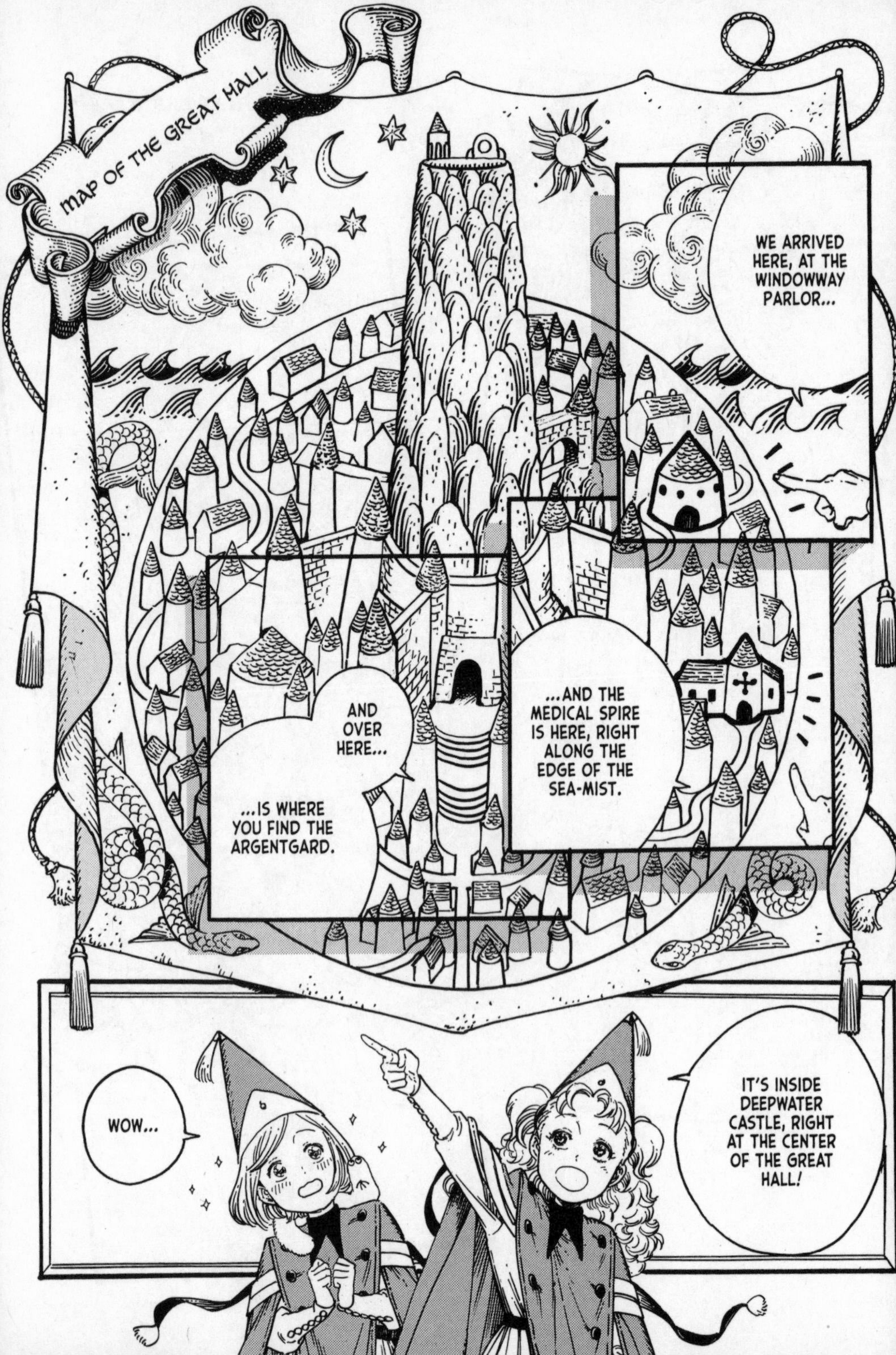
MAP OF THE GREAT HALL
WE ARRIVED HERE, AT THE WINDOWWAY PARLOR...
...AND THE MEDICAL SPIRE IS HERE, RIGHT ALONG THE EDGE OF THE SEA-MIST.
AND OVER HERE...
...IS WHERE YOU FIND THE ARGENTGARD.
IT'S INSIDE DEEPWATER CASTLE, RIGHT AT THE CENTER OF THE GREAT HALL!
WOW...

Chapter 32

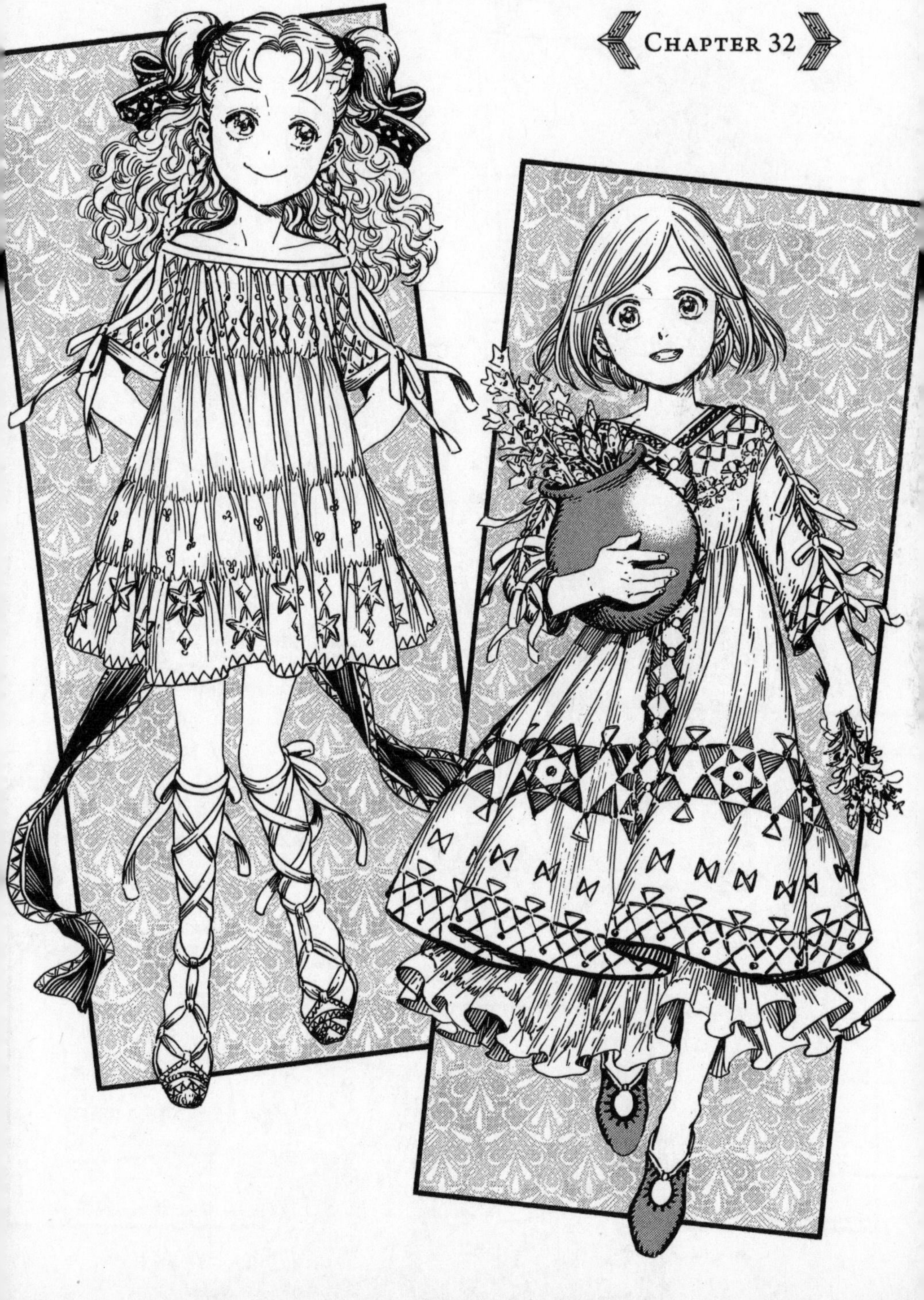

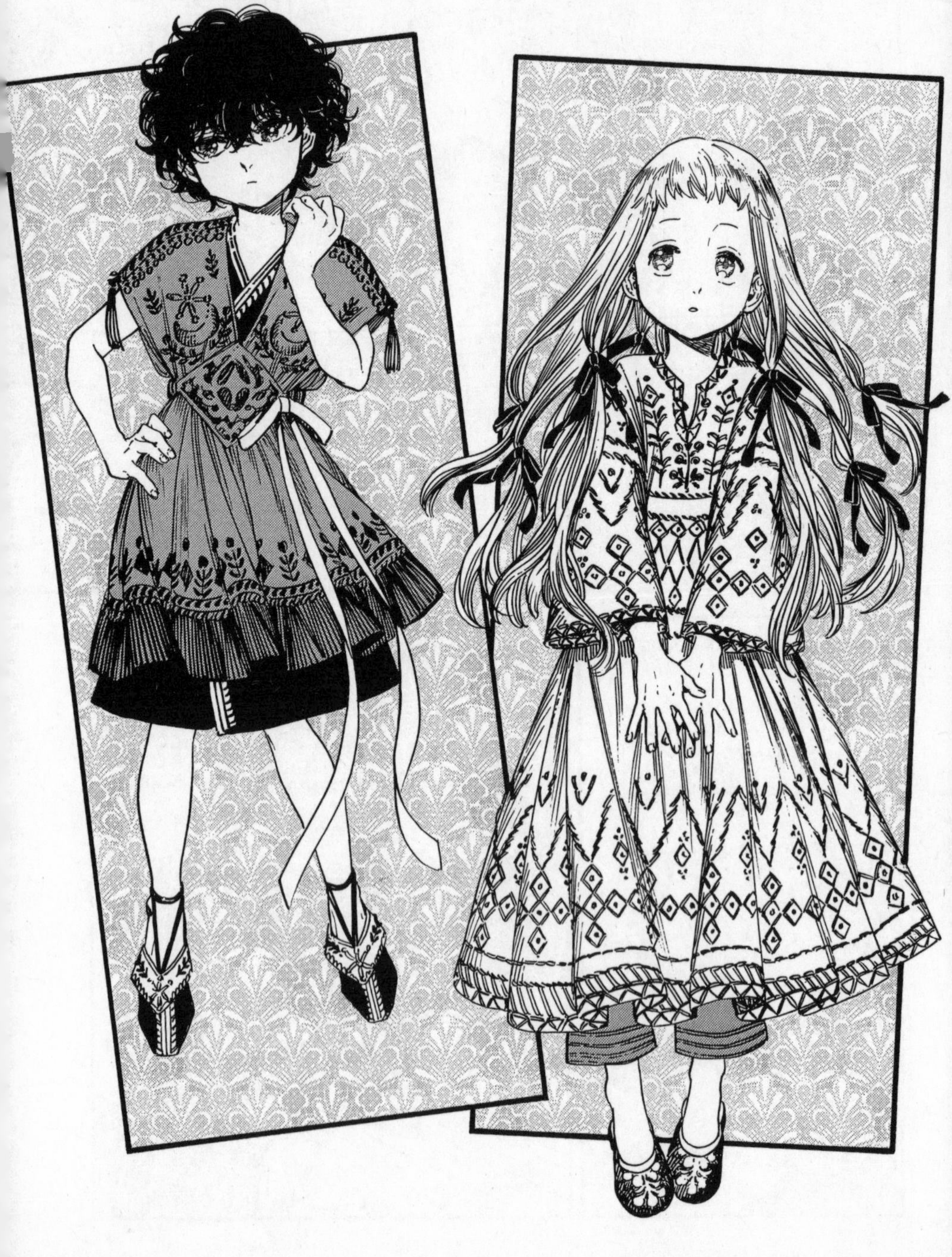

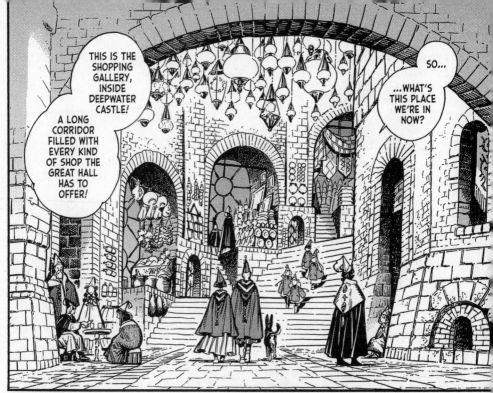

SO...
...WHAT'S THIS PLACE WE'RE IN NOW?
THIS IS THE SHOPPING GALLERY, INSIDE DEEPWATER CASTLE!
A LONG CORRIDOR FILLED WITH EVERY KIND OF SHOP THE GREAT HALL HAS TO OFFER!
EACH ALCOVE HAS SHOPS FOR FOOD OR COMPONENTS...
...AND SOME EVEN SELL CUSTOM-MADE CONTRAPTIONS!
YOU CAN ALSO FIND LIMITED-EDITION GREAT HALL MEMORABILIA!
YOU MEAN LIKE *SOUVENIRS*?!
WHOOOOA!

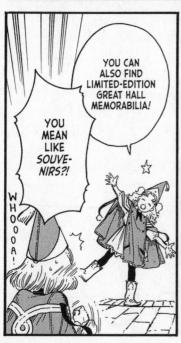

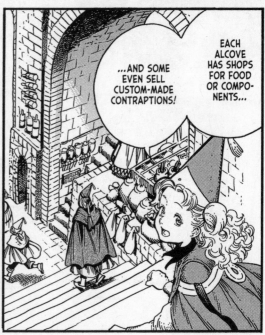

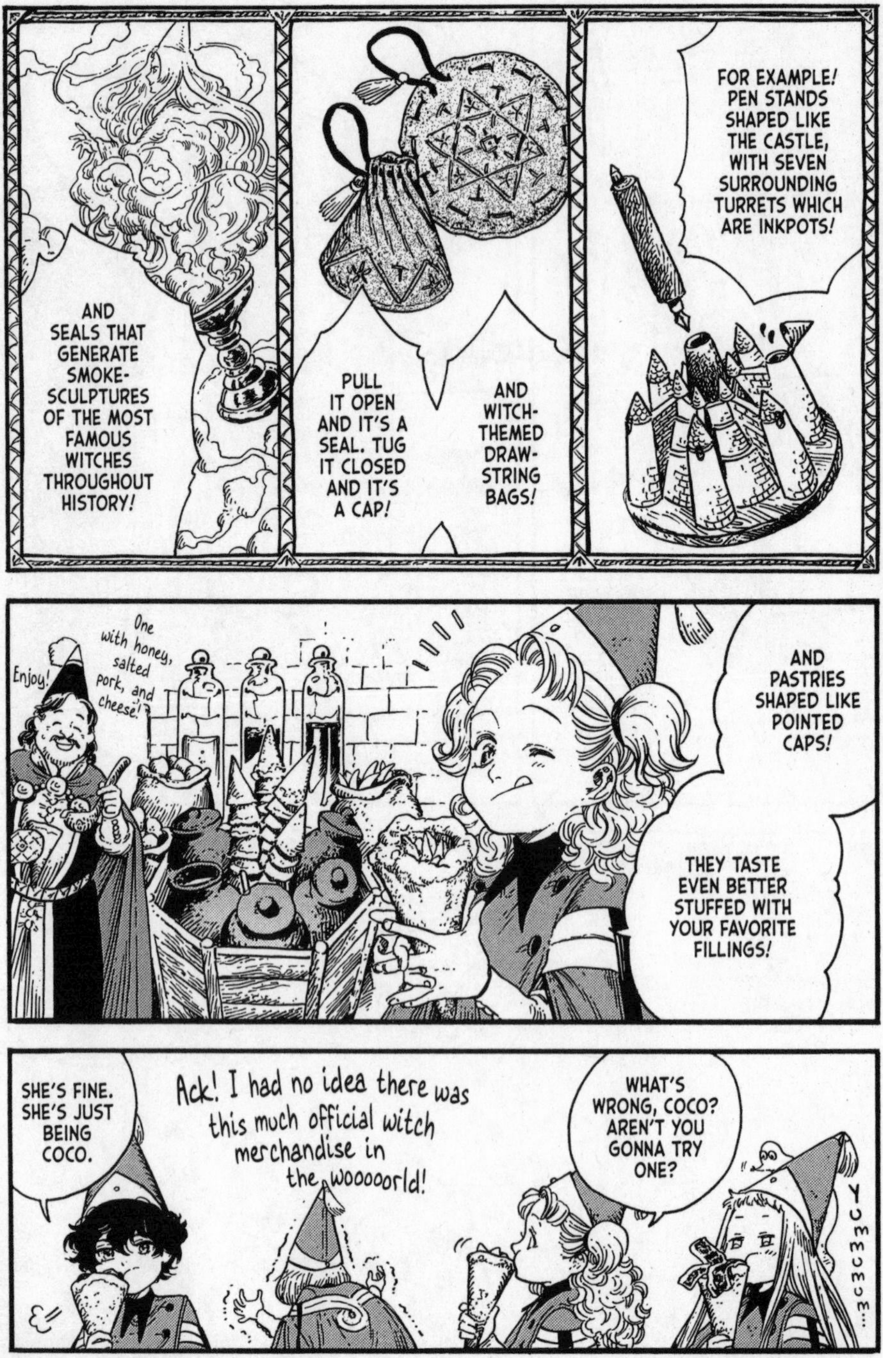
FOR EXAMPLE! PEN STANDS SHAPED LIKE THE CASTLE, WITH SEVEN SURROUNDING TURRETS WHICH ARE INKPOTS!
AND WITCH-THEMED DRAW-STRING BAGS!
PULL IT OPEN AND IT'S A SEAL. TUG IT CLOSED AND IT'S A CAP!
AND SEALS THAT GENERATE SMOKE-SCULPTURES OF THE MOST FAMOUS WITCHES THROUGHOUT HISTORY!
AND PASTRIES SHAPED LIKE POINTED CAPS!
THEY TASTE EVEN BETTER STUFFED WITH YOUR FAVORITE FILLINGS!
One with honey, salted pork, and cheese!
Enjoy!
WHAT'S WRONG, COCO? AREN'T YOU GONNA TRY ONE?
YUMMMM...
Ack! I had no idea there was this much official witch merchandise in the wooooorld!
SHE'S FINE. SHE'S JUST BEING COCO.

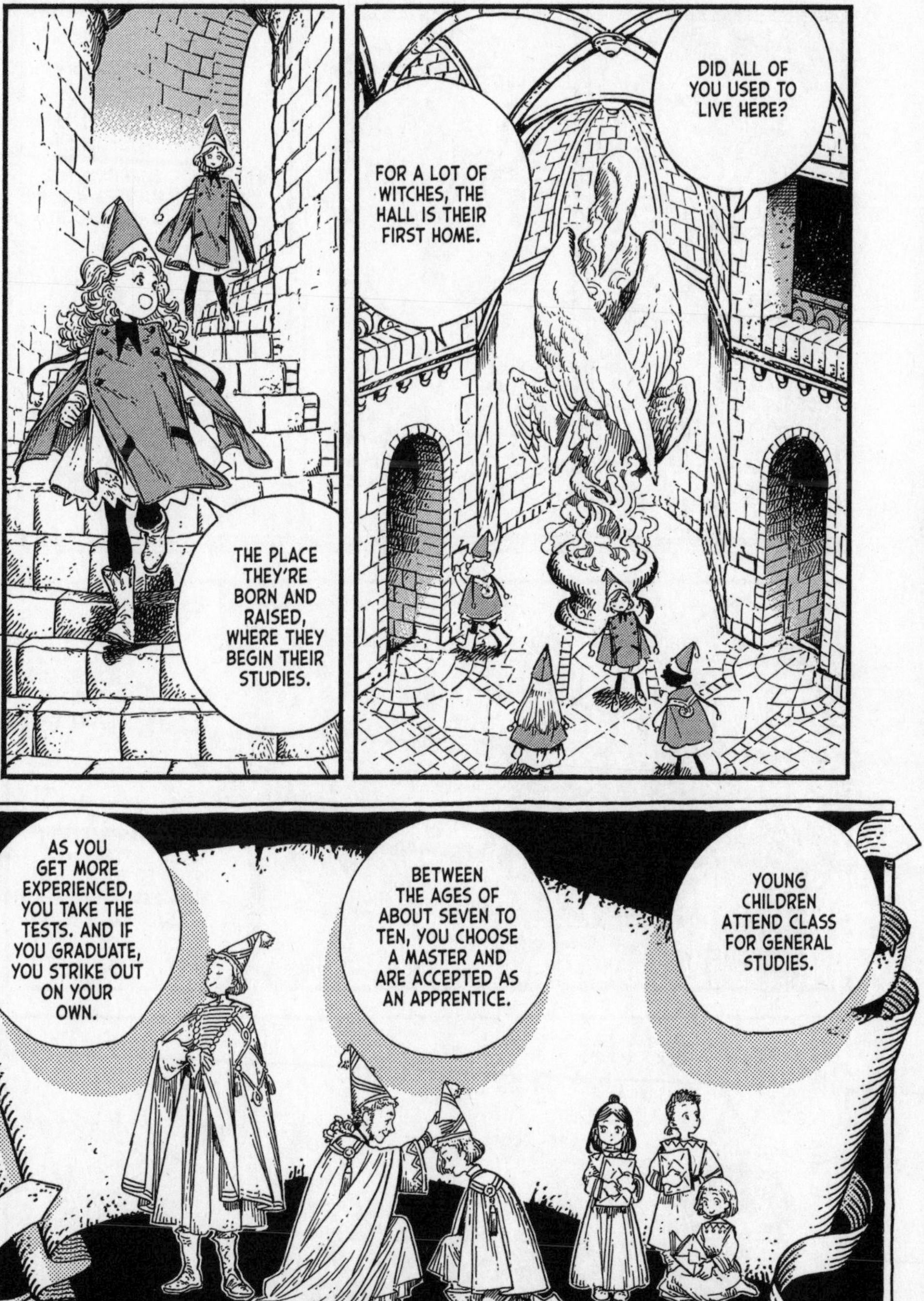
DID ALL OF YOU USED TO LIVE HERE?
FOR A LOT OF WITCHES, THE HALL IS THEIR FIRST HOME.
THE PLACE THEY'RE BORN AND RAISED, WHERE THEY BEGIN THEIR STUDIES.
YOUNG CHILDREN ATTEND CLASS FOR GENERAL STUDIES.
BETWEEN THE AGES OF ABOUT SEVEN TO TEN, YOU CHOOSE A MASTER AND ARE ACCEPTED AS AN APPRENTICE.
AS YOU GET MORE EXPERIENCED, YOU TAKE THE TESTS. AND IF YOU GRADUATE, YOU STRIKE OUT ON YOUR OWN.

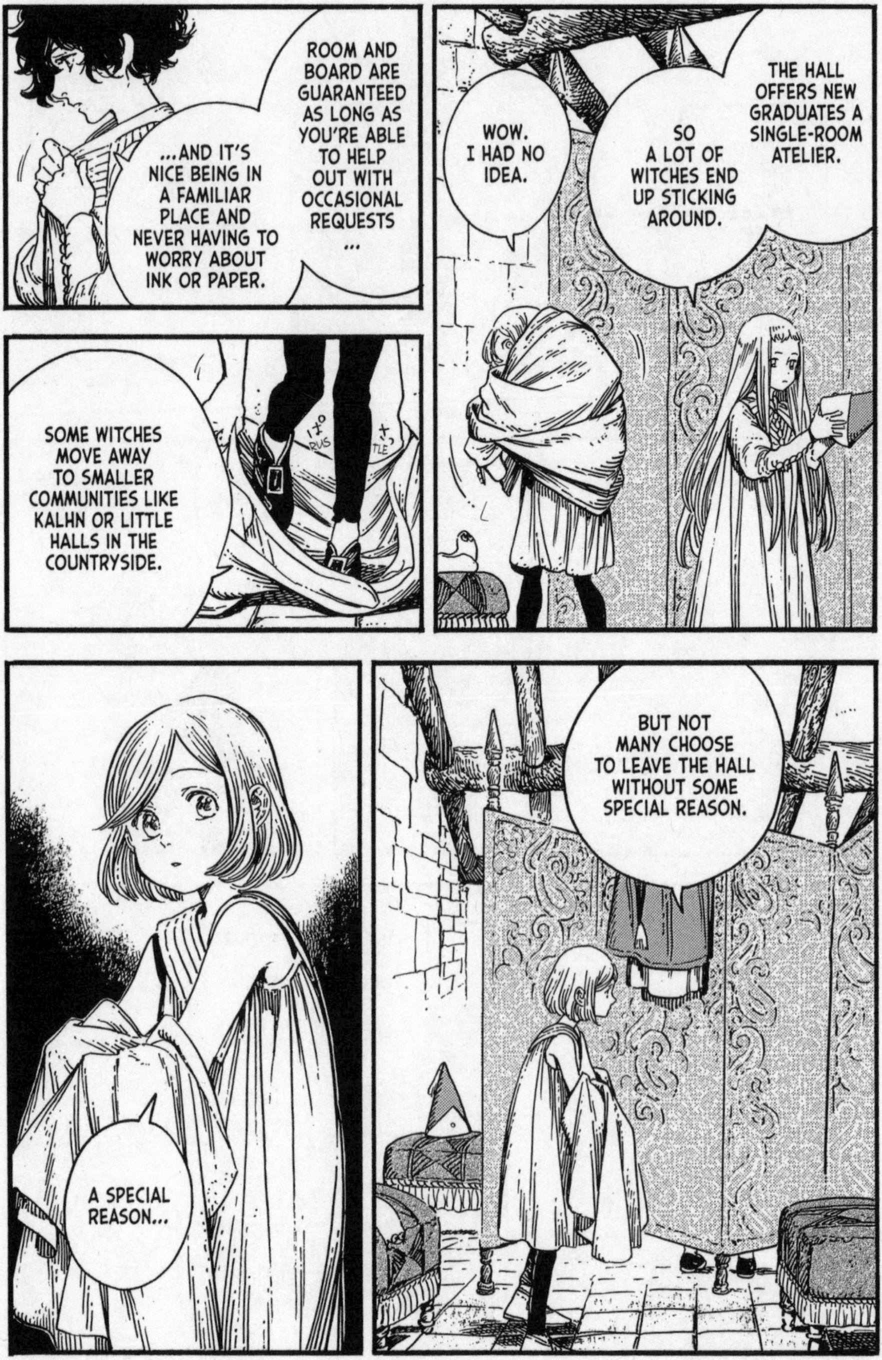
THE HALL OFFERS NEW GRADUATES A SINGLE-ROOM ATELIER.
SO A LOT OF WITCHES END UP STICKING AROUND.
WOW. I HAD NO IDEA.
ROOM AND BOARD ARE GUARANTEED AS LONG AS YOU'RE ABLE TO HELP OUT WITH OCCASIONAL REQUESTS ...
...AND IT'S NICE BEING IN A FAMILIAR PLACE AND NEVER HAVING TO WORRY ABOUT INK OR PAPER.
SOME WITCHES MOVE AWAY TO SMALLER COMMUNITIES LIKE KALHN OR LITTLE HALLS IN THE COUNTRYSIDE.
BUT NOT MANY CHOOSE TO LEAVE THE HALL WITHOUT SOME SPECIAL REASON.
A SPECIAL REASON...

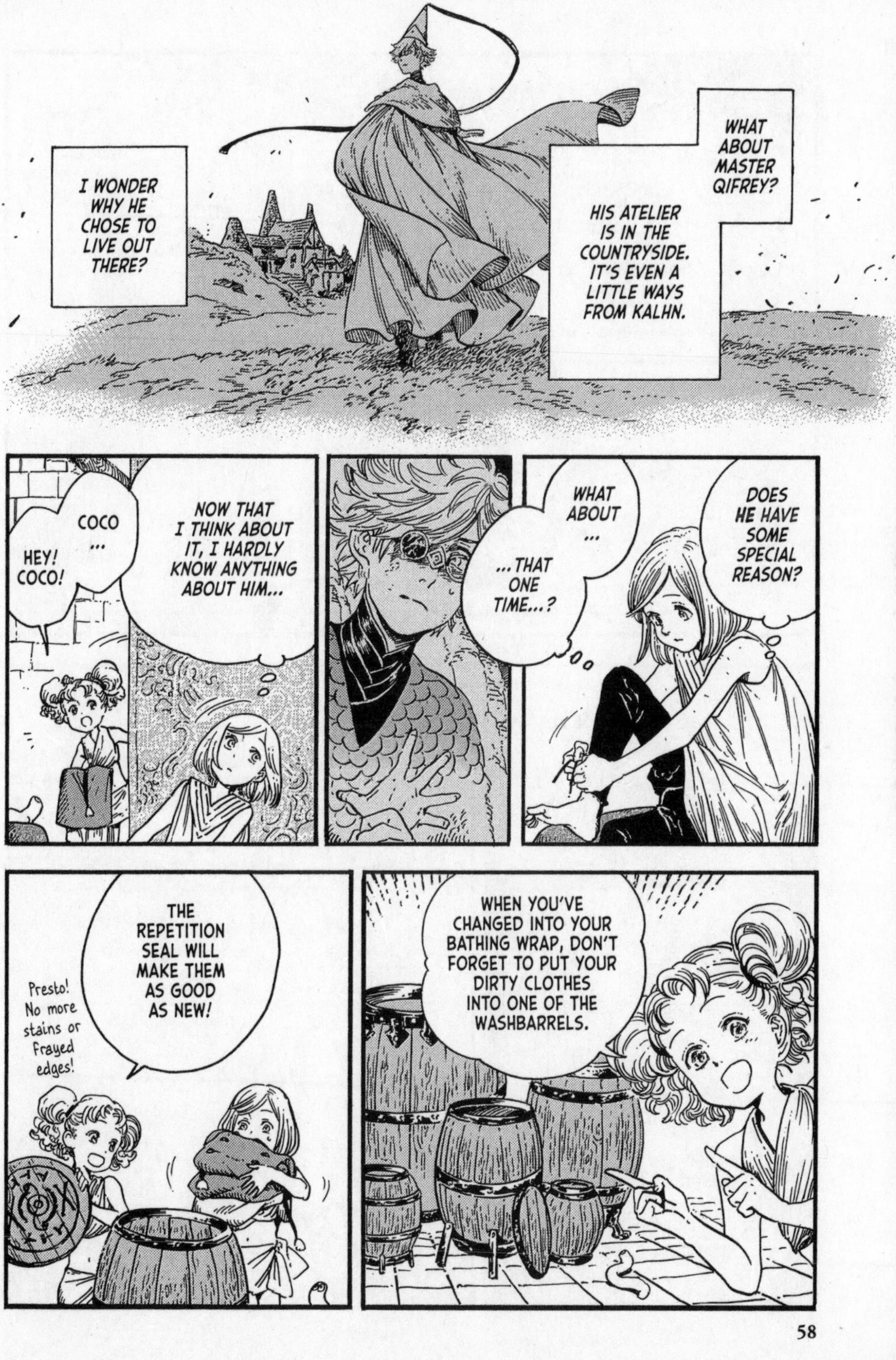
WHAT ABOUT MASTER QIFREY?
HIS ATELIER IS IN THE COUNTRYSIDE. IT'S EVEN A LITTLE WAYS FROM KALHN.
I WONDER WHY HE CHOSE TO LIVE OUT THERE?
DOES HE HAVE SOME SPECIAL REASON?
WHAT ABOUT ...
...THAT ONE TIME...?
NOW THAT I THINK ABOUT IT, I HARDLY KNOW ANYTHING ABOUT HIM...
COCO ...
HEY! COCO!
WHEN YOU'VE CHANGED INTO YOUR BATHING WRAP, DON'T FORGET TO PUT YOUR DIRTY CLOTHES INTO ONE OF THE WASHBARRELS.
THE REPETITION SEAL WILL MAKE THEM AS GOOD AS NEW!
Presto! No more stains or Frayed edges!

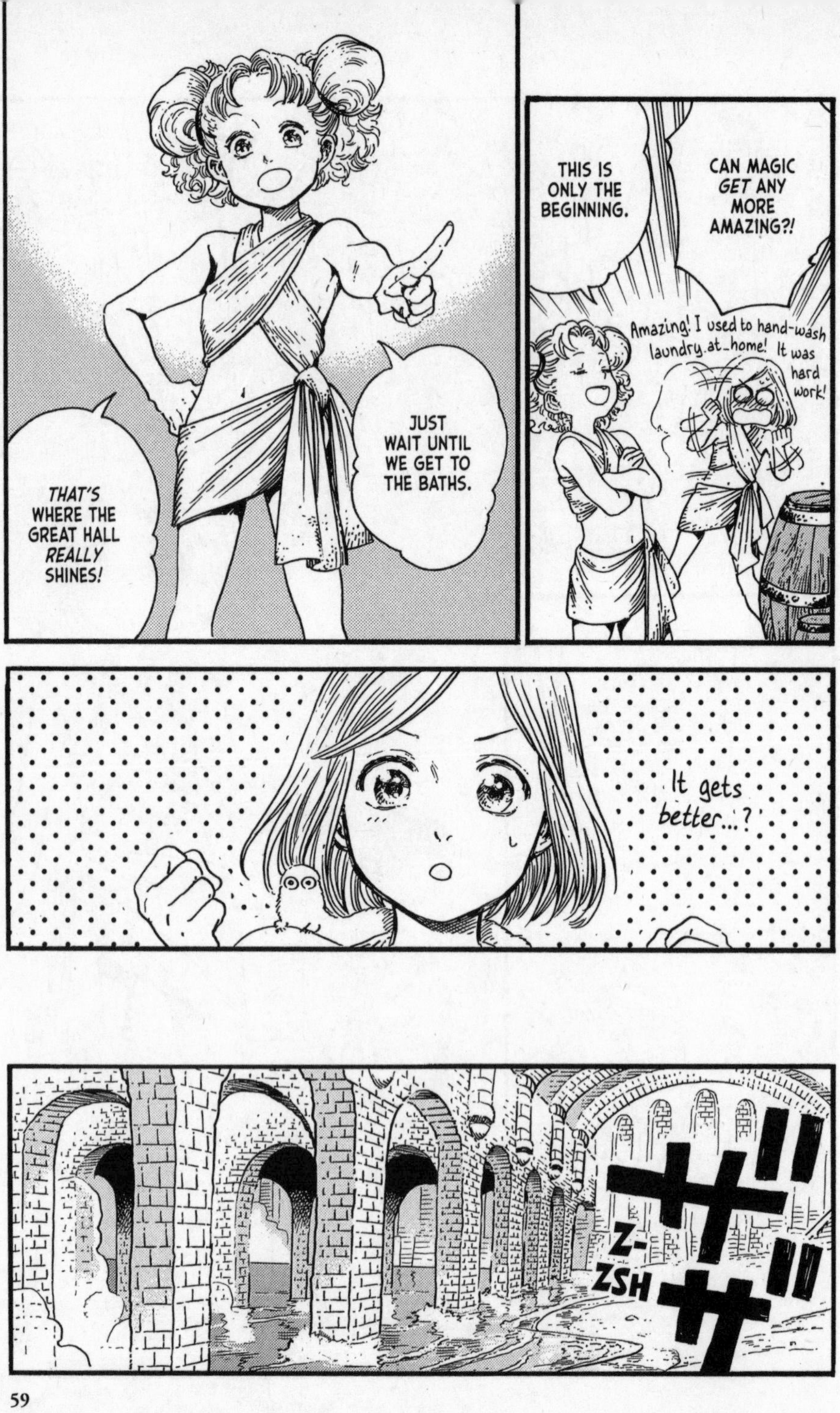
CAN MAGIC *GET* ANY MORE AMAZING?!
THIS IS ONLY THE BEGINNING.
Amazing! I used to hand-wash laundry at home! It was hard work!
JUST WAIT UNTIL WE GET TO THE BATHS.
THAT'S WHERE THE GREAT HALL *REALLY* SHINES!
It gets better...?
ザザ
Z-ZSH

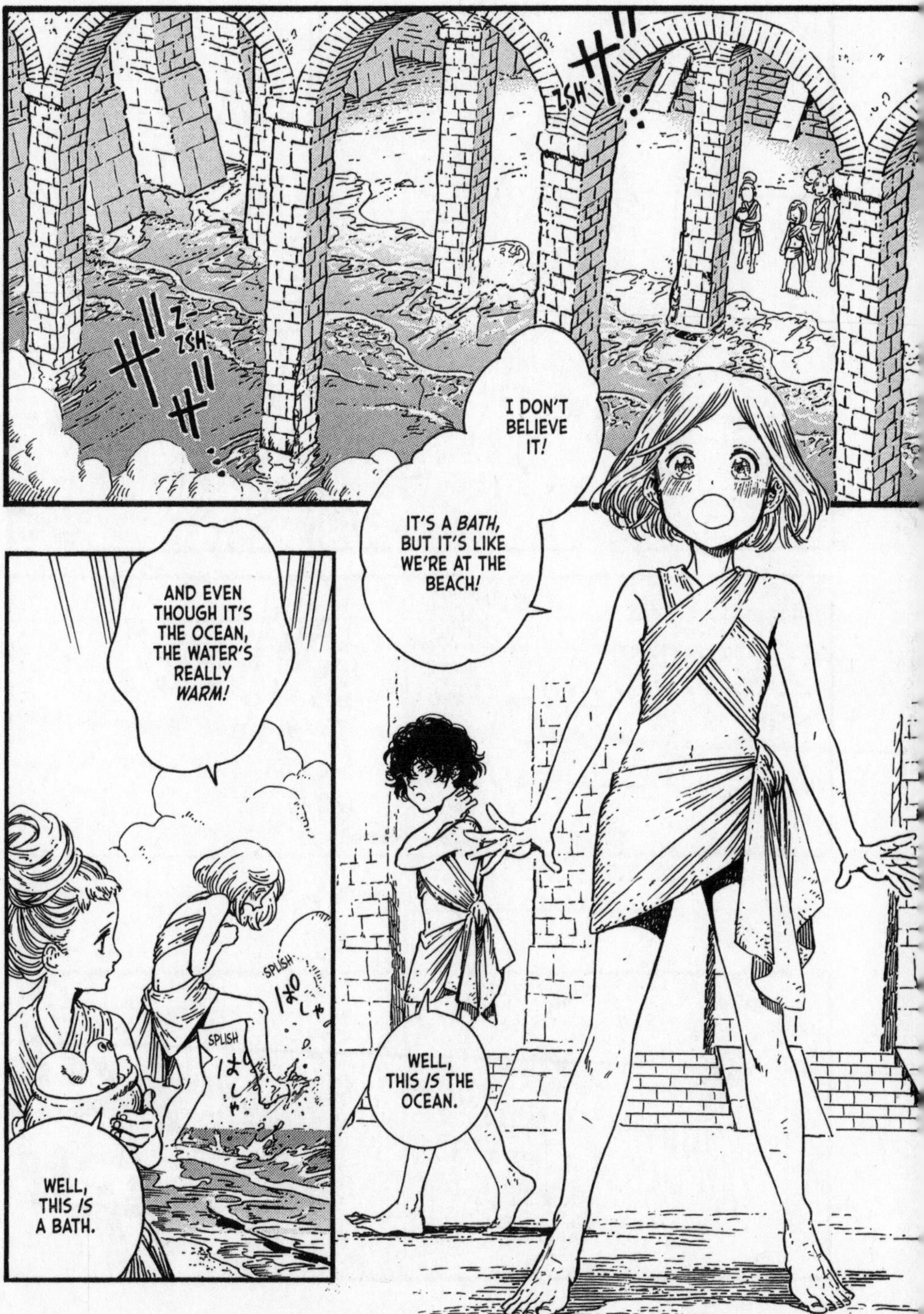
ZSH
Z-ZSH
I DON'T BELIEVE IT!
IT'S A *BATH*, BUT IT'S LIKE WE'RE AT THE BEACH!
WELL, THIS *IS* THE OCEAN.
AND EVEN THOUGH IT'S THE OCEAN, THE WATER'S REALLY *WARM!*
SPLISH
SPLISH
WELL, THIS *IS* A BATH.

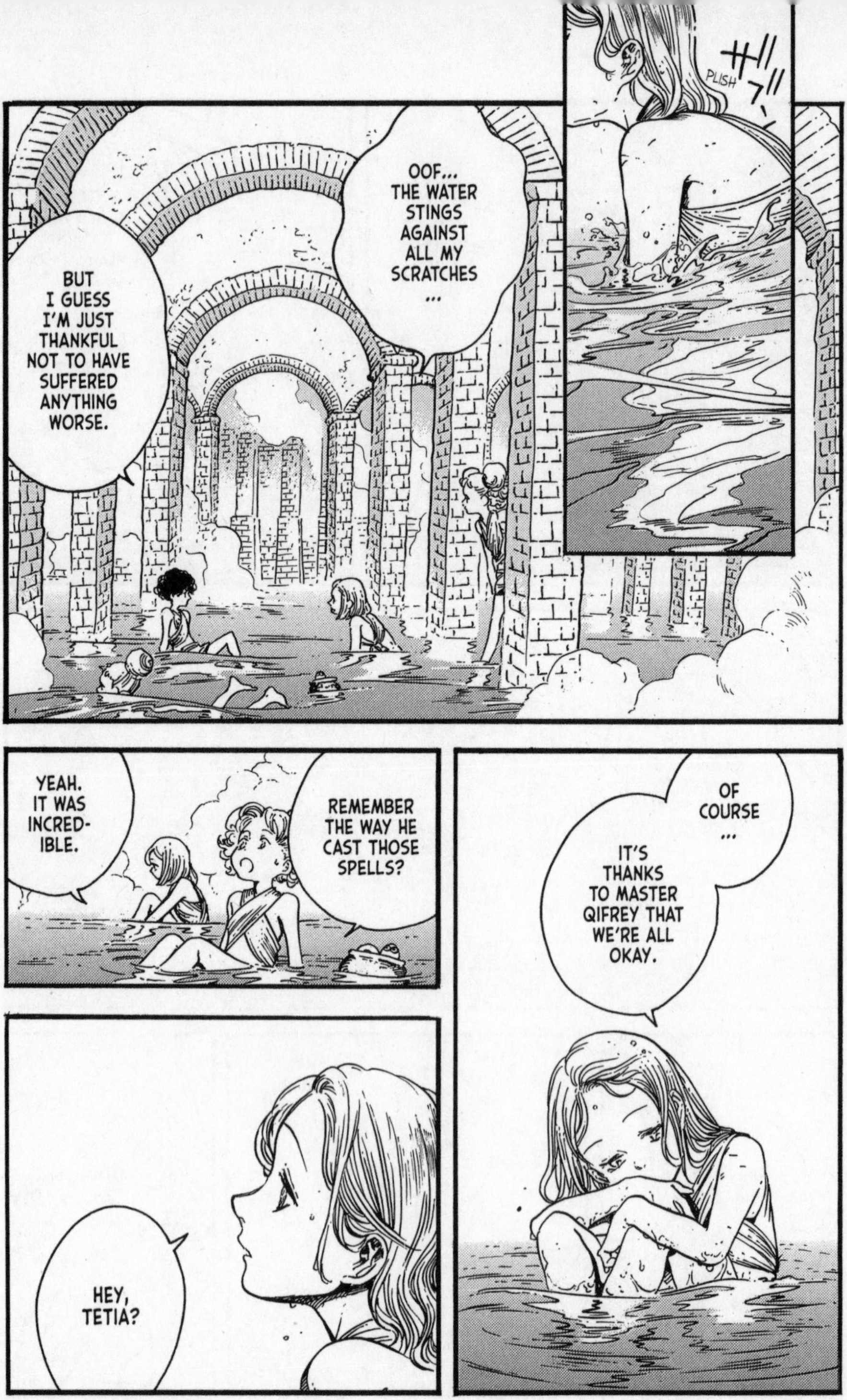
PLISH
OOF... THE WATER STINGS AGAINST ALL MY SCRATCHES ...
BUT I GUESS I'M JUST THANKFUL NOT TO HAVE SUFFERED ANYTHING WORSE.
OF COURSE ...
IT'S THANKS TO MASTER QIFREY THAT WE'RE ALL OKAY.
REMEMBER THE WAY HE CAST THOSE SPELLS?
YEAH. IT WAS INCRED-IBLE.
HEY, TETIA?

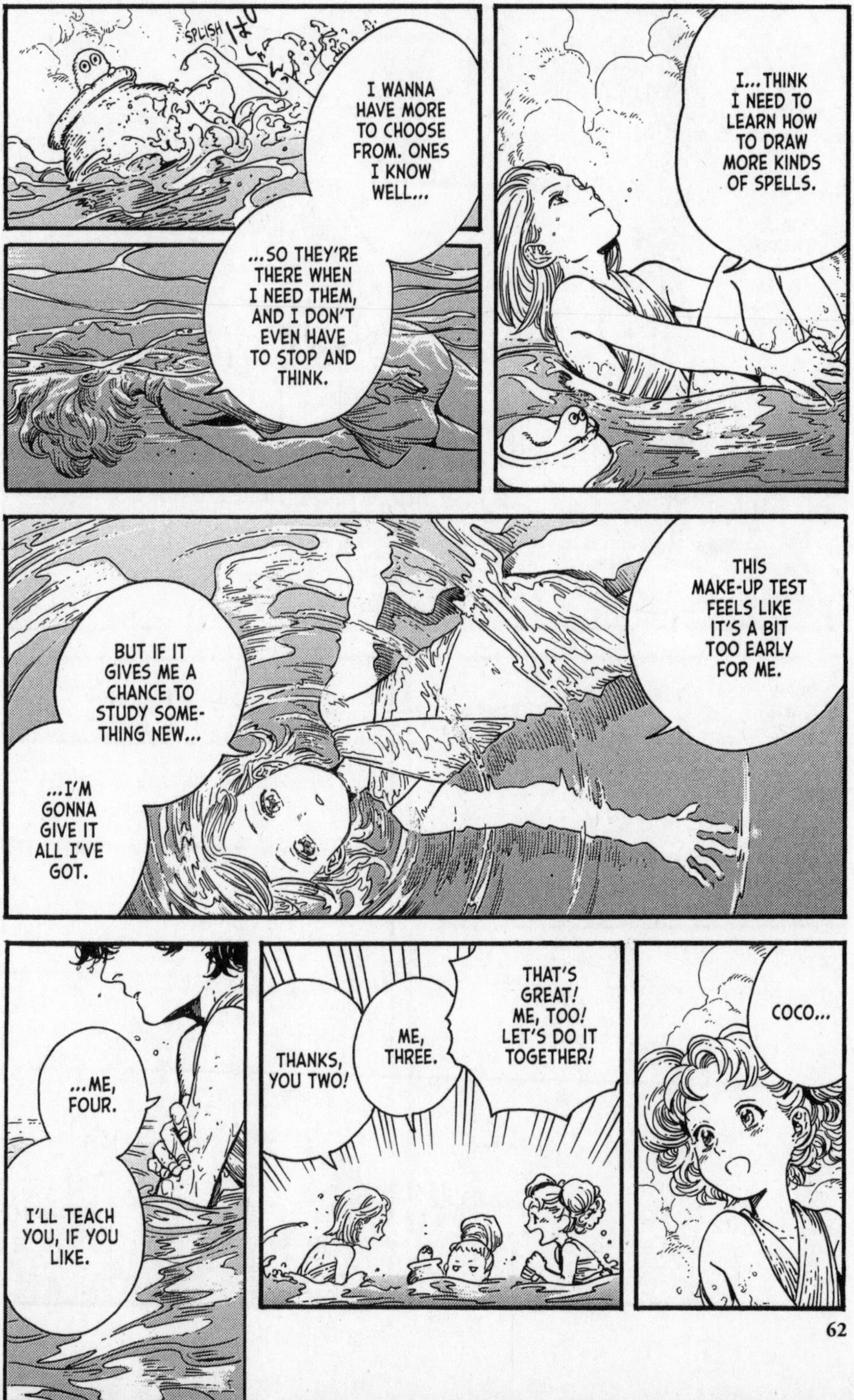
I...THINK I NEED TO LEARN HOW TO DRAW MORE KINDS OF SPELLS.
SPLISH
I WANNA HAVE MORE TO CHOOSE FROM. ONES I KNOW WELL...
...SO THEY'RE THERE WHEN I NEED THEM, AND I DON'T EVEN HAVE TO STOP AND THINK.
THIS MAKE-UP TEST FEELS LIKE IT'S A BIT TOO EARLY FOR ME.
BUT IF IT GIVES ME A CHANCE TO STUDY SOME-THING NEW...
...I'M GONNA GIVE IT ALL I'VE GOT.
COCO...
THAT'S GREAT! ME, TOO! LET'S DO IT TOGETHER!
ME, THREE.
THANKS, YOU TWO!
...ME, FOUR.
I'LL TEACH YOU, IF YOU LIKE.

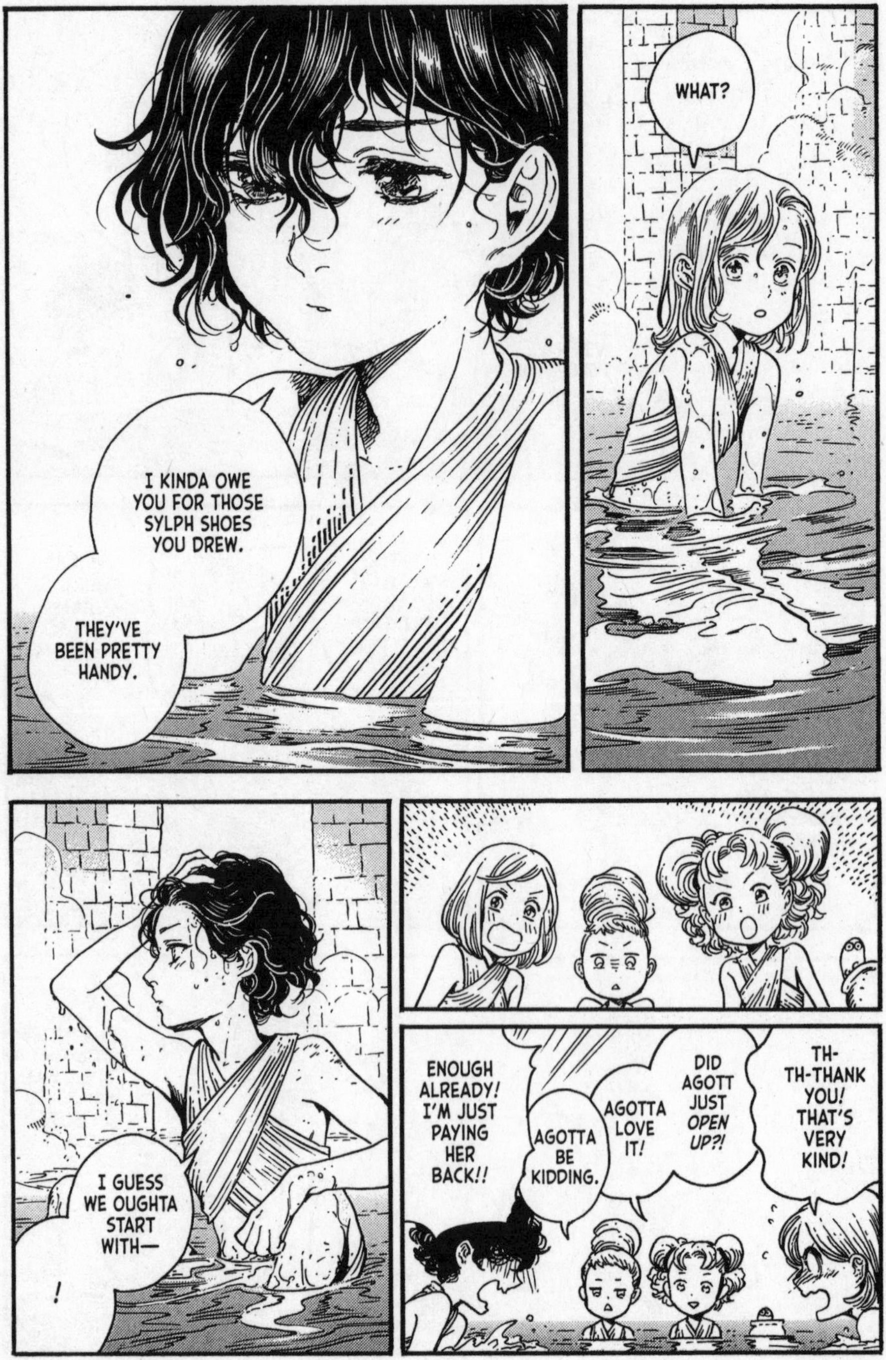
WHAT?
I KINDA OWE YOU FOR THOSE SYLPH SHOES YOU DREW.
THEY'VE BEEN PRETTY HANDY.
TH-TH-THANK YOU! THAT'S VERY KIND!
DID AGOTT JUST OPEN UP?!
AGOTTA LOVE IT!
AGOTTA BE KIDDING.
ENOUGH ALREADY! I'M JUST PAYING HER BACK!!
I GUESS WE OUGHTA START WITH—
!

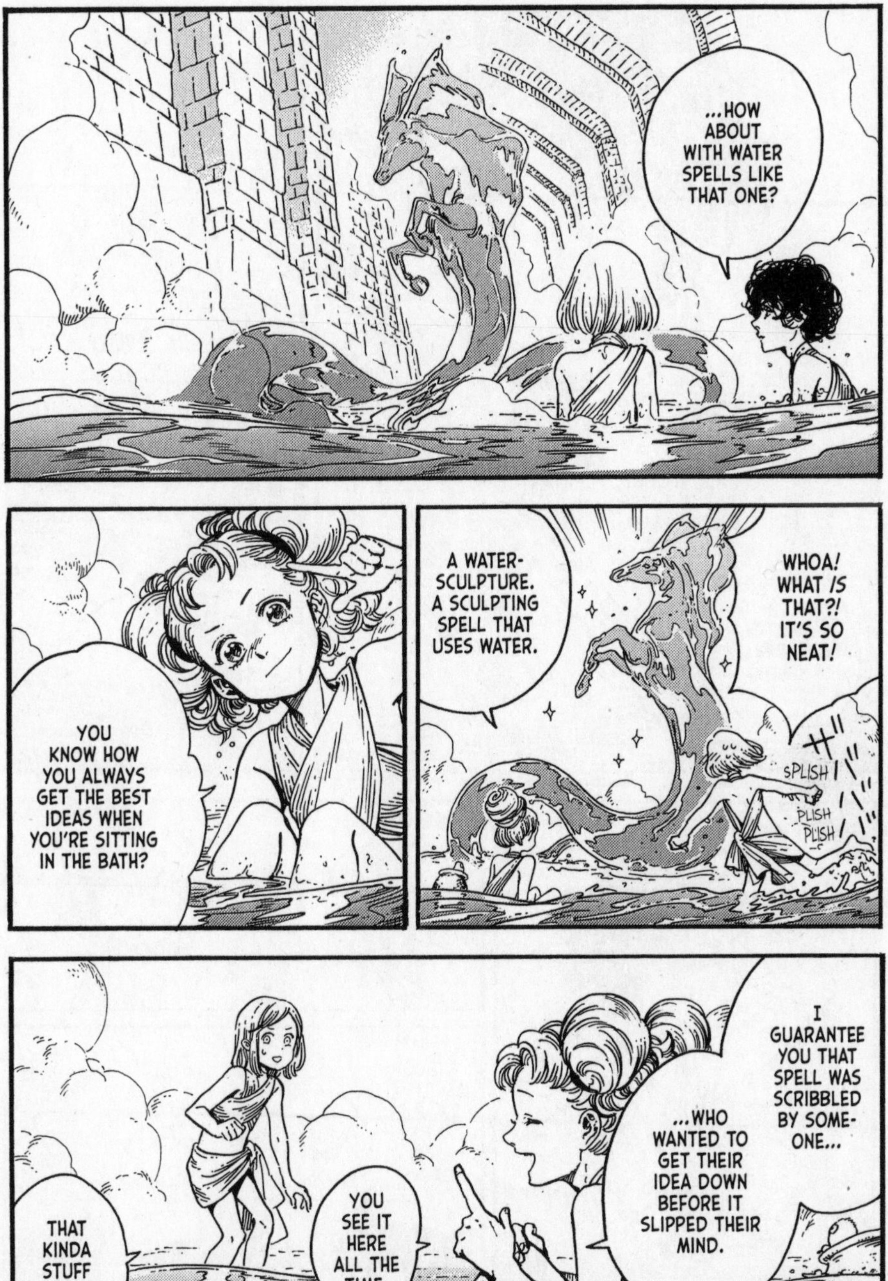
...HOW ABOUT WITH WATER SPELLS LIKE THAT ONE?
WHOA! WHAT *IS* THAT?! IT'S SO NEAT!
SPLISH
PLISH
PLISH
A WATER-SCULPTURE. A SCULPTING SPELL THAT USES WATER.
YOU KNOW HOW YOU ALWAYS GET THE BEST IDEAS WHEN YOU'RE SITTING IN THE BATH?
I GUARANTEE YOU THAT SPELL WAS SCRIBBLED BY SOME-ONE...
...WHO WANTED TO GET THEIR IDEA DOWN BEFORE IT SLIPPED THEIR MIND.
YOU SEE IT HERE ALL THE TIME.
THAT KINDA STUFF HAPPENS *OFTEN*...?

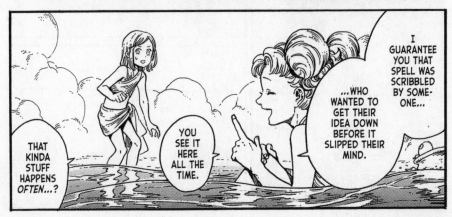

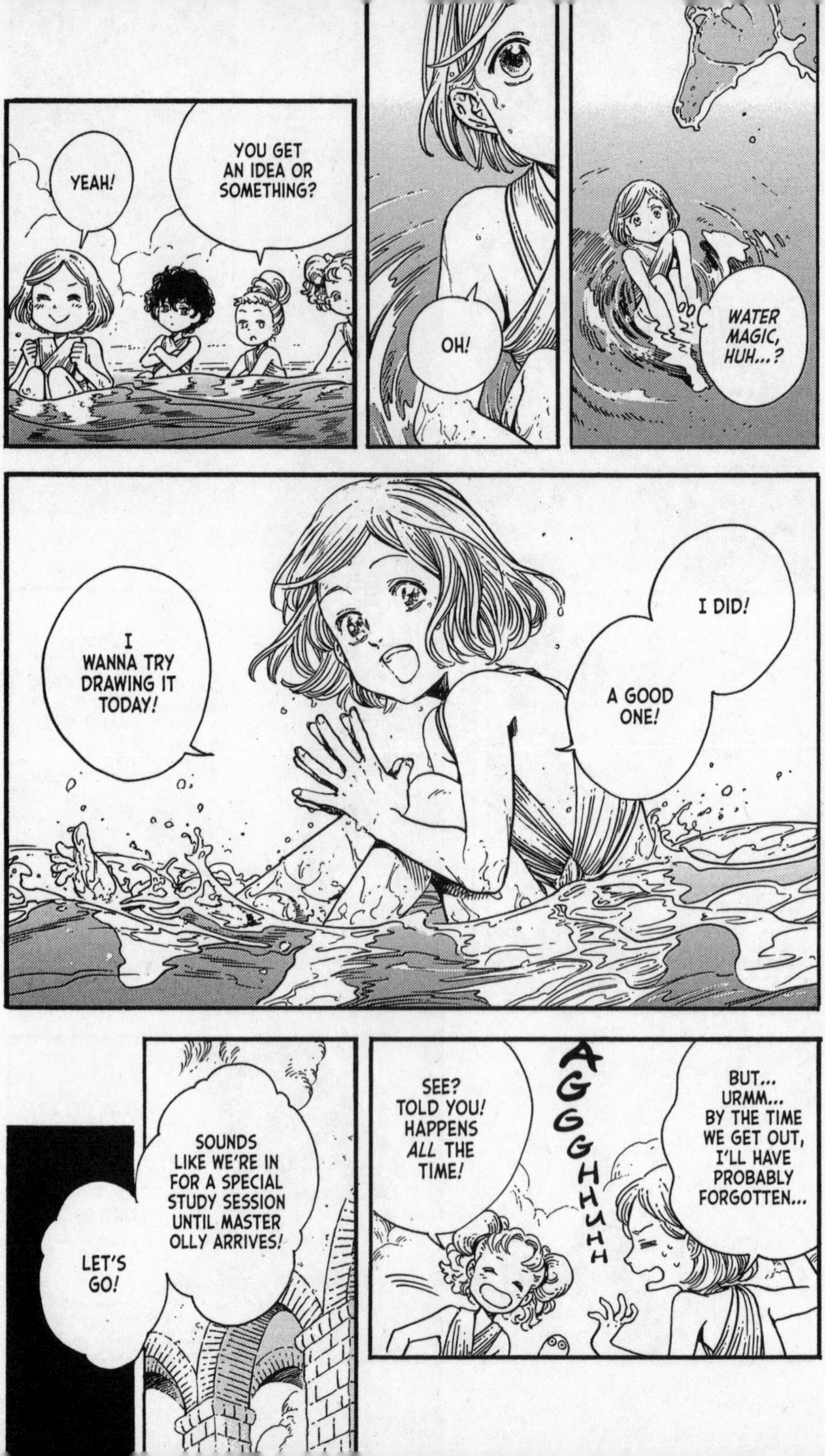
WATER MAGIC, HUH...?
OH!
YOU GET AN IDEA OR SOMETHING?
YEAH!
I DID!
A GOOD ONE!
I WANNA TRY DRAWING IT TODAY!
BUT... URMM... BY THE TIME WE GET OUT, I'LL HAVE PROBABLY FORGOTTEN...
AGGGHHUHH
SEE? TOLD YOU! HAPPENS *ALL* THE TIME!
SOUNDS LIKE WE'RE IN FOR A SPECIAL STUDY SESSION UNTIL MASTER OLLY ARRIVES!
LET'S GO!

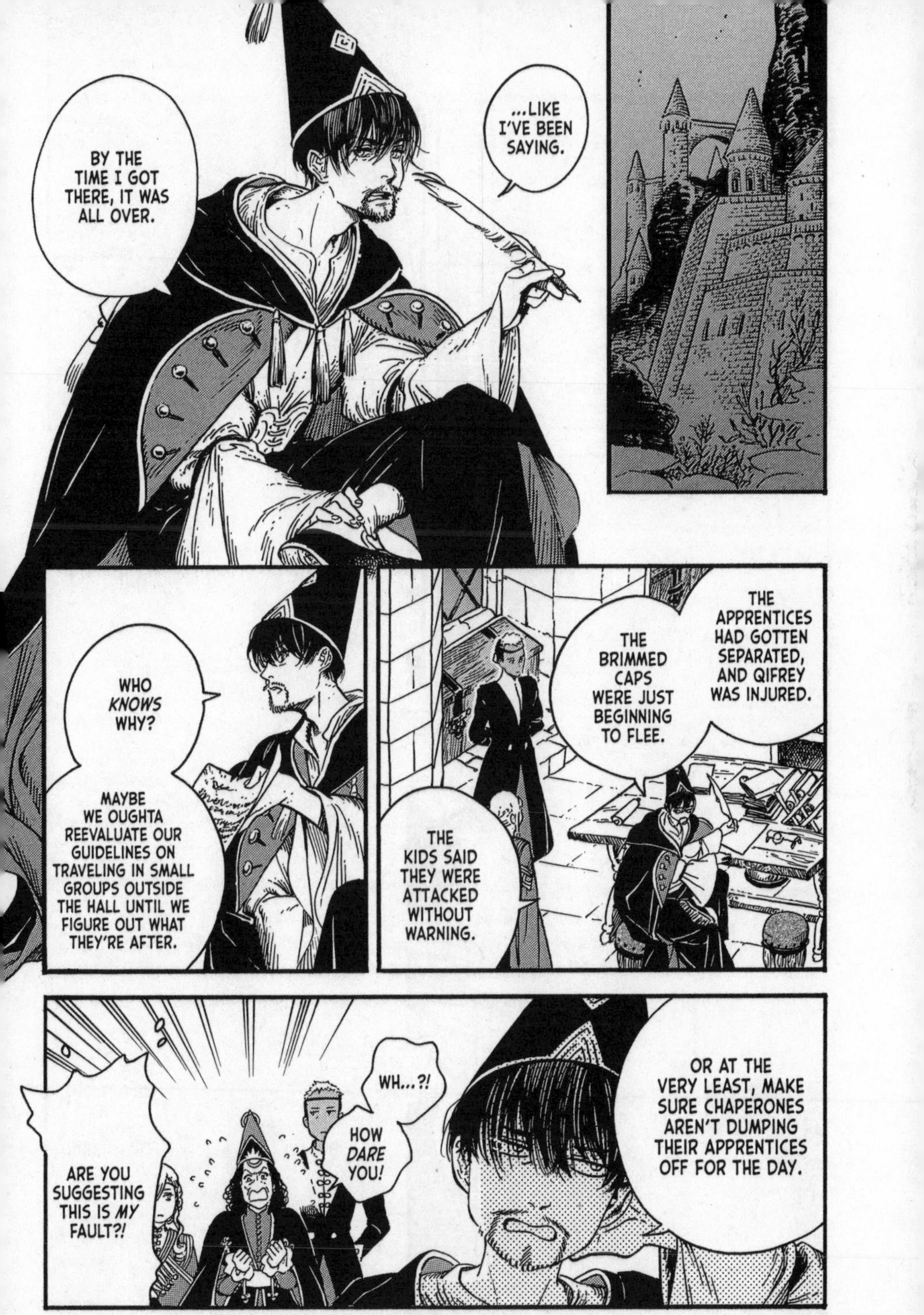
...LIKE I'VE BEEN SAYING.
BY THE TIME I GOT THERE, IT WAS ALL OVER.
THE APPRENTICES HAD GOTTEN SEPARATED, AND QIFREY WAS INJURED.
THE BRIMMED CAPS WERE JUST BEGINNING TO FLEE.
THE KIDS SAID THEY WERE ATTACKED WITHOUT WARNING.
WHO *KNOWS* WHY?
MAYBE WE OUGHTA REEVALUATE OUR GUIDELINES ON TRAVELING IN SMALL GROUPS OUTSIDE THE HALL UNTIL WE FIGURE OUT WHAT THEY'RE AFTER.
OR AT THE VERY LEAST, MAKE SURE CHAPERONES AREN'T DUMPING THEIR APPRENTICES OFF FOR THE DAY.
WH...?!
HOW *DARE* YOU!
ARE YOU SUGGESTING THIS IS *MY* FAULT?!

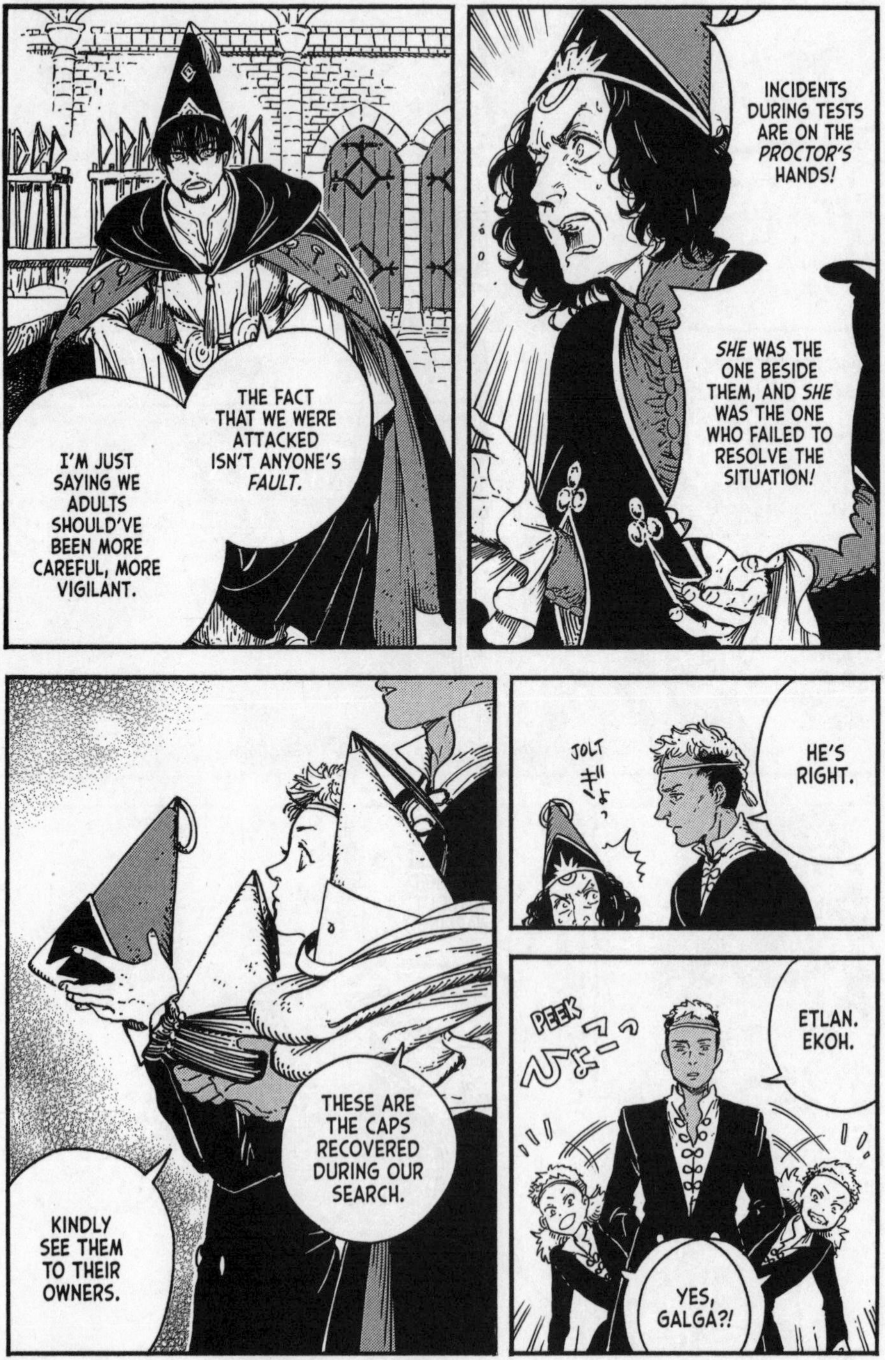
INCIDENTS DURING TESTS ARE ON THE *PROCTOR'S* HANDS!
SHE WAS THE ONE BESIDE THEM, AND *SHE* WAS THE ONE WHO FAILED TO RESOLVE THE SITUATION!
THE FACT THAT WE WERE ATTACKED ISN'T ANYONE'S *FAULT.*
I'M JUST SAYING WE ADULTS SHOULD'VE BEEN MORE CAREFUL, MORE VIGILANT.
HE'S RIGHT.
JOLT
ぎょっ
ETLAN. EKOH.
PEEK
YES, GALGA?!
THESE ARE THE CAPS RECOVERED DURING OUR SEARCH.
KINDLY SEE THEM TO THEIR OWNERS.

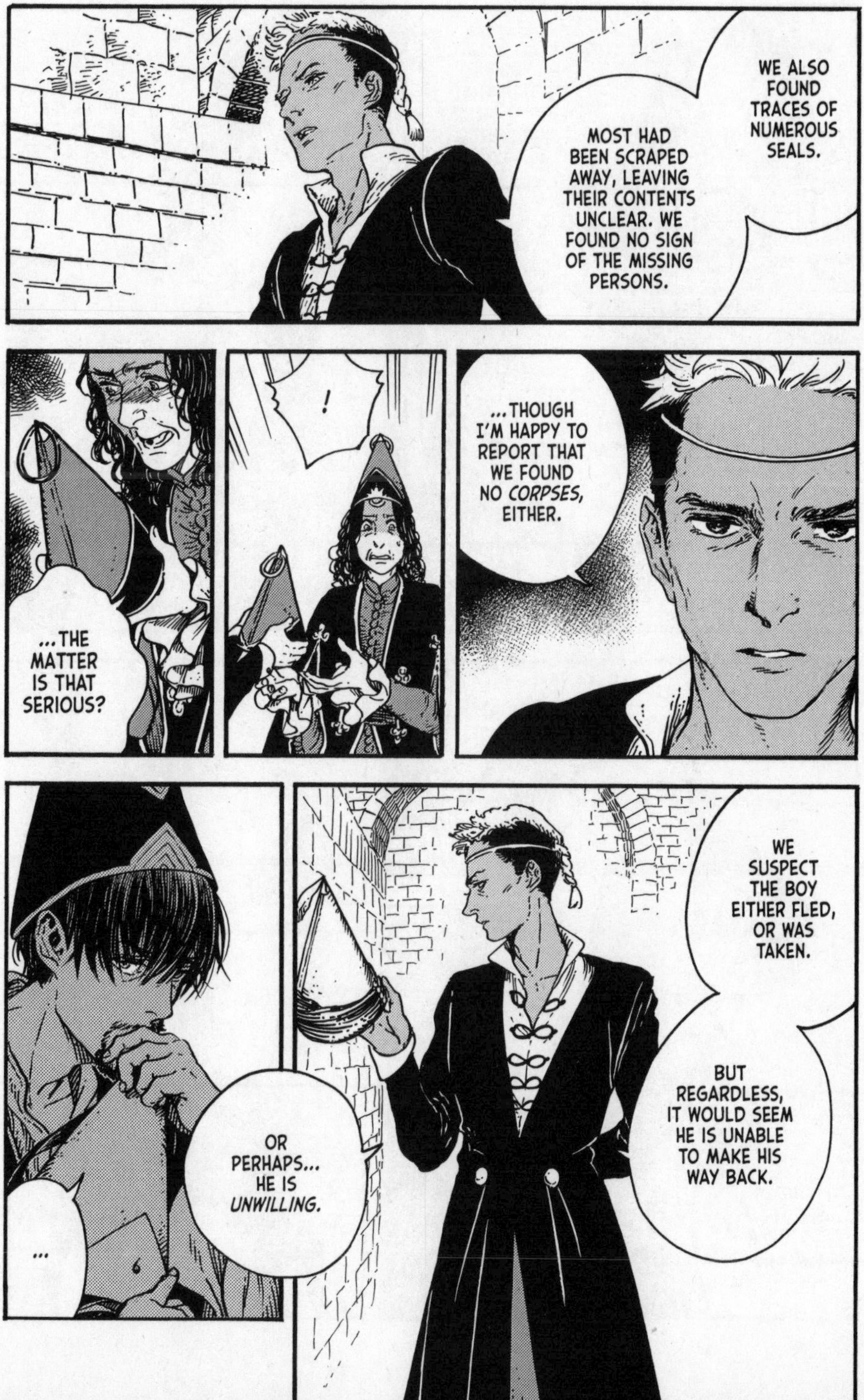
WE ALSO FOUND TRACES OF NUMEROUS SEALS.
MOST HAD BEEN SCRAPED AWAY, LEAVING THEIR CONTENTS UNCLEAR. WE FOUND NO SIGN OF THE MISSING PERSONS.
...THOUGH I'M HAPPY TO REPORT THAT WE FOUND NO *CORPSES*, EITHER.
!
...THE MATTER IS THAT SERIOUS?
WE SUSPECT THE BOY EITHER FLED, OR WAS TAKEN.
BUT REGARDLESS, IT WOULD SEEM HE IS UNABLE TO MAKE HIS WAY BACK.
OR PERHAPS... HE IS *UNWILLING*.
...

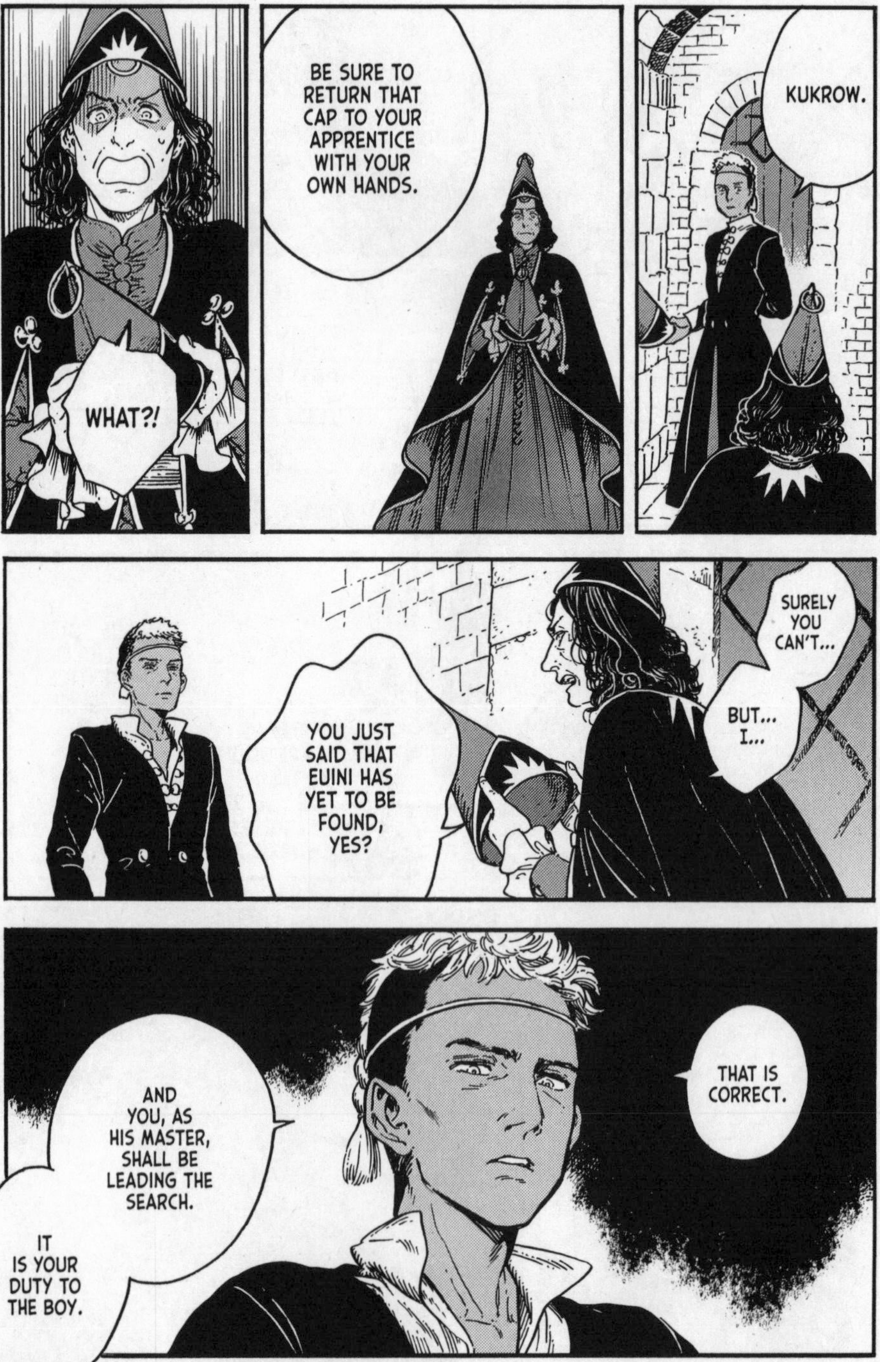
KUKROW.
BE SURE TO RETURN THAT CAP TO YOUR APPRENTICE WITH YOUR OWN HANDS.
WHAT?!
SURELY YOU CAN'T...
BUT... I...
YOU JUST SAID THAT EUINI HAS YET TO BE FOUND, YES?
THAT IS CORRECT.
AND YOU, AS HIS MASTER, SHALL BE LEADING THE SEARCH.
IT IS YOUR DUTY TO THE BOY.

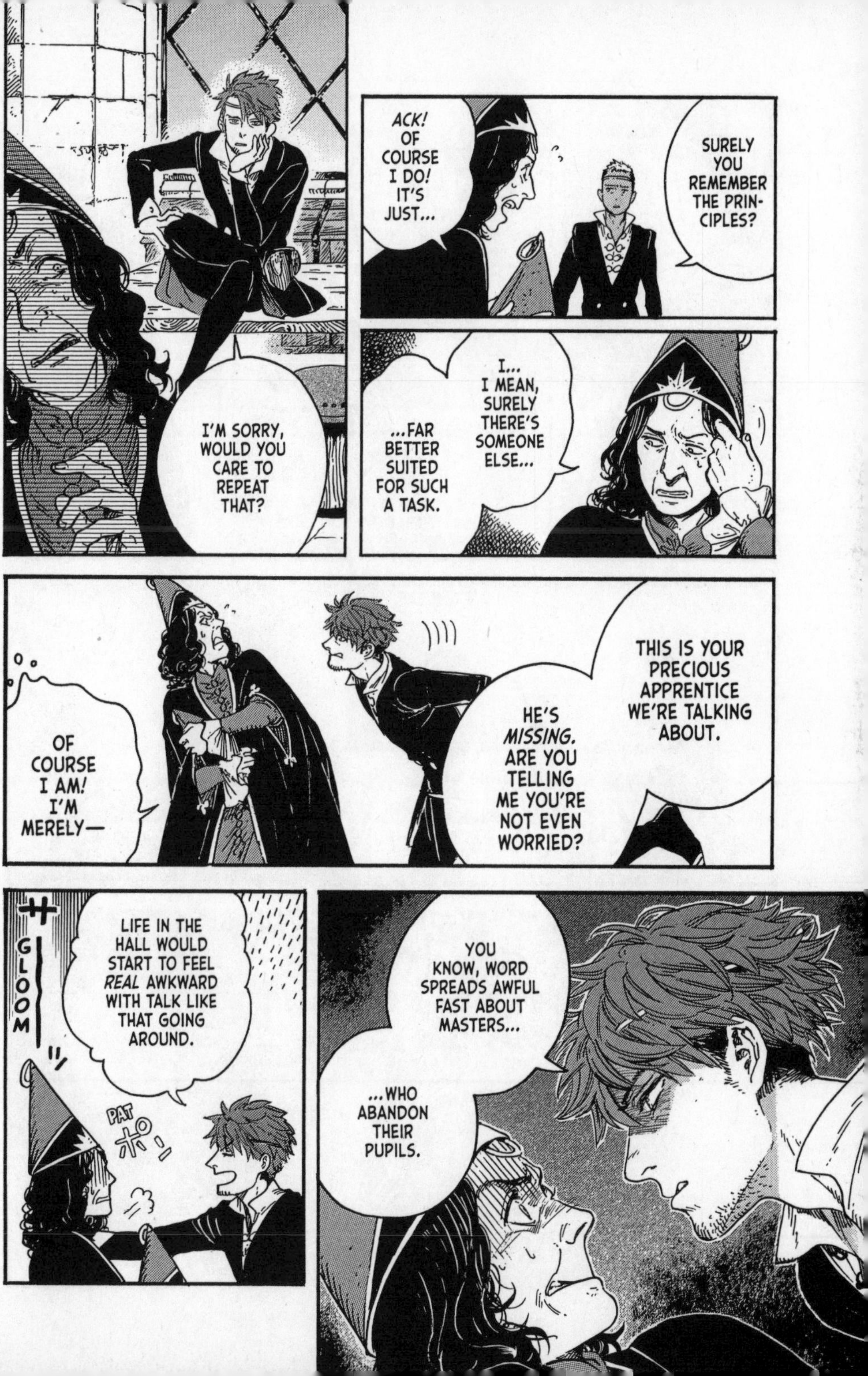
SURELY YOU REMEMBER THE PRIN-CIPLES?
ACK! OF COURSE I DO! IT'S JUST...
I... I MEAN, SURELY THERE'S SOMEONE ELSE...
...FAR BETTER SUITED FOR SUCH A TASK.
I'M SORRY, WOULD YOU CARE TO REPEAT THAT?
THIS IS YOUR PRECIOUS APPRENTICE WE'RE TALKING ABOUT.
HE'S *MISSING.* ARE YOU TELLING ME YOU'RE NOT EVEN WORRIED?
OF COURSE I AM! I'M MERELY—
YOU KNOW, WORD SPREADS AWFUL FAST ABOUT MASTERS...
...WHO ABANDON THEIR PUPILS.
LIFE IN THE HALL WOULD START TO FEEL *REAL* AWKWARD WITH TALK LIKE THAT GOING AROUND.
GLOOM
PAT

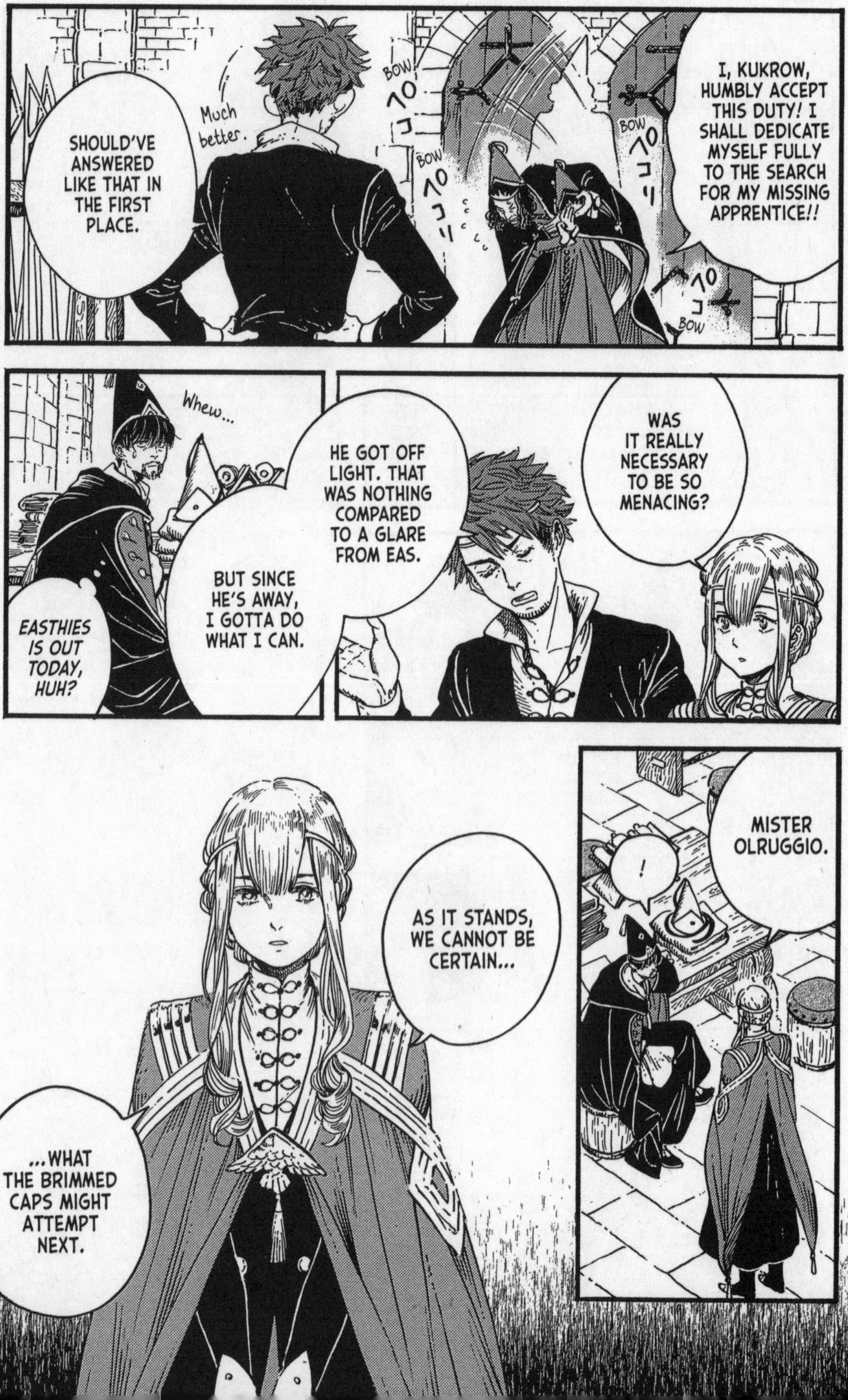
I, KUKROW, HUMBLY ACCEPT THIS DUTY! I SHALL DEDICATE MYSELF FULLY TO THE SEARCH FOR MY MISSING APPRENTICE!!
BOW ヘコ
BOW ヘコリ
BOW ヘコリ
ヘコ BOW
BOW ヘコ
Much better.
SHOULD'VE ANSWERED LIKE THAT IN THE FIRST PLACE.
WAS IT REALLY NECESSARY TO BE SO MENACING?
HE GOT OFF LIGHT. THAT WAS NOTHING COMPARED TO A GLARE FROM EAS.
BUT SINCE HE'S AWAY, I GOTTA DO WHAT I CAN.
Whew...
EASTHIES IS OUT TODAY, HUH?
MISTER OLRUGGIO.
!
AS IT STANDS, WE CANNOT BE CERTAIN...
...WHAT THE BRIMMED CAPS MIGHT ATTEMPT NEXT.

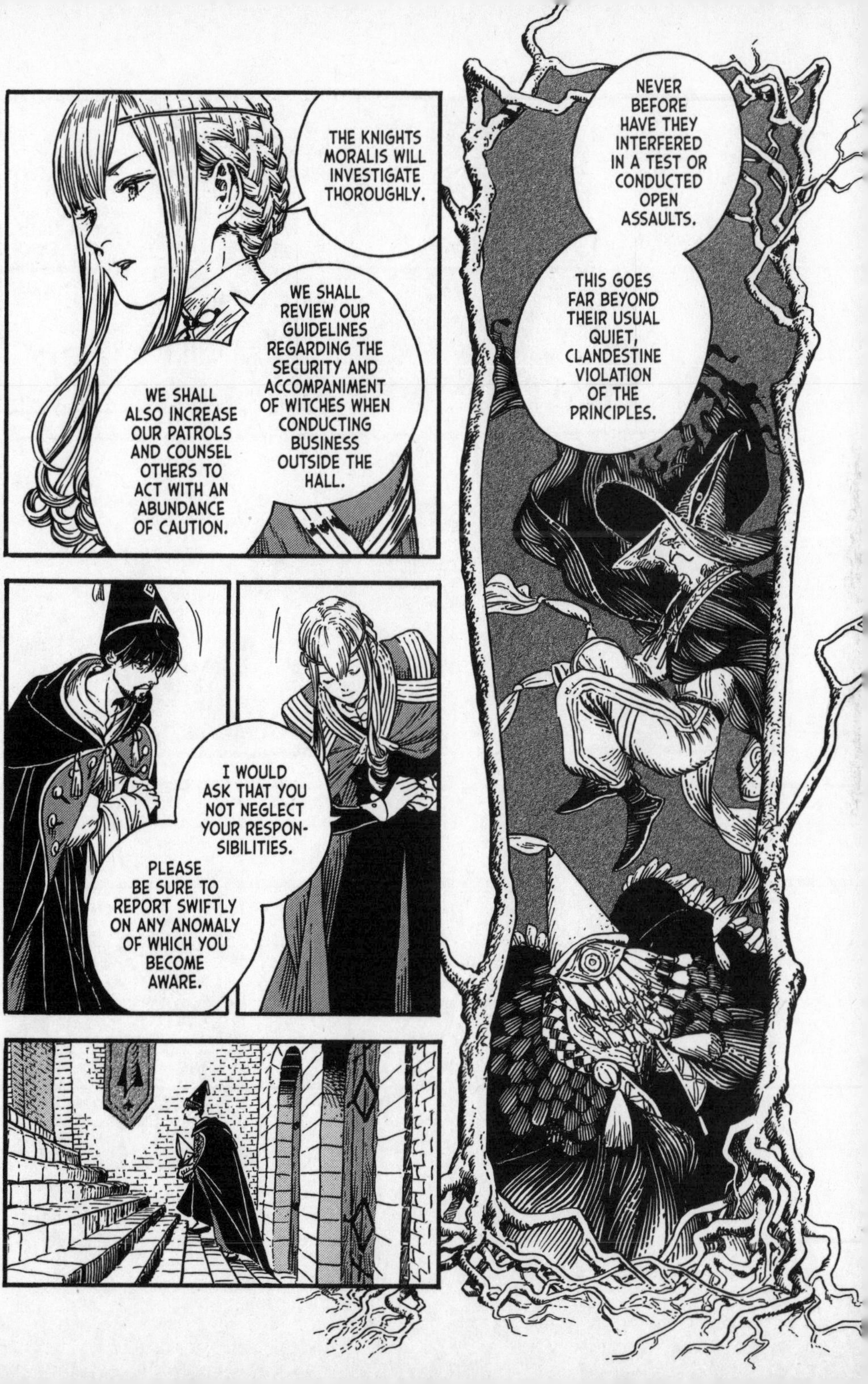
NEVER BEFORE HAVE THEY INTERFERED IN A TEST OR CONDUCTED OPEN ASSAULTS.
THIS GOES FAR BEYOND THEIR USUAL QUIET, CLANDESTINE VIOLATION OF THE PRINCIPLES.
THE KNIGHTS MORALIS WILL INVESTIGATE THOROUGHLY.
WE SHALL REVIEW OUR GUIDELINES REGARDING THE SECURITY AND ACCOMPANIMENT OF WITCHES WHEN CONDUCTING BUSINESS OUTSIDE THE HALL.
WE SHALL ALSO INCREASE OUR PATROLS AND COUNSEL OTHERS TO ACT WITH AN ABUNDANCE OF CAUTION.
I WOULD ASK THAT YOU NOT NEGLECT YOUR RESPONSIBILITIES.
PLEASE BE SURE TO REPORT SWIFTLY ON ANY ANOMALY OF WHICH YOU BECOME AWARE.

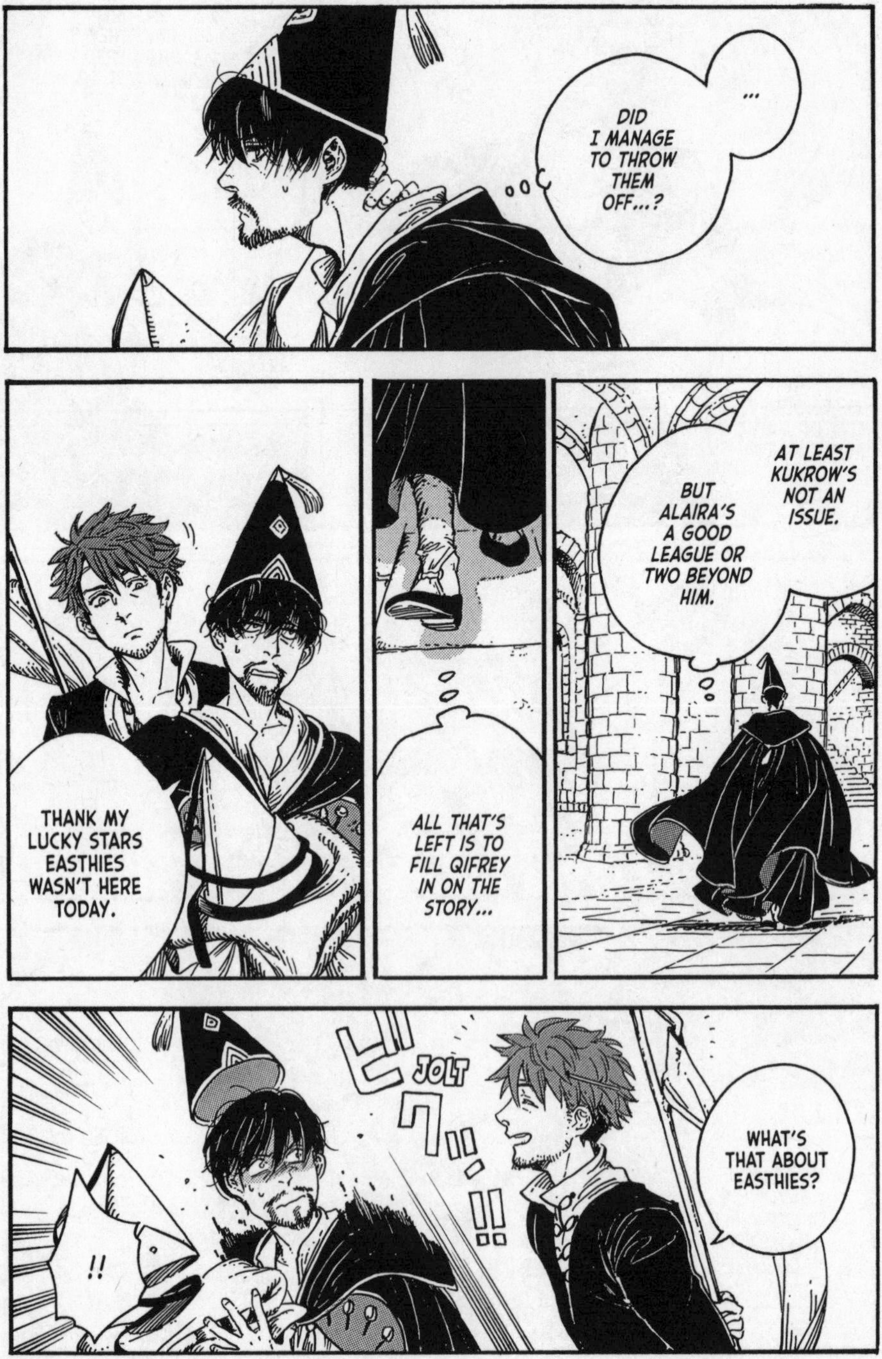
...
DID I MANAGE TO THROW THEM OFF...?
AT LEAST KUKROW'S NOT AN ISSUE.
BUT ALAIRA'S A GOOD LEAGUE OR TWO BEYOND HIM.
ALL THAT'S LEFT IS TO FILL QIFREY IN ON THE STORY...
THANK MY LUCKY STARS EASTHIES WASN'T HERE TODAY.
WHAT'S THAT ABOUT EASTHIES?
JOLT
!!
!!

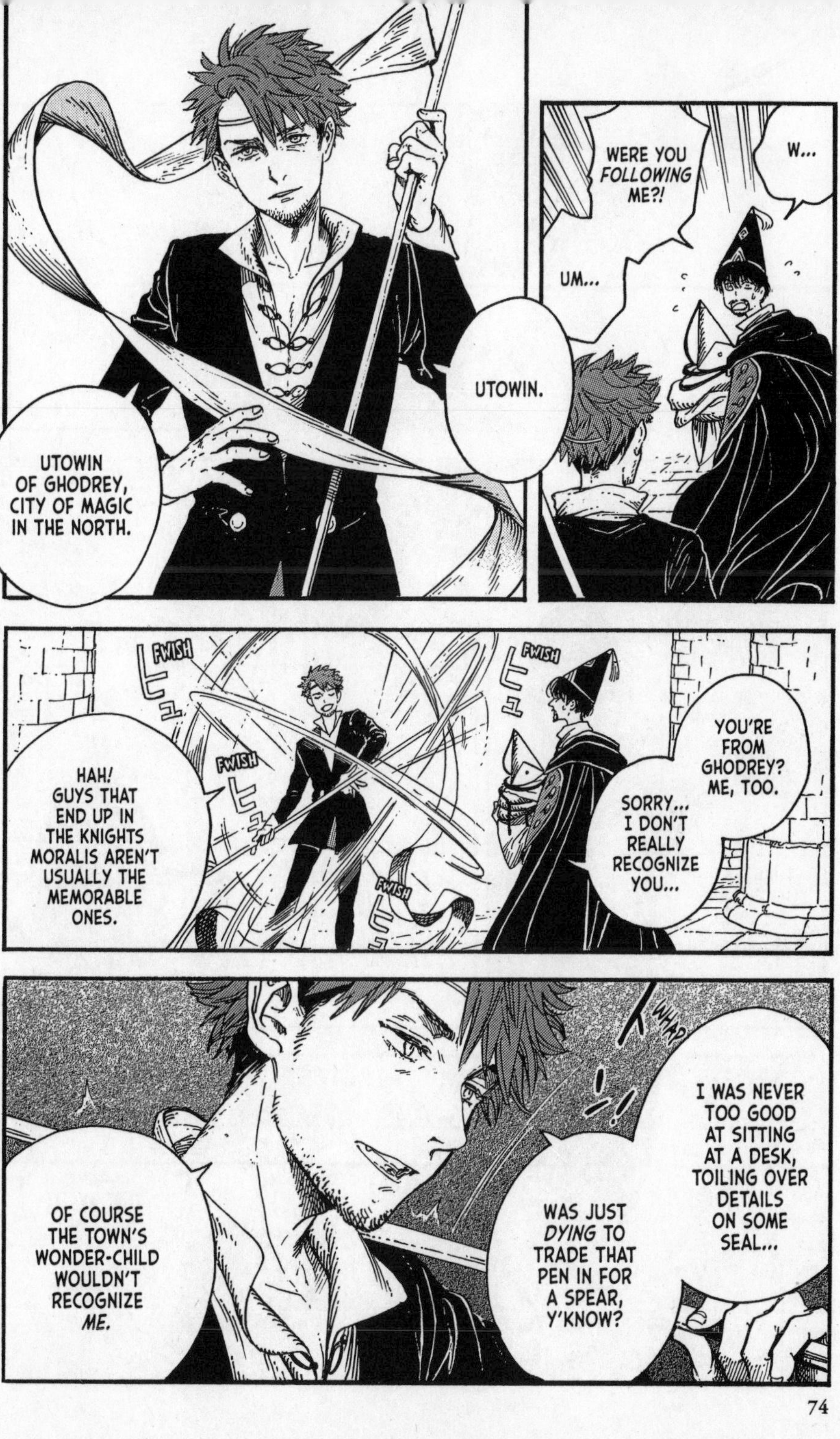
W...
WERE YOU *FOLLOWING* ME?!
UM...
UTOWIN.
UTOWIN OF GHODREY, CITY OF MAGIC IN THE NORTH.
FWISH
YOU'RE FROM GHODREY? ME, TOO.
SORRY... I DON'T REALLY RECOGNIZE YOU...
FWISH
FWISH
HAH! GUYS THAT END UP IN THE KNIGHTS MORALIS AREN'T USUALLY THE MEMORABLE ONES.
FWISH
WHAP
I WAS NEVER TOO GOOD AT SITTING AT A DESK, TOILING OVER DETAILS ON SOME SEAL...
WAS JUST *DYING* TO TRADE THAT PEN IN FOR A SPEAR, Y'KNOW?
OF COURSE THE TOWN'S WONDER-CHILD WOULDN'T RECOGNIZE *ME*.

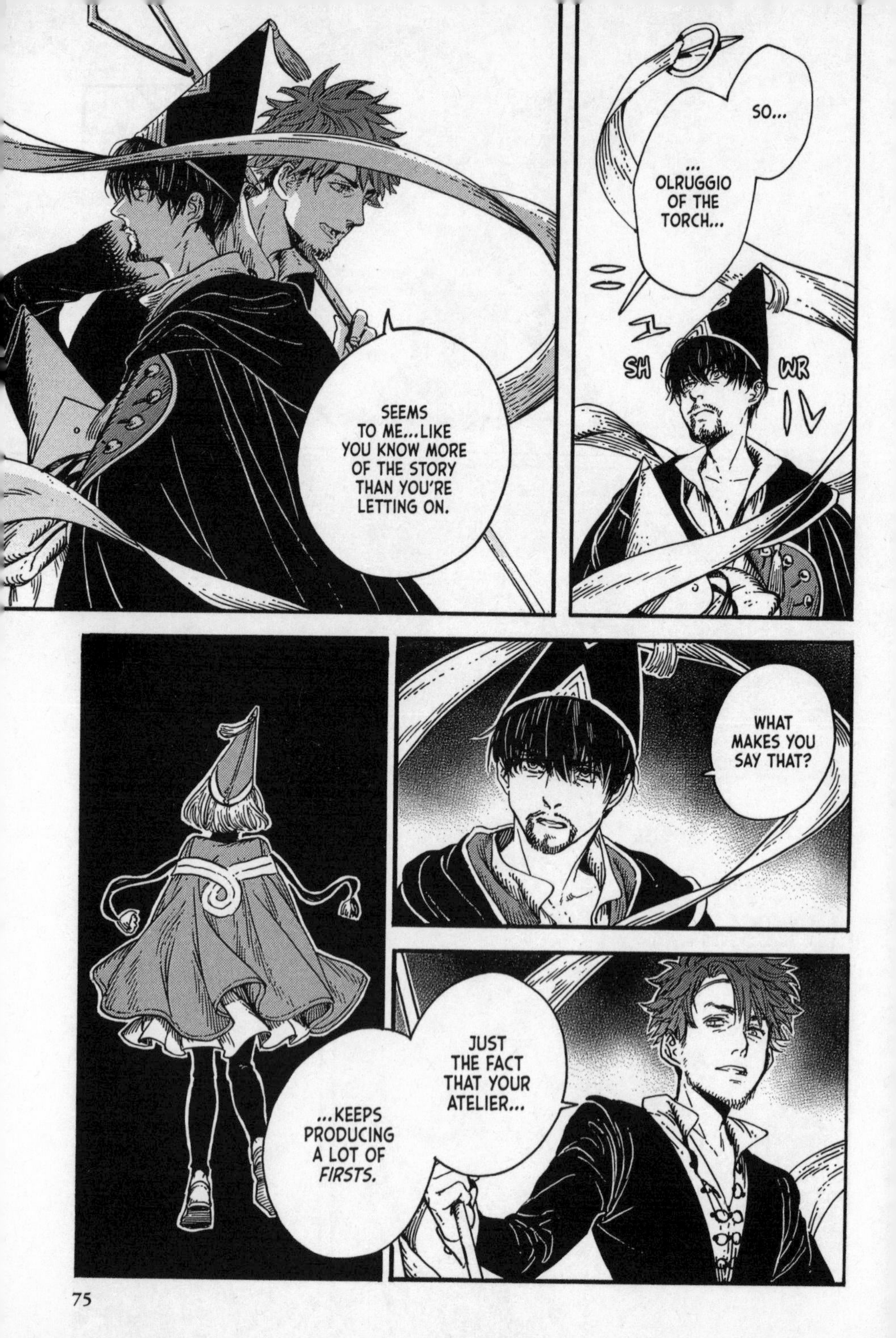
SO...
...OLRUGGIO OF THE TORCH...
SH WR
SEEMS TO ME...LIKE YOU KNOW MORE OF THE STORY THAN YOU'RE LETTING ON.
WHAT MAKES YOU SAY THAT?
JUST THE FACT THAT YOUR ATELIER...
...KEEPS PRODUCING A LOT OF *FIRSTS.*

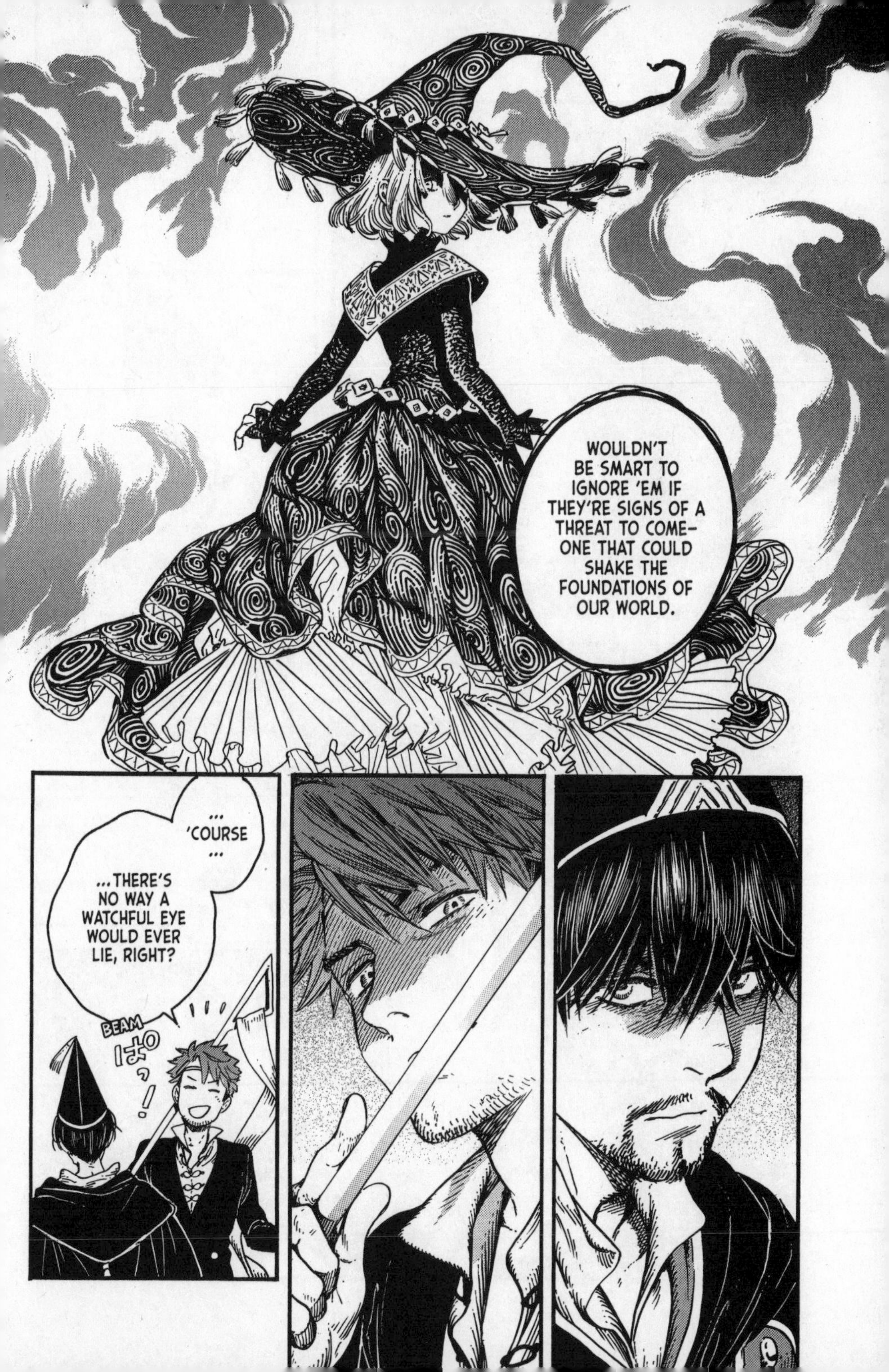
WOULDN'T BE SMART TO IGNORE 'EM IF THEY'RE SIGNS OF A THREAT TO COME—ONE THAT COULD SHAKE THE FOUNDATIONS OF OUR WORLD.
... 'COURSE ...
...THERE'S NO WAY A WATCHFUL EYE WOULD EVER LIE, RIGHT?
BEAM
ぱっ!

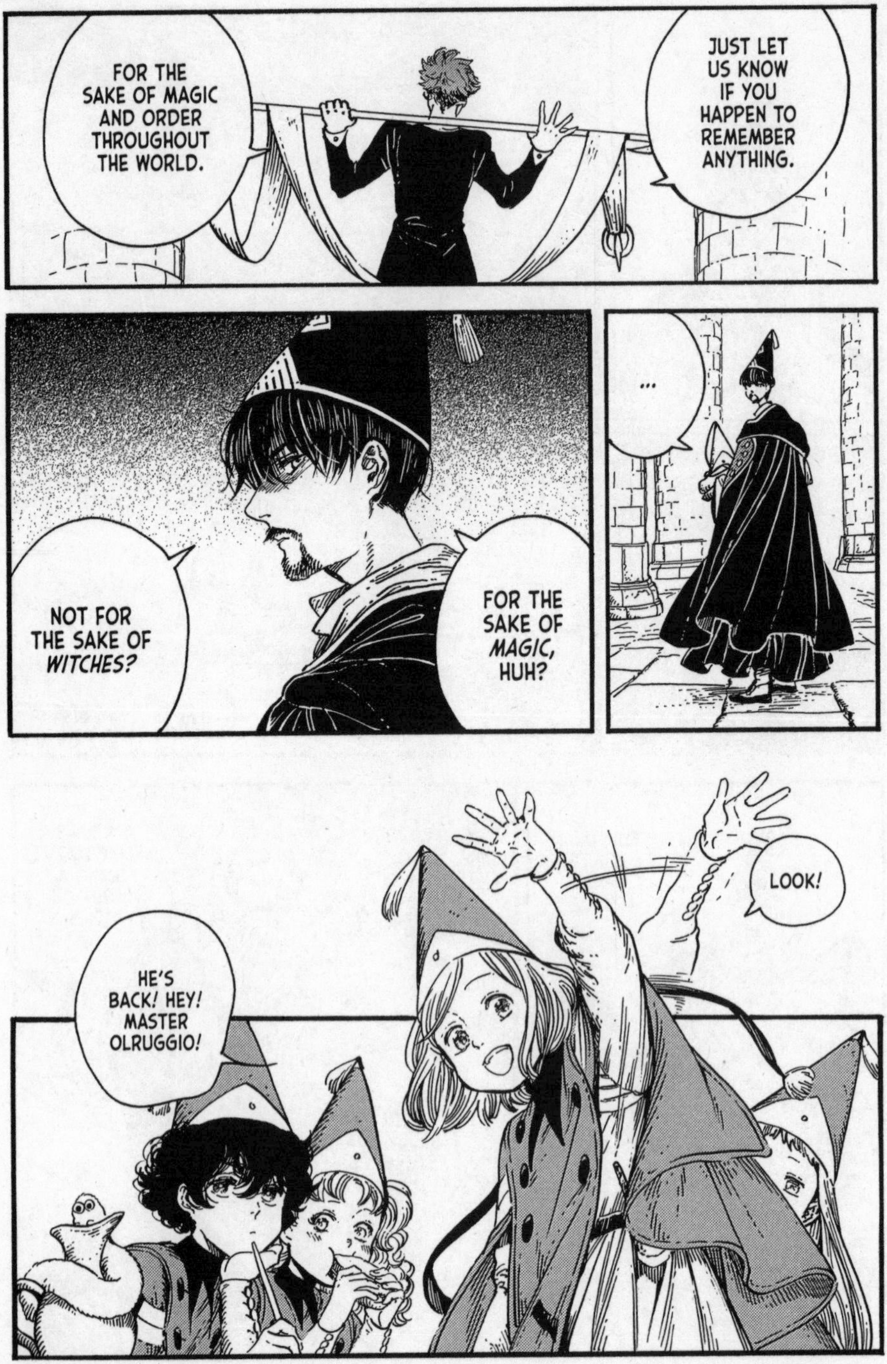
JUST LET US KNOW IF YOU HAPPEN TO REMEMBER ANYTHING.
FOR THE SAKE OF MAGIC AND ORDER THROUGHOUT THE WORLD.
...
FOR THE SAKE OF *MAGIC*, HUH?
NOT FOR THE SAKE OF *WITCHES?*
LOOK!
HE'S BACK! HEY! MASTER OLRUGGIO!

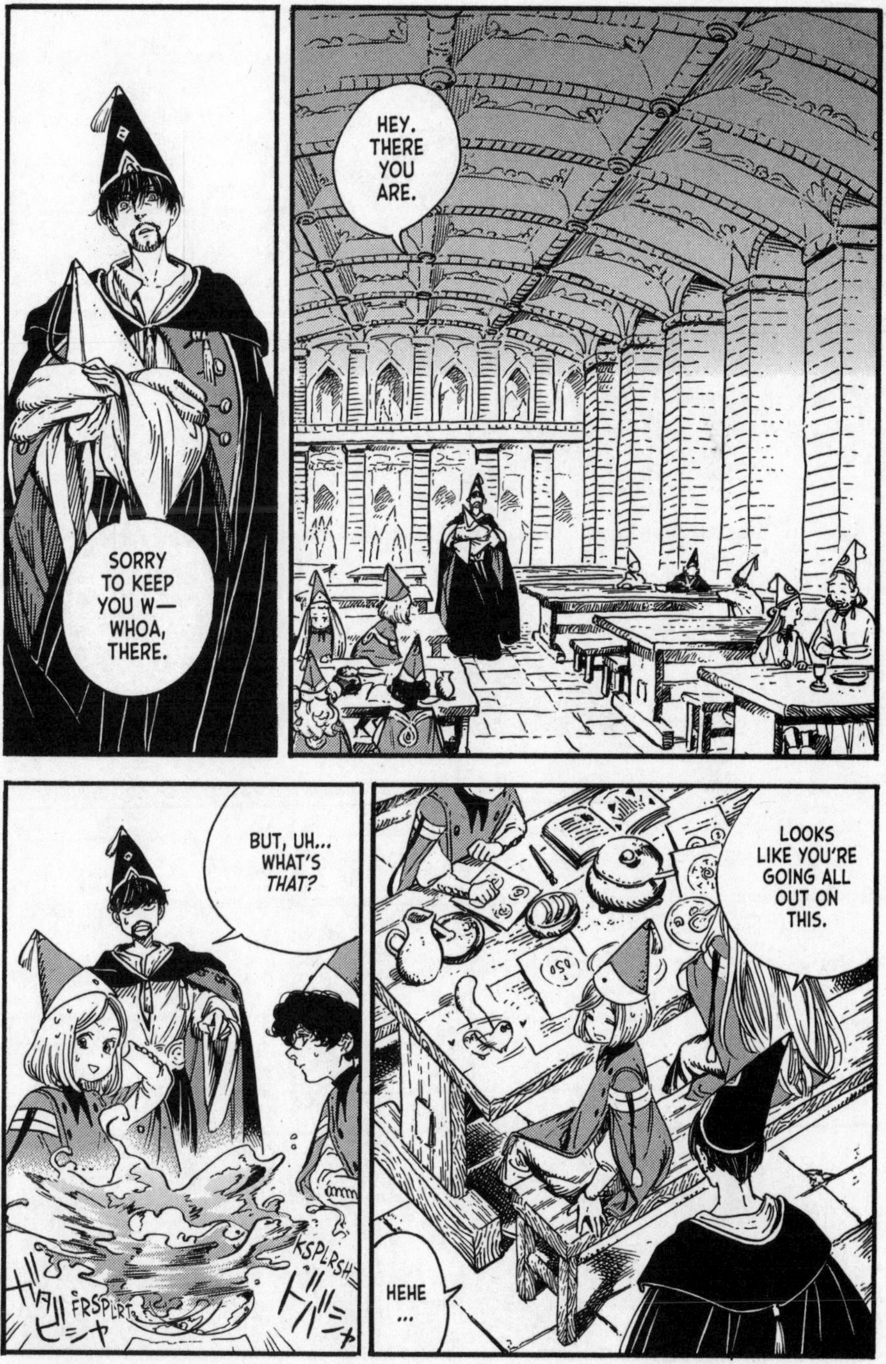
HEY. THERE YOU ARE.
SORRY TO KEEP YOU W— WHOA, THERE.
LOOKS LIKE YOU'RE GOING ALL OUT ON THIS.
HEHE ...
BUT, UH... WHAT'S *THAT?*
KSPLRSH
FRSPLRT

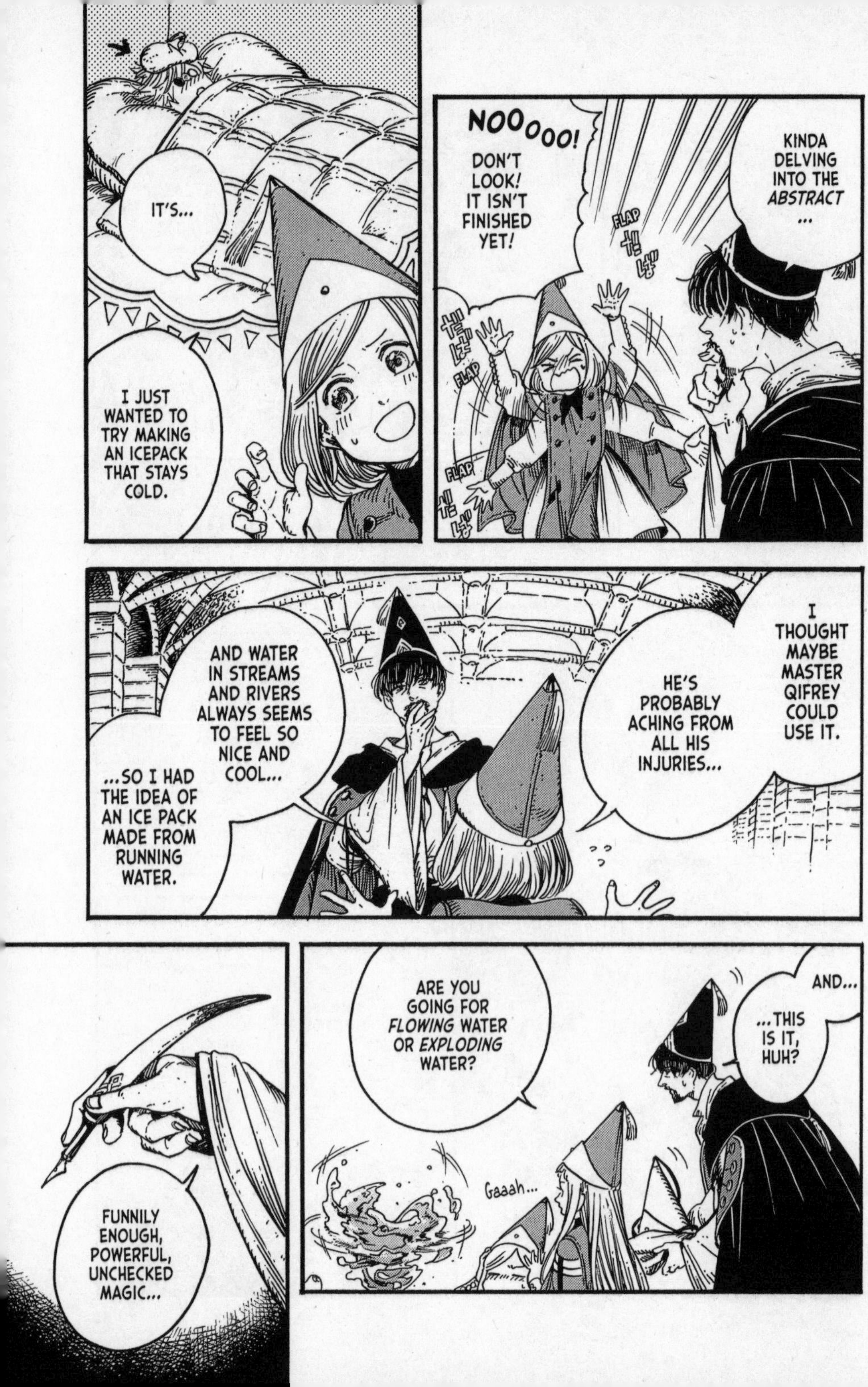
KINDA DELVING INTO THE *ABSTRACT* ...
NOOOOO!
DON'T LOOK! IT ISN'T FINISHED YET!
FLAP
FLAP
FLAP
IT'S...
I JUST WANTED TO TRY MAKING AN ICEPACK THAT STAYS COLD.
I THOUGHT MAYBE MASTER QIFREY COULD USE IT.
HE'S PROBABLY ACHING FROM ALL HIS INJURIES...
AND WATER IN STREAMS AND RIVERS ALWAYS SEEMS TO FEEL SO NICE AND COOL...
...SO I HAD THE IDEA OF AN ICE PACK MADE FROM RUNNING WATER.
AND...
...THIS IS IT, HUH?
ARE YOU GOING FOR *FLOWING* WATER OR *EXPLODING* WATER?
Gaaah...
FUNNILY ENOUGH, POWERFUL, UNCHECKED MAGIC...

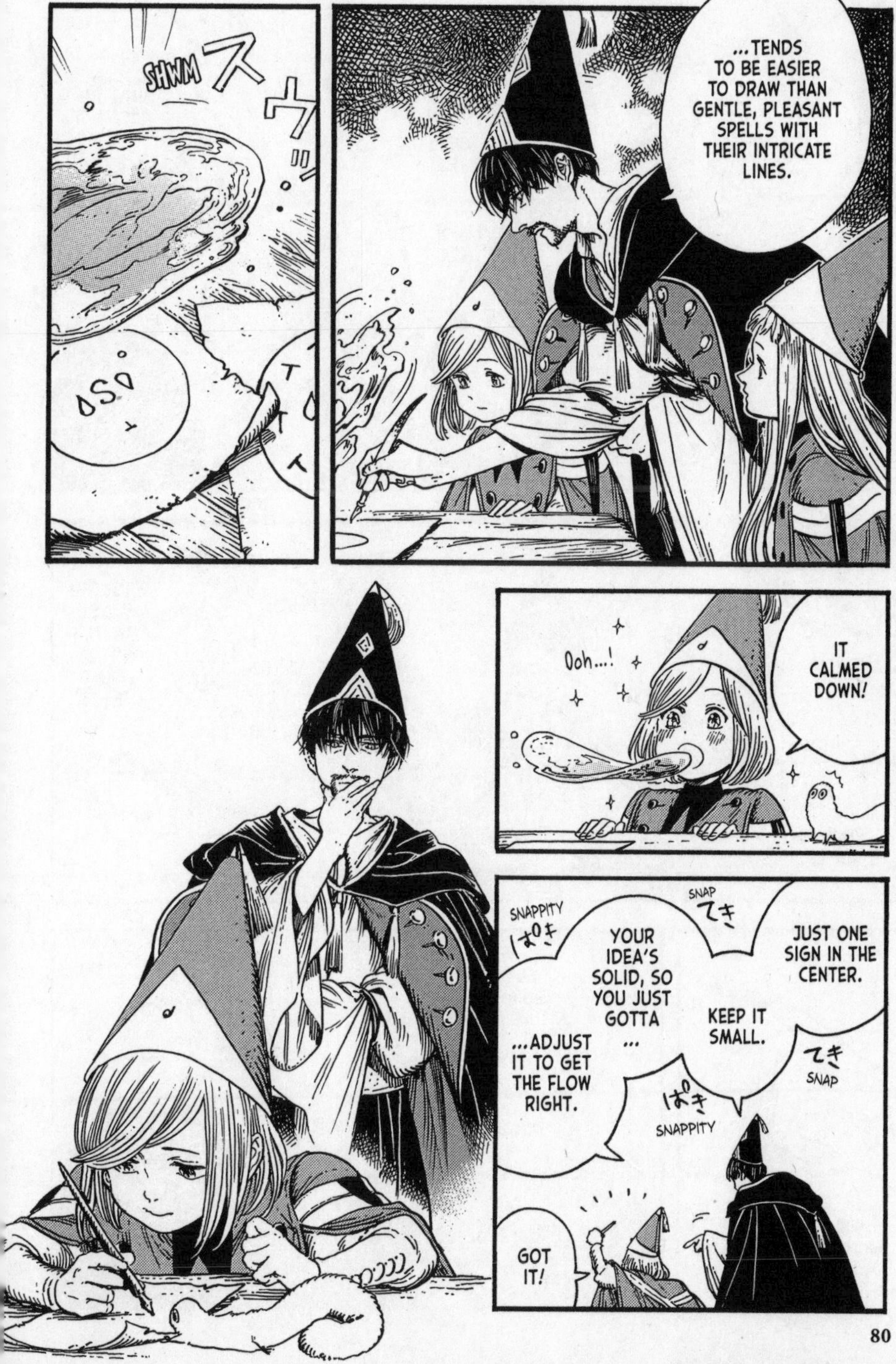
...TENDS TO BE EASIER TO DRAW THAN GENTLE, PLEASANT SPELLS WITH THEIR INTRICATE LINES.
SHWM スウッ
Ooh...!
IT CALMED DOWN!
JUST ONE SIGN IN THE CENTER.
SNAP てき
KEEP IT SMALL.
YOUR IDEA'S SOLID, SO YOU JUST GOTTA ...
SNAPPITY ぱき
...ADJUST IT TO GET THE FLOW RIGHT.
てき SNAP
ぱき SNAPPITY
GOT IT!

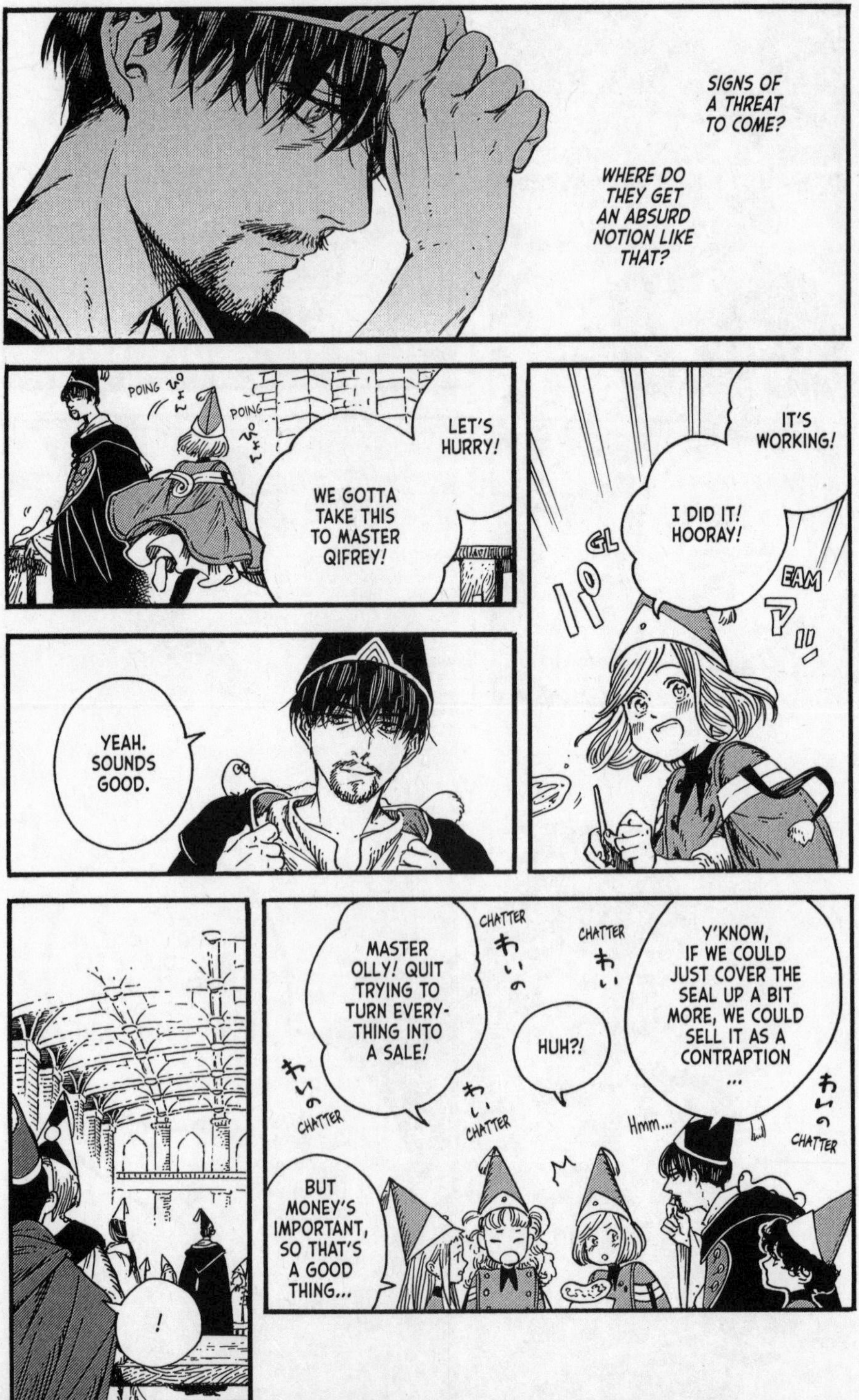

SIGNS OF A THREAT TO COME?
WHERE DO THEY GET AN ABSURD NOTION LIKE THAT?
IT'S WORKING!
I DID IT! HOORAY!
GL
EAM
LET'S HURRY!
WE GOTTA TAKE THIS TO MASTER QIFREY!
POING
POING
YEAH. SOUNDS GOOD.
Y'KNOW, IF WE COULD JUST COVER THE SEAL UP A BIT MORE, WE COULD SELL IT AS A CONTRAPTION ...
CHATTER
CHATTER
HUH?!
MASTER OLLY! QUIT TRYING TO TURN EVERY-THING INTO A SALE!
CHATTER
CHATTER
CHATTER
Hmm...
BUT MONEY'S IMPORTANT, SO THAT'S A GOOD THING...
!

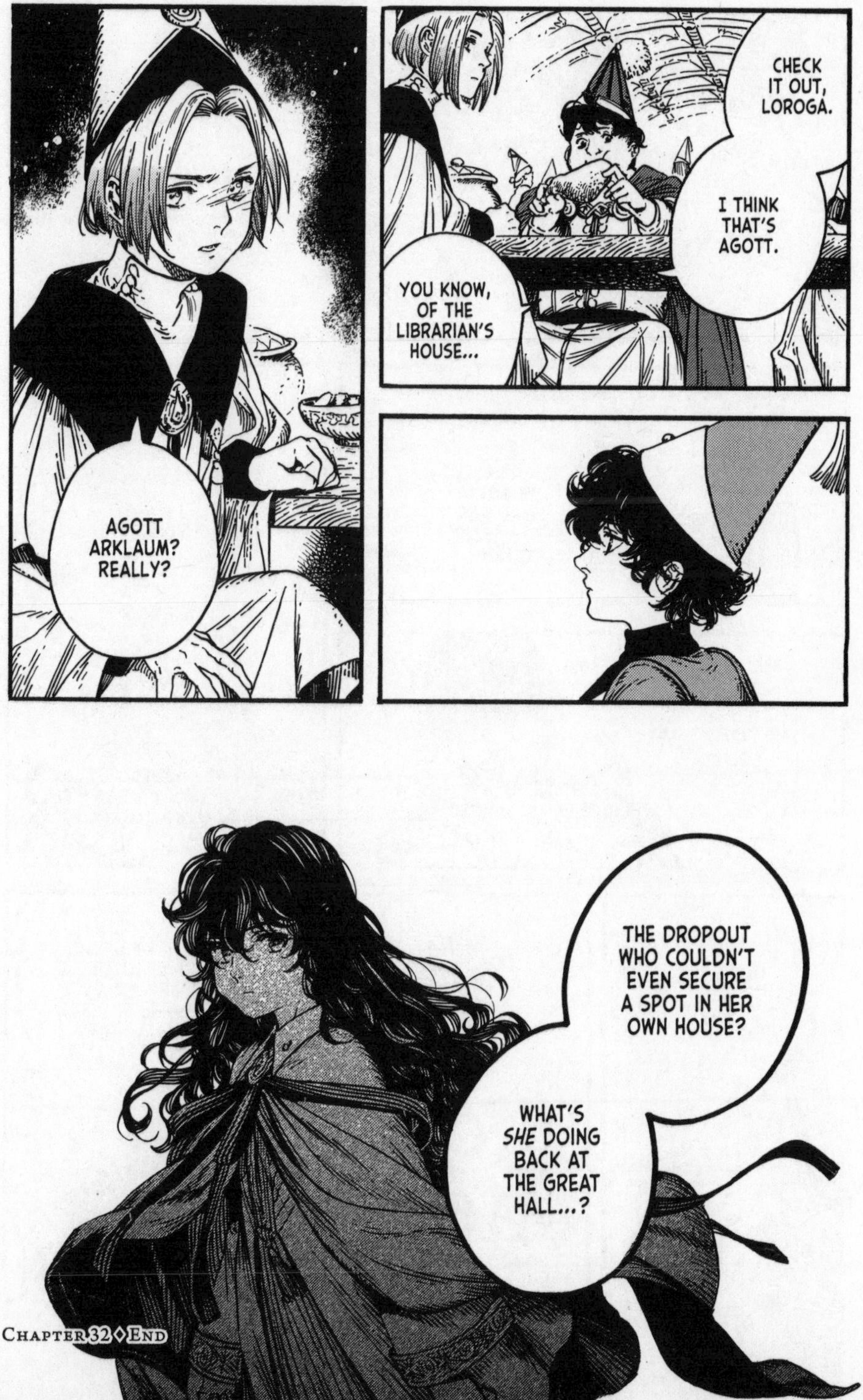
CHECK IT OUT, LOROGA.
I THINK THAT'S AGOTT.
YOU KNOW, OF THE LIBRARIAN'S HOUSE...
AGOTT ARKLAUM? REALLY?
THE DROPOUT WHO COULDN'T EVEN SECURE A SPOT IN HER OWN HOUSE?
WHAT'S *SHE* DOING BACK AT THE GREAT HALL...?

Chapter 32 ◇ End

Witch Hat Atelier

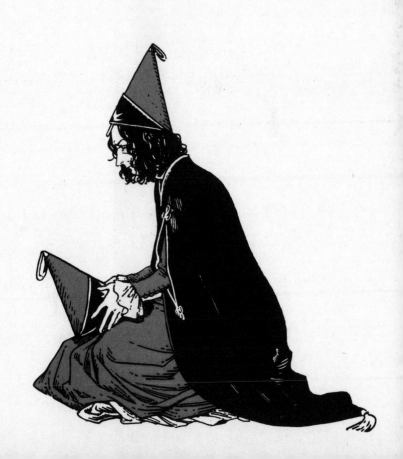

Chapter 33

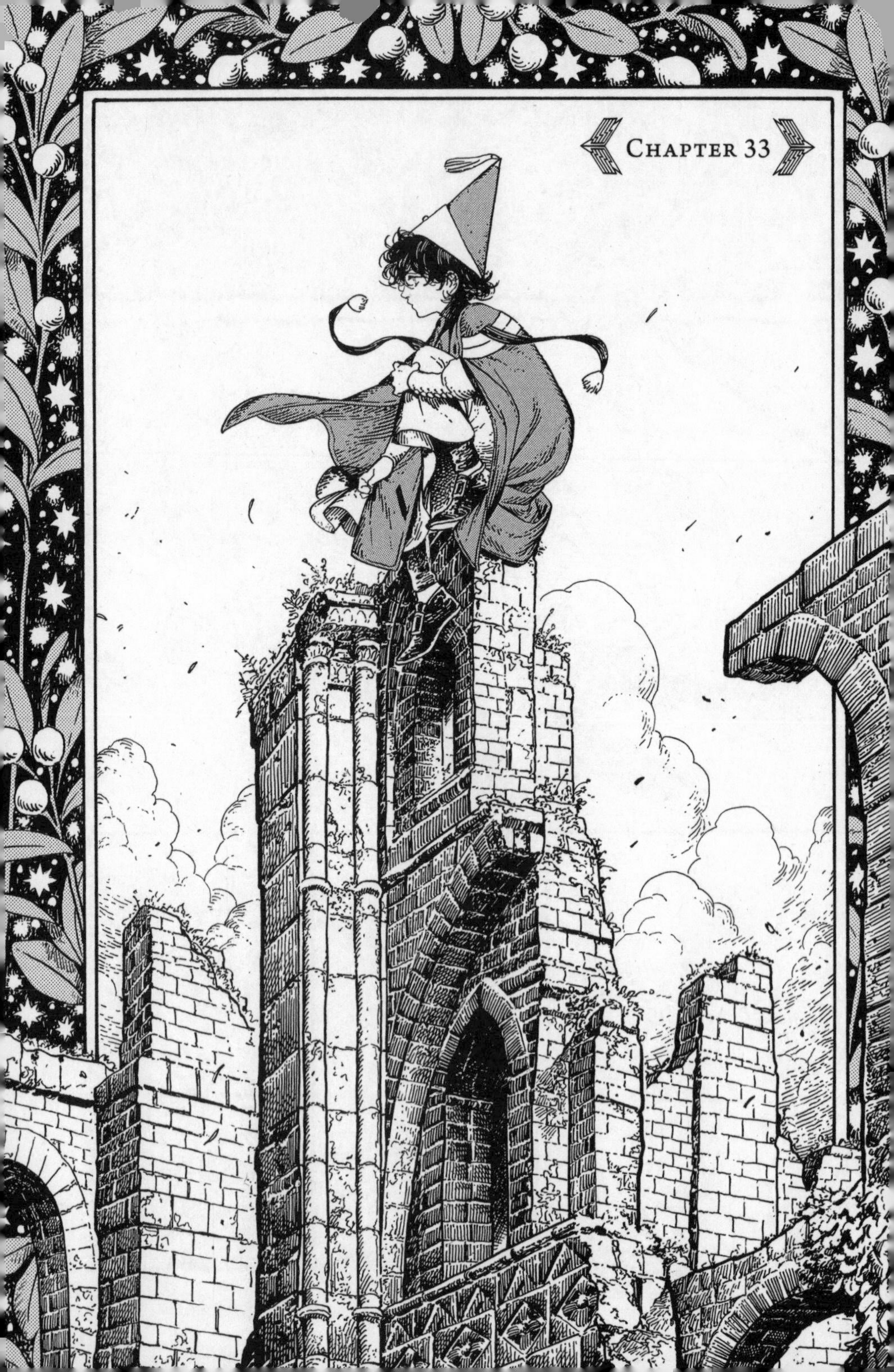

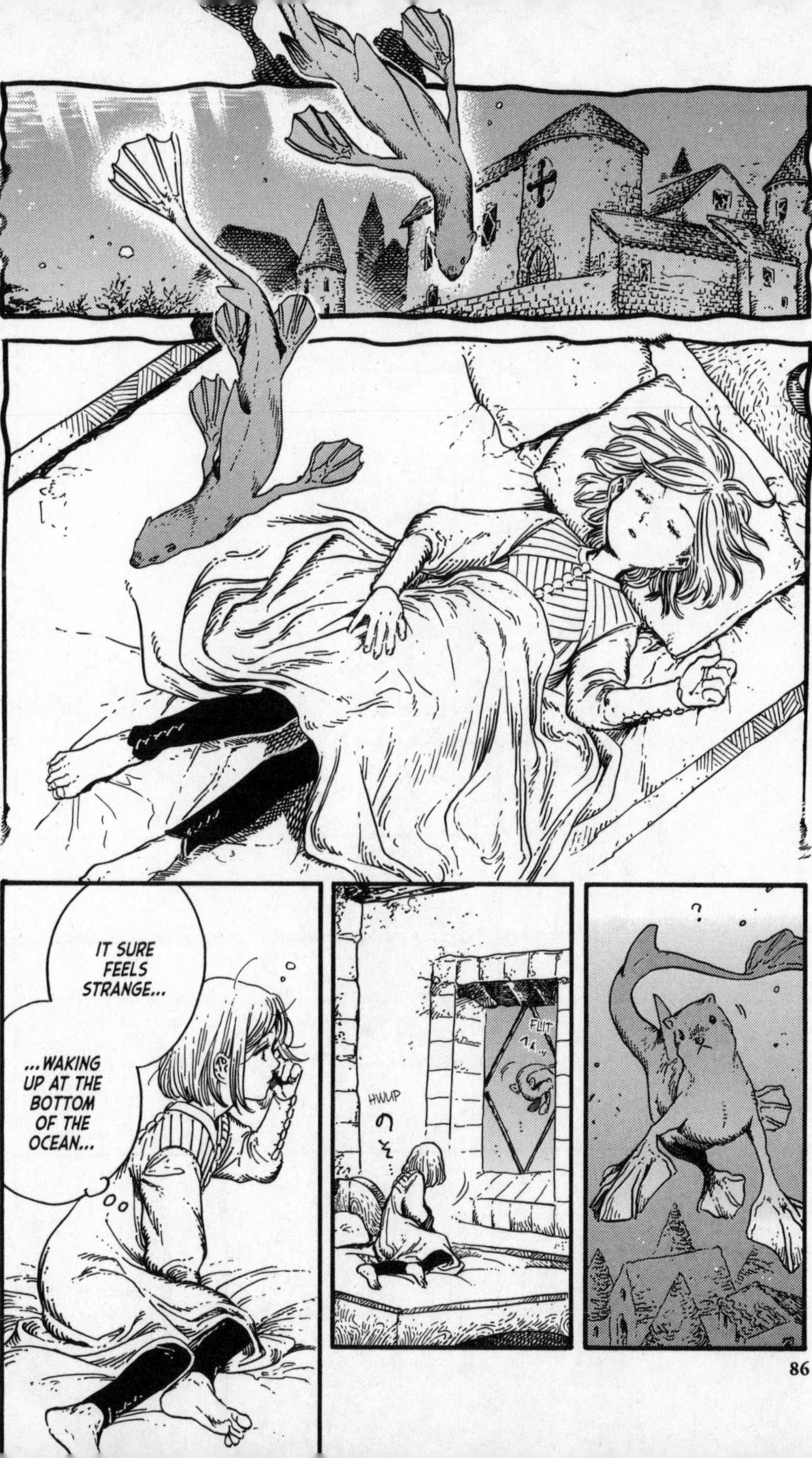
?
FLIT
HWUP
の
IT SURE FEELS STRANGE...
...WAKING UP AT THE BOTTOM OF THE OCEAN...

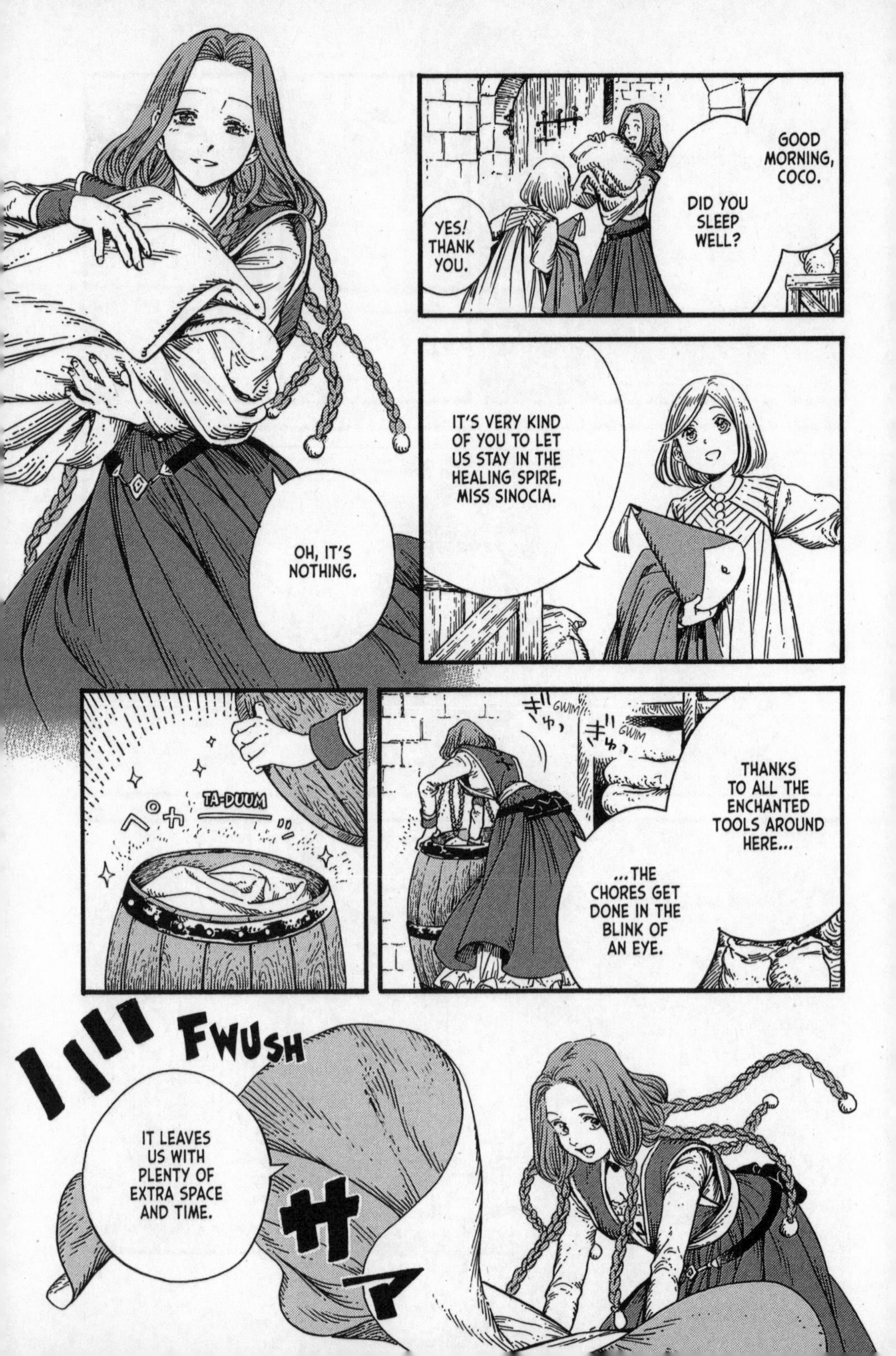
GOOD MORNING, COCO.
DID YOU SLEEP WELL?
YES! THANK YOU.
IT'S VERY KIND OF YOU TO LET US STAY IN THE HEALING SPIRE, MISS SINOCIA.
OH, IT'S NOTHING.
GWIM
GWIM
THANKS TO ALL THE ENCHANTED TOOLS AROUND HERE...
...THE CHORES GET DONE IN THE BLINK OF AN EYE.
TA-DUUM
FWUSH
IT LEAVES US WITH PLENTY OF EXTRA SPACE AND TIME.

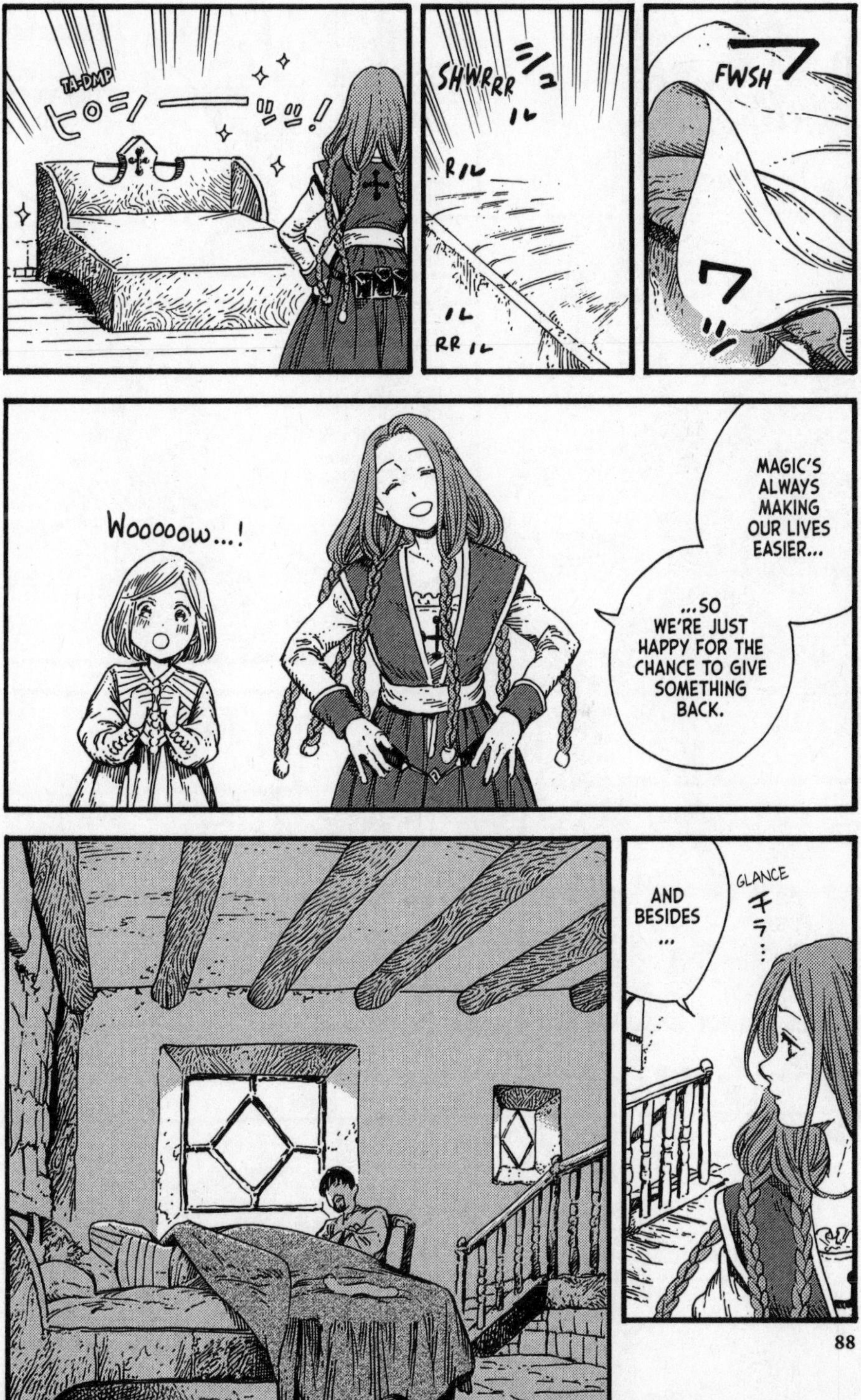
FWSH
SHWRRR
RRル
RR ル
TA-DMP
MAGIC'S ALWAYS MAKING OUR LIVES EASIER...
...SO WE'RE JUST HAPPY FOR THE CHANCE TO GIVE SOMETHING BACK.
Wooooow...!
GLANCE
チラ…
AND BESIDES ...

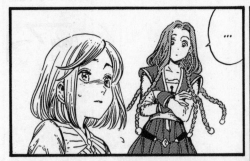

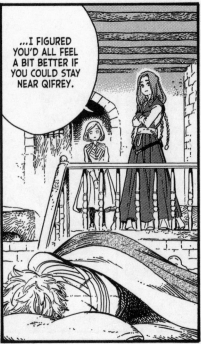

...I FIGURED YOU'D ALL FEEL A BIT BETTER IF YOU COULD STAY NEAR QIFREY.
...
NOW, NOW! ENOUGH OF THAT FRETTING!
CLAMP
ガシッ
TURN THAT FROWN UPSIDE DOWN!
YOUR TEST BEGINS TODAY, RIGHT?
LEAVE THE DOCTORING TO SINOCIA, BEST CARETAKER UNDER THE SEA!
YOU'VE GOTTA FOCUS ON BEING A WITCH!
...RIGHT!

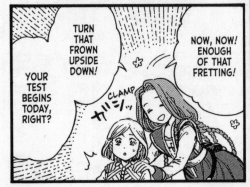

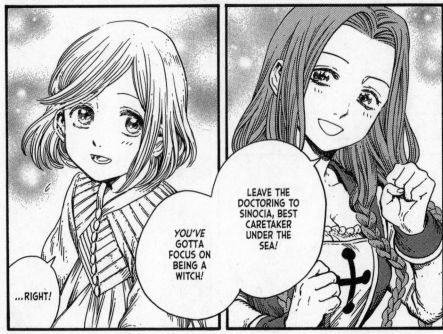

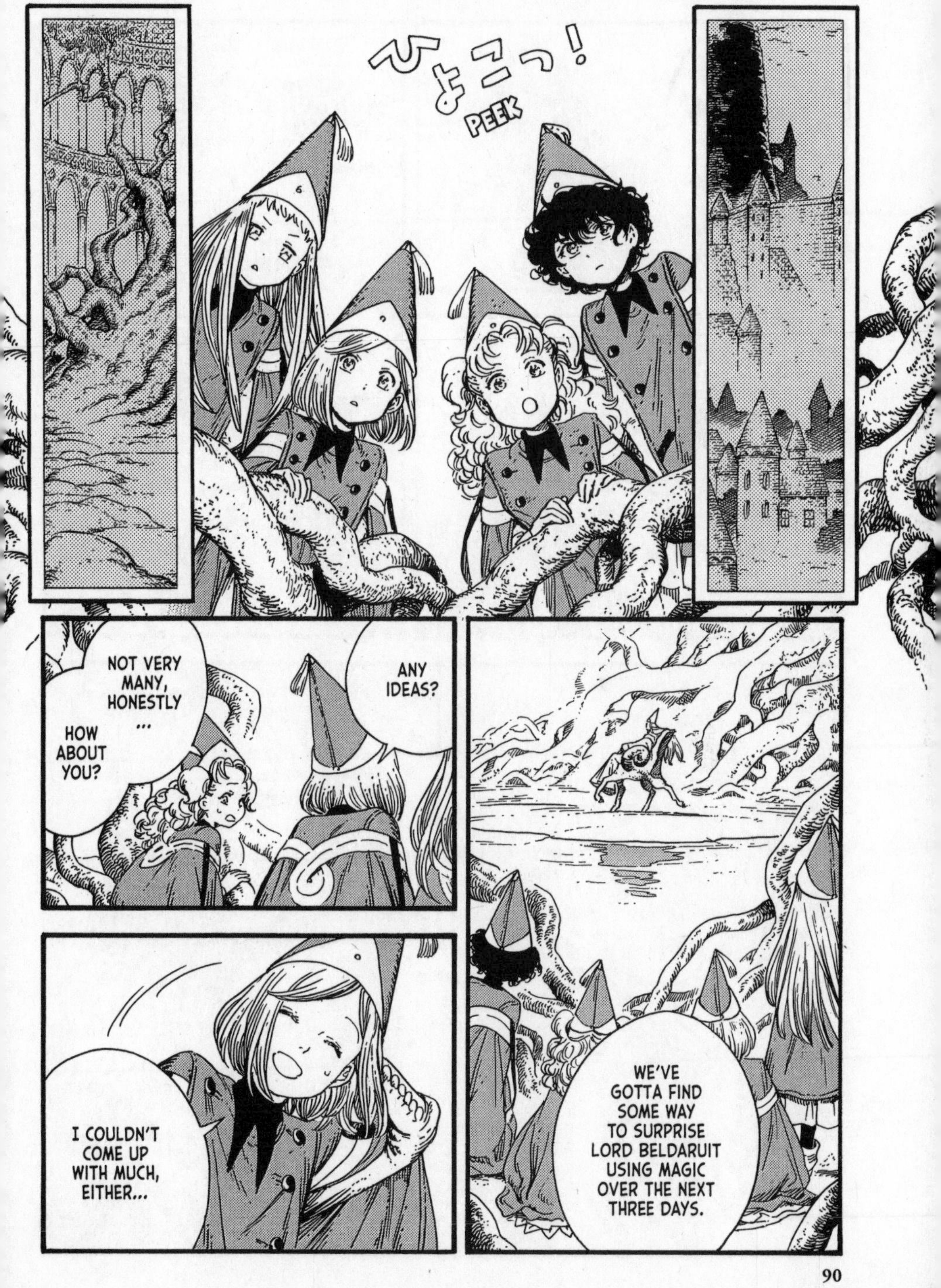
ひょこっ!
PEEK
ANY IDEAS?
NOT VERY MANY, HONESTLY ...
HOW ABOUT YOU?
WE'VE GOTTA FIND SOME WAY TO SURPRISE LORD BELDARUIT USING MAGIC OVER THE NEXT THREE DAYS.
I COULDN'T COME UP WITH MUCH, EITHER...

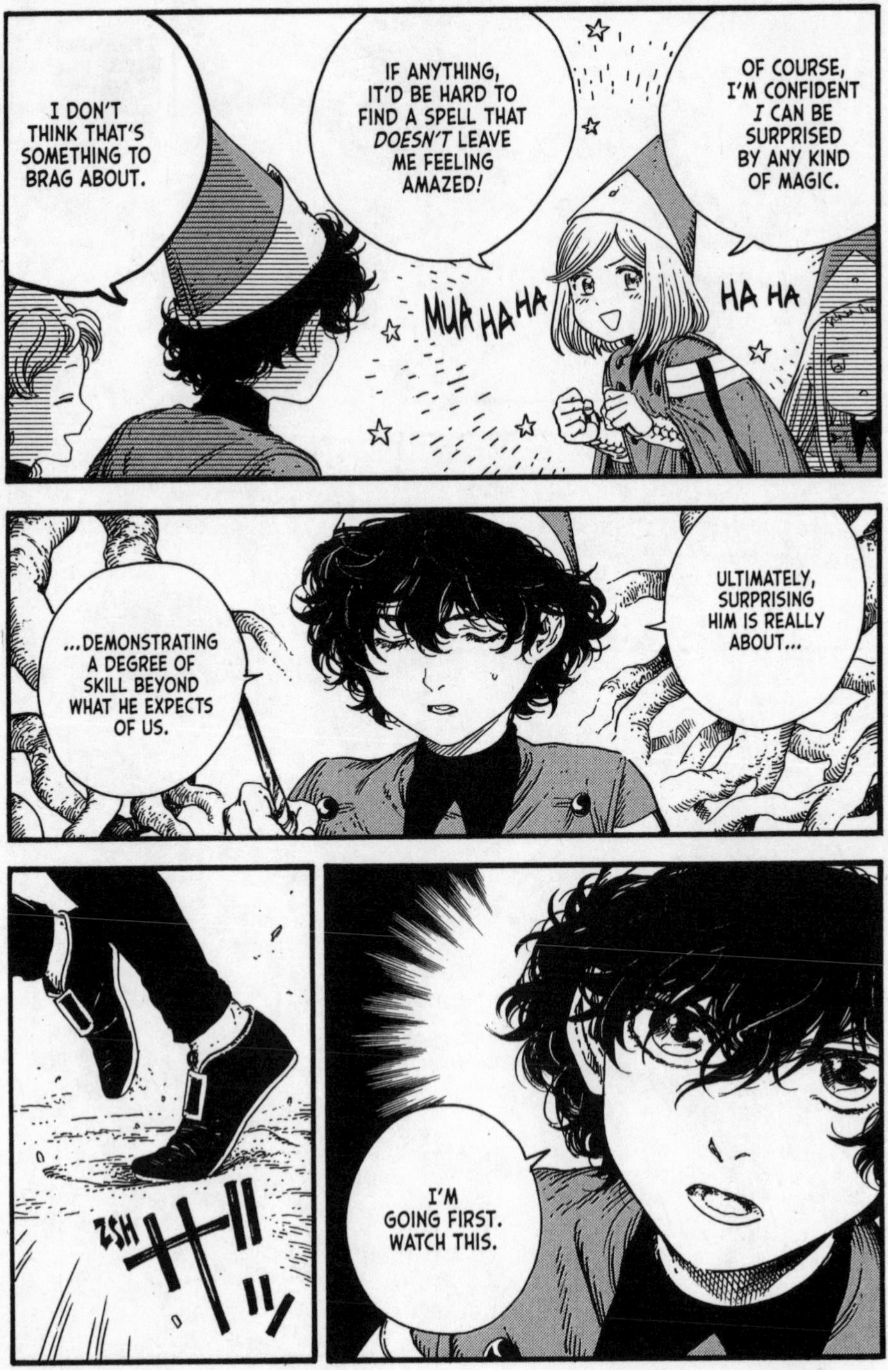
OF COURSE, I'M CONFIDENT *I* CAN BE SURPRISED BY ANY KIND OF MAGIC.
IF ANYTHING, IT'D BE HARD TO FIND A SPELL THAT *DOESN'T* LEAVE ME FEELING AMAZED!
HA HA
MUA HA HA
I DON'T THINK THAT'S SOMETHING TO BRAG ABOUT.
ULTIMATELY, SURPRISING HIM IS REALLY ABOUT...
...DEMONSTRATING A DEGREE OF SKILL BEYOND WHAT HE EXPECTS OF US.
I'M GOING FIRST. WATCH THIS.
ZSH

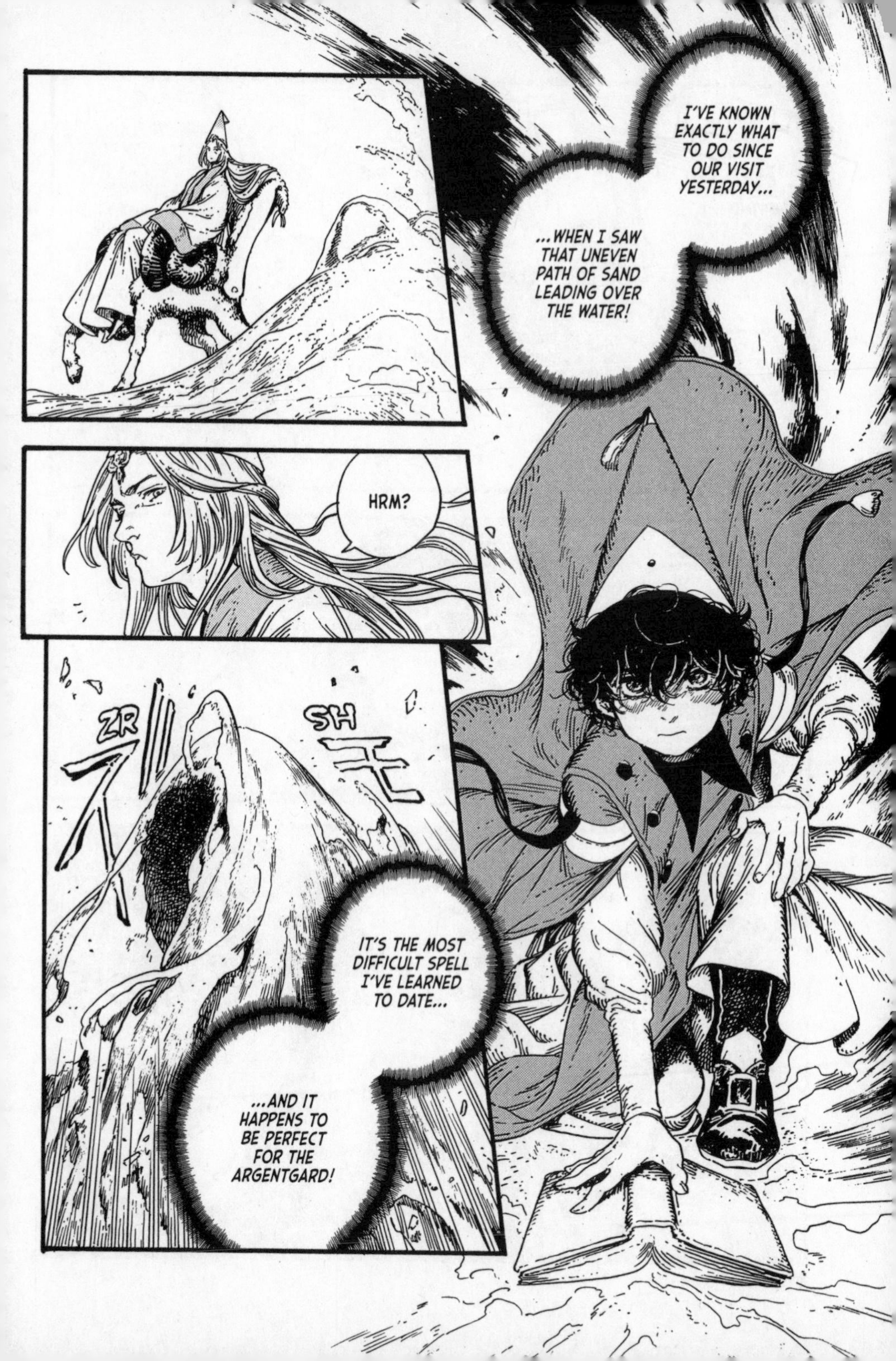
I'VE KNOWN EXACTLY WHAT TO DO SINCE OUR VISIT YESTERDAY...
...WHEN I SAW THAT UNEVEN PATH OF SAND LEADING OVER THE WATER!
IT'S THE MOST DIFFICULT SPELL I'VE LEARNED TO DATE...
...AND IT HAPPENS TO BE PERFECT FOR THE ARGENTGARD!
HRM?
ZR
SH

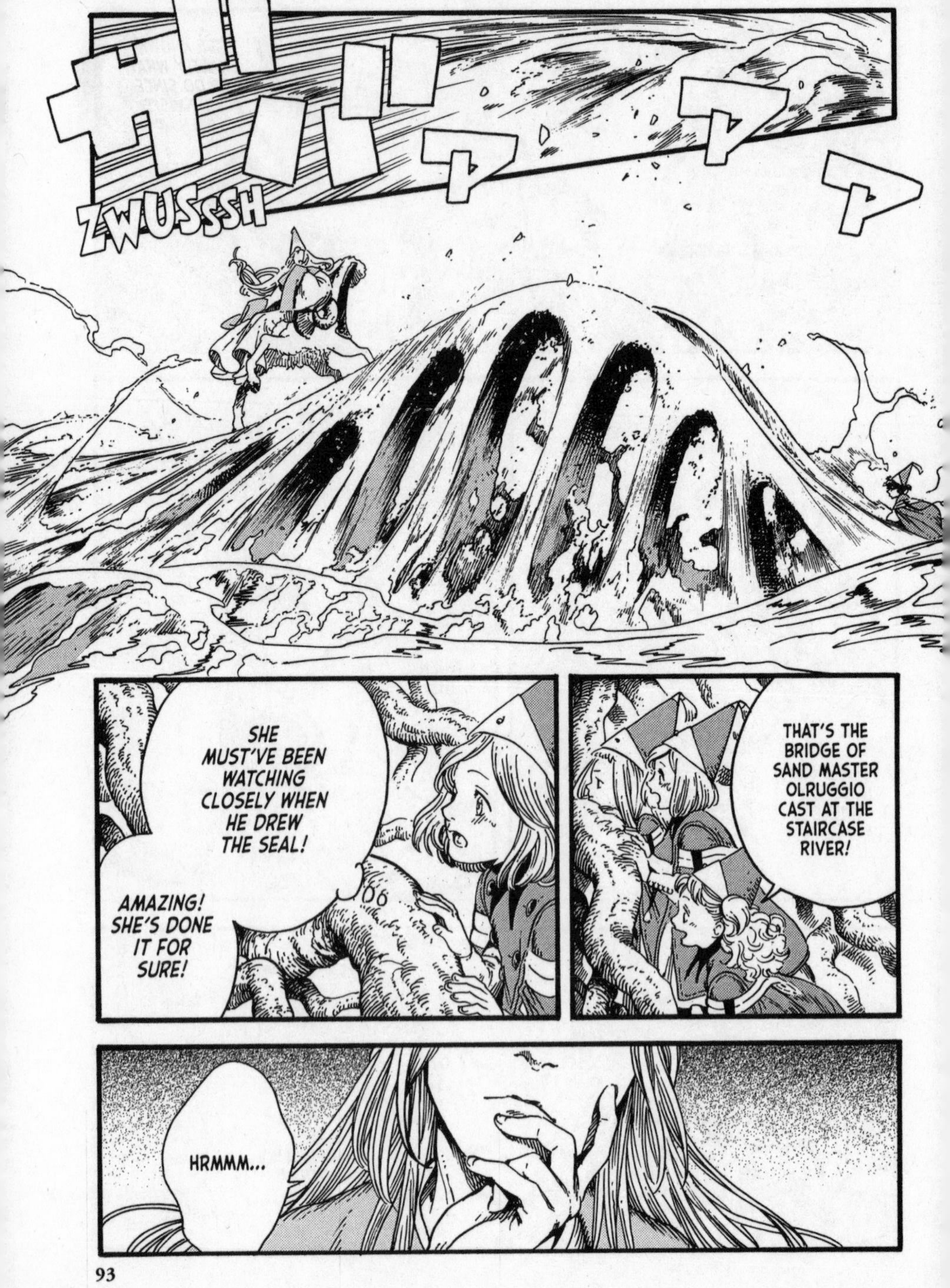
ZWUSSSH
THAT'S THE BRIDGE OF SAND MASTER OLRUGGIO CAST AT THE STAIRCASE RIVER!
SHE MUST'VE BEEN WATCHING CLOSELY WHEN HE DREW THE SEAL!
AMAZING! SHE'S DONE IT FOR SURE!
HRMMM...

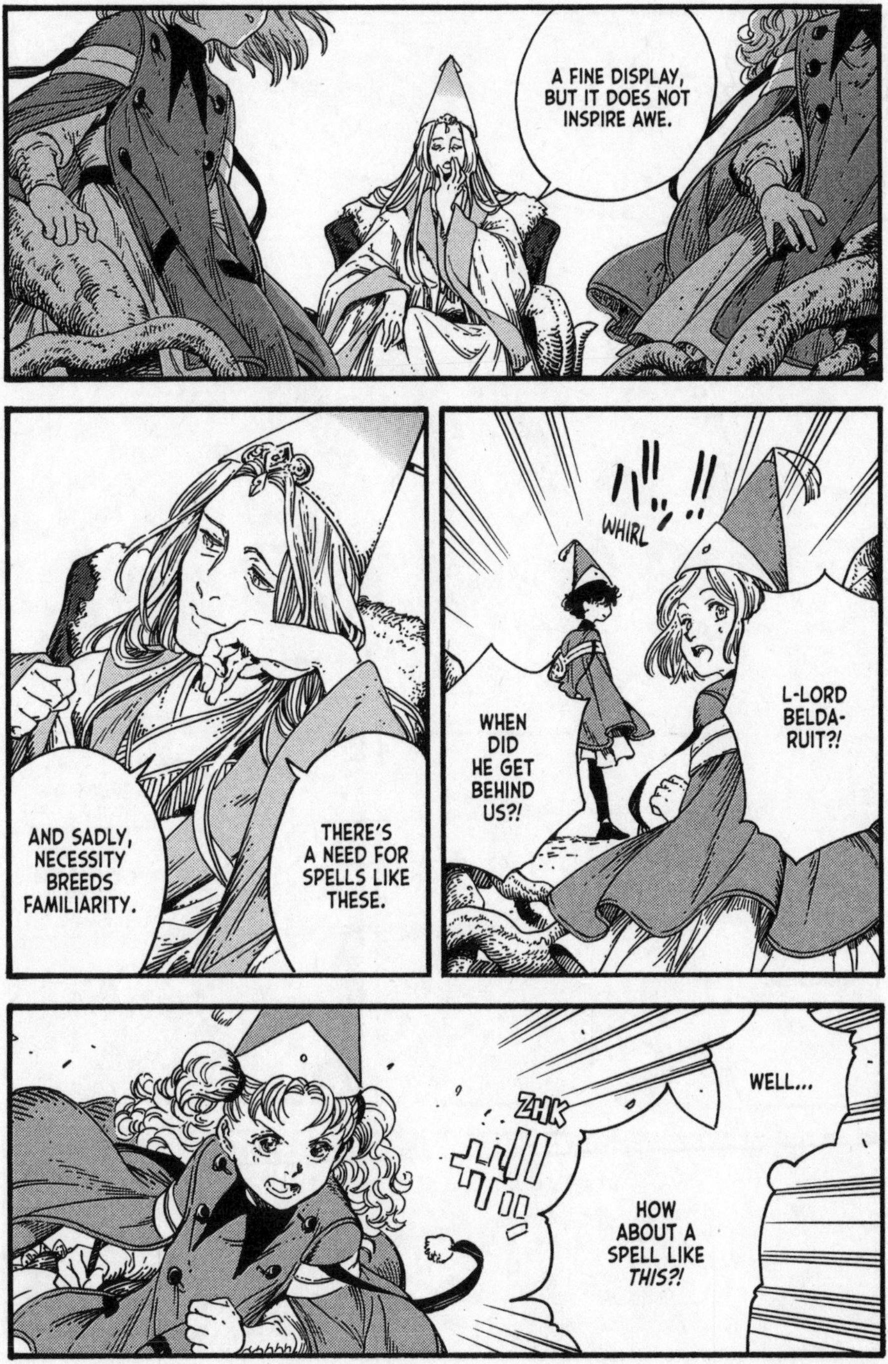
A FINE DISPLAY, BUT IT DOES NOT INSPIRE AWE.
WHIRL
L-LORD BELDA-RUIT?!
WHEN DID HE GET BEHIND US?!
THERE'S A NEED FOR SPELLS LIKE THESE.
AND SADLY, NECESSITY BREEDS FAMILIARITY.
WELL...
HOW ABOUT A SPELL LIKE *THIS?!*
ZHK

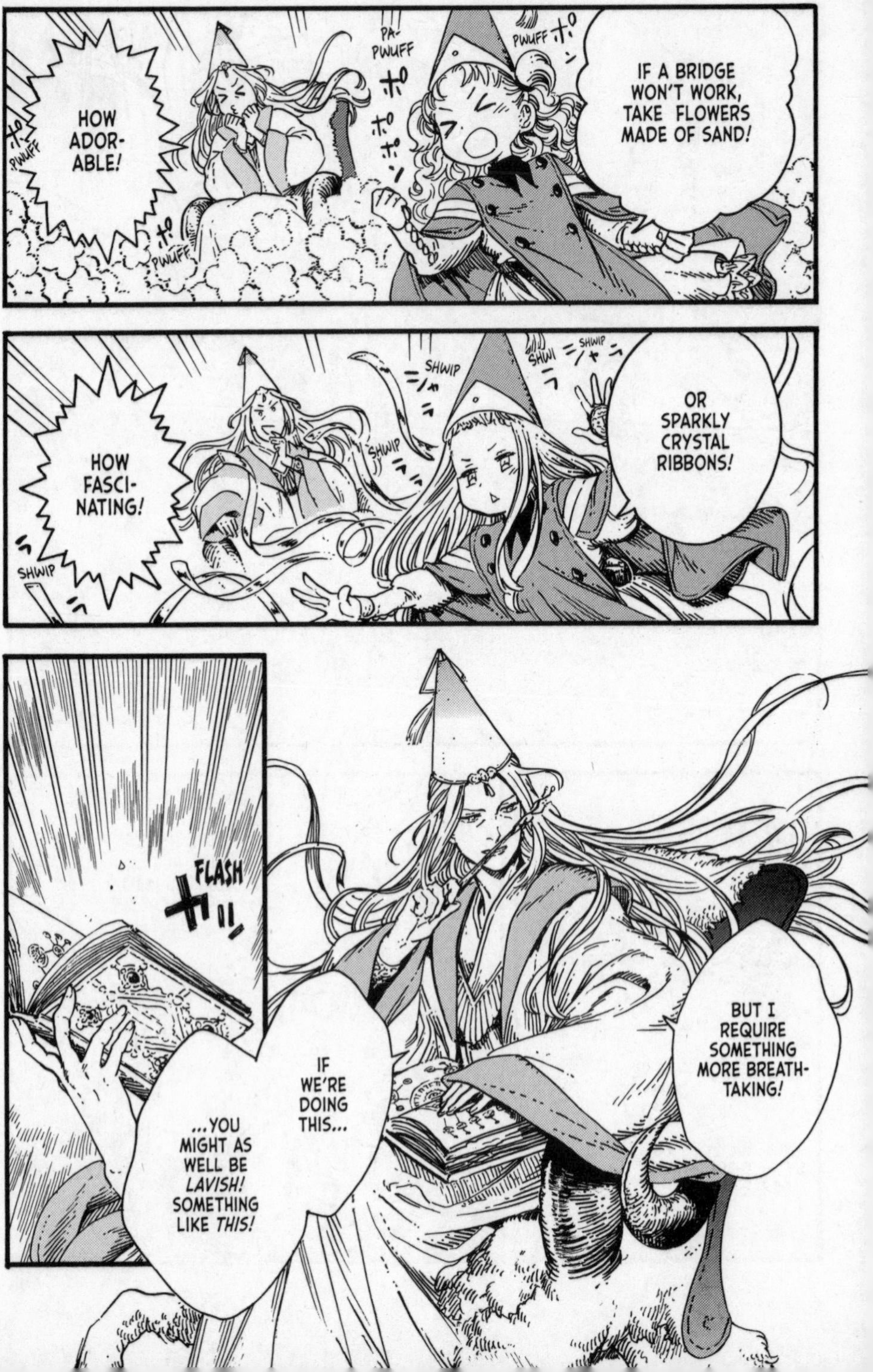
IF A BRIDGE WON'T WORK, TAKE FLOWERS MADE OF SAND!
PWUFF ポン
PA-PWUFF ポ
ポポン
HOW ADORABLE!
ポ PWUFF
ポ PWUFF
OR SPARKLY CRYSTAL RIBBONS!
SHWI
SHWIP シャ
SHWIP シャ
SHWIP
HOW FASCINATING!
SHWIP
BUT I REQUIRE SOMETHING MORE BREATHTAKING!
IF WE'RE DOING THIS...
...YOU MIGHT AS WELL BE *LAVISH!* SOMETHING LIKE *THIS!*
FLASH

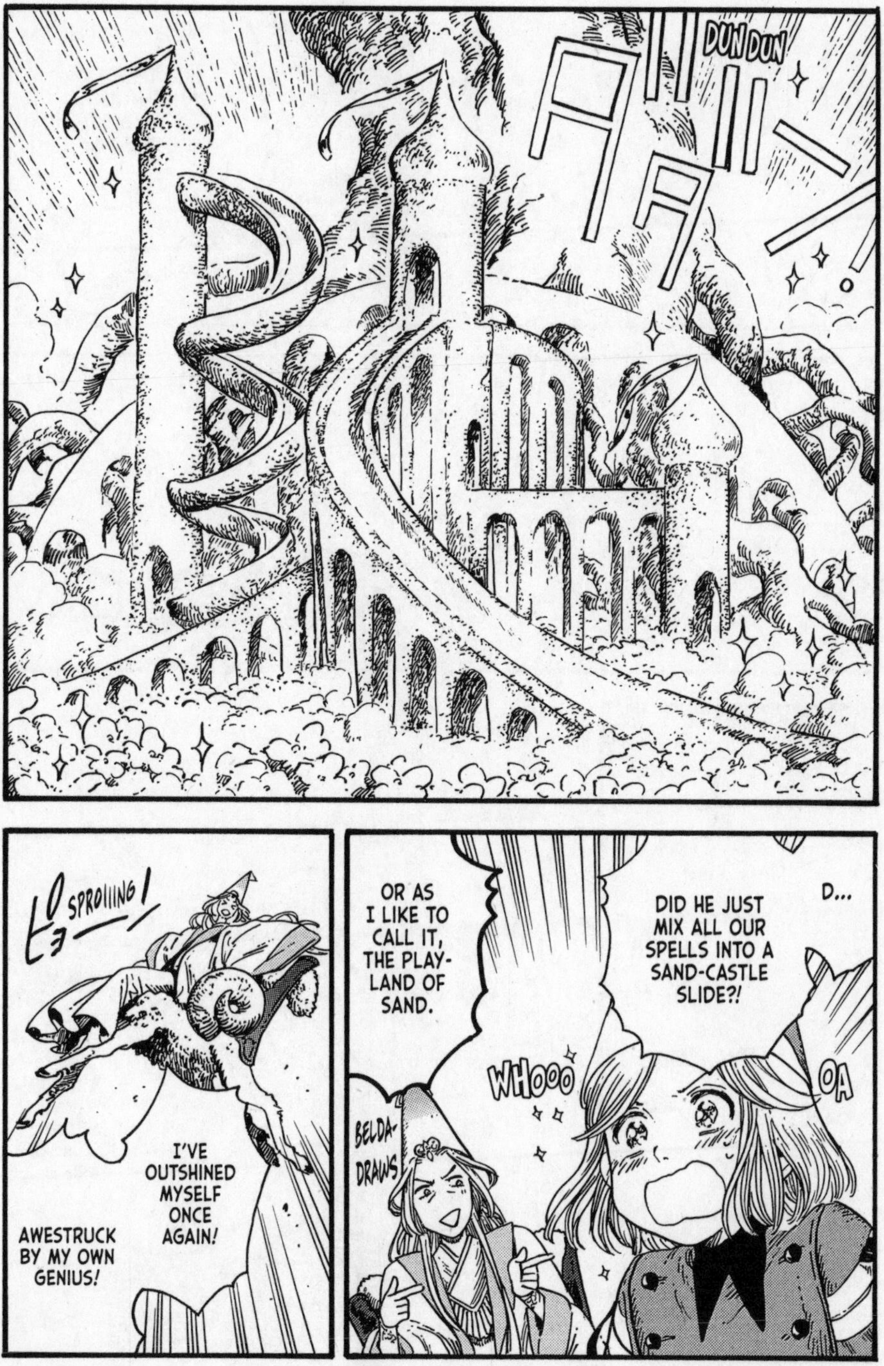
DUN DUN
D...
DID HE JUST MIX ALL OUR SPELLS INTO A SAND-CASTLE SLIDE?!
OR AS I LIKE TO CALL IT, THE PLAY-LAND OF SAND.
OA
WHOOO
BELDA-DRAWS
SPROIIING!
I'VE OUTSHINED MYSELF ONCE AGAIN!
AWESTRUCK BY MY OWN GENIUS!

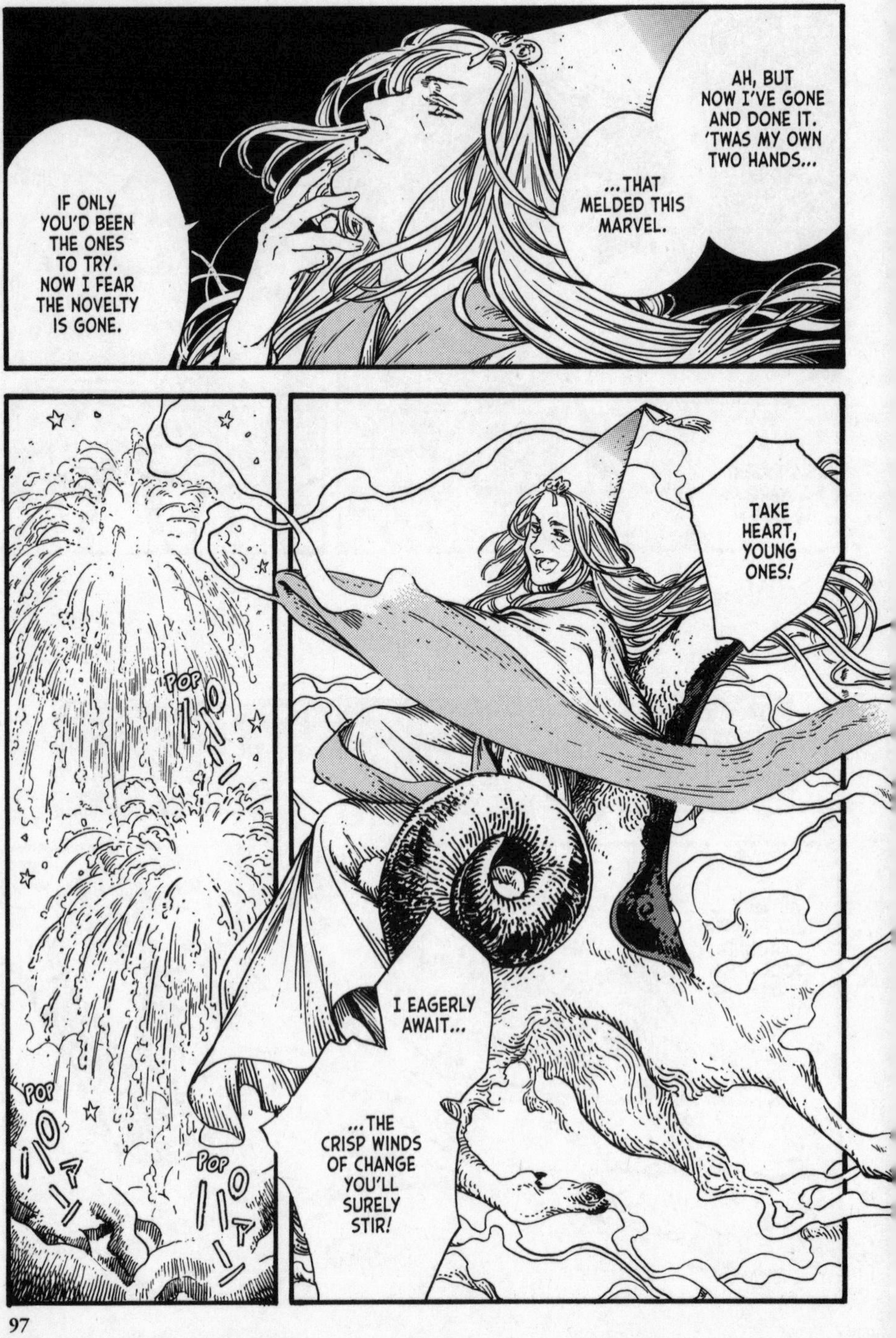
AH, BUT NOW I'VE GONE AND DONE IT. 'TWAS MY OWN TWO HANDS...
...THAT MELDED THIS MARVEL.
IF ONLY YOU'D BEEN THE ONES TO TRY. NOW I FEAR THE NOVELTY IS GONE.
TAKE HEART, YOUNG ONES!
I EAGERLY AWAIT...
...THE CRISP WINDS OF CHANGE YOU'LL SURELY STIR!
POP
POP
POP

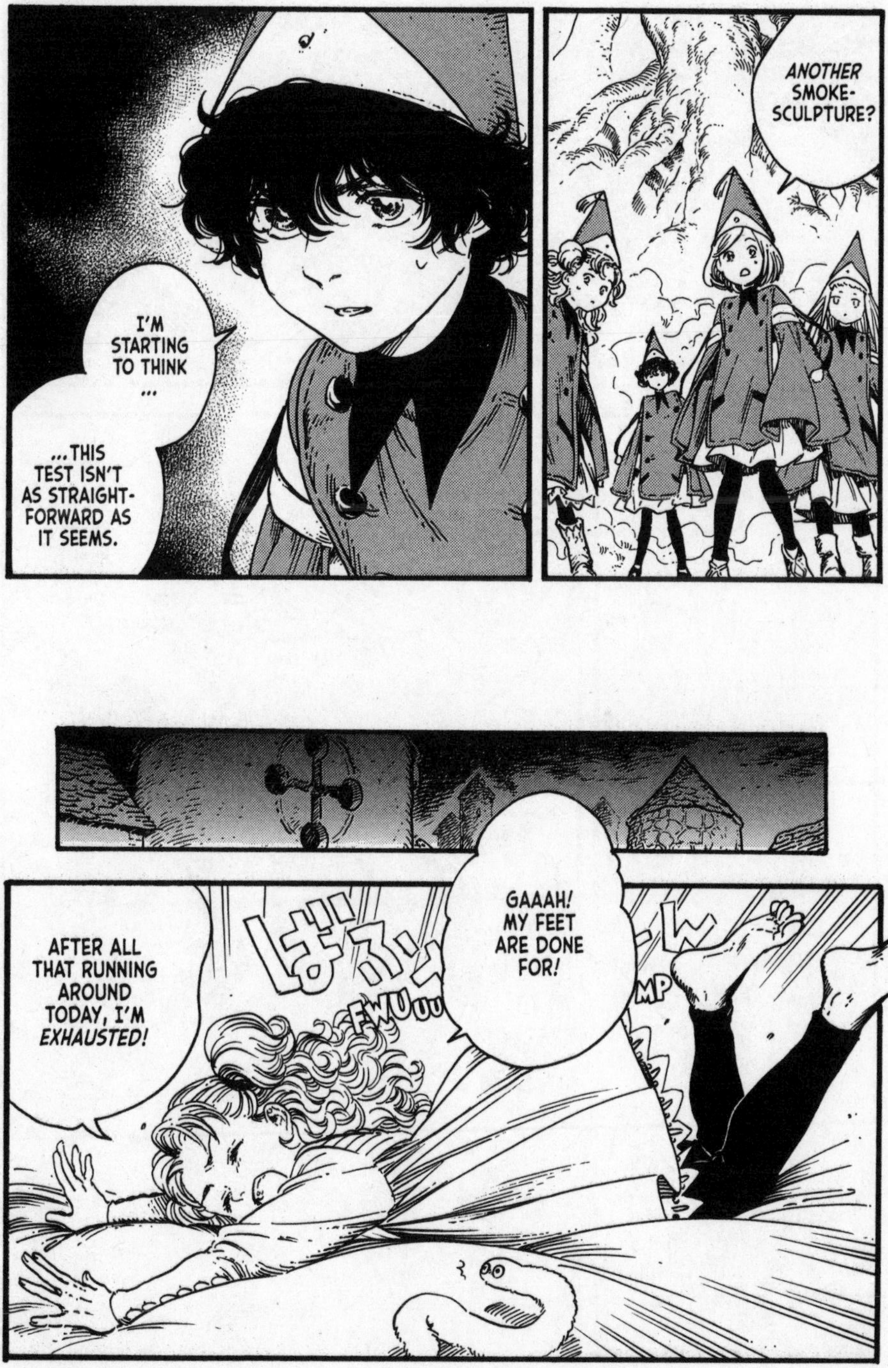
ANOTHER SMOKE-SCULPTURE?
I'M STARTING TO THINK ...
...THIS TEST ISN'T AS STRAIGHT-FORWARD AS IT SEEMS.
GAAAH! MY FEET ARE DONE FOR!
AFTER ALL THAT RUNNING AROUND TODAY, I'M EXHAUSTED!

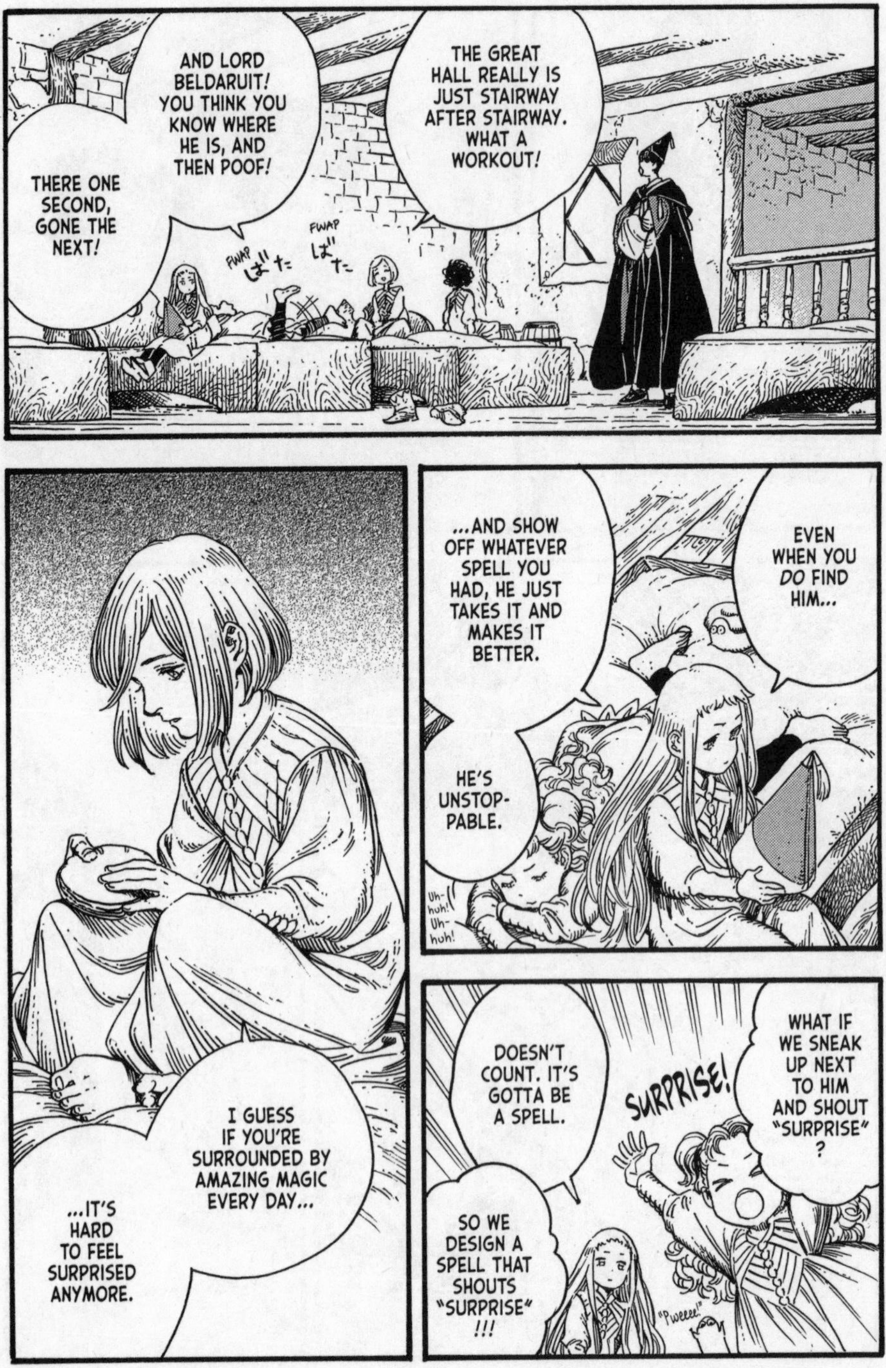
THE GREAT HALL REALLY IS JUST STAIRWAY AFTER STAIRWAY. WHAT A WORKOUT!
AND LORD BELDARUIT! YOU THINK YOU KNOW WHERE HE IS, AND THEN POOF!
THERE ONE SECOND, GONE THE NEXT!
FWAP ばた
FWAP ばた
EVEN WHEN YOU *DO* FIND HIM...
...AND SHOW OFF WHATEVER SPELL YOU HAD, HE JUST TAKES IT AND MAKES IT BETTER.
HE'S UNSTOP-PABLE.
Uh-huh! Uh-huh!
WHAT IF WE SNEAK UP NEXT TO HIM AND SHOUT "SURPRISE"?
SURPRISE!
DOESN'T COUNT. IT'S GOTTA BE A SPELL.
SO WE DESIGN A SPELL THAT SHOUTS "SURPRISE"!!!
"Pweeee!"
I GUESS IF YOU'RE SURROUNDED BY AMAZING MAGIC EVERY DAY...
...IT'S HARD TO FEEL SURPRISED ANYMORE.

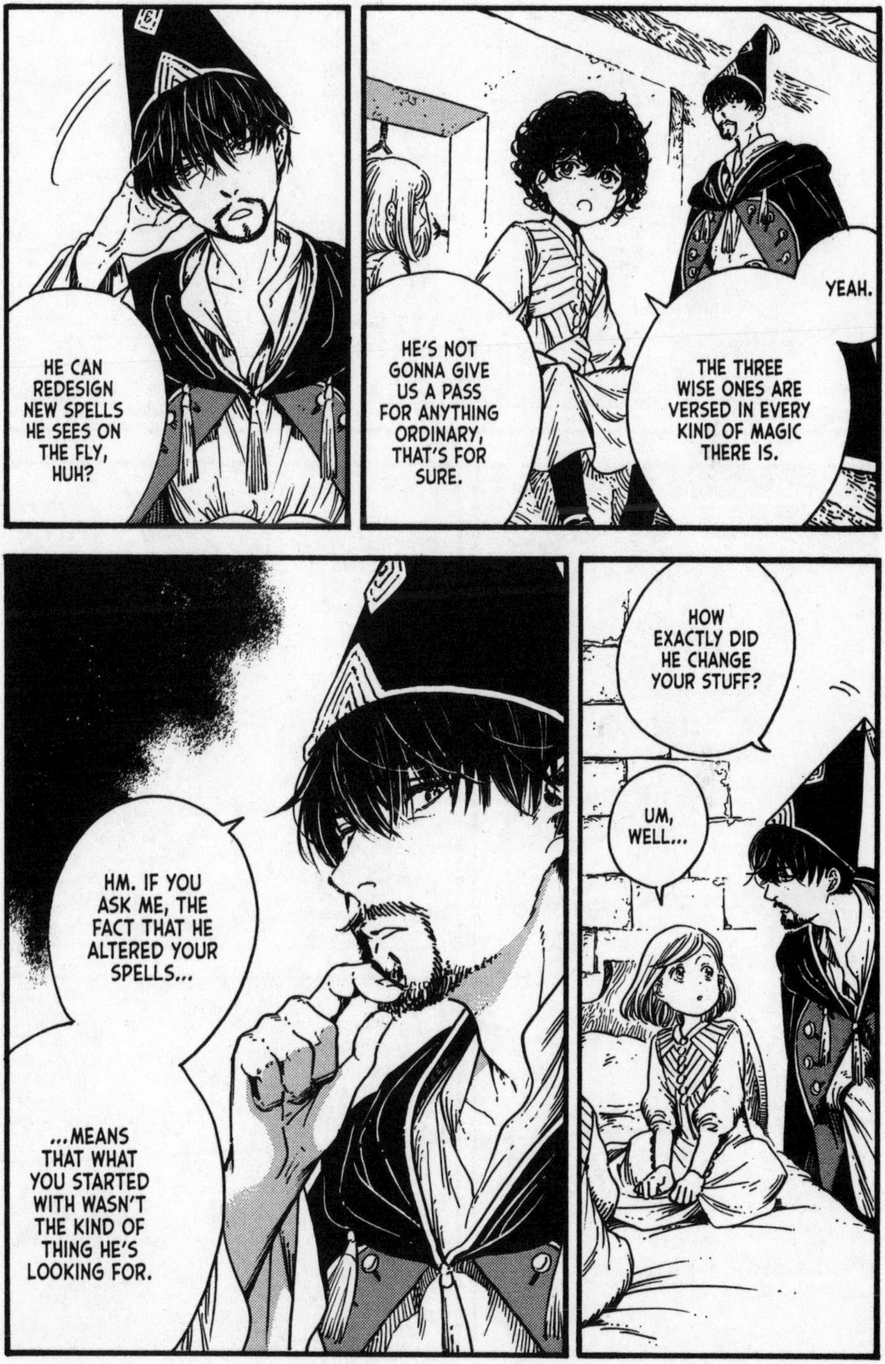

YEAH.
THE THREE WISE ONES ARE VERSED IN EVERY KIND OF MAGIC THERE IS.
HE'S NOT GONNA GIVE US A PASS FOR ANYTHING ORDINARY, THAT'S FOR SURE.
HE CAN REDESIGN NEW SPELLS HE SEES ON THE FLY, HUH?
HOW EXACTLY DID HE CHANGE YOUR STUFF?
UM, WELL...
HM. IF YOU ASK ME, THE FACT THAT HE ALTERED YOUR SPELLS...
...MEANS THAT WHAT YOU STARTED WITH WASN'T THE KIND OF THING HE'S LOOKING FOR.

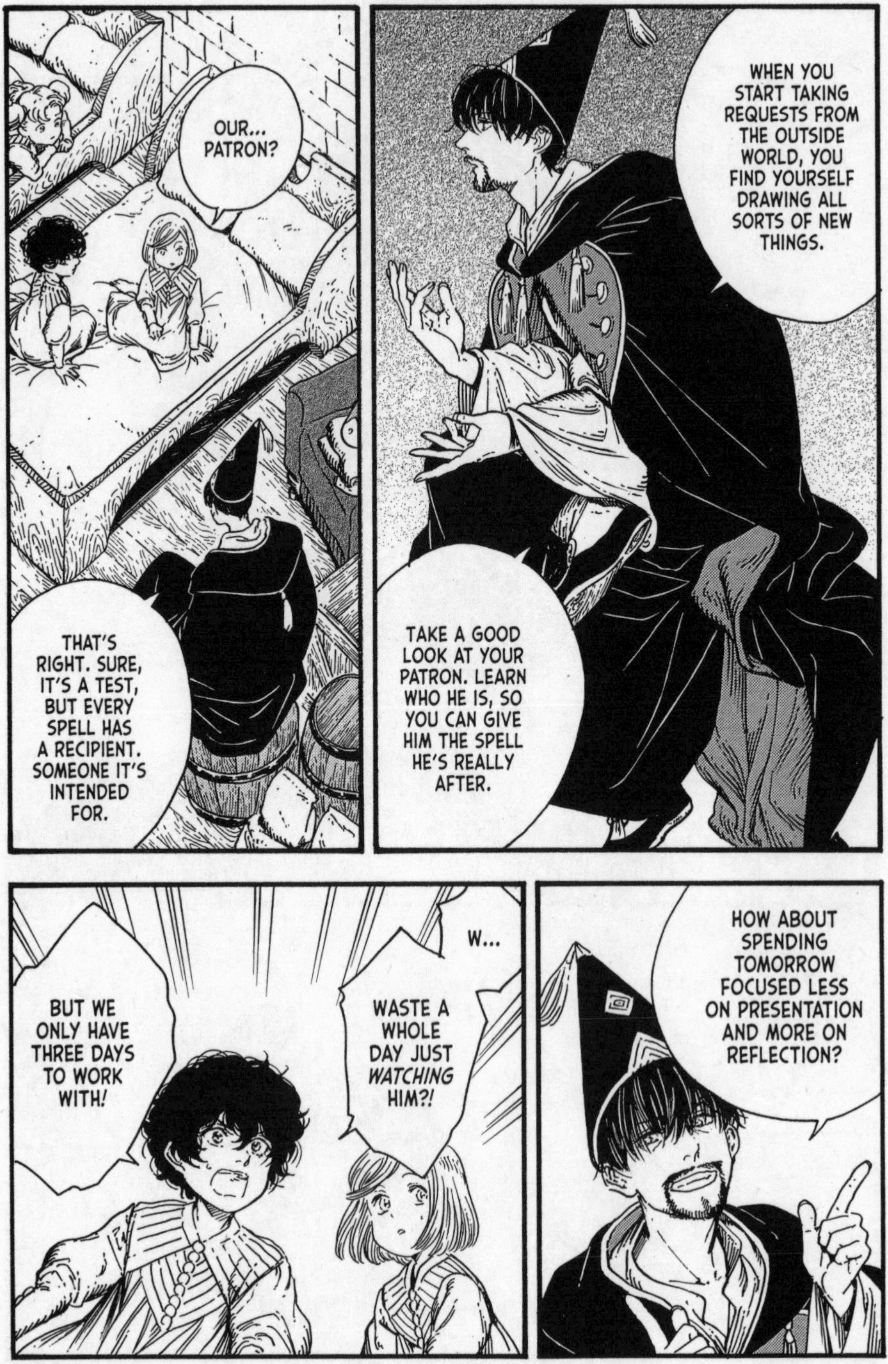
WHEN YOU START TAKING REQUESTS FROM THE OUTSIDE WORLD, YOU FIND YOURSELF DRAWING ALL SORTS OF NEW THINGS.
TAKE A GOOD LOOK AT YOUR PATRON. LEARN WHO HE IS, SO YOU CAN GIVE HIM THE SPELL HE'S REALLY AFTER.
OUR... PATRON?
THAT'S RIGHT. SURE, IT'S A TEST, BUT EVERY SPELL HAS A RECIPIENT. SOMEONE IT'S INTENDED FOR.
HOW ABOUT SPENDING TOMORROW FOCUSED LESS ON PRESENTATION AND MORE ON REFLECTION?
W...
WASTE A WHOLE DAY JUST *WATCHING* HIM?!
BUT WE ONLY HAVE THREE DAYS TO WORK WITH!

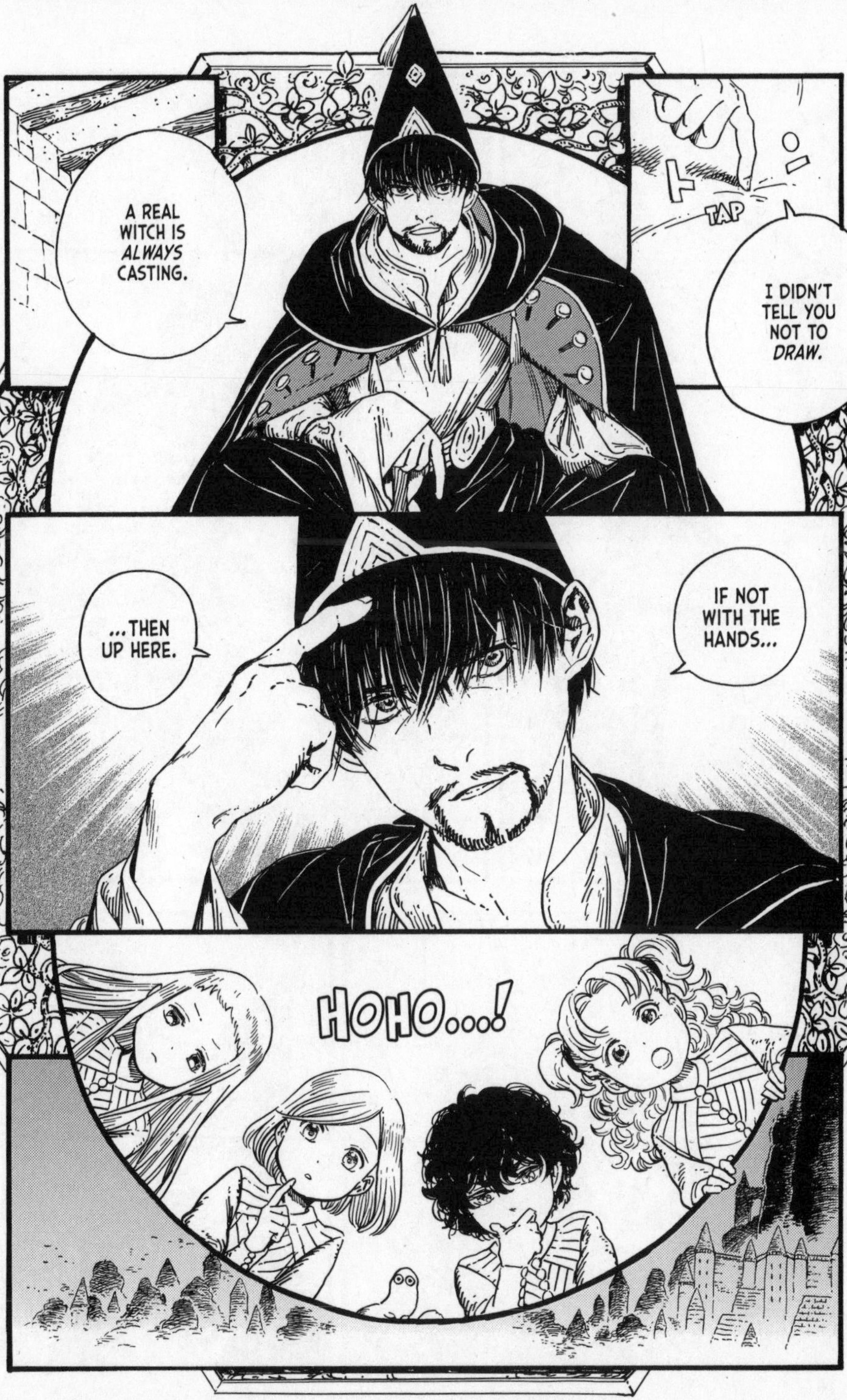
TAP
I DIDN'T TELL YOU NOT TO *DRAW.*
A REAL WITCH IS *ALWAYS* CASTING.
IF NOT WITH THE HANDS...
...THEN UP HERE.
HOHO...!

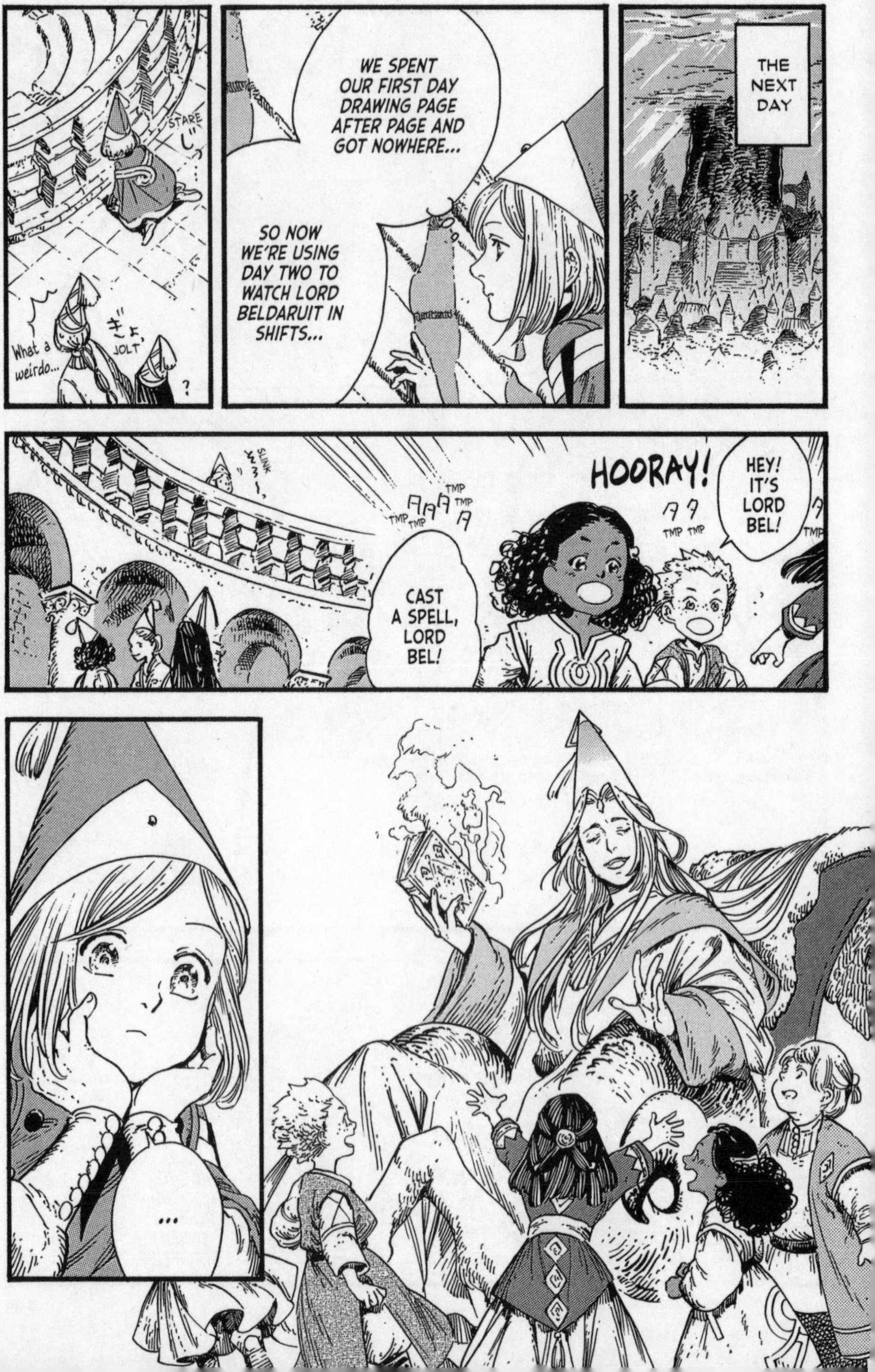
THE NEXT DAY
WE SPENT OUR FIRST DAY DRAWING PAGE AFTER PAGE AND GOT NOWHERE...
SO NOW WE'RE USING DAY TWO TO WATCH LORD BELDARUIT IN SHIFTS...
STARE
What a weirdo...
JOLT
?
HEY! IT'S LORD BEL!
TMP
TMP TMP
HOORAY!
CAST A SPELL, LORD BEL!
TMP TMP TMP TMP
SLINK
...

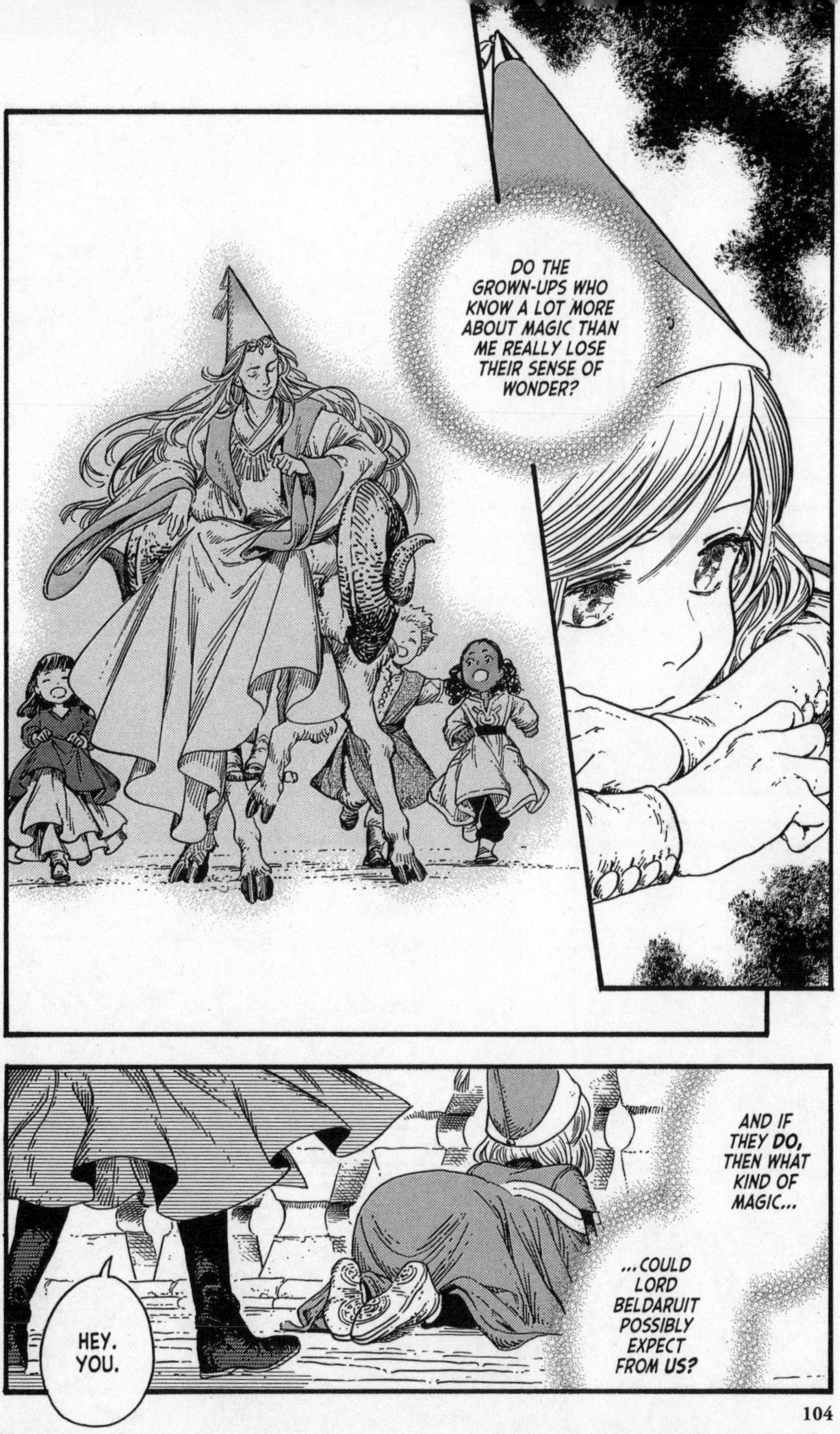
DO THE GROWN-UPS WHO KNOW A LOT MORE ABOUT MAGIC THAN ME REALLY LOSE THEIR SENSE OF WONDER?
AND IF THEY DO, THEN WHAT KIND OF MAGIC...
...COULD LORD BELDARUIT POSSIBLY EXPECT FROM US?
HEY. YOU.

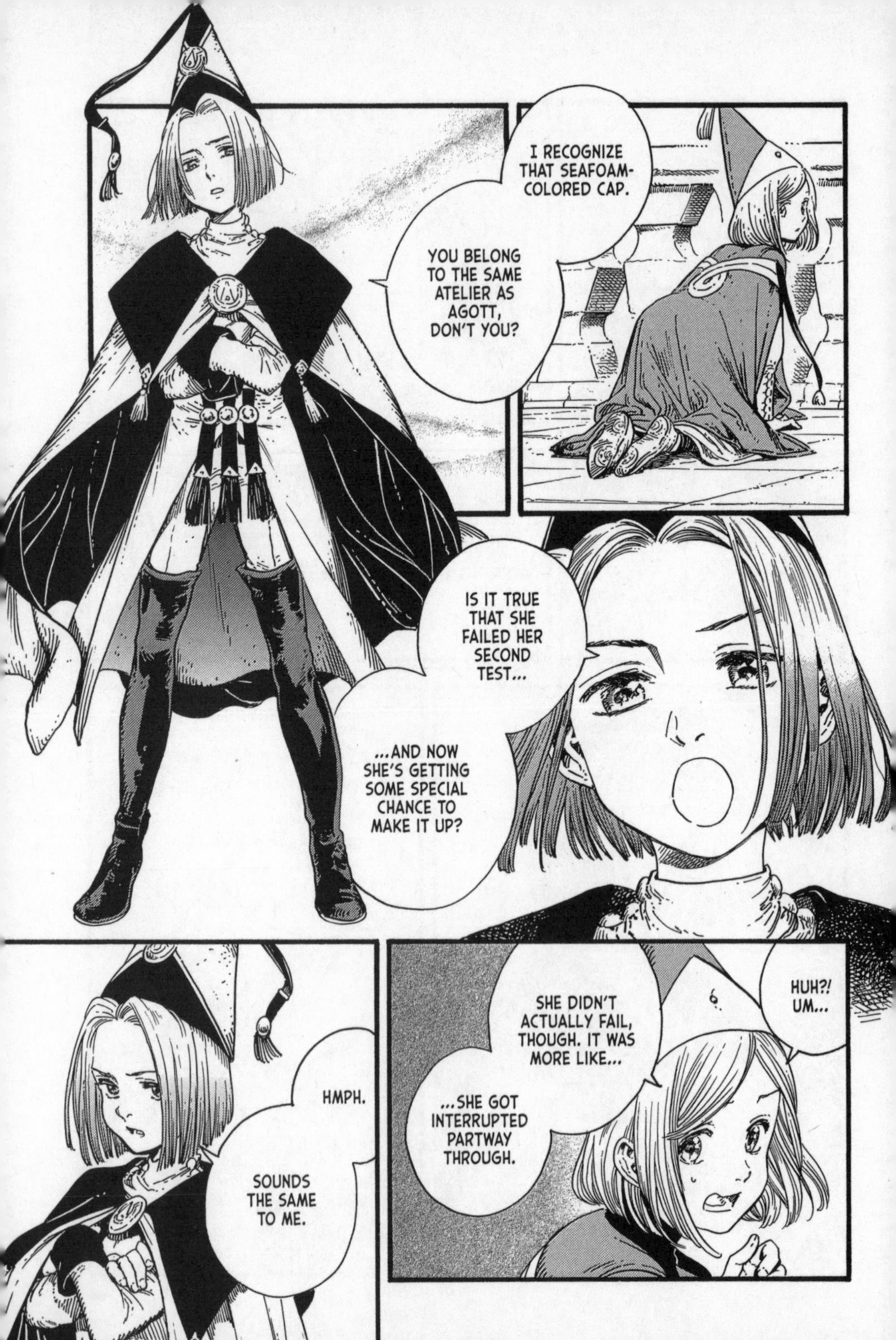
I RECOGNIZE THAT SEAFOAM-COLORED CAP.
YOU BELONG TO THE SAME ATELIER AS AGOTT, DON'T YOU?
IS IT TRUE THAT SHE FAILED HER SECOND TEST...
...AND NOW SHE'S GETTING SOME SPECIAL CHANCE TO MAKE IT UP?
HUH?! UM...
SHE DIDN'T ACTUALLY FAIL, THOUGH. IT WAS MORE LIKE...
...SHE GOT INTERRUPTED PARTWAY THROUGH.
HMPH.
SOUNDS THE SAME TO ME.

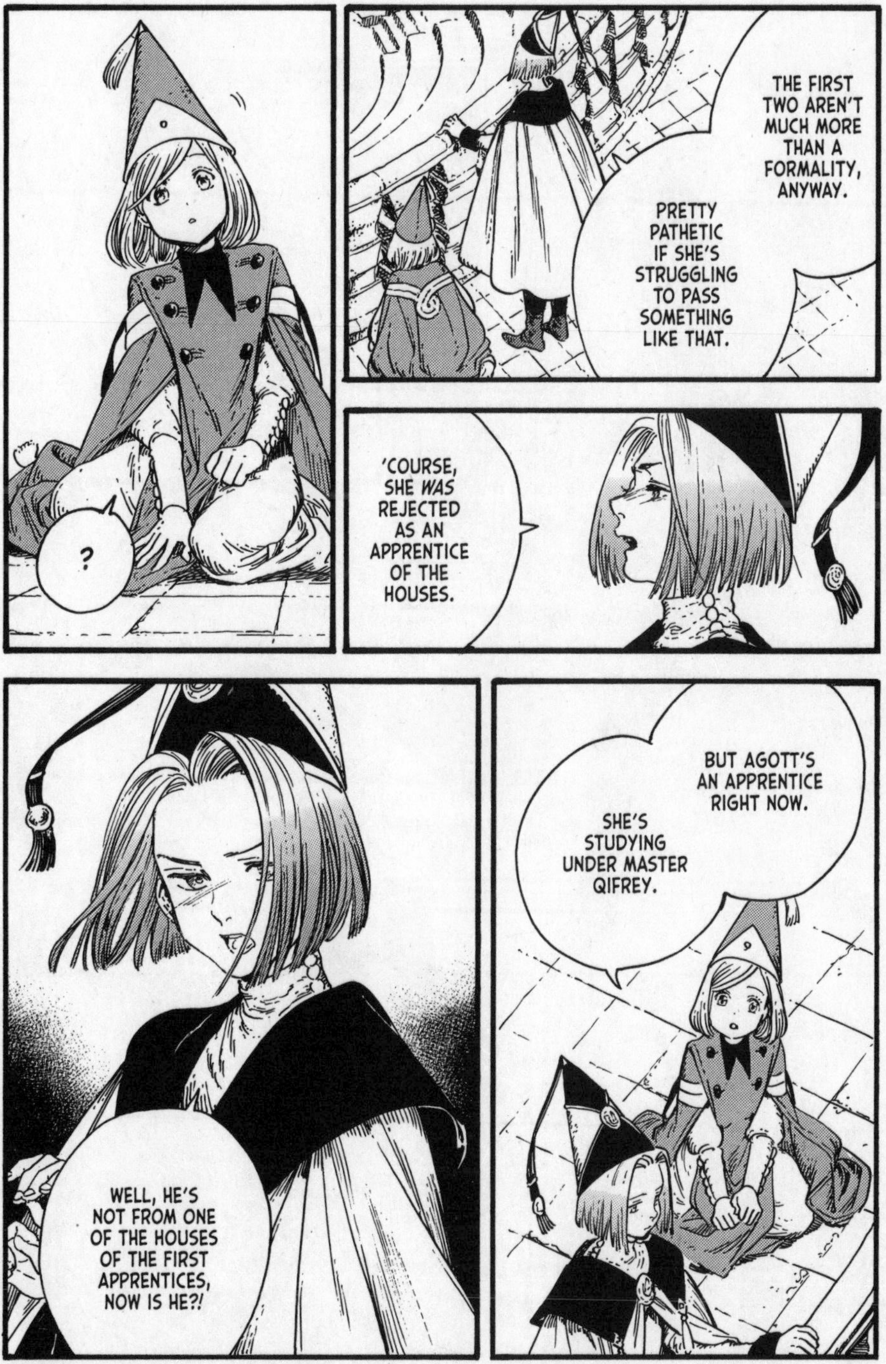
THE FIRST TWO AREN'T MUCH MORE THAN A FORMALITY, ANYWAY.
PRETTY PATHETIC IF SHE'S STRUGGLING TO PASS SOMETHING LIKE THAT.
'COURSE, SHE *WAS* REJECTED AS AN APPRENTICE OF THE HOUSES.
?
BUT AGOTT'S AN APPRENTICE RIGHT NOW.
SHE'S STUDYING UNDER MASTER QIFREY.
WELL, HE'S NOT FROM ONE OF THE HOUSES OF THE FIRST APPRENTICES, NOW IS HE?!

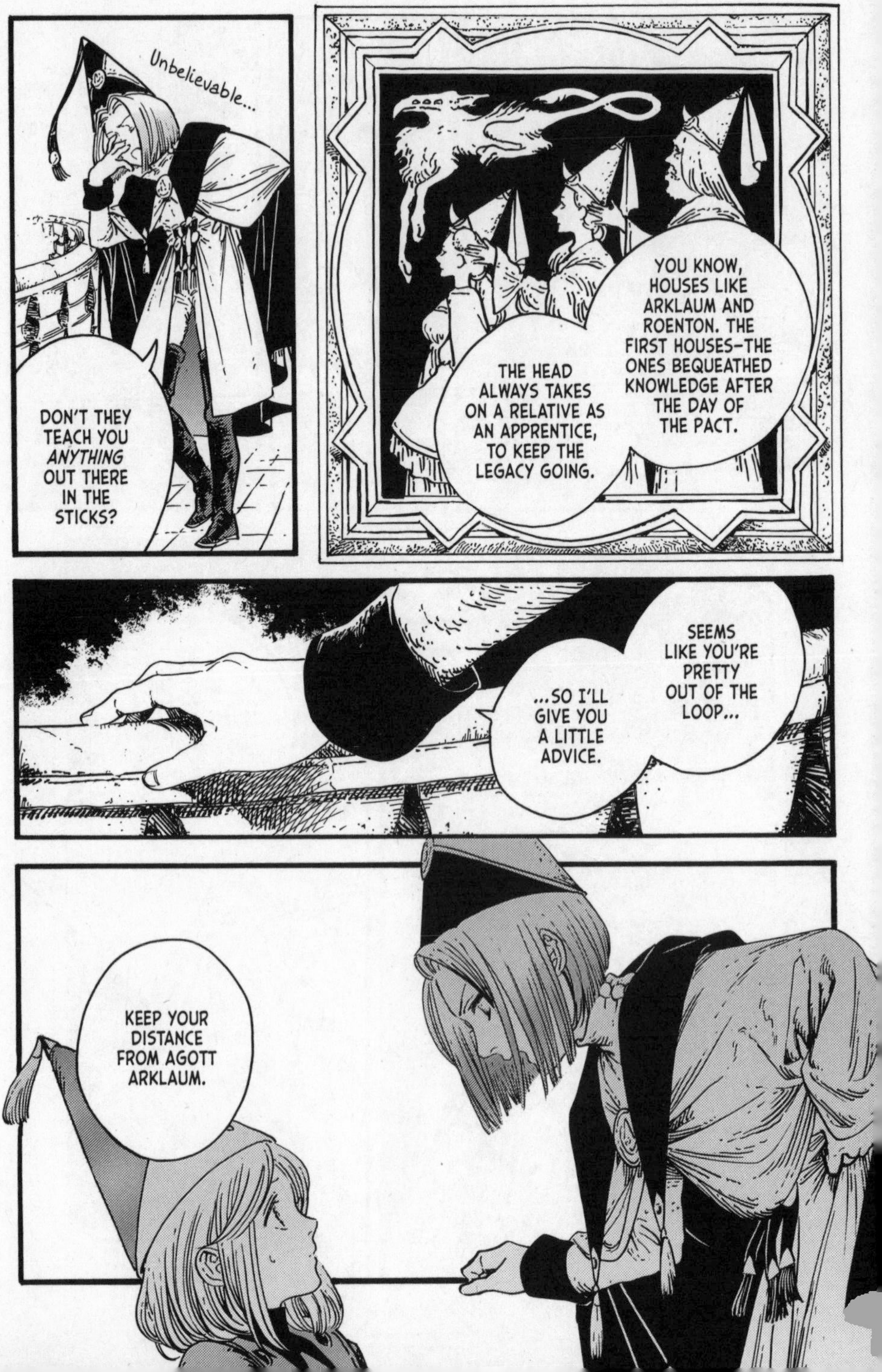
YOU KNOW, HOUSES LIKE ARKLAUM AND ROENTON. THE FIRST HOUSES—THE ONES BEQUEATHED KNOWLEDGE AFTER THE DAY OF THE PACT.
THE HEAD ALWAYS TAKES ON A RELATIVE AS AN APPRENTICE, TO KEEP THE LEGACY GOING.
Unbelievable...
DON'T THEY TEACH YOU *ANYTHING* OUT THERE IN THE STICKS?
SEEMS LIKE YOU'RE PRETTY OUT OF THE LOOP...
...SO I'LL GIVE YOU A LITTLE ADVICE.
KEEP YOUR DISTANCE FROM AGOTT ARKLAUM.

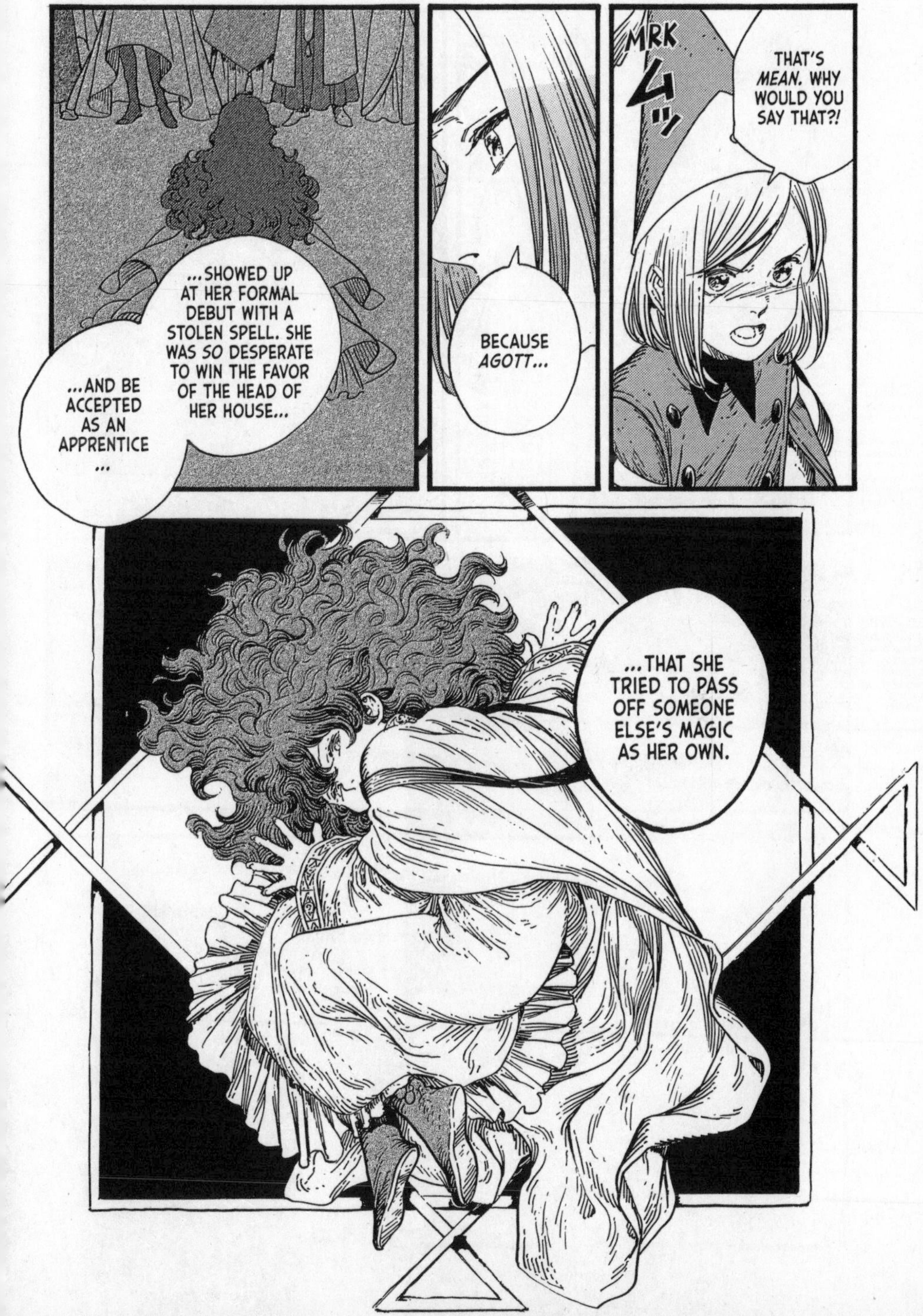
MRK
ムッ
THAT'S MEAN. WHY WOULD YOU SAY THAT?!
BECAUSE AGOTT...
...SHOWED UP AT HER FORMAL DEBUT WITH A STOLEN SPELL. SHE WAS SO DESPERATE TO WIN THE FAVOR OF THE HEAD OF HER HOUSE...
...AND BE ACCEPTED AS AN APPRENTICE...
...THAT SHE TRIED TO PASS OFF SOMEONE ELSE'S MAGIC AS HER OWN.

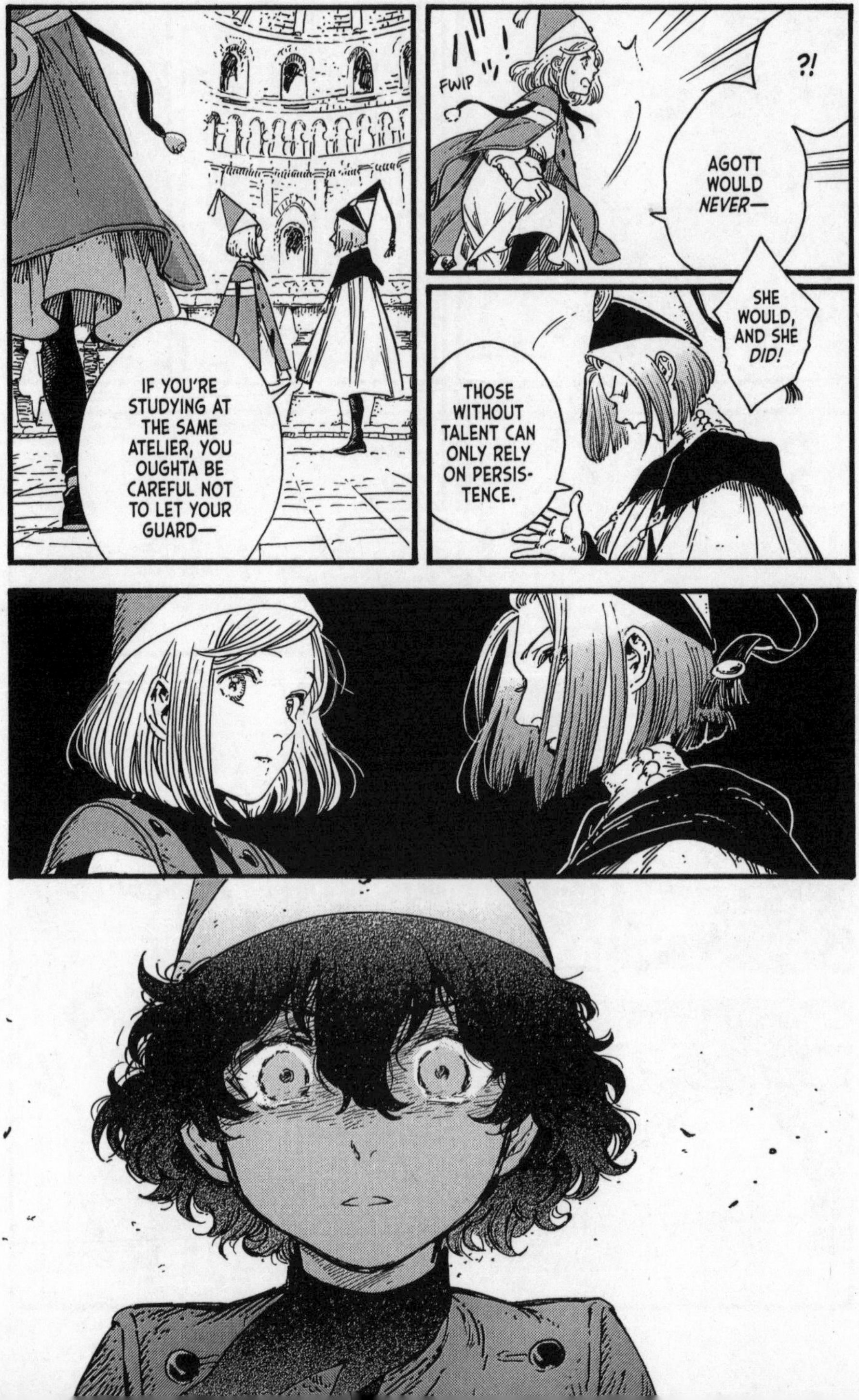
?!
AGOTT WOULD NEVER—
FWIP
SHE WOULD, AND SHE DID!
THOSE WITHOUT TALENT CAN ONLY RELY ON PERSIS-TENCE.
IF YOU'RE STUDYING AT THE SAME ATELIER, YOU OUGHTA BE CAREFUL NOT TO LET YOUR GUARD—

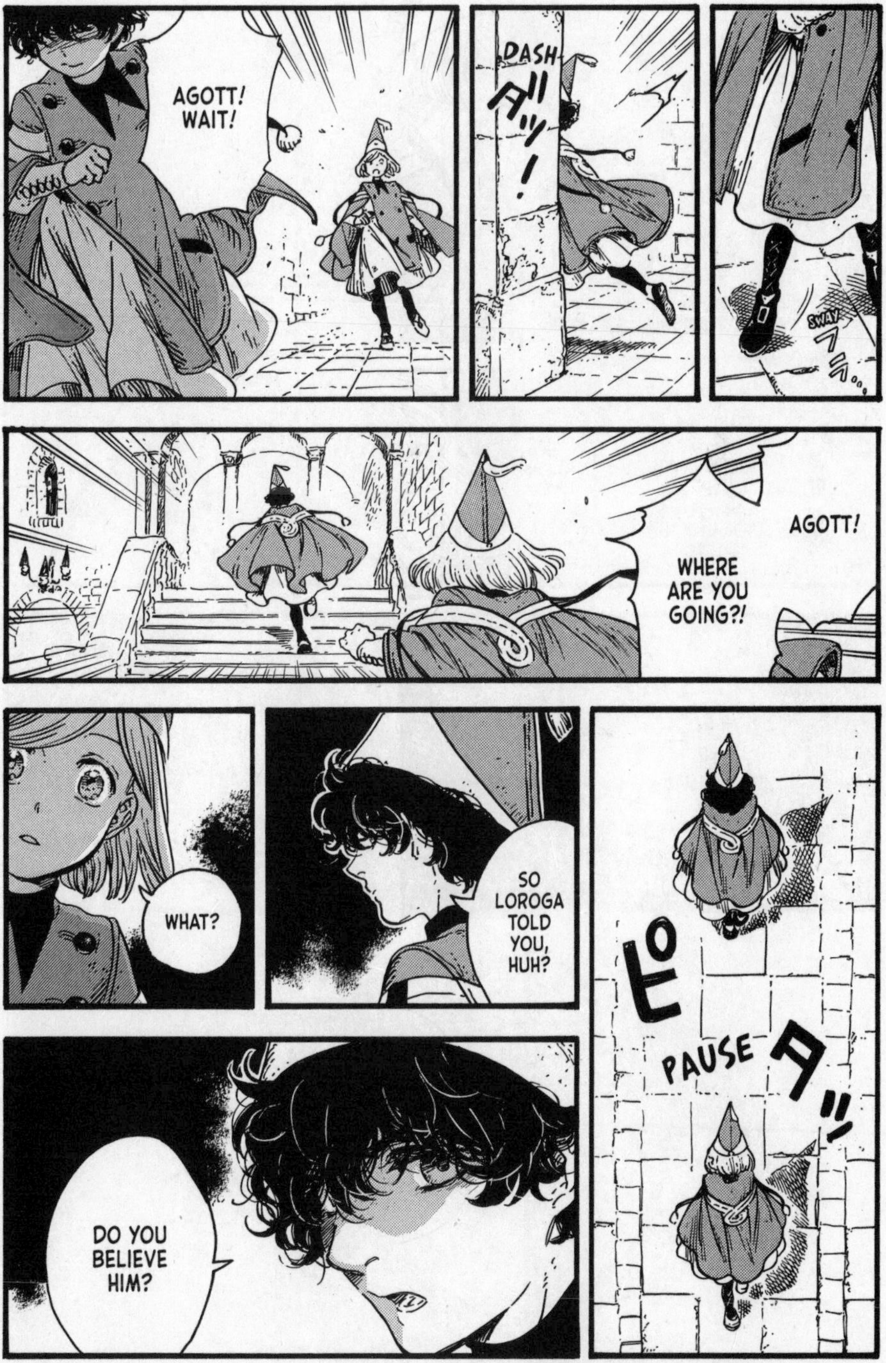
SWAY
フラ...
DASH
ダッ!
AGOTT! WAIT!
AGOTT!
WHERE ARE YOU GOING?!
ピタッ
PAUSE
SO LOROGA TOLD YOU, HUH?
WHAT?
DO YOU BELIEVE HIM?

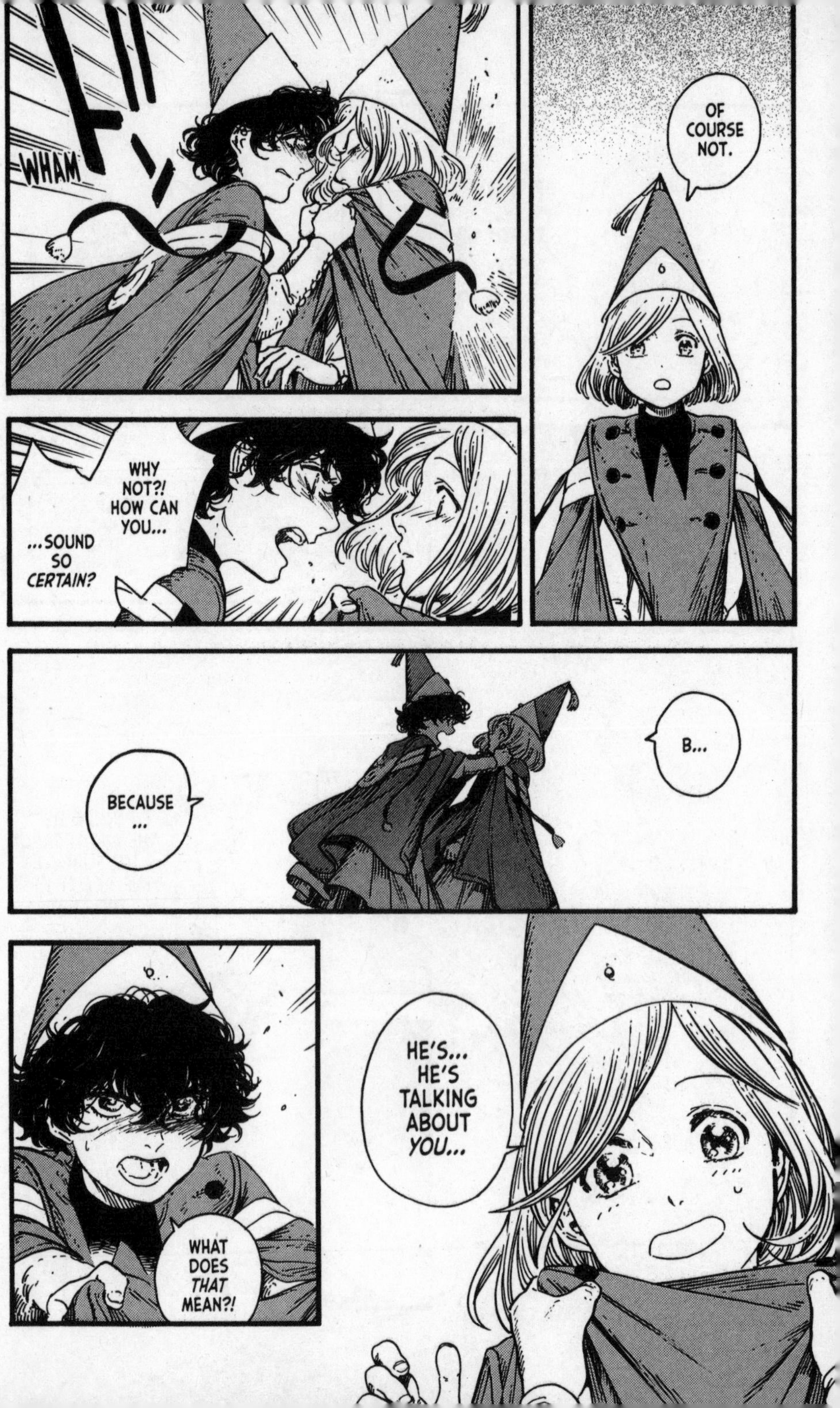
OF COURSE NOT.
WHAM
WHY NOT?! HOW CAN YOU...
...SOUND SO CERTAIN?
B...
BECAUSE ...
HE'S... HE'S TALKING ABOUT YOU...
WHAT DOES THAT MEAN?!

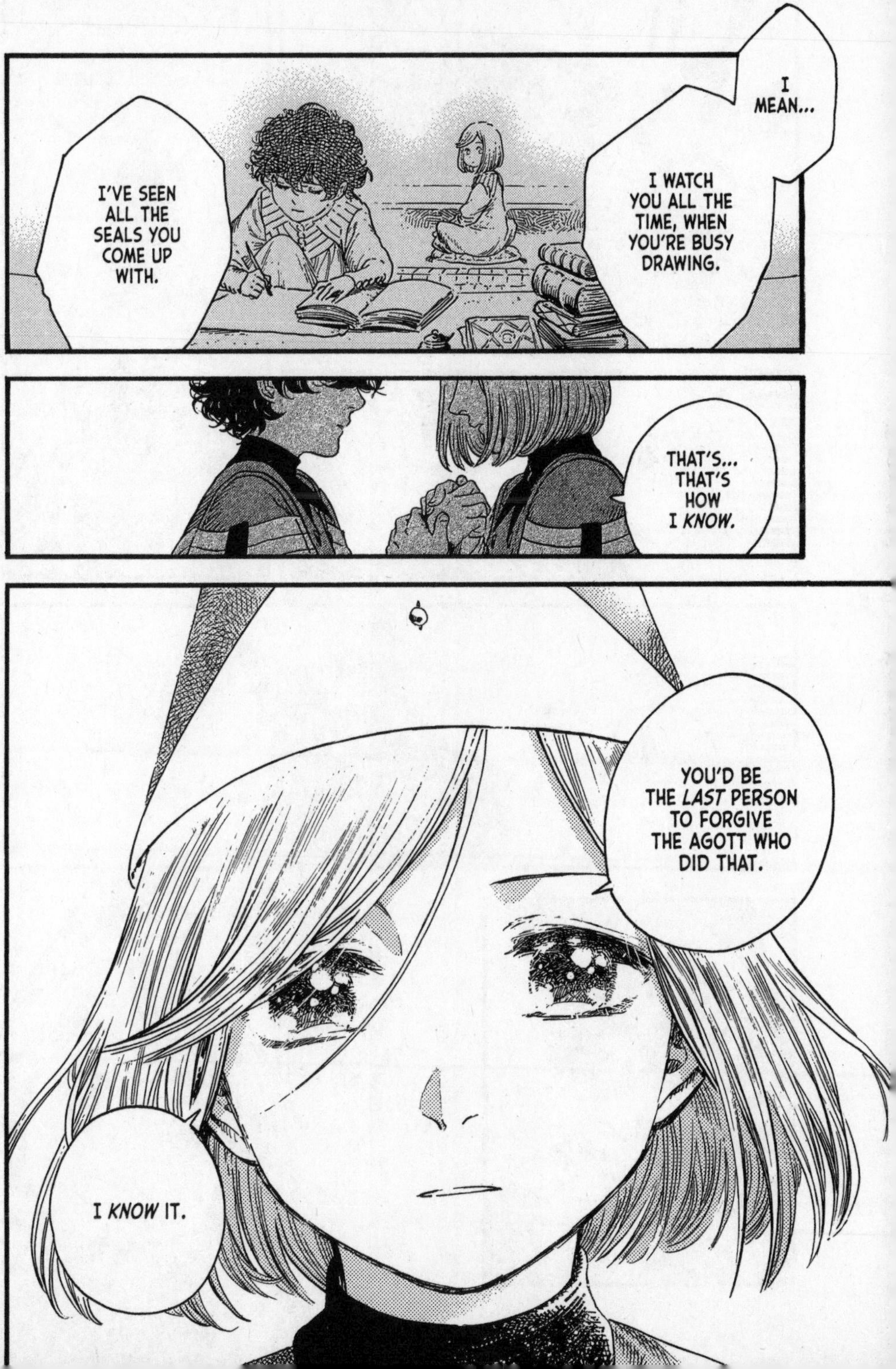
I MEAN...
I WATCH YOU ALL THE TIME, WHEN YOU'RE BUSY DRAWING.
I'VE SEEN ALL THE SEALS YOU COME UP WITH.
THAT'S... THAT'S HOW I *KNOW.*
YOU'D BE THE *LAST* PERSON TO FORGIVE THE AGOTT WHO DID THAT.
I *KNOW* IT.

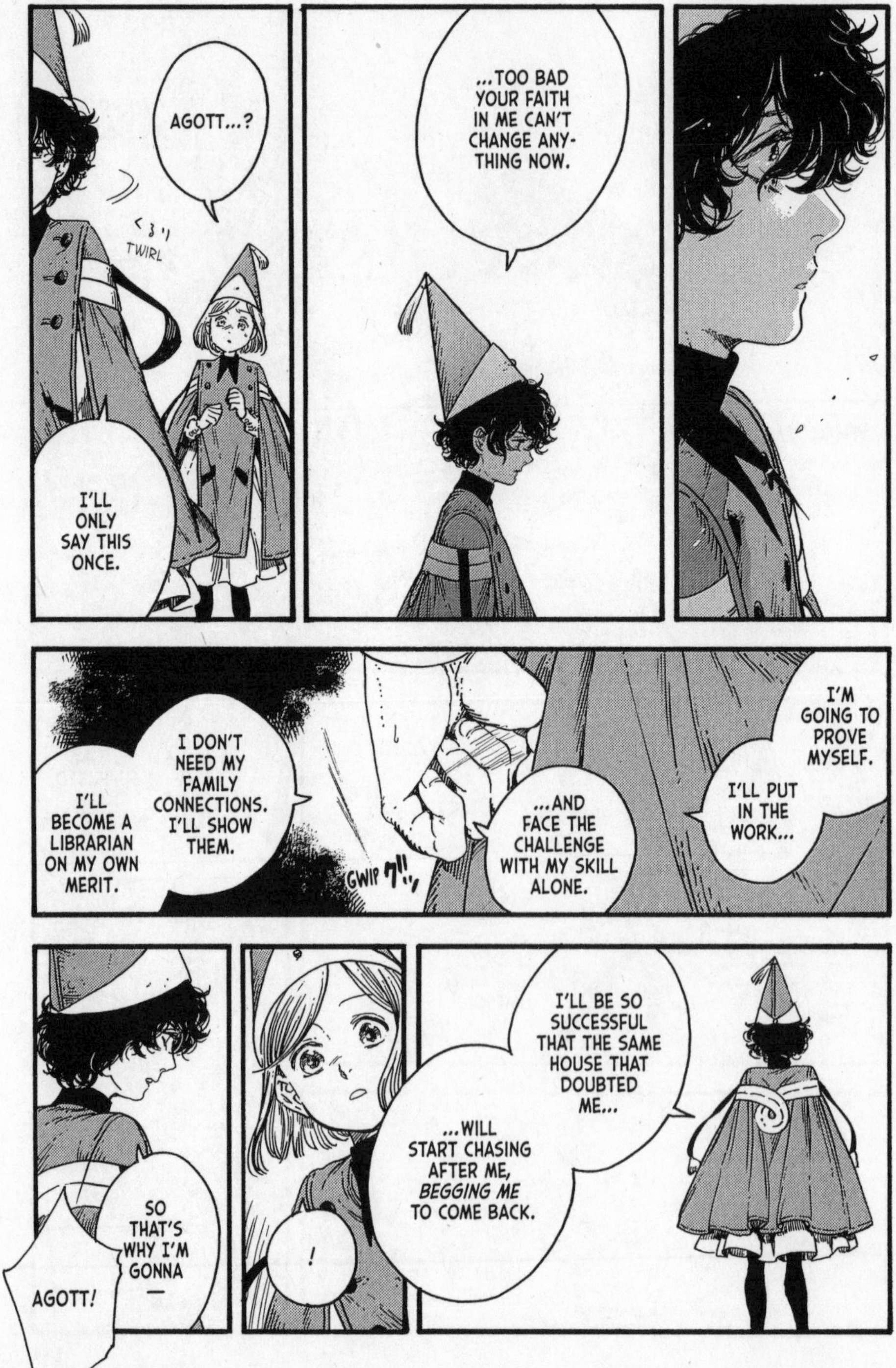
...TOO BAD YOUR FAITH IN ME CAN'T CHANGE ANY-THING NOW.
AGOTT...?
くるり TWIRL
I'LL ONLY SAY THIS ONCE.
I'M GOING TO PROVE MYSELF.
I'LL PUT IN THE WORK...
...AND FACE THE CHALLENGE WITH MY SKILL ALONE.
GWIP ギュッ
I DON'T NEED MY FAMILY CONNECTIONS. I'LL SHOW THEM.
I'LL BECOME A LIBRARIAN ON MY OWN MERIT.
I'LL BE SO SUCCESSFUL THAT THE SAME HOUSE THAT DOUBTED ME...
...WILL START CHASING AFTER ME, *BEGGING ME* TO COME BACK.
!
SO THAT'S WHY I'M GONNA —
AGOTT!

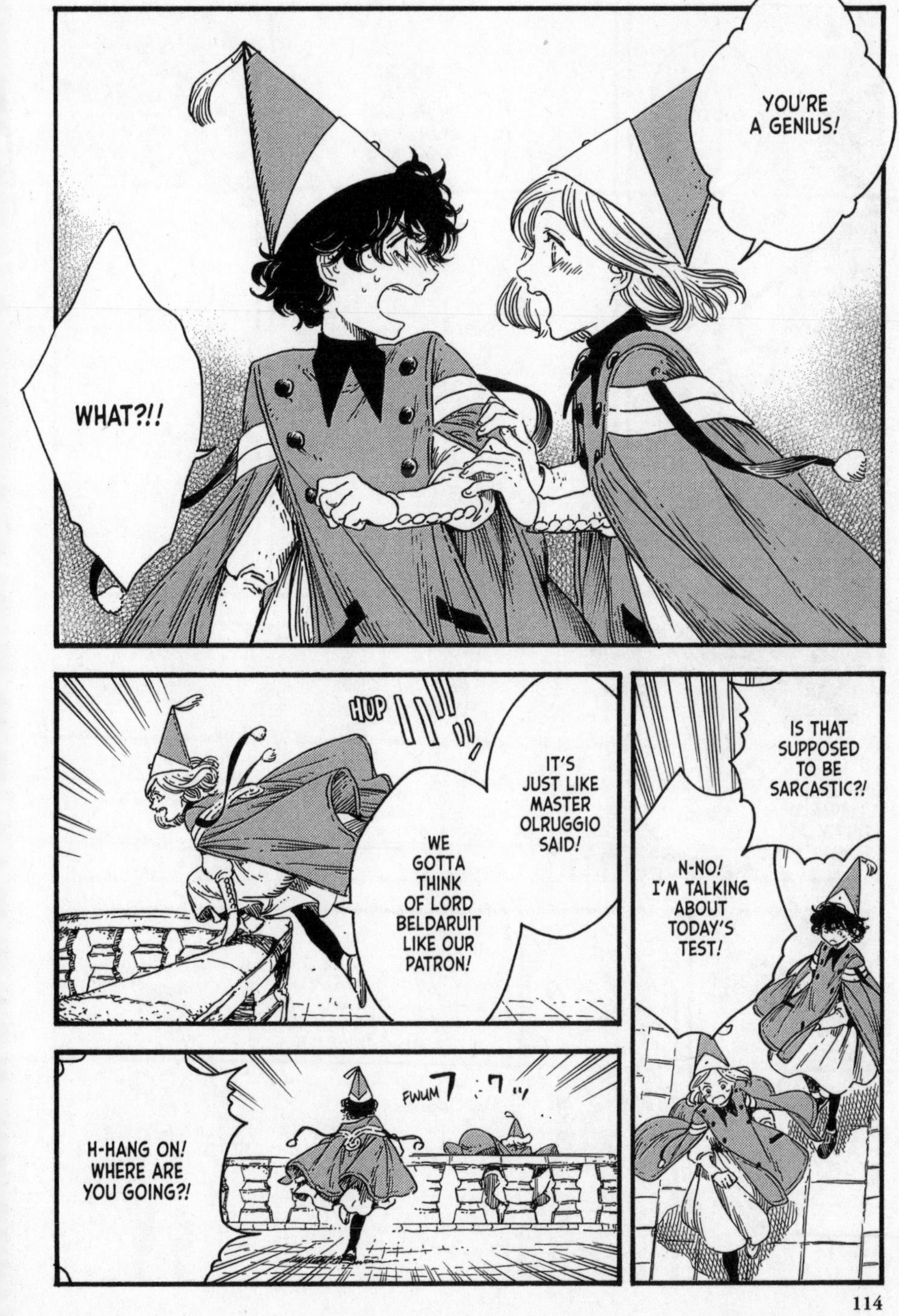
YOU'RE A GENIUS!
WHAT?!!
IS THAT SUPPOSED TO BE SARCASTIC?!
N-NO! I'M TALKING ABOUT TODAY'S TEST!
HUP
IT'S JUST LIKE MASTER OLRUGGIO SAID!
WE GOTTA THINK OF LORD BELDARUIT LIKE OUR PATRON!
FWUM
H-HANG ON! WHERE ARE YOU GOING?!

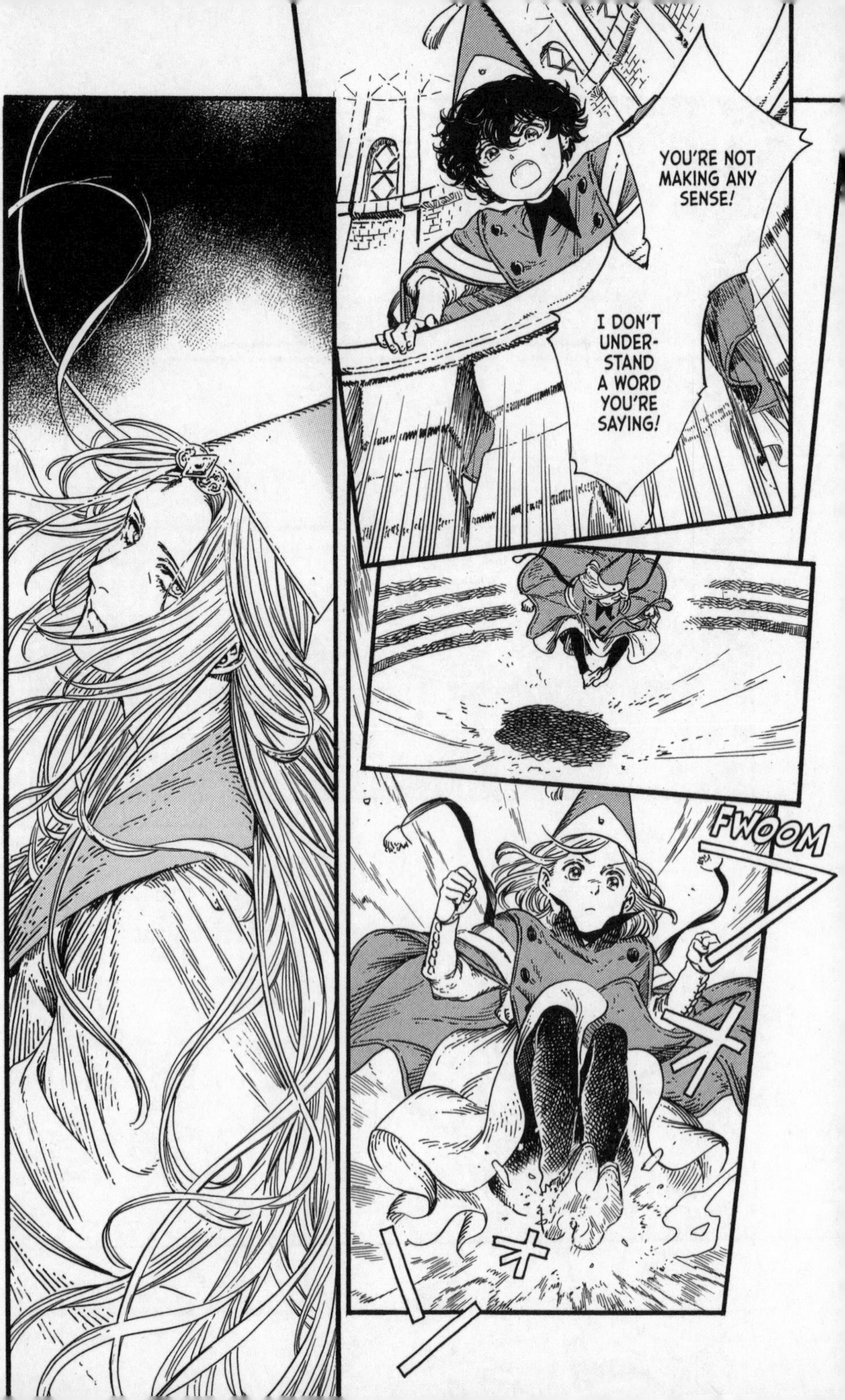
YOU'RE NOT MAKING ANY SENSE!
I DON'T UNDER-STAND A WORD YOU'RE SAYING!
FWOOM

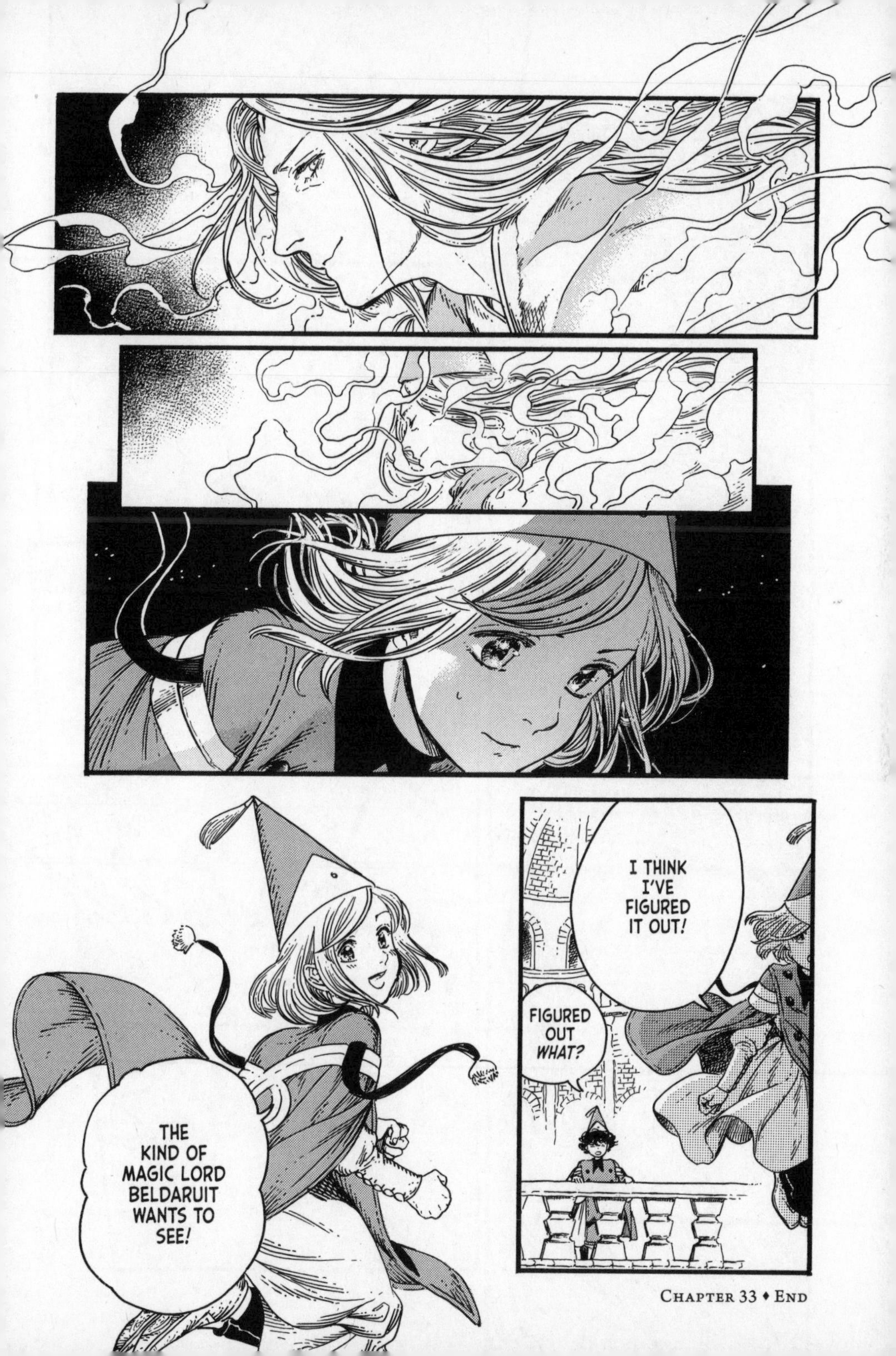
I THINK I'VE FIGURED IT OUT!
FIGURED OUT *WHAT?*
THE KIND OF MAGIC LORD BELDARUIT WANTS TO SEE!

Chapter 33 ♦ End

Witch Hat Atelier

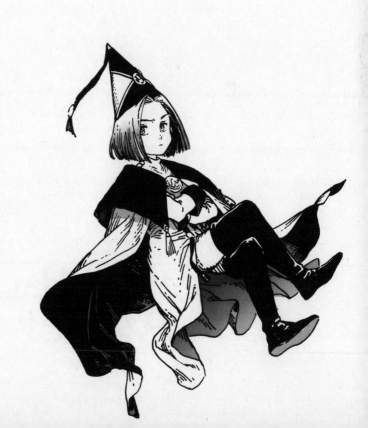

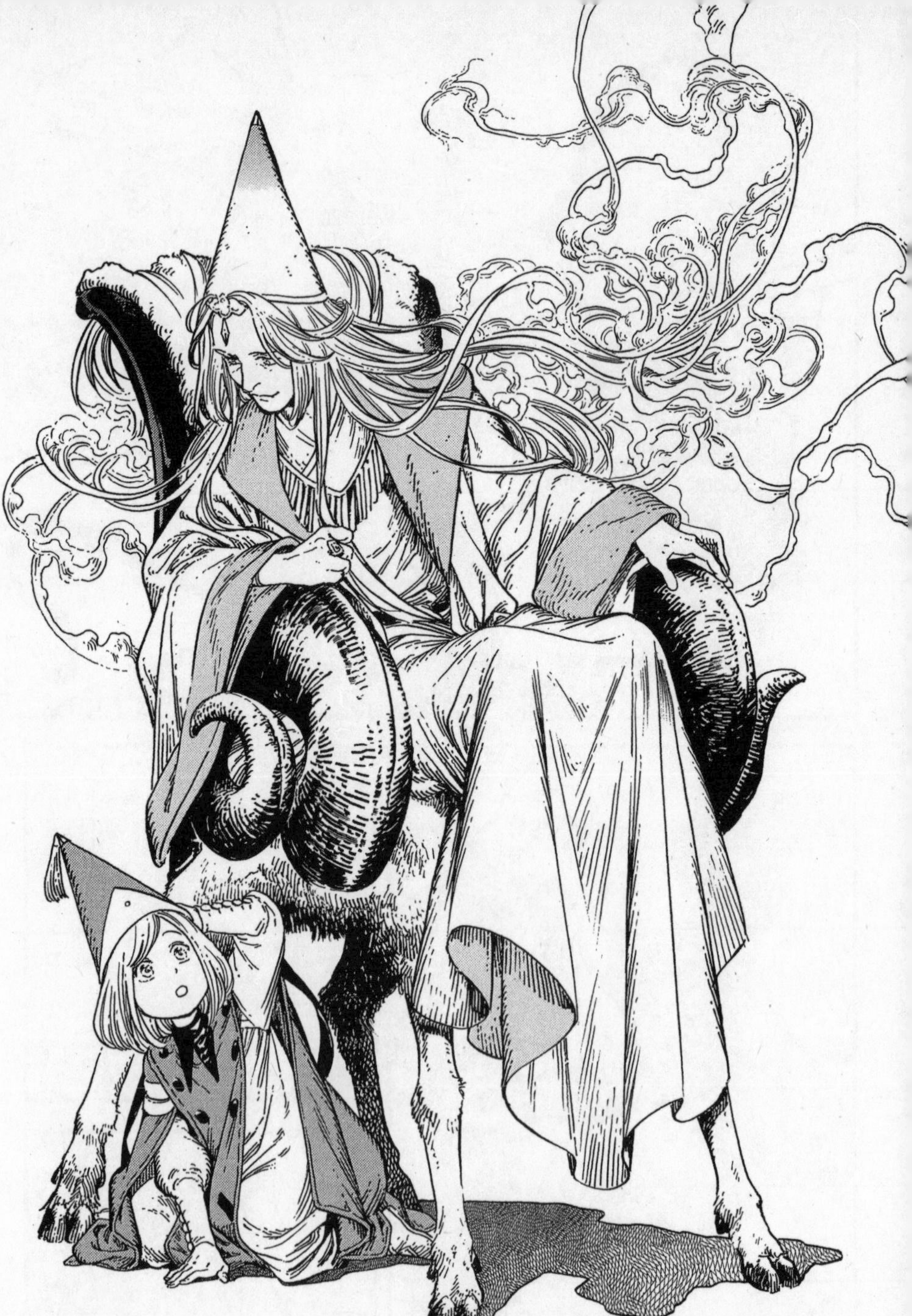

Chapter 34

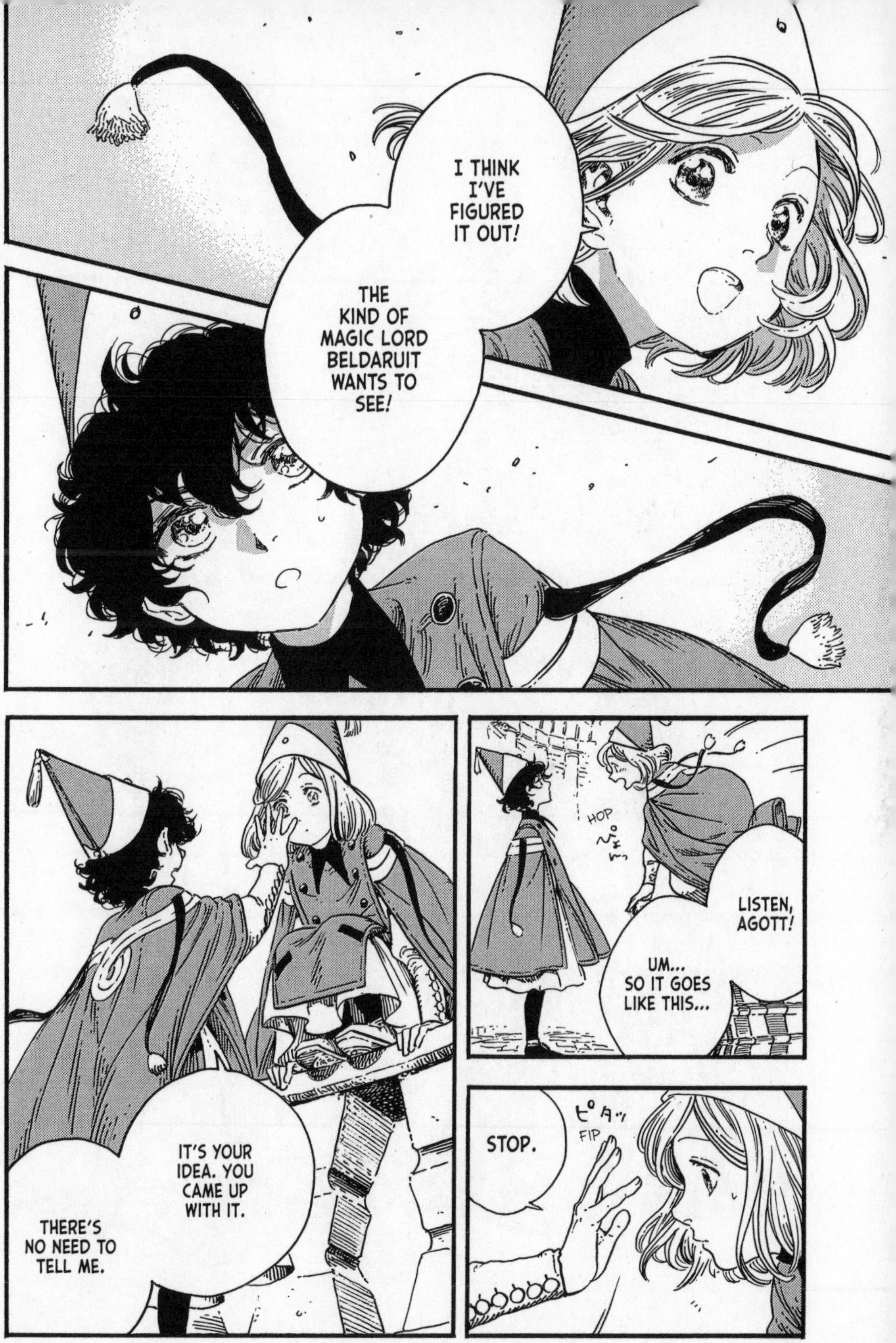
I THINK I'VE FIGURED IT OUT!
THE KIND OF MAGIC LORD BELDARUIT WANTS TO SEE!
HOP
LISTEN, AGOTT!
UM... SO IT GOES LIKE THIS...
ピタッ
FIP
STOP.
IT'S YOUR IDEA. YOU CAME UP WITH IT.
THERE'S NO NEED TO TELL ME.

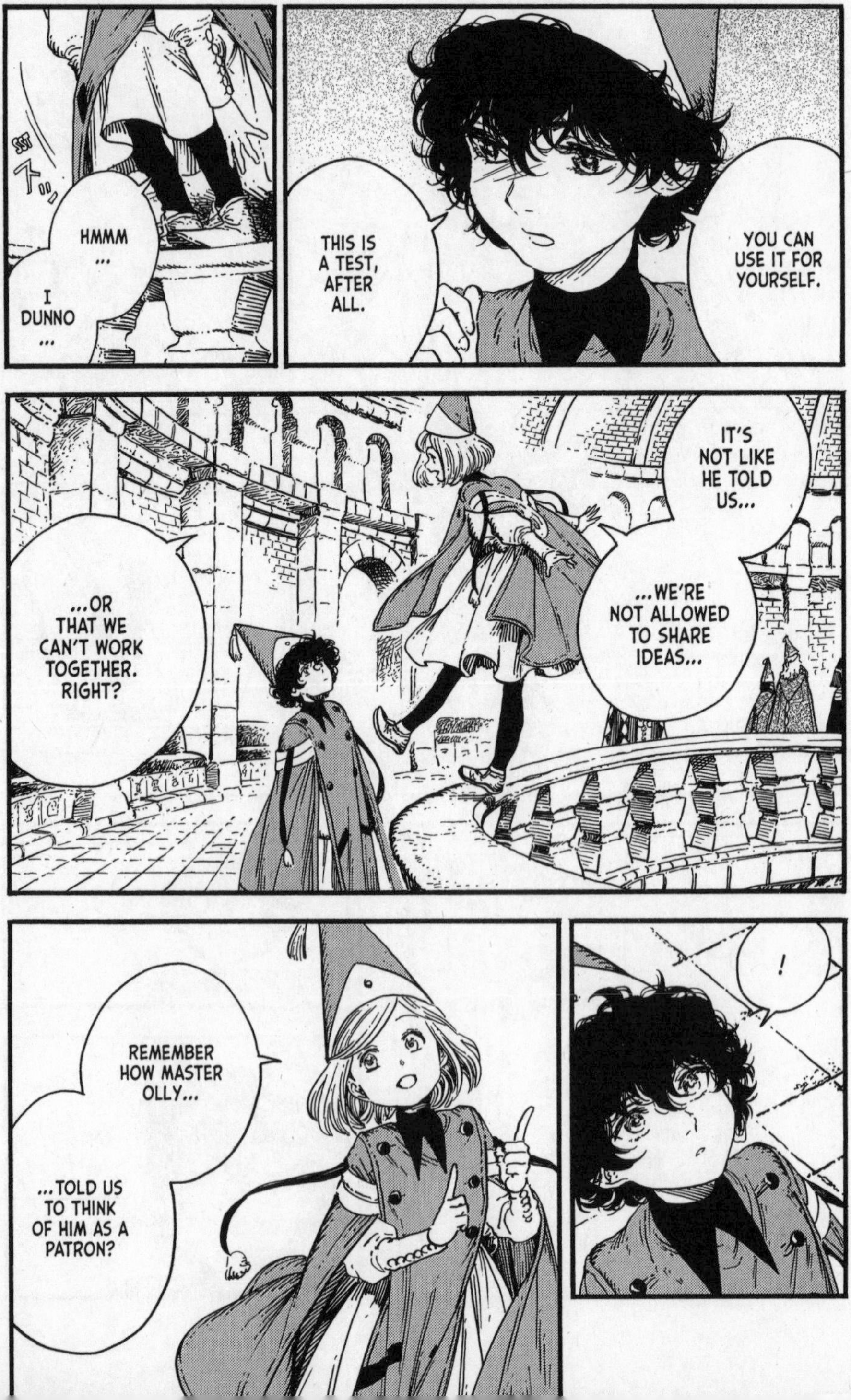
YOU CAN USE IT FOR YOURSELF.
THIS IS A TEST, AFTER ALL.
SST
HMMM ...
I DUNNO ...
IT'S NOT LIKE HE TOLD US...
...WE'RE NOT ALLOWED TO SHARE IDEAS...
...OR THAT WE CAN'T WORK TOGETHER. RIGHT?
!
REMEMBER HOW MASTER OLLY...
...TOLD US TO THINK OF HIM AS A PATRON?

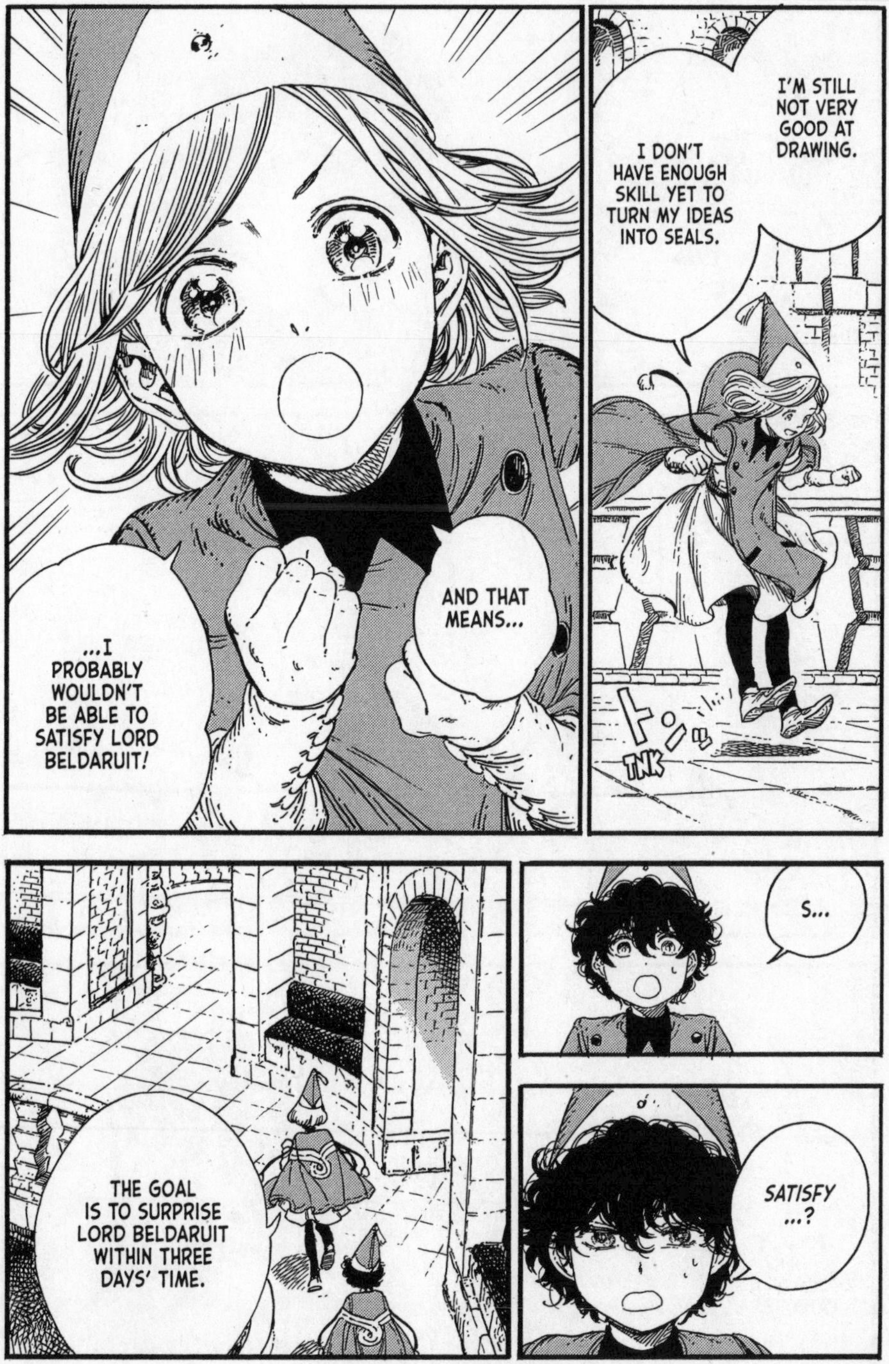
I'M STILL NOT VERY GOOD AT DRAWING.
I DON'T HAVE ENOUGH SKILL YET TO TURN MY IDEAS INTO SEALS.
TNK
AND THAT MEANS...
...I PROBABLY WOULDN'T BE ABLE TO SATISFY LORD BELDARUIT!
S...
SATISFY ...?
THE GOAL IS TO SURPRISE LORD BELDARUIT WITHIN THREE DAYS' TIME.

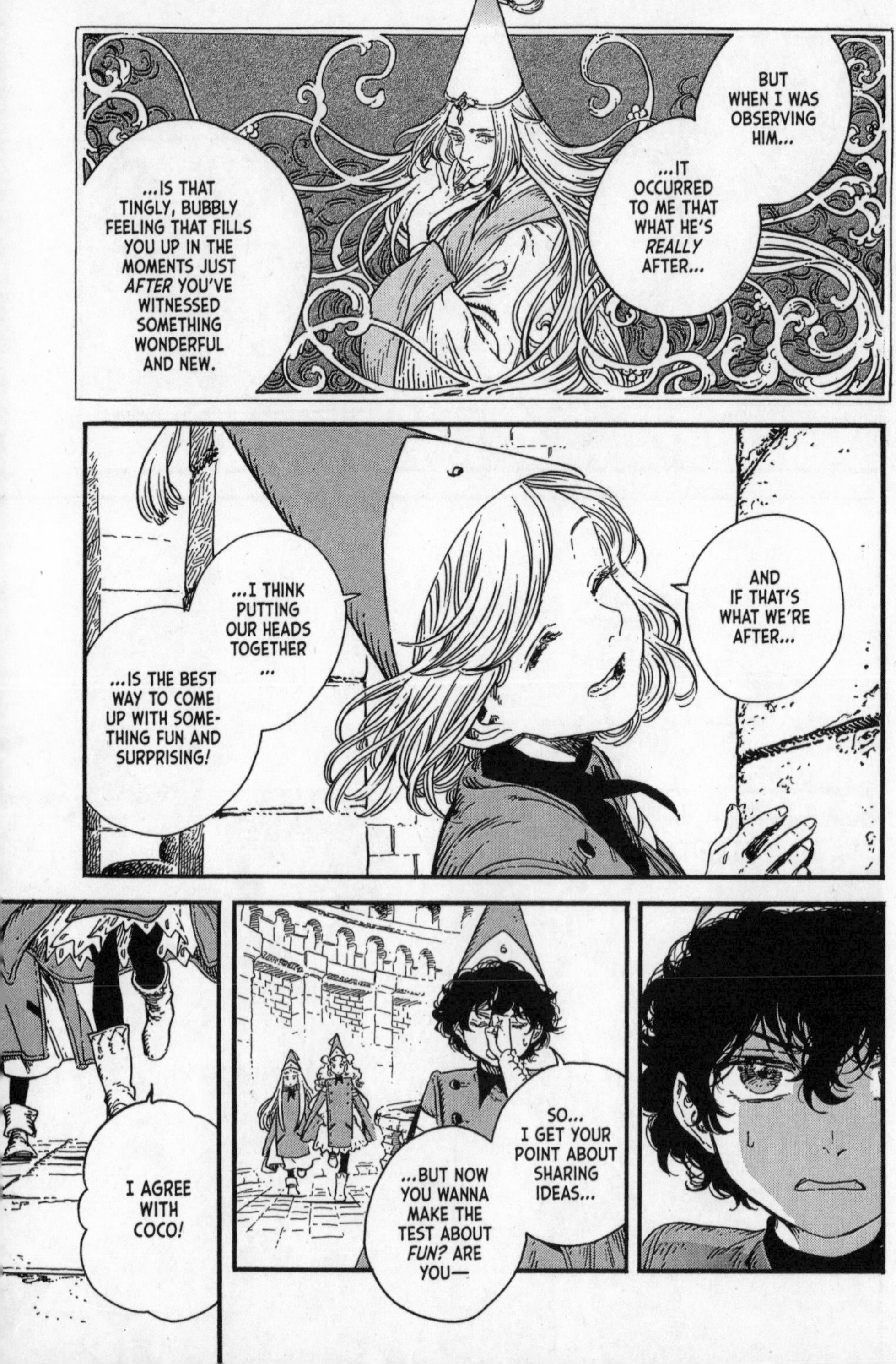
BUT WHEN I WAS OBSERVING HIM...
...IT OCCURRED TO ME THAT WHAT HE'S *REALLY* AFTER...
...IS THAT TINGLY, BUBBLY FEELING THAT FILLS YOU UP IN THE MOMENTS JUST *AFTER* YOU'VE WITNESSED SOMETHING WONDERFUL AND NEW.
AND IF THAT'S WHAT WE'RE AFTER...
...I THINK PUTTING OUR HEADS TOGETHER ...
...IS THE BEST WAY TO COME UP WITH SOME-THING FUN AND SURPRISING!
SO... I GET YOUR POINT ABOUT SHARING IDEAS...
...BUT NOW YOU WANNA MAKE THE TEST ABOUT *FUN?* ARE YOU—
I AGREE WITH COCO!

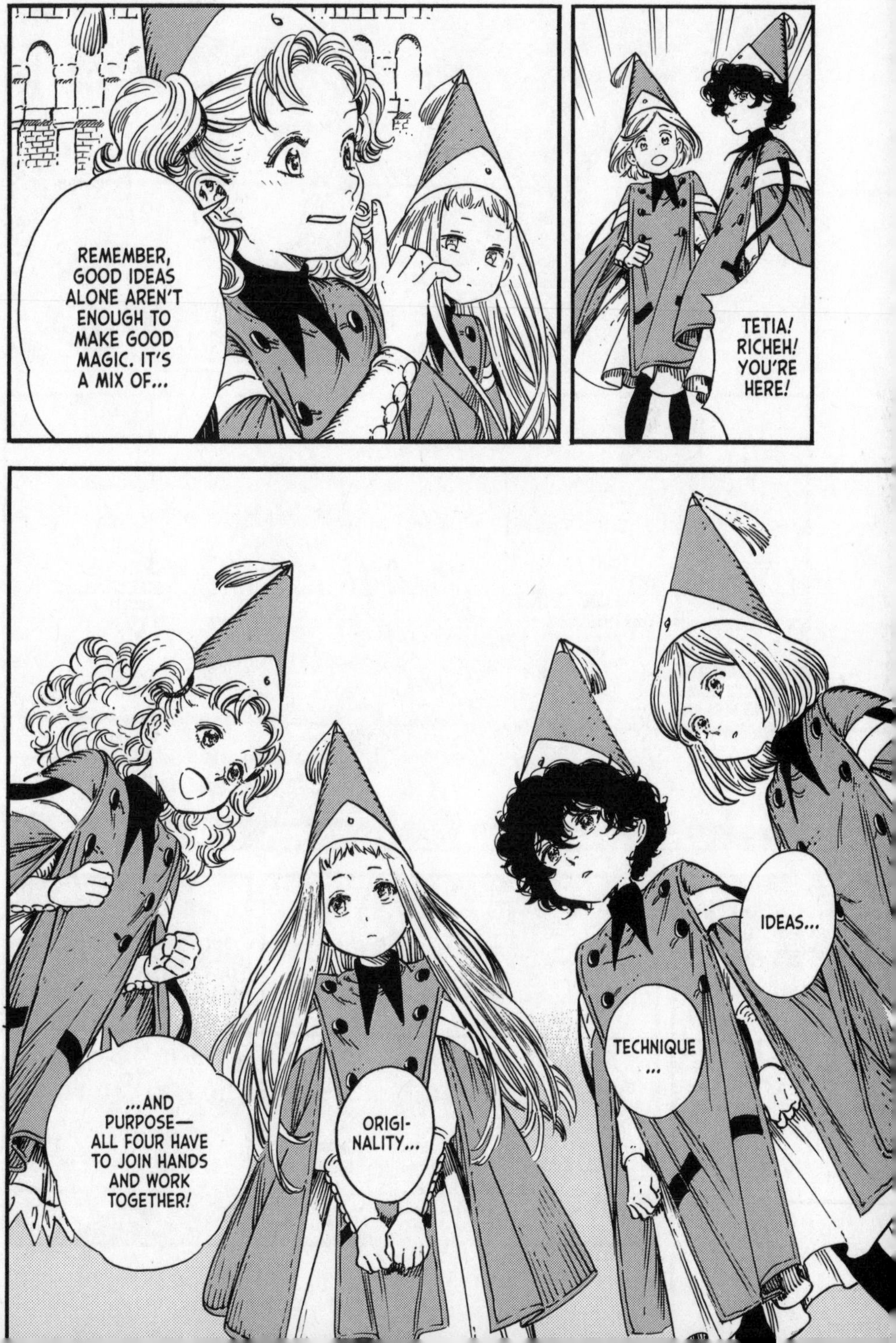

TETIA! RICHEH! YOU'RE HERE!
REMEMBER, GOOD IDEAS ALONE AREN'T ENOUGH TO MAKE GOOD MAGIC. IT'S A MIX OF...
IDEAS...
TECHNIQUE ...
ORIGI-NALITY...
...AND PURPOSE—ALL FOUR HAVE TO JOIN HANDS AND WORK TOGETHER!

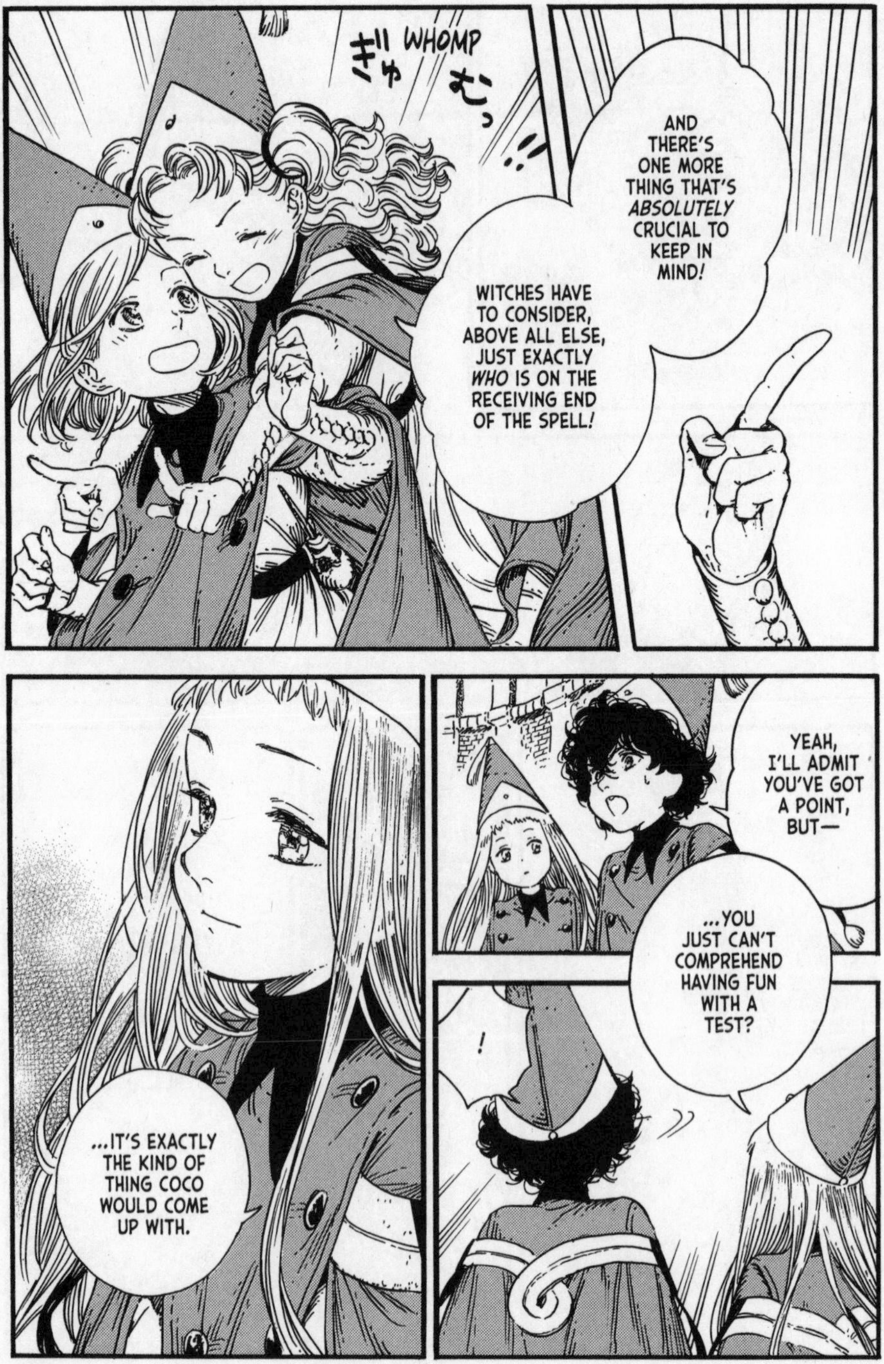
AND THERE'S ONE MORE THING THAT'S *ABSOLUTELY* CRUCIAL TO KEEP IN MIND!
WITCHES HAVE TO CONSIDER, ABOVE ALL ELSE, JUST EXACTLY *WHO* IS ON THE RECEIVING END OF THE SPELL!
ぎゅむっ WHOMP
!!
YEAH, I'LL ADMIT YOU'VE GOT A POINT, BUT—
...YOU JUST CAN'T COMPREHEND HAVING FUN WITH A TEST?
!
...IT'S EXACTLY THE KIND OF THING COCO WOULD COME UP WITH.

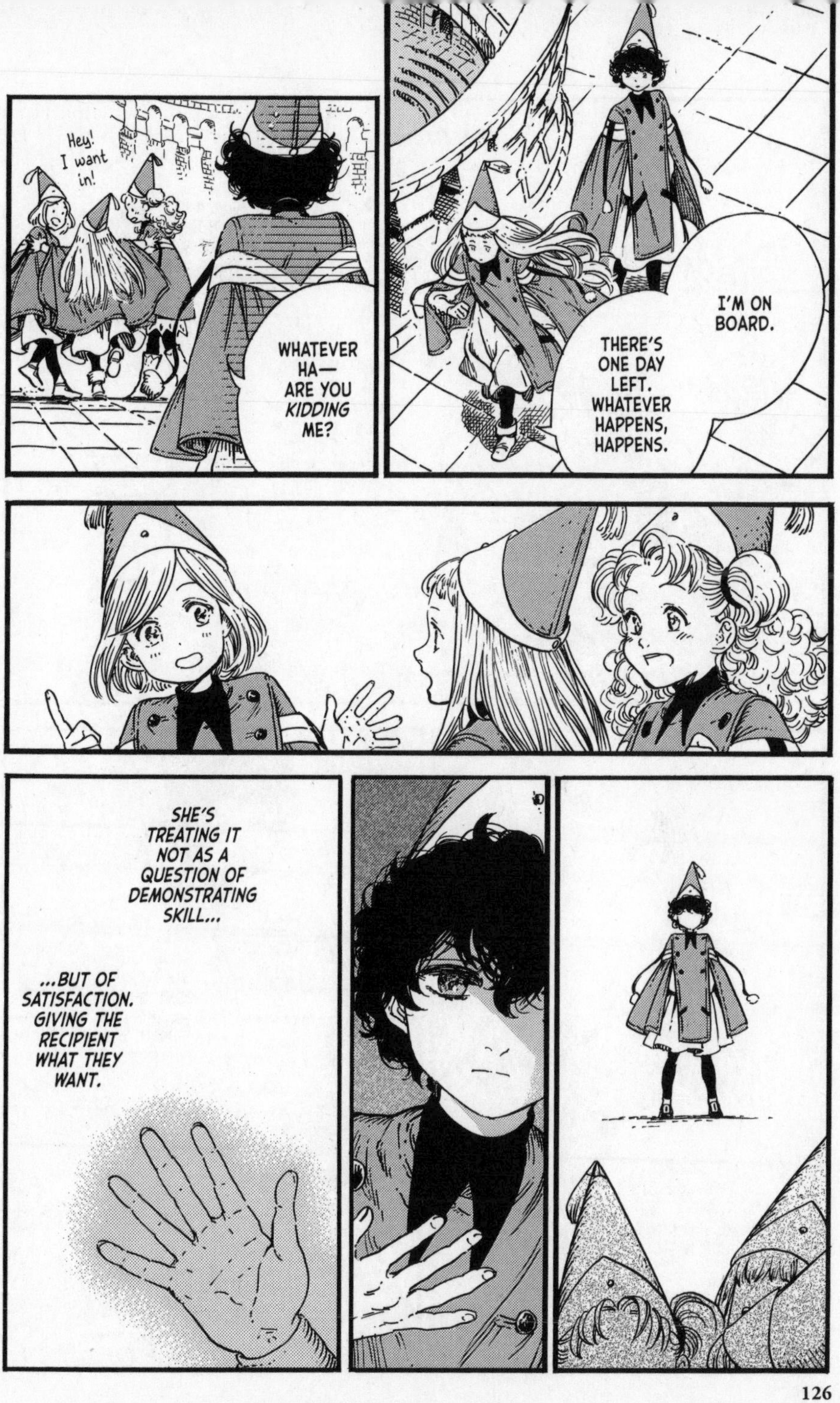
I'M ON BOARD.
THERE'S ONE DAY LEFT. WHATEVER HAPPENS, HAPPENS.
WHATEVER HA— ARE YOU *KIDDING* ME?
Hey! I want in!
SHE'S TREATING IT NOT AS A QUESTION OF DEMONSTRATING SKILL...
...BUT OF SATISFACTION. GIVING THE RECIPIENT WHAT THEY WANT.

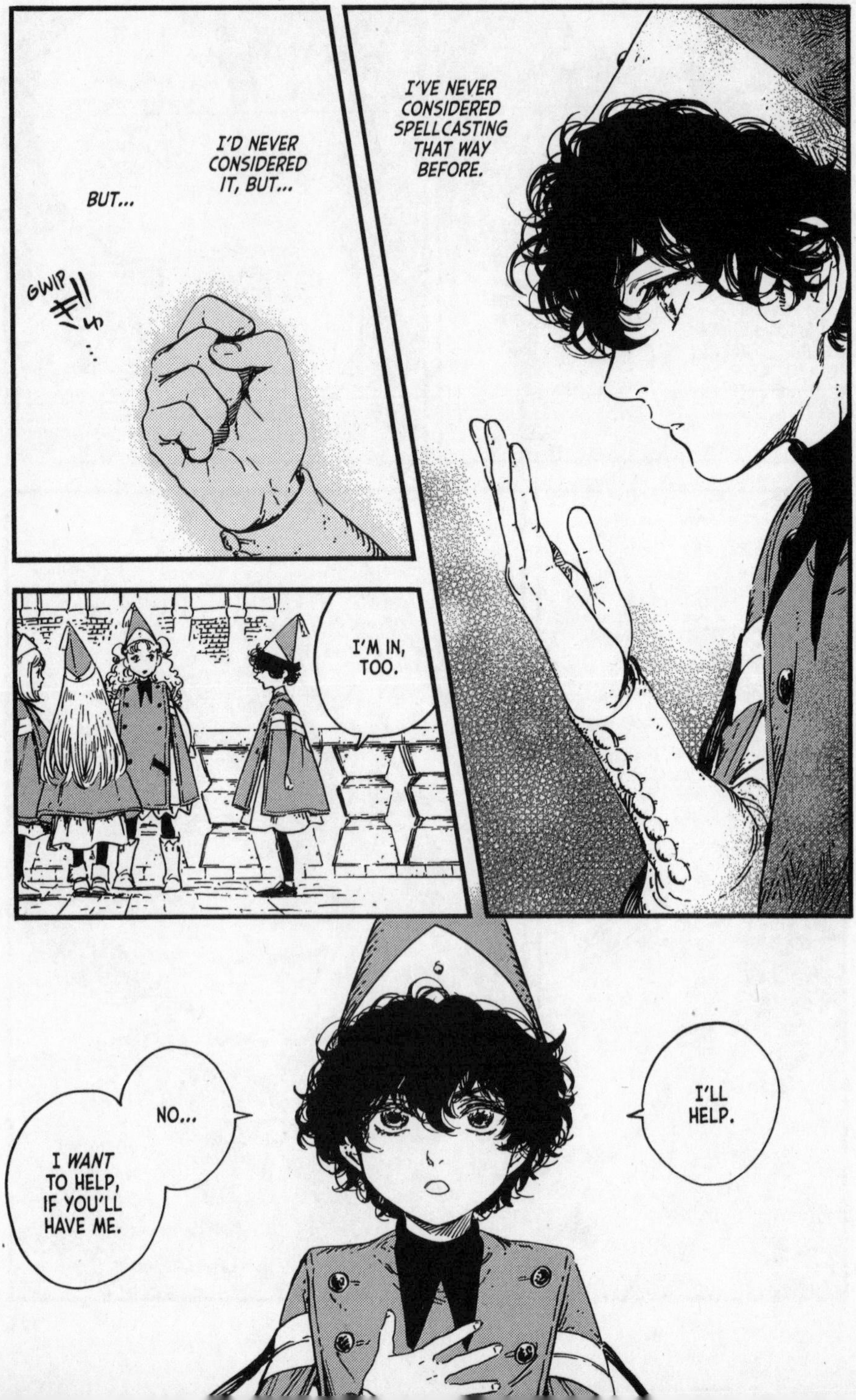
I'VE NEVER CONSIDERED SPELLCASTING THAT WAY BEFORE.
I'D NEVER CONSIDERED IT, BUT...
BUT...
GWIP
I'M IN, TOO.
I'LL HELP.
NO...
I *WANT* TO HELP, IF YOU'LL HAVE ME.

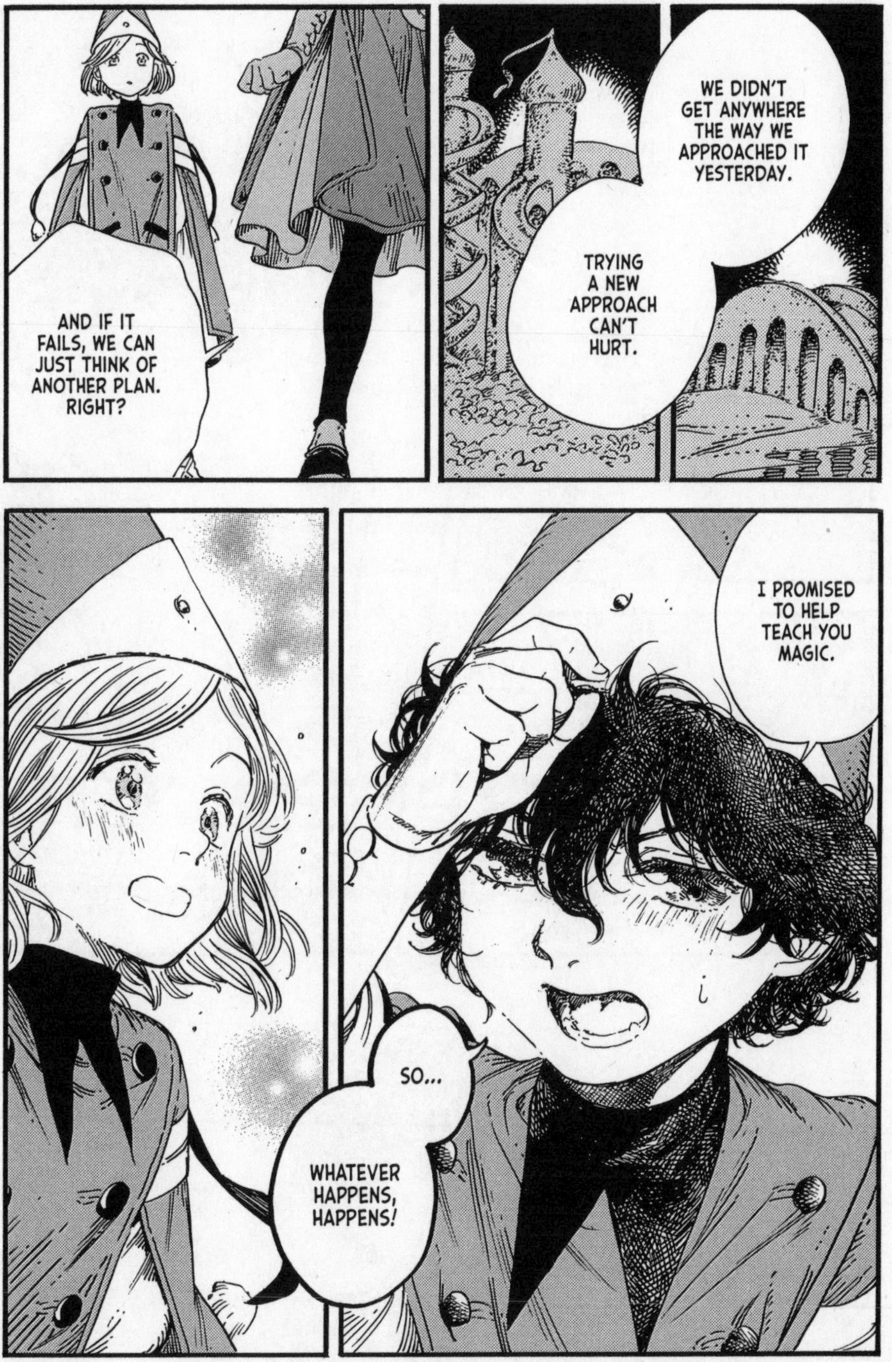
WE DIDN'T GET ANYWHERE THE WAY WE APPROACHED IT YESTERDAY.
TRYING A NEW APPROACH CAN'T HURT.
AND IF IT FAILS, WE CAN JUST THINK OF ANOTHER PLAN. RIGHT?
I PROMISED TO HELP TEACH YOU MAGIC.
SO...
WHATEVER HAPPENS, HAPPENS!

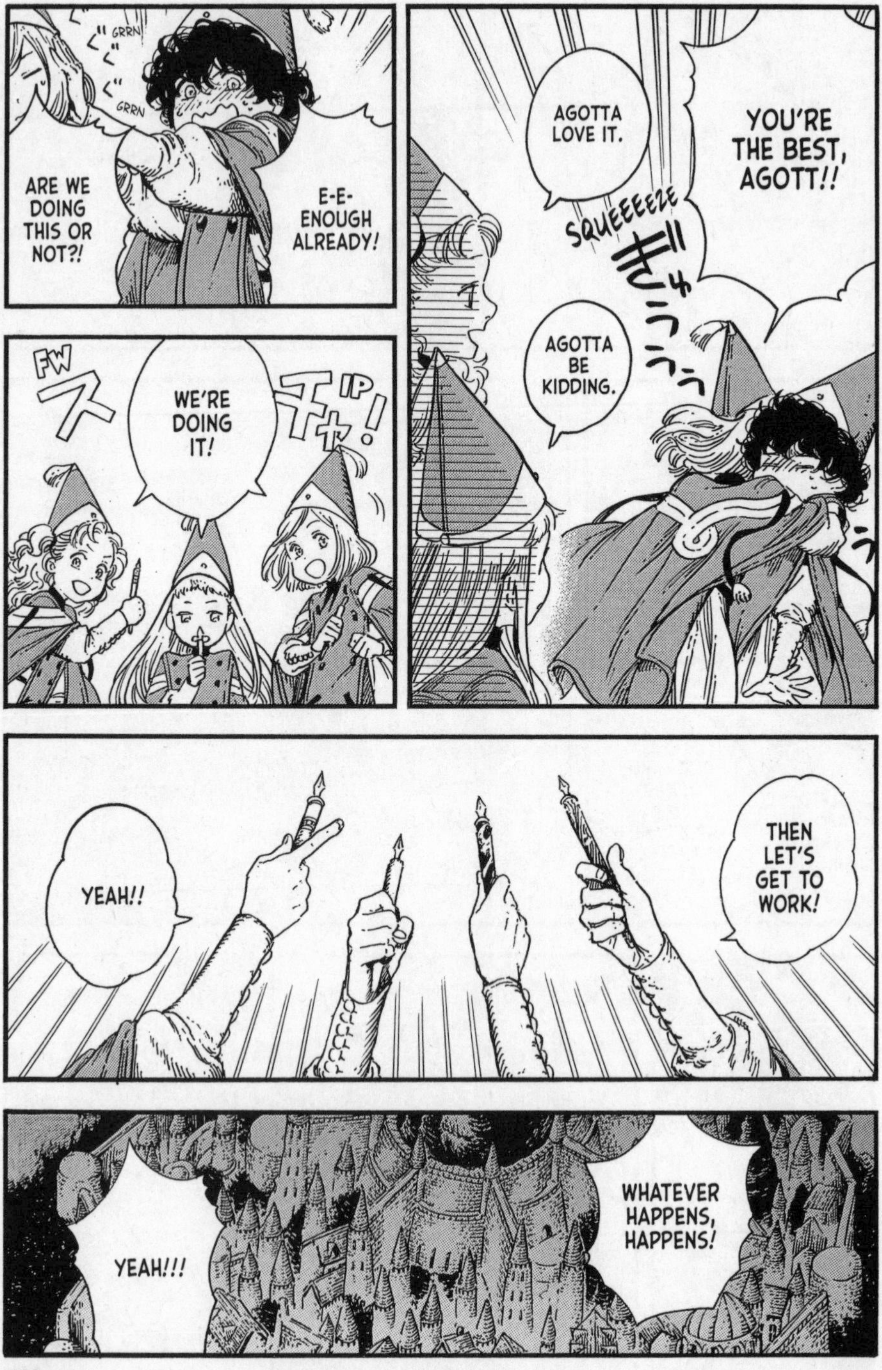
YOU'RE THE BEST, AGOTT!!
AGOTTA LOVE IT.
SQUEEEEZE
ぎゅううう
AGOTTA BE KIDDING.
E-E- ENOUGH ALREADY!
GRRN
GRRN
ARE WE DOING THIS OR NOT?!
IP
チャ
WE'RE DOING IT!
FW
ス
THEN LET'S GET TO WORK!
YEAH!!
WHATEVER HAPPENS, HAPPENS!
YEAH!!!

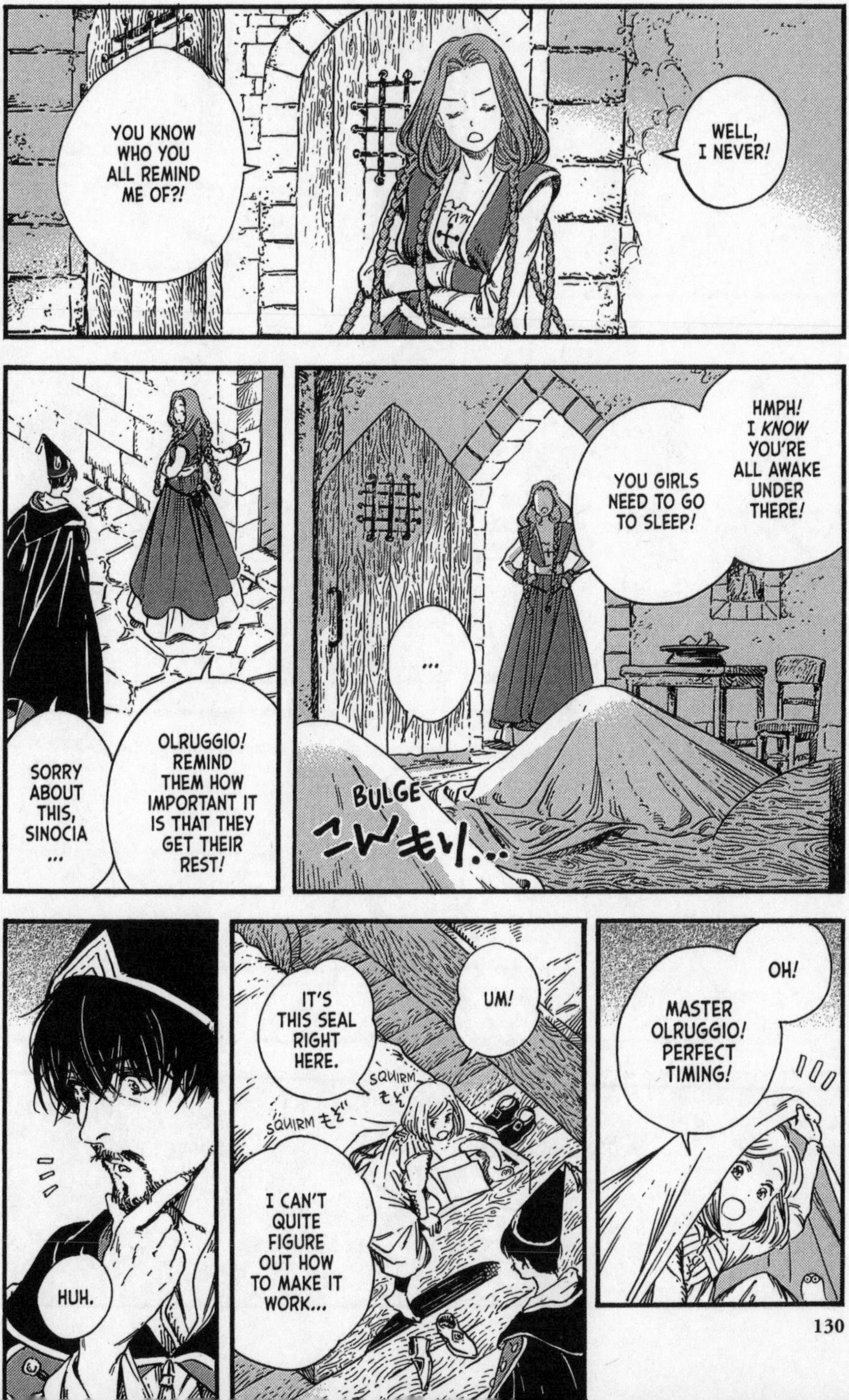
WELL, I NEVER!
YOU KNOW WHO YOU ALL REMIND ME OF?!
HMPH! I *KNOW* YOU'RE ALL AWAKE UNDER THERE!
YOU GIRLS NEED TO GO TO SLEEP!
...
BULGE こんもり…
OLRUGGIO! REMIND THEM HOW IMPORTANT IT IS THAT THEY GET THEIR REST!
SORRY ABOUT THIS, SINOCIA ...
OH!
MASTER OLRUGGIO! PERFECT TIMING!
UM!
IT'S THIS SEAL RIGHT HERE.
SQUIRM もぞ
SQUIRM もぞ
I CAN'T QUITE FIGURE OUT HOW TO MAKE IT WORK...
HUH.

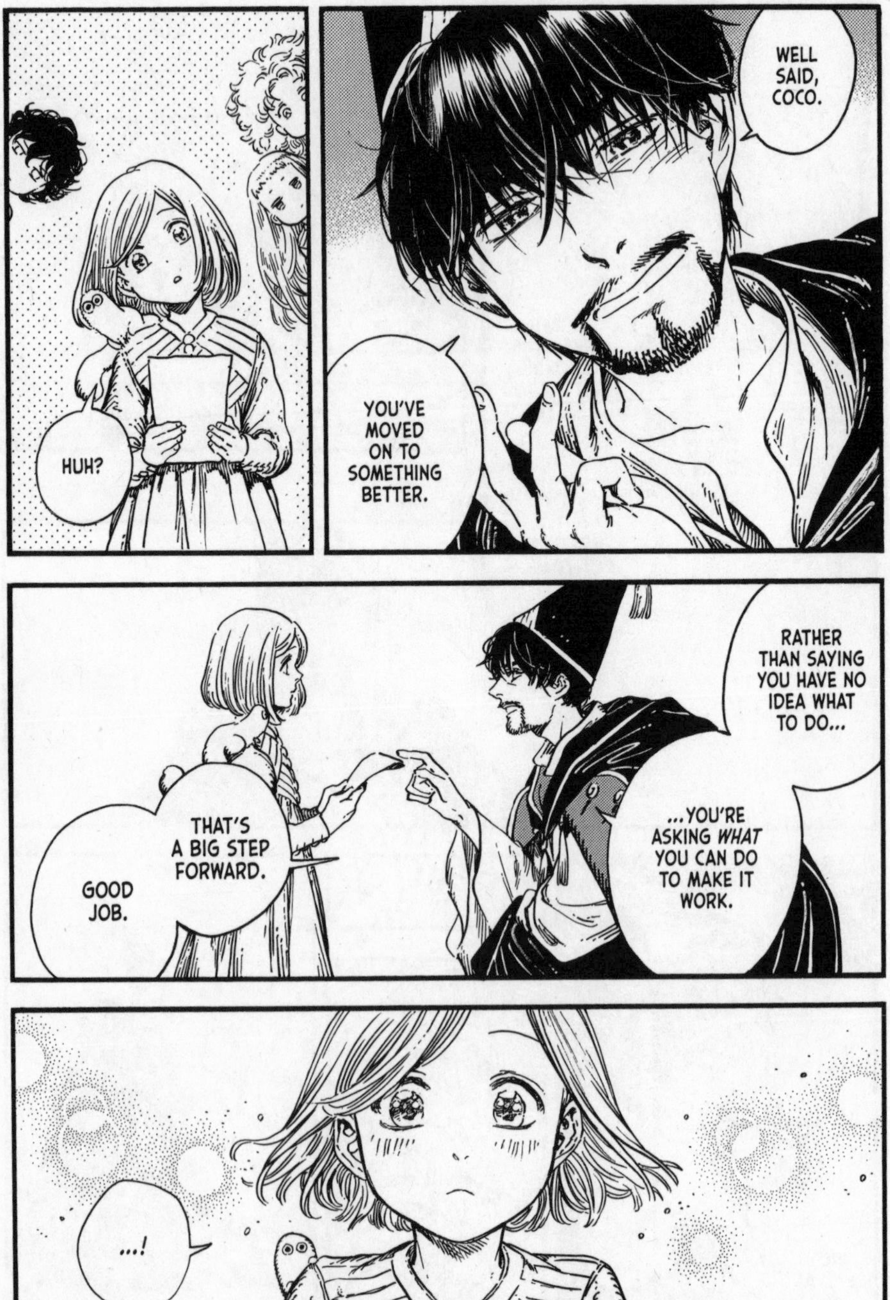
WELL SAID, COCO.
YOU'VE MOVED ON TO SOMETHING BETTER.
HUH?
RATHER THAN SAYING YOU HAVE NO IDEA WHAT TO DO...
...YOU'RE ASKING *WHAT* YOU CAN DO TO MAKE IT WORK.
THAT'S A BIG STEP FORWARD.
GOOD JOB.
...!

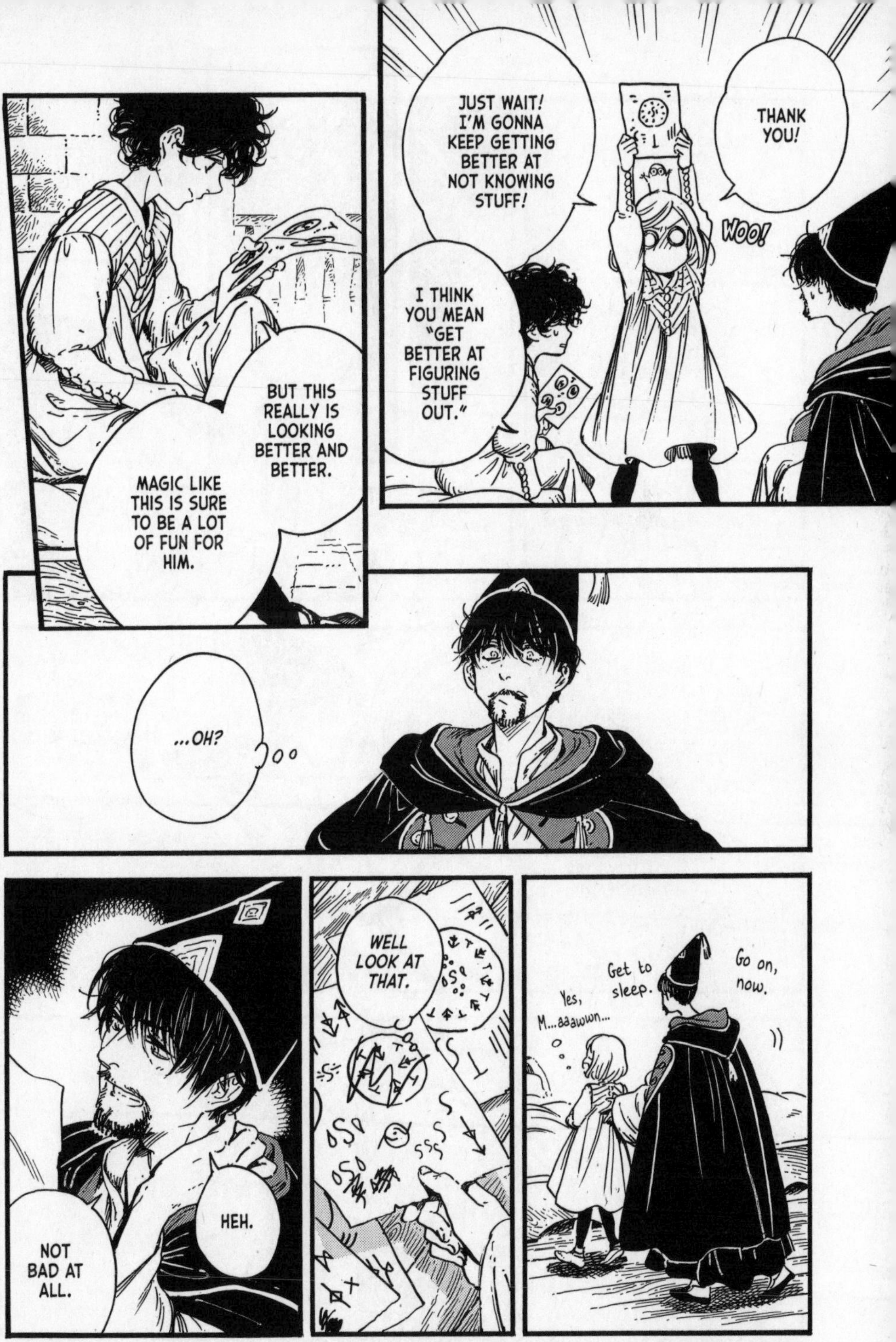
THANK YOU!
WOO!
JUST WAIT! I'M GONNA KEEP GETTING BETTER AT NOT KNOWING STUFF!
I THINK YOU MEAN "GET BETTER AT FIGURING STUFF OUT."
BUT THIS REALLY IS LOOKING BETTER AND BETTER.
MAGIC LIKE THIS IS SURE TO BE A LOT OF FUN FOR HIM.
...OH?
Go on, now.
Get to sleep.
Yes, M...aaawwn...
WELL LOOK AT THAT.
HEH.
NOT BAD AT ALL.

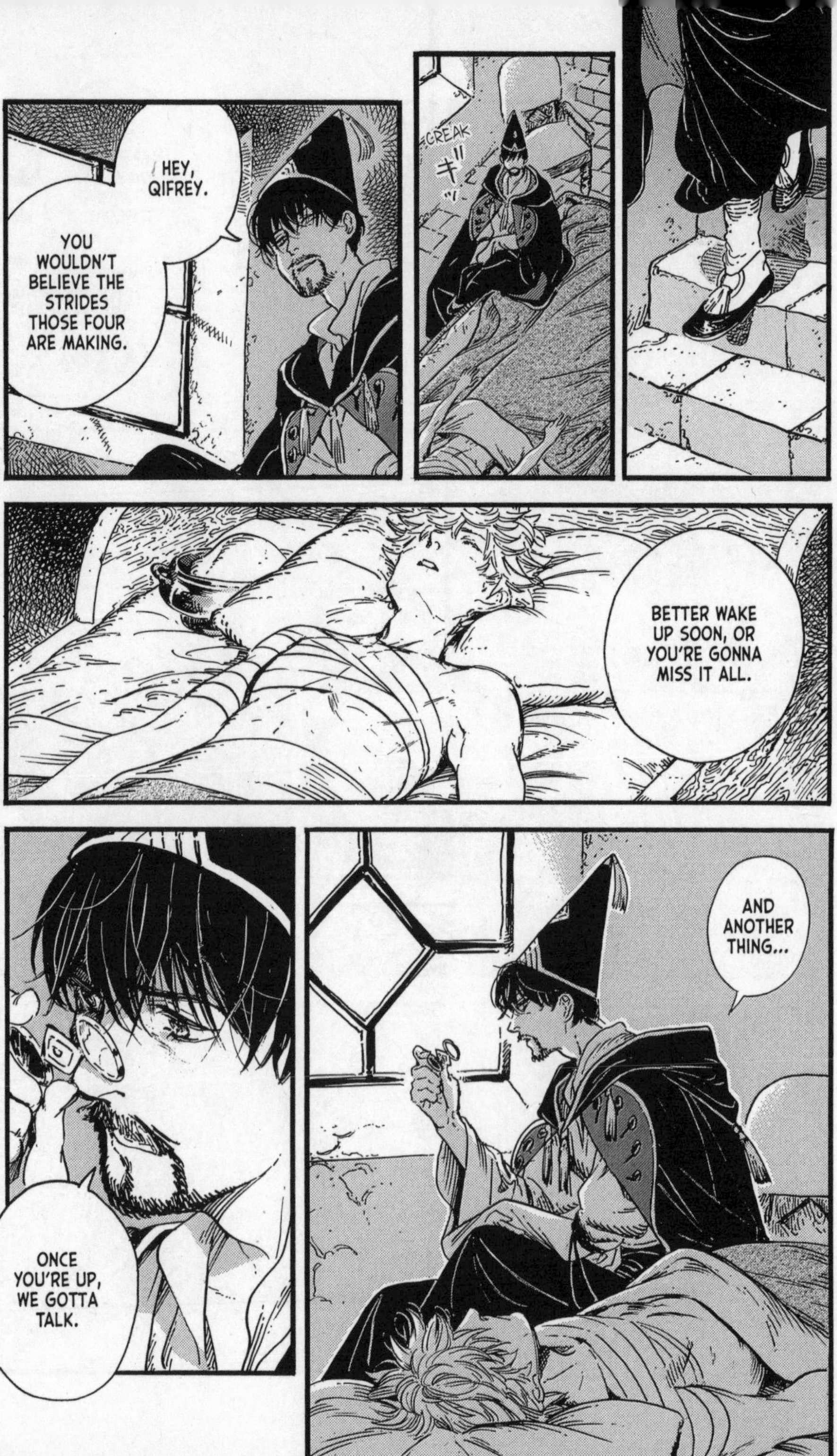
CREAK
ギッ
HEY, QIFREY.
YOU WOULDN'T BELIEVE THE STRIDES THOSE FOUR ARE MAKING.
BETTER WAKE UP SOON, OR YOU'RE GONNA MISS IT ALL.
AND ANOTHER THING...
ONCE YOU'RE UP, WE GOTTA TALK.

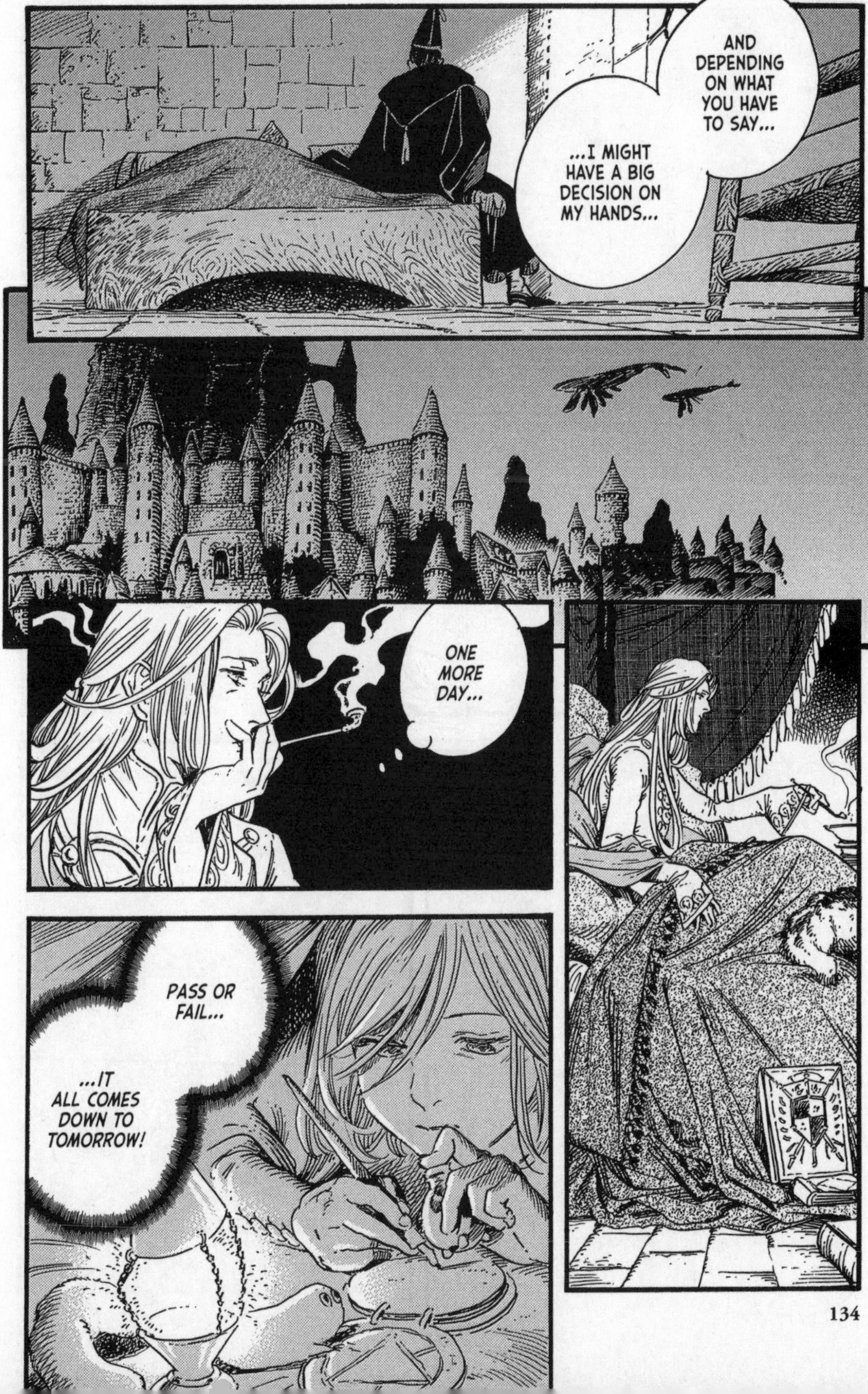
AND DEPENDING ON WHAT YOU HAVE TO SAY...
...I MIGHT HAVE A BIG DECISION ON MY HANDS...
ONE MORE DAY...
PASS OR FAIL...
...IT ALL COMES DOWN TO TOMORROW!

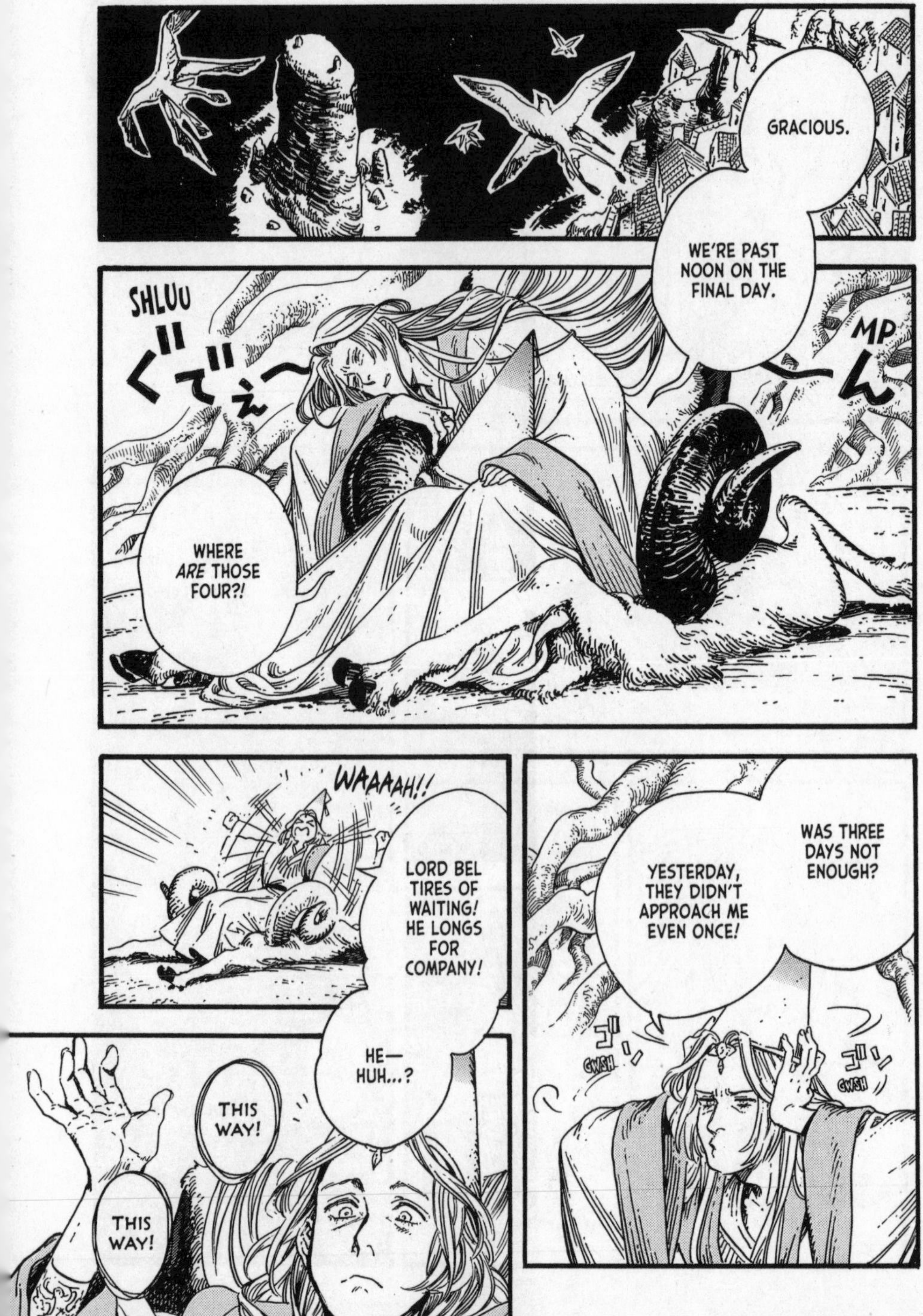
GRACIOUS.
WE'RE PAST NOON ON THE FINAL DAY.
MP
ん
SHLUU
ぐでぇ〜
WHERE *ARE* THOSE FOUR?!
WAS THREE DAYS NOT ENOUGH?
YESTERDAY, THEY DIDN'T APPROACH ME EVEN ONCE!
ゴン
GWSH
ゴン
GWSH
WAAAAH!!
LORD BEL TIRES OF WAITING! HE LONGS FOR COMPANY!
HE— HUH...?
THIS WAY!
THIS WAY!

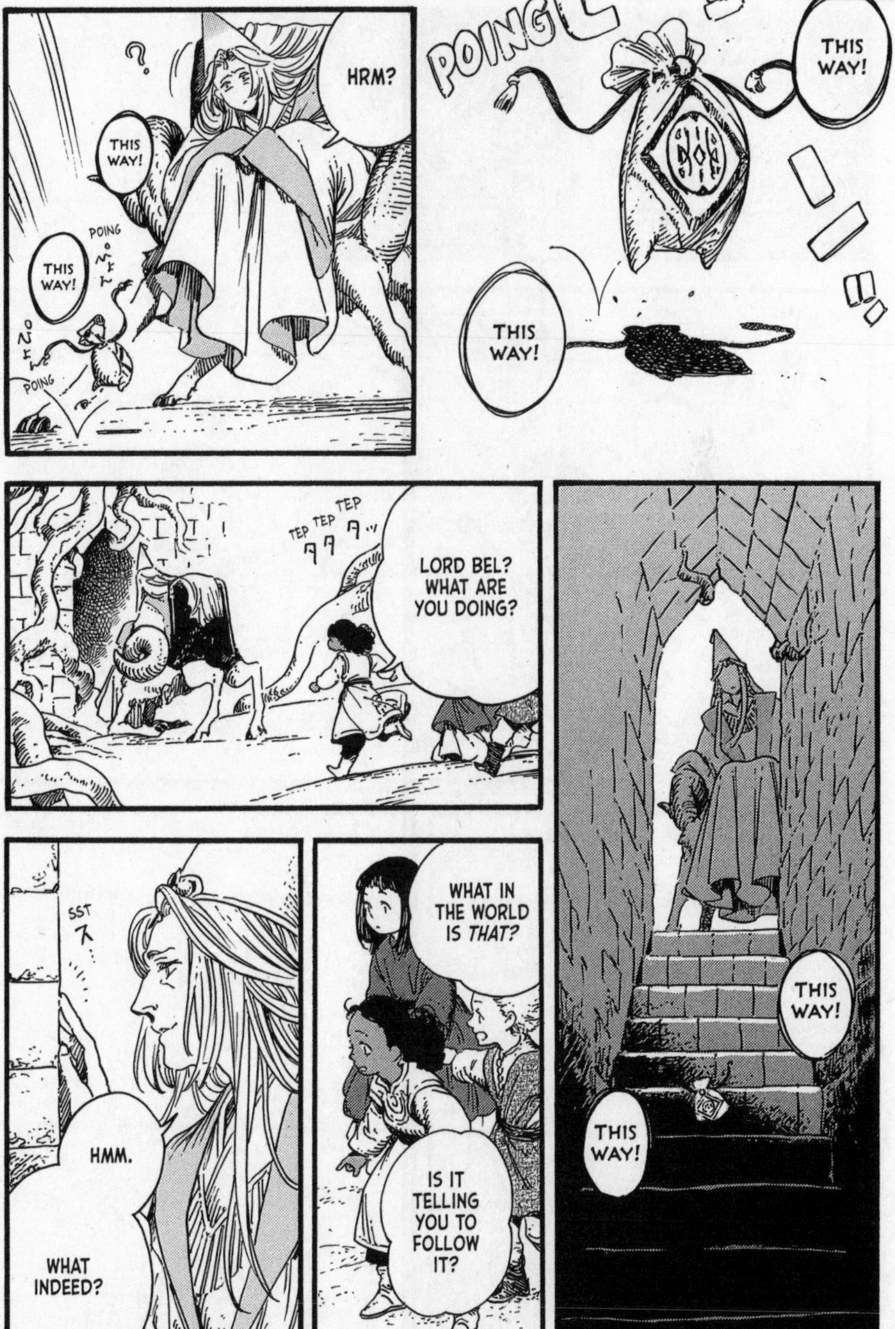
POING
THIS WAY!
THIS WAY!
HRM?
THIS WAY!
POING
THIS WAY!
POING
THIS WAY!
THIS WAY!
TEP TEP TEP
LORD BEL? WHAT ARE YOU DOING?
WHAT IN THE WORLD IS *THAT?*
IS IT TELLING YOU TO FOLLOW IT?
SST
HMM.
WHAT INDEED?

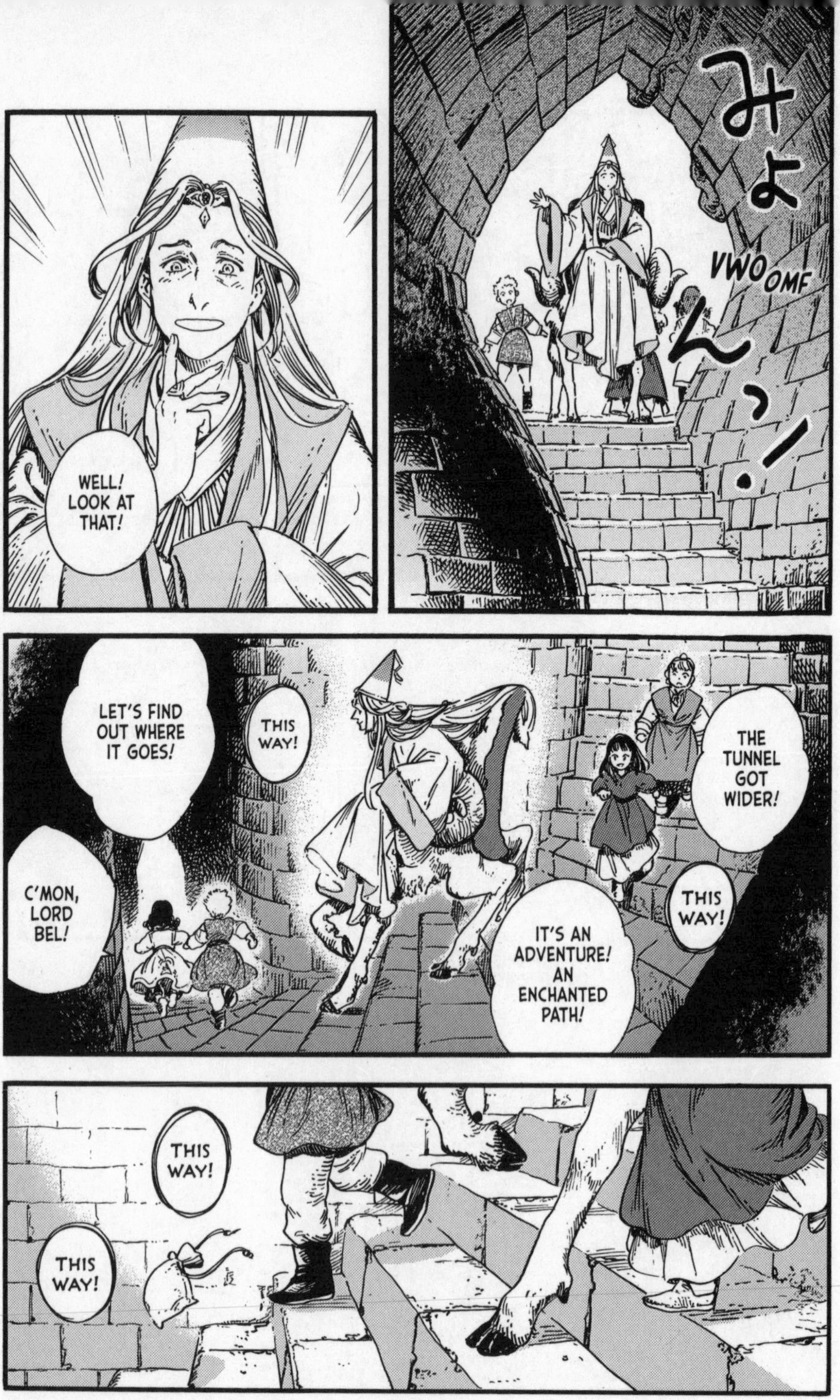
みょんっ!
VWOOMF
WELL! LOOK AT THAT!
THE TUNNEL GOT WIDER!
THIS WAY!
IT'S AN ADVENTURE! AN ENCHANTED PATH!
THIS WAY!
LET'S FIND OUT WHERE IT GOES!
C'MON, LORD BEL!
THIS WAY!
THIS WAY!

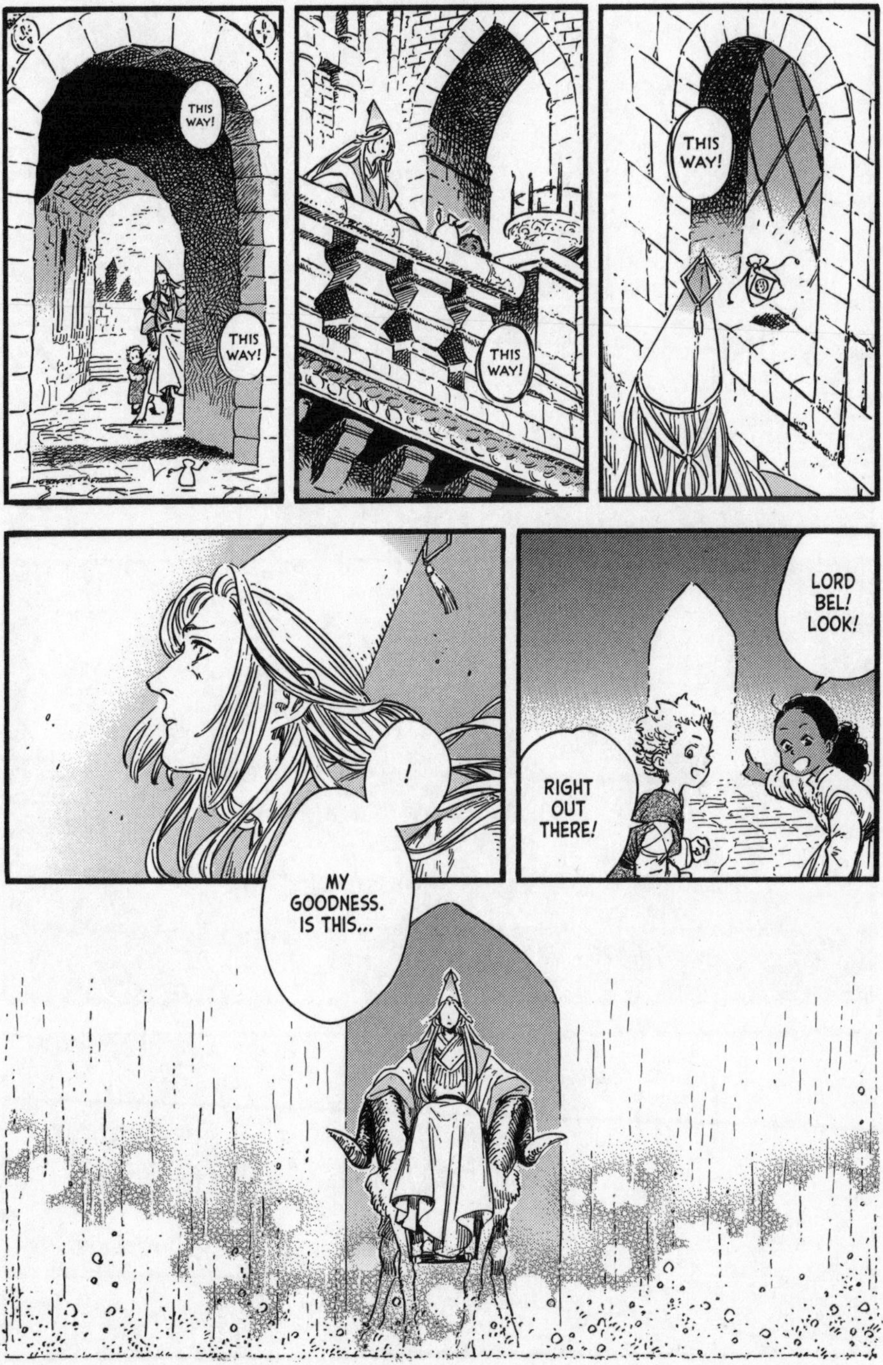
THIS WAY!
THIS WAY!
THIS WAY!
THIS WAY!
LORD BEL! LOOK!
RIGHT OUT THERE!
!
MY GOODNESS. IS THIS...

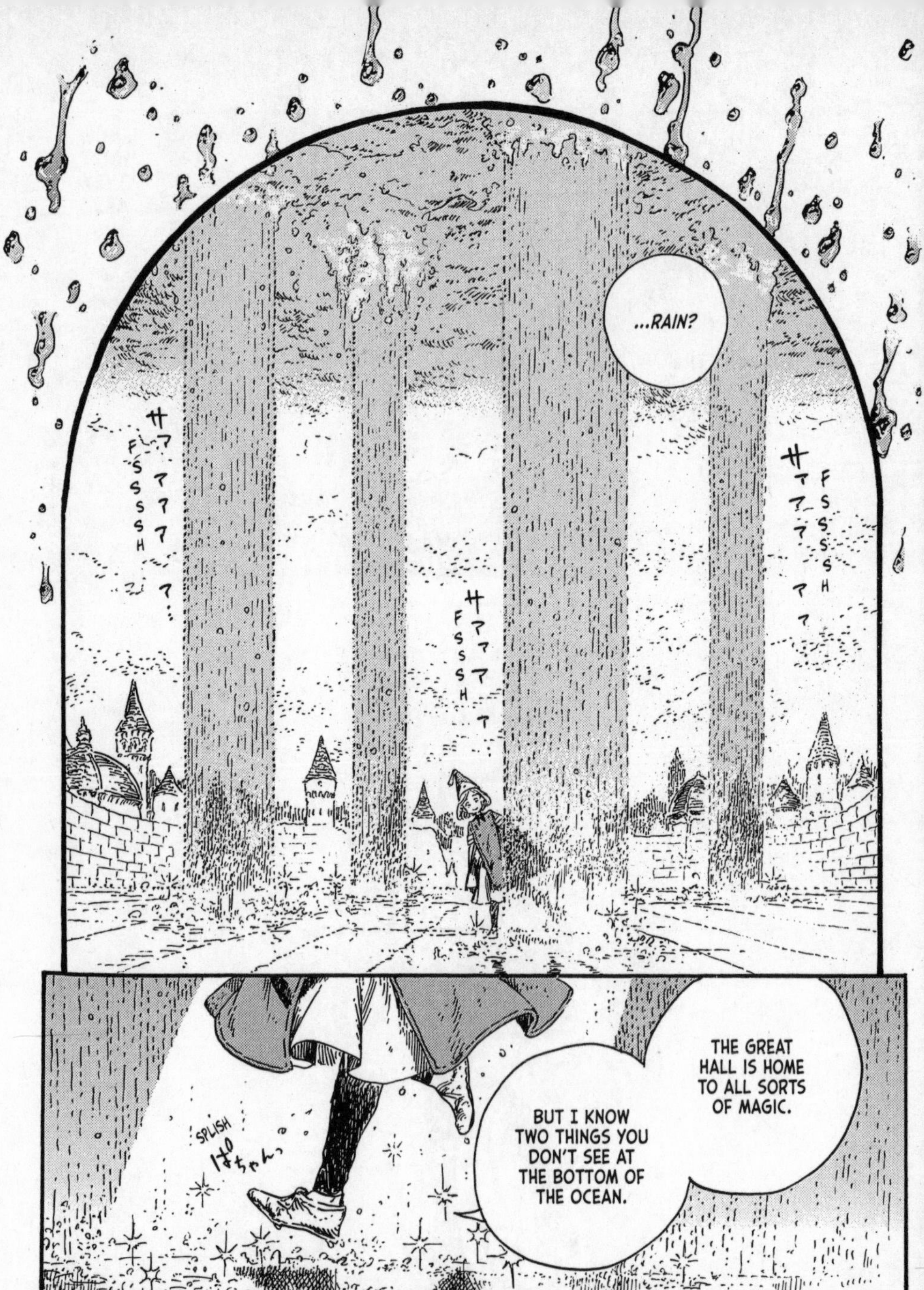
FSSSH
FSSSH
FSSSH
...RAIN?
THE GREAT HALL IS HOME TO ALL SORTS OF MAGIC.
BUT I KNOW TWO THINGS YOU DON'T SEE AT THE BOTTOM OF THE OCEAN.
SPLISH

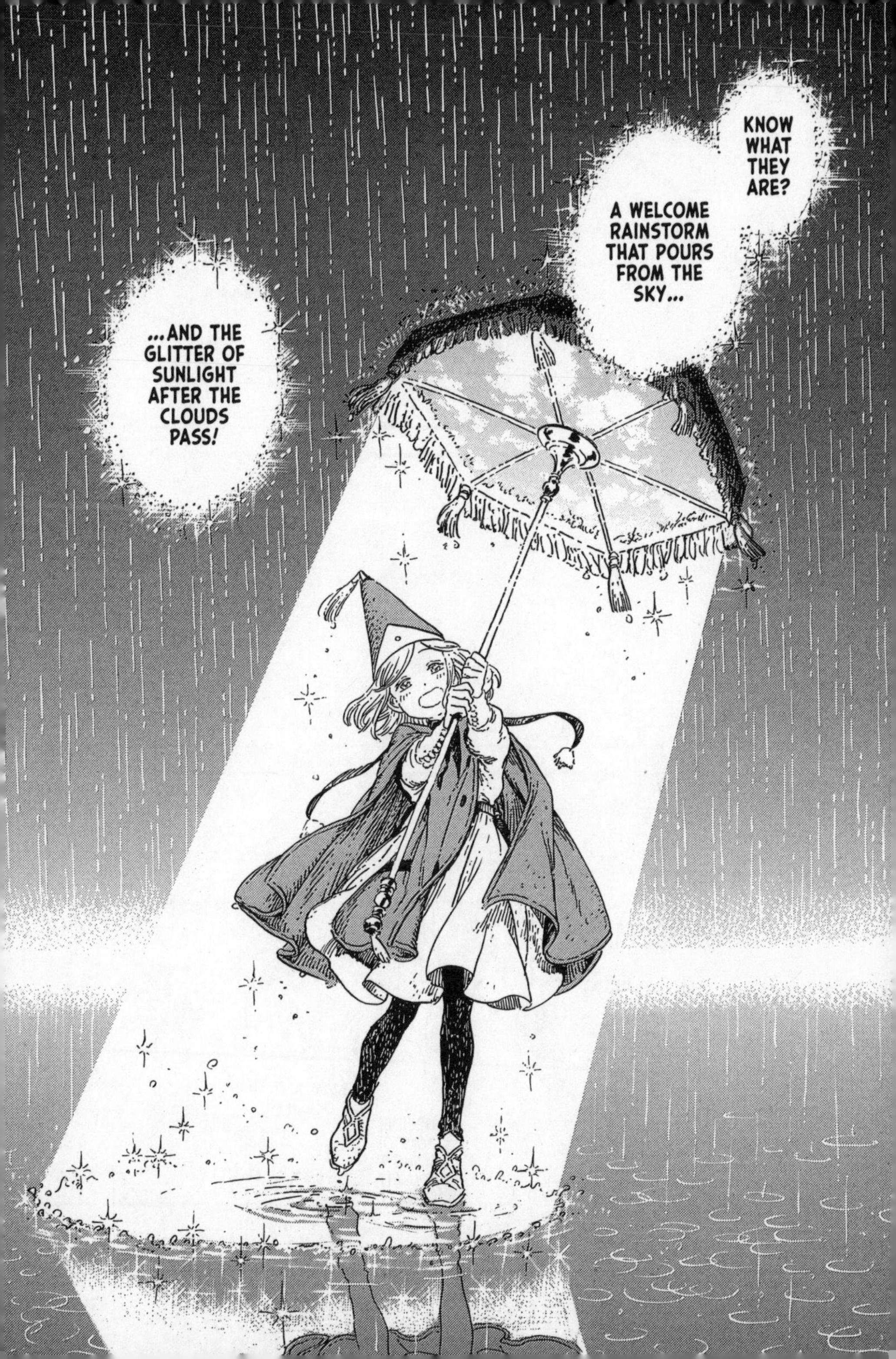
KNOW WHAT THEY ARE?
A WELCOME RAINSTORM THAT POURS FROM THE SKY...
...AND THE GLITTER OF SUNLIGHT AFTER THE CLOUDS PASS!

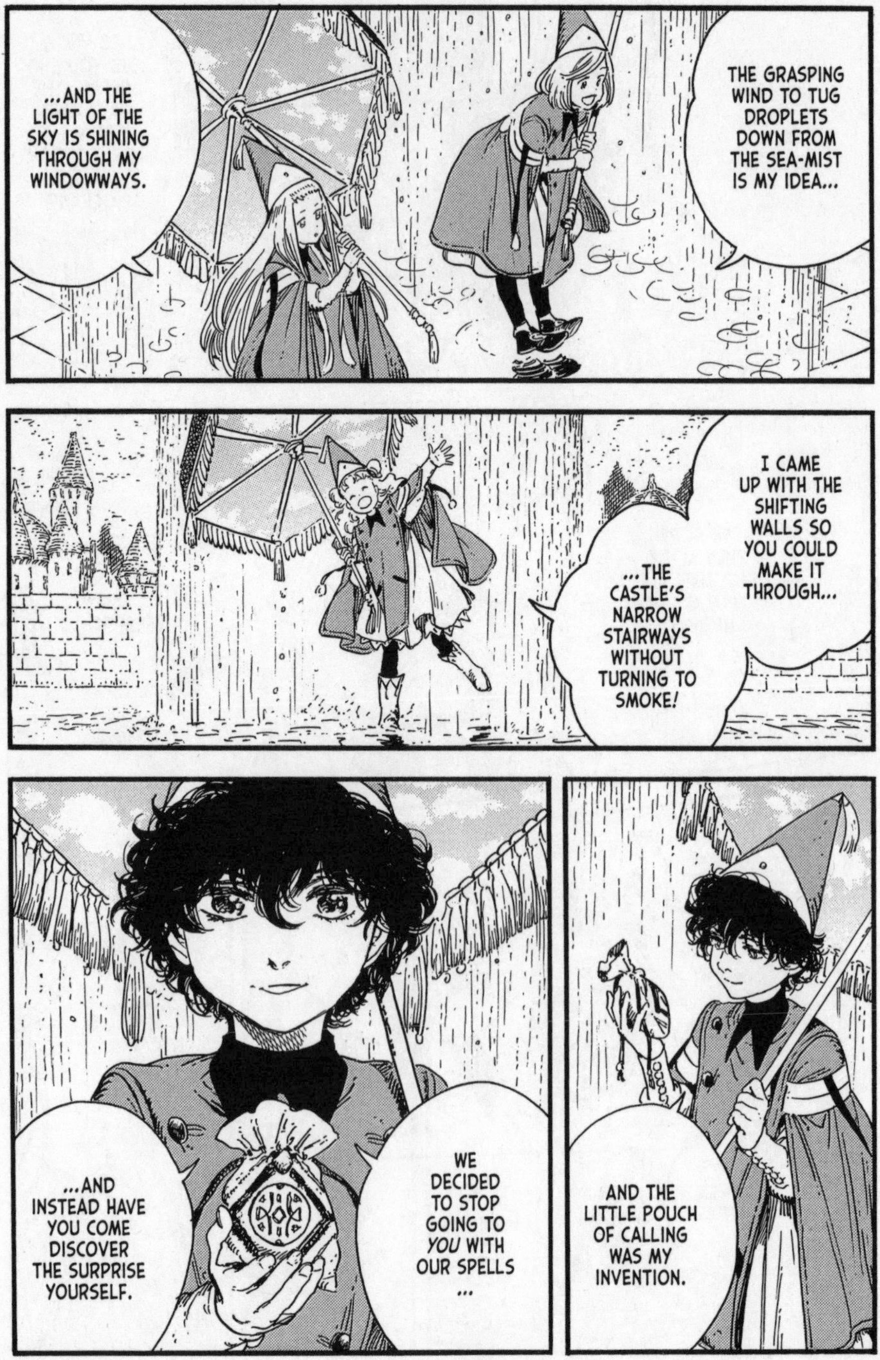
THE GRASPING WIND TO TUG DROPLETS DOWN FROM THE SEA-MIST IS MY IDEA...
...AND THE LIGHT OF THE SKY IS SHINING THROUGH MY WINDOWWAYS.
I CAME UP WITH THE SHIFTING WALLS SO YOU COULD MAKE IT THROUGH...
...THE CASTLE'S NARROW STAIRWAYS WITHOUT TURNING TO SMOKE!
AND THE LITTLE POUCH OF CALLING WAS MY INVENTION.
WE DECIDED TO STOP GOING TO *YOU* WITH OUR SPELLS ...
...AND INSTEAD HAVE YOU COME DISCOVER THE SURPRISE YOURSELF.

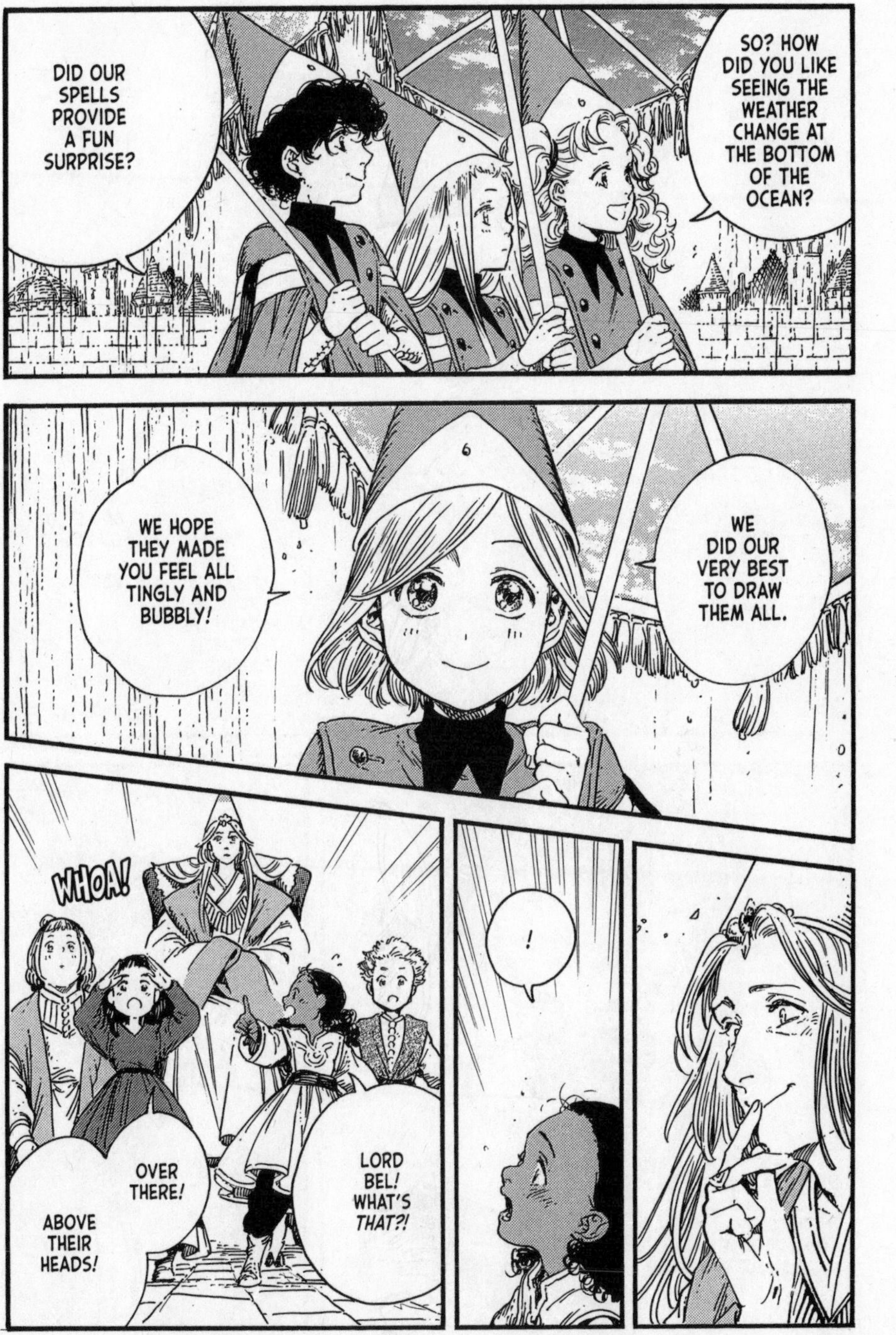
SO? HOW DID YOU LIKE SEEING THE WEATHER CHANGE AT THE BOTTOM OF THE OCEAN?
DID OUR SPELLS PROVIDE A FUN SURPRISE?
WE DID OUR VERY BEST TO DRAW THEM ALL.
WE HOPE THEY MADE YOU FEEL ALL TINGLY AND BUBBLY!
!
WHOA!
LORD BEL! WHAT'S *THAT?!*
OVER THERE!
ABOVE THEIR HEADS!

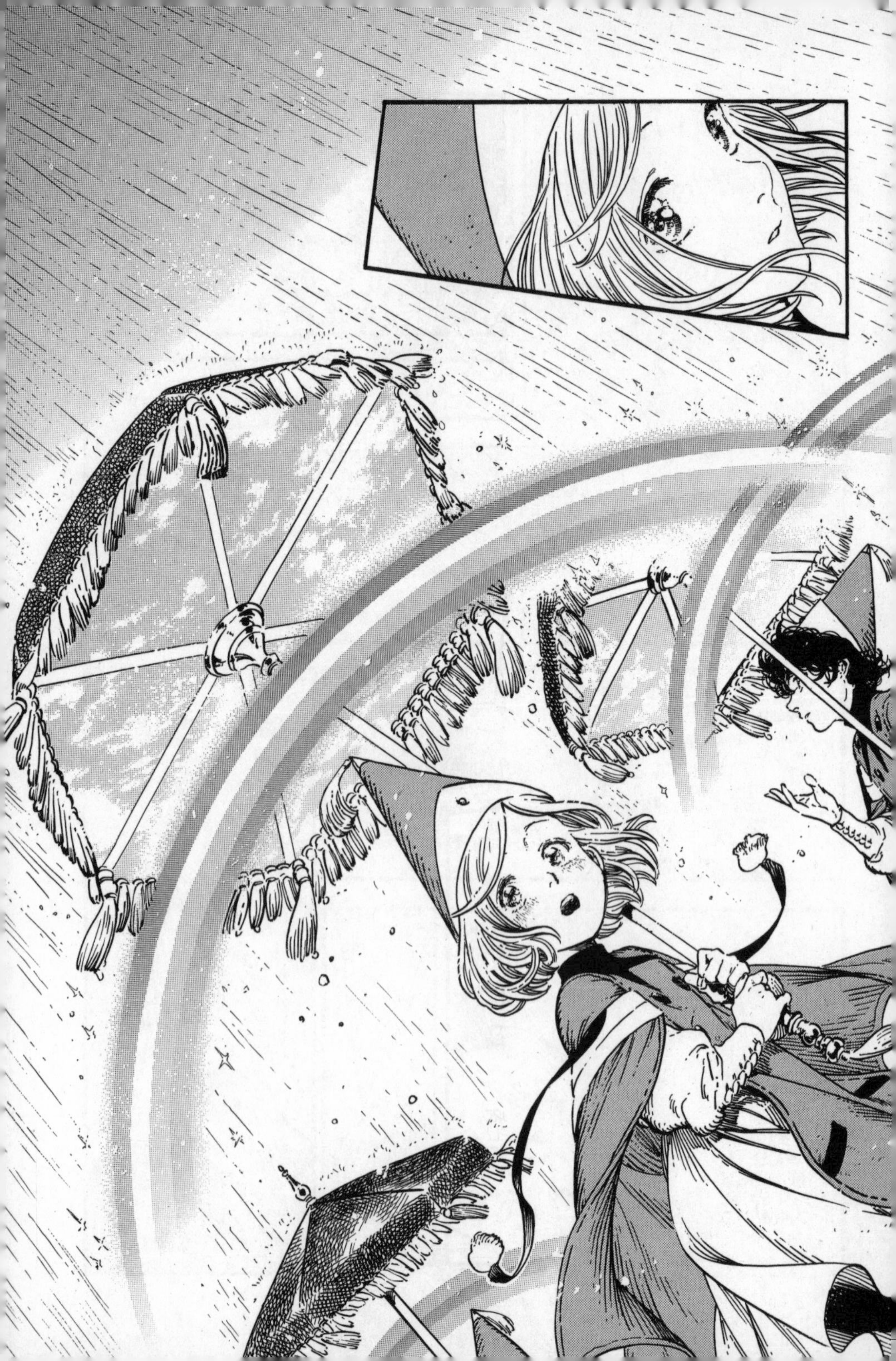

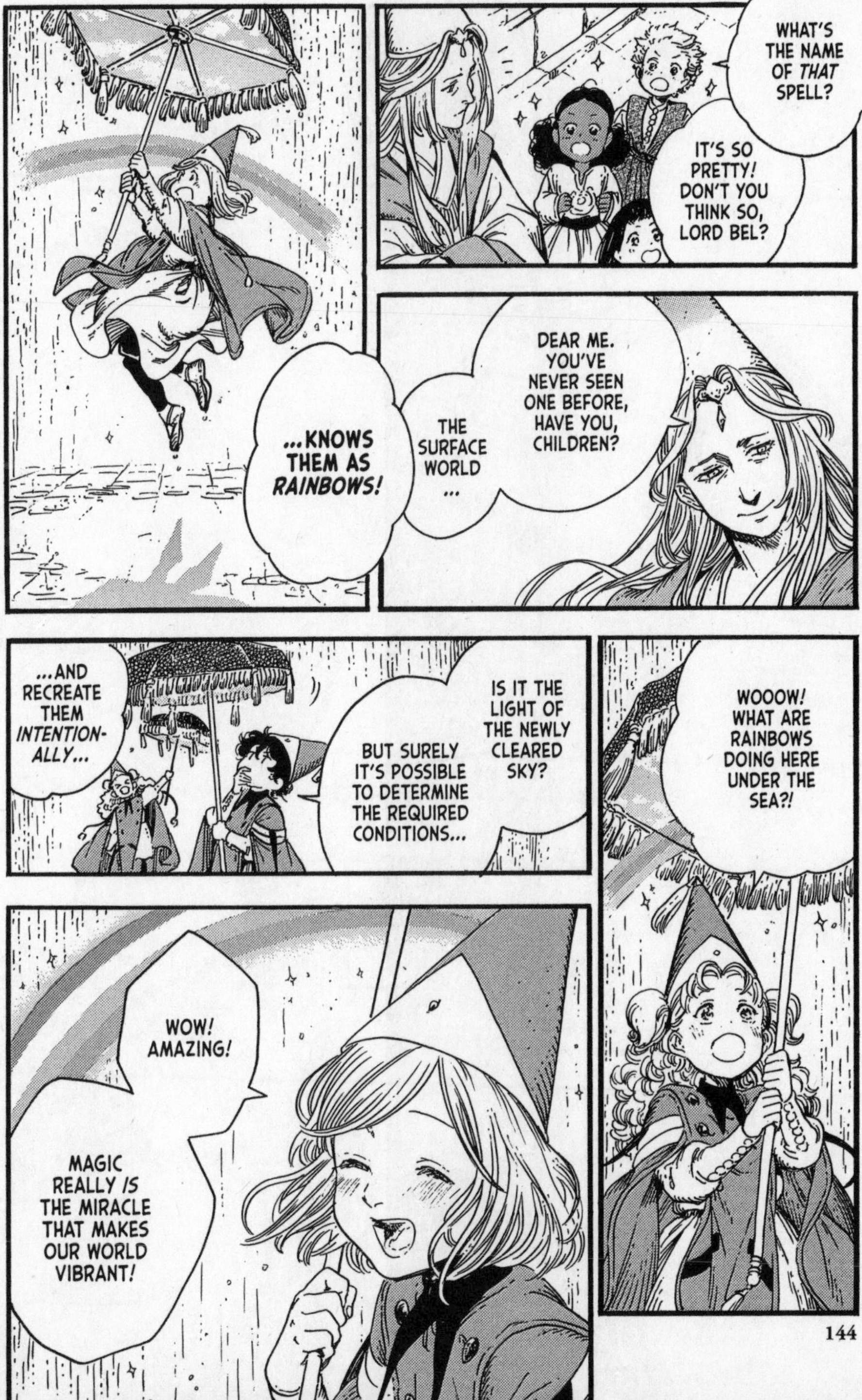
WHAT'S THE NAME OF *THAT* SPELL?
IT'S SO PRETTY! DON'T YOU THINK SO, LORD BEL?
DEAR ME. YOU'VE NEVER SEEN ONE BEFORE, HAVE YOU, CHILDREN?
THE SURFACE WORLD ...
...KNOWS THEM AS *RAINBOWS!*
WOOOW! WHAT ARE RAINBOWS DOING HERE UNDER THE SEA?!
IS IT THE LIGHT OF THE NEWLY CLEARED SKY?
BUT SURELY IT'S POSSIBLE TO DETERMINE THE REQUIRED CONDITIONS...
...AND RECREATE THEM *INTENTION-ALLY*...
WOW! *AMAZING!*
MAGIC REALLY *IS* THE MIRACLE THAT MAKES OUR WORLD VIBRANT!

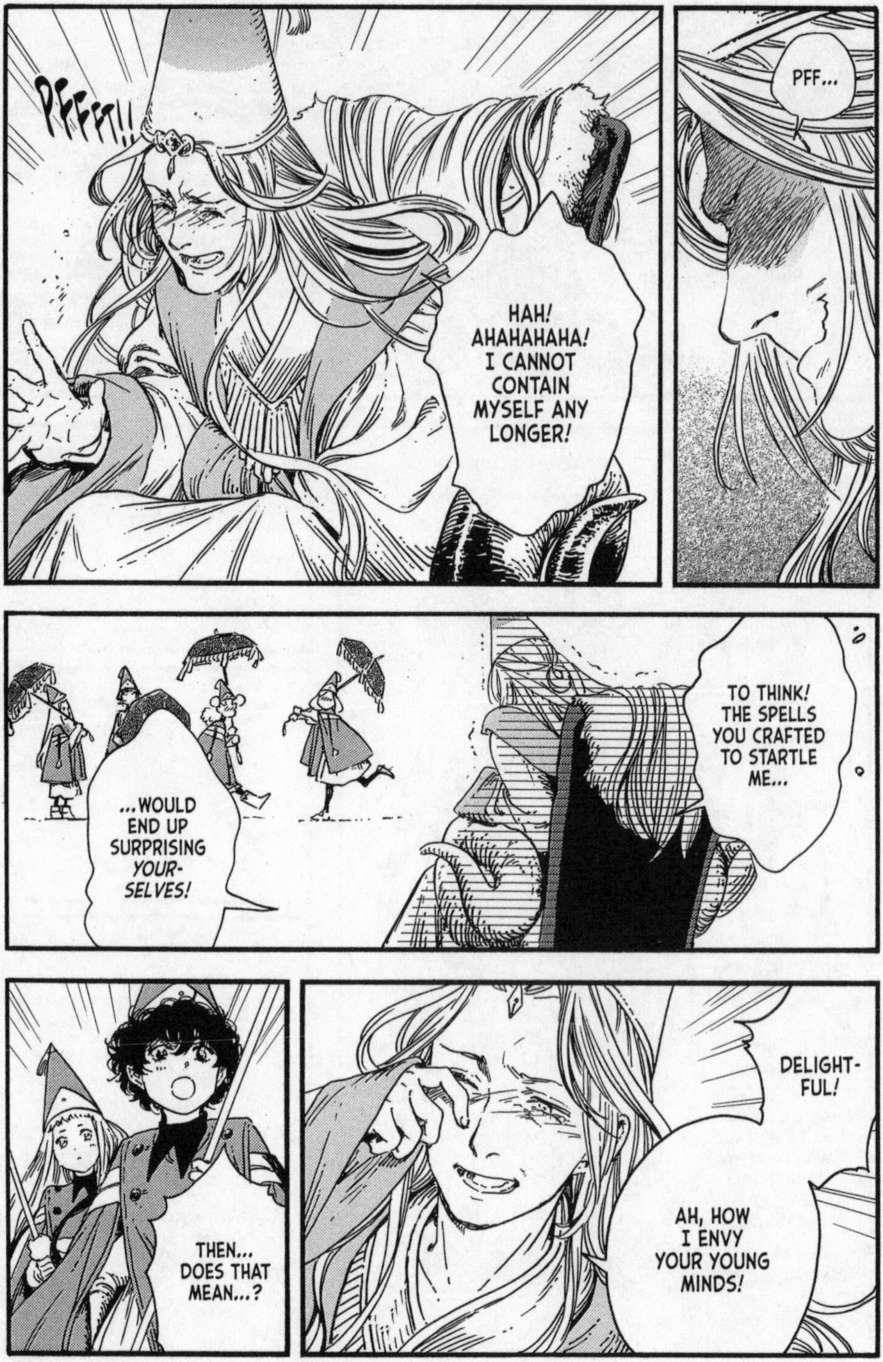
PFF...
PFFFT!!
HAH! AHAHAHAHA! I CANNOT CONTAIN MYSELF ANY LONGER!
TO THINK! THE SPELLS YOU CRAFTED TO STARTLE ME...
...WOULD END UP SURPRISING YOUR-SELVES!
DELIGHT-FUL!
AH, HOW I ENVY YOUR YOUNG MINDS!
THEN... DOES THAT MEAN...?

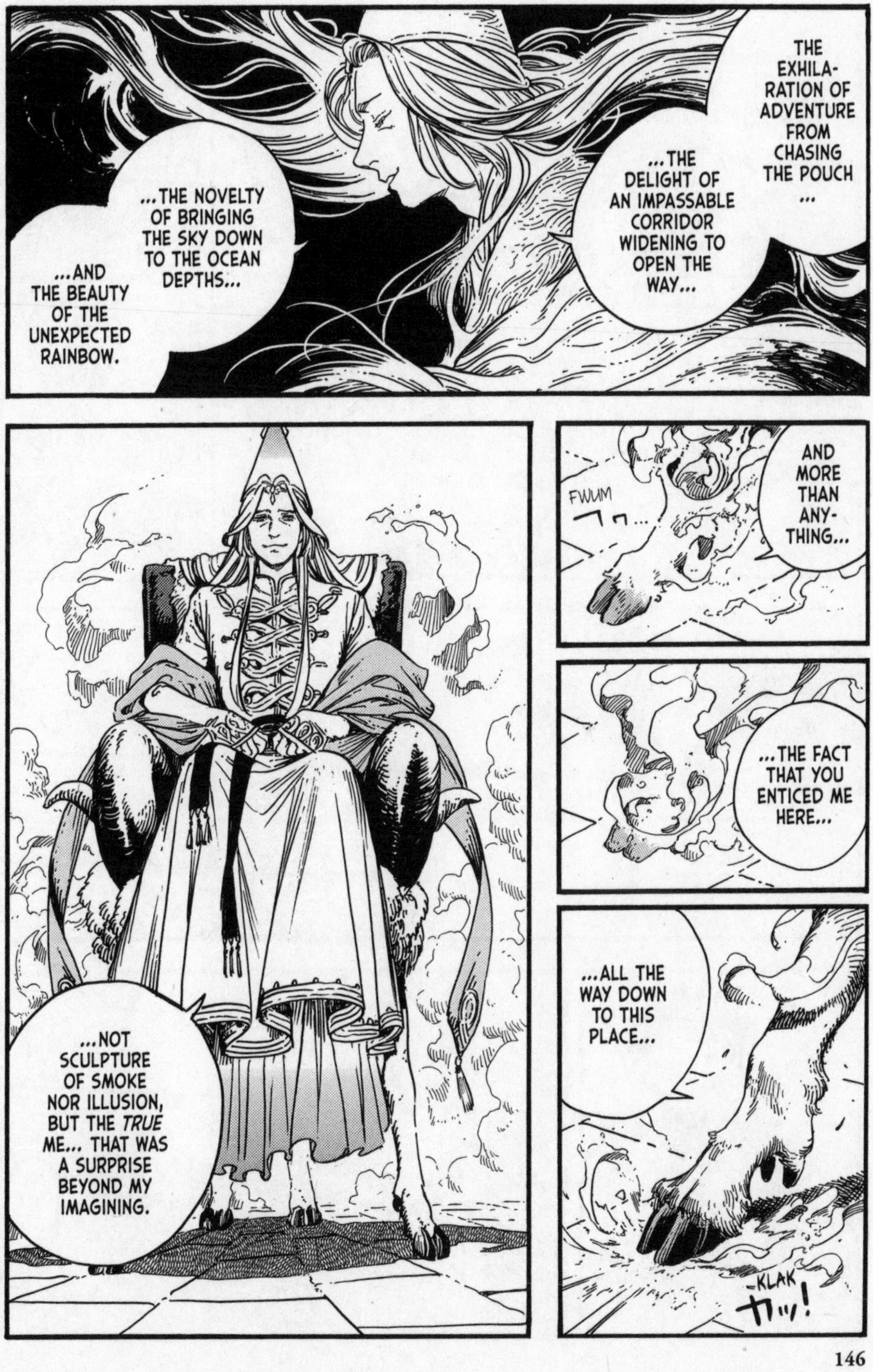
THE EXHILA-RATION OF ADVENTURE FROM CHASING THE POUCH ...
...THE DELIGHT OF AN IMPASSABLE CORRIDOR WIDENING TO OPEN THE WAY...
...THE NOVELTY OF BRINGING THE SKY DOWN TO THE OCEAN DEPTHS...
...AND THE BEAUTY OF THE UNEXPECTED RAINBOW.
AND MORE THAN ANY-THING...
FWUM
...THE FACT THAT YOU ENTICED ME HERE...
...ALL THE WAY DOWN TO THIS PLACE...
KLAK
...NOT SCULPTURE OF SMOKE NOR ILLUSION, BUT THE *TRUE* ME... THAT WAS A SURPRISE BEYOND MY IMAGINING.

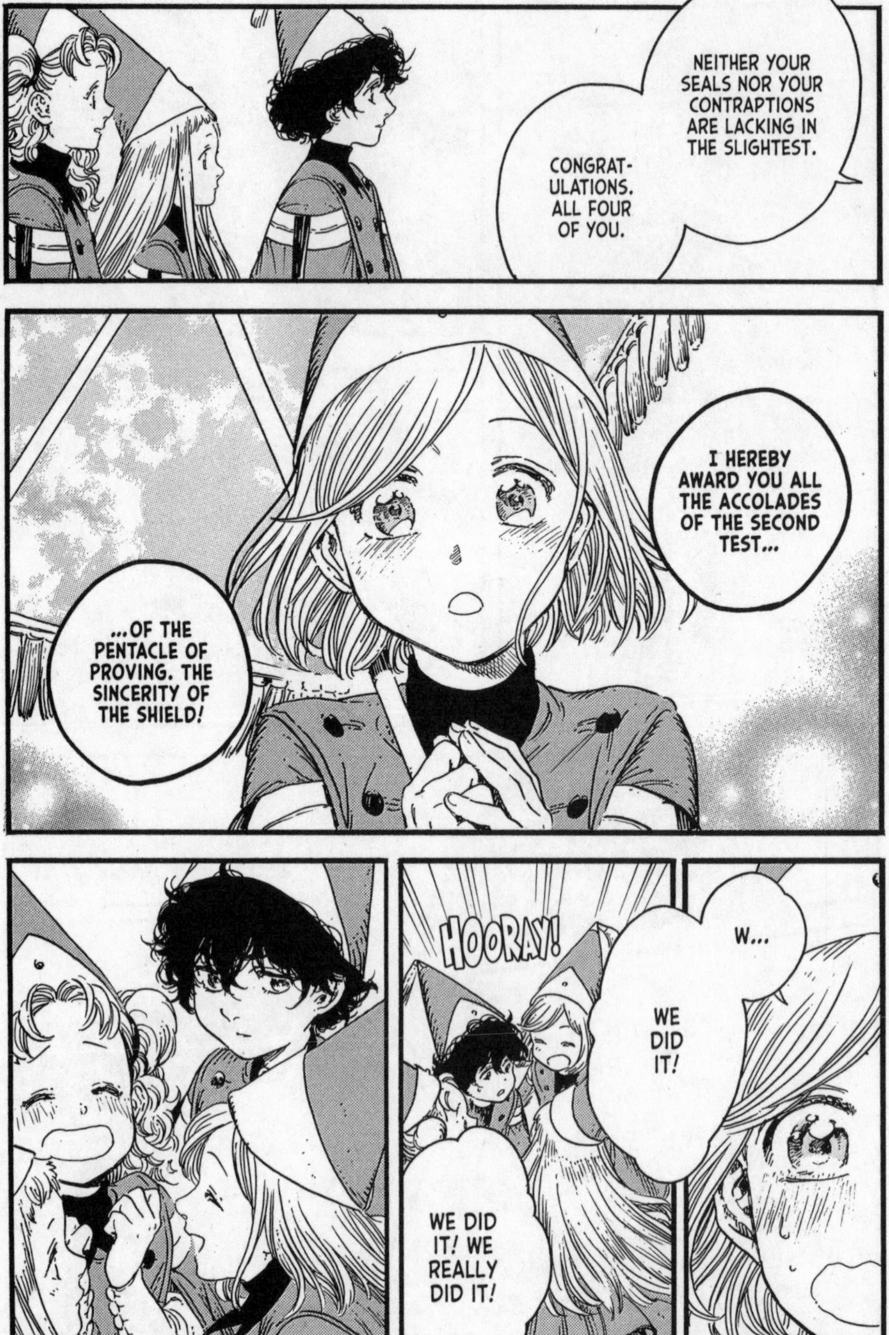
NEITHER YOUR SEALS NOR YOUR CONTRAPTIONS ARE LACKING IN THE SLIGHTEST.
CONGRAT-ULATIONS. ALL FOUR OF YOU.
I HEREBY AWARD YOU ALL THE ACCOLADES OF THE SECOND TEST...
...OF THE PENTACLE OF PROVING. THE SINCERITY OF THE SHIELD!
W...
WE DID IT!
HOORAY!
WE DID IT! WE REALLY DID IT!

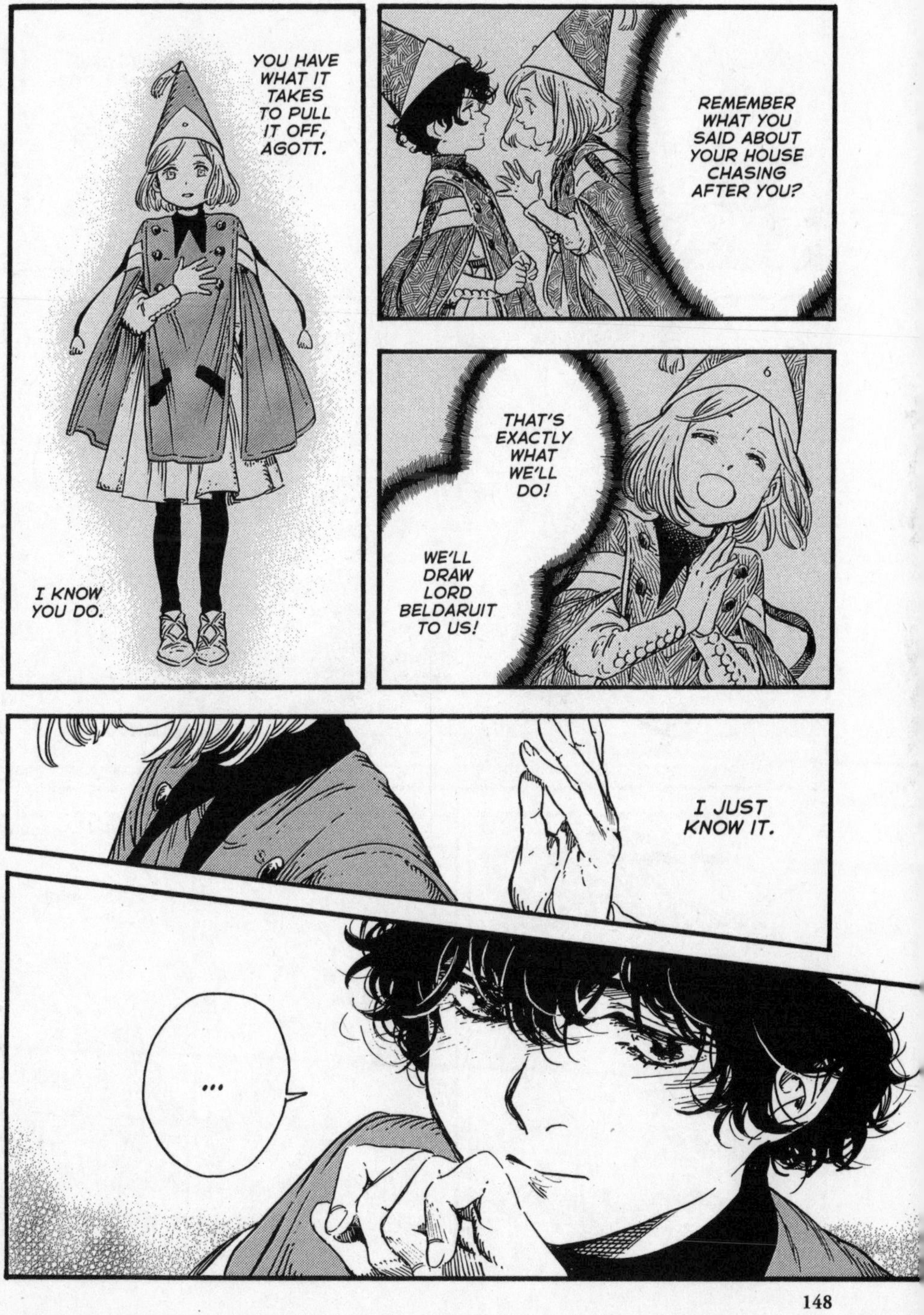
REMEMBER WHAT YOU SAID ABOUT YOUR HOUSE CHASING AFTER YOU?
THAT'S EXACTLY WHAT WE'LL DO!
WE'LL DRAW LORD BELDARUIT TO US!
YOU HAVE WHAT IT TAKES TO PULL IT OFF, AGOTT.
I KNOW YOU DO.
I JUST KNOW IT.
...

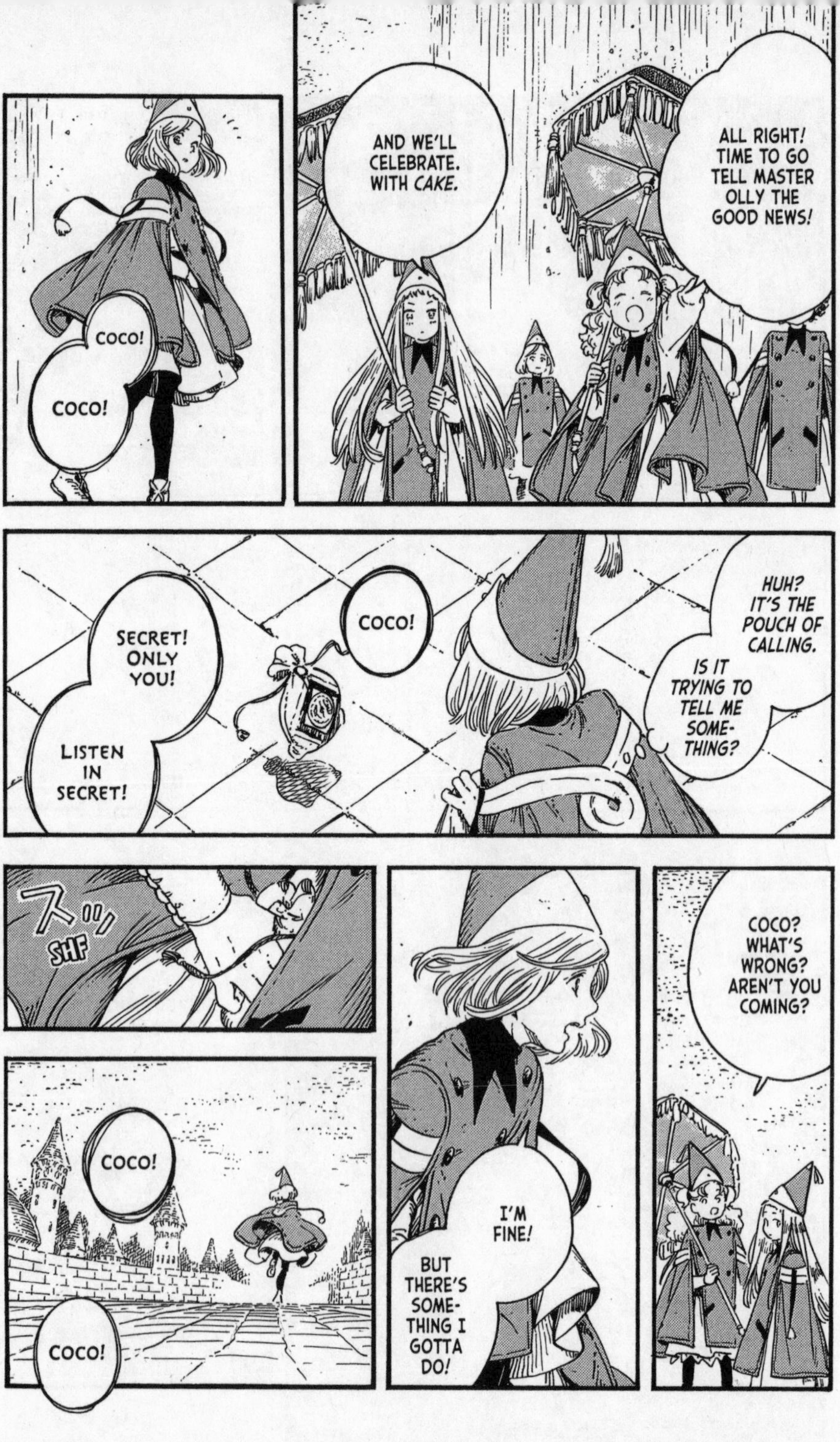
ALL RIGHT! TIME TO GO TELL MASTER OLLY THE GOOD NEWS!
AND WE'LL CELEBRATE. WITH *CAKE.*
COCO!
COCO!
HUH? IT'S THE POUCH OF CALLING.
IS IT TRYING TO TELL ME SOME-THING?
COCO!
SECRET! ONLY YOU!
LISTEN IN SECRET!
COCO? WHAT'S WRONG? AREN'T YOU COMING?
I'M FINE!
BUT THERE'S SOME-THING I GOTTA DO!
スッ
SHF
COCO!
COCO!

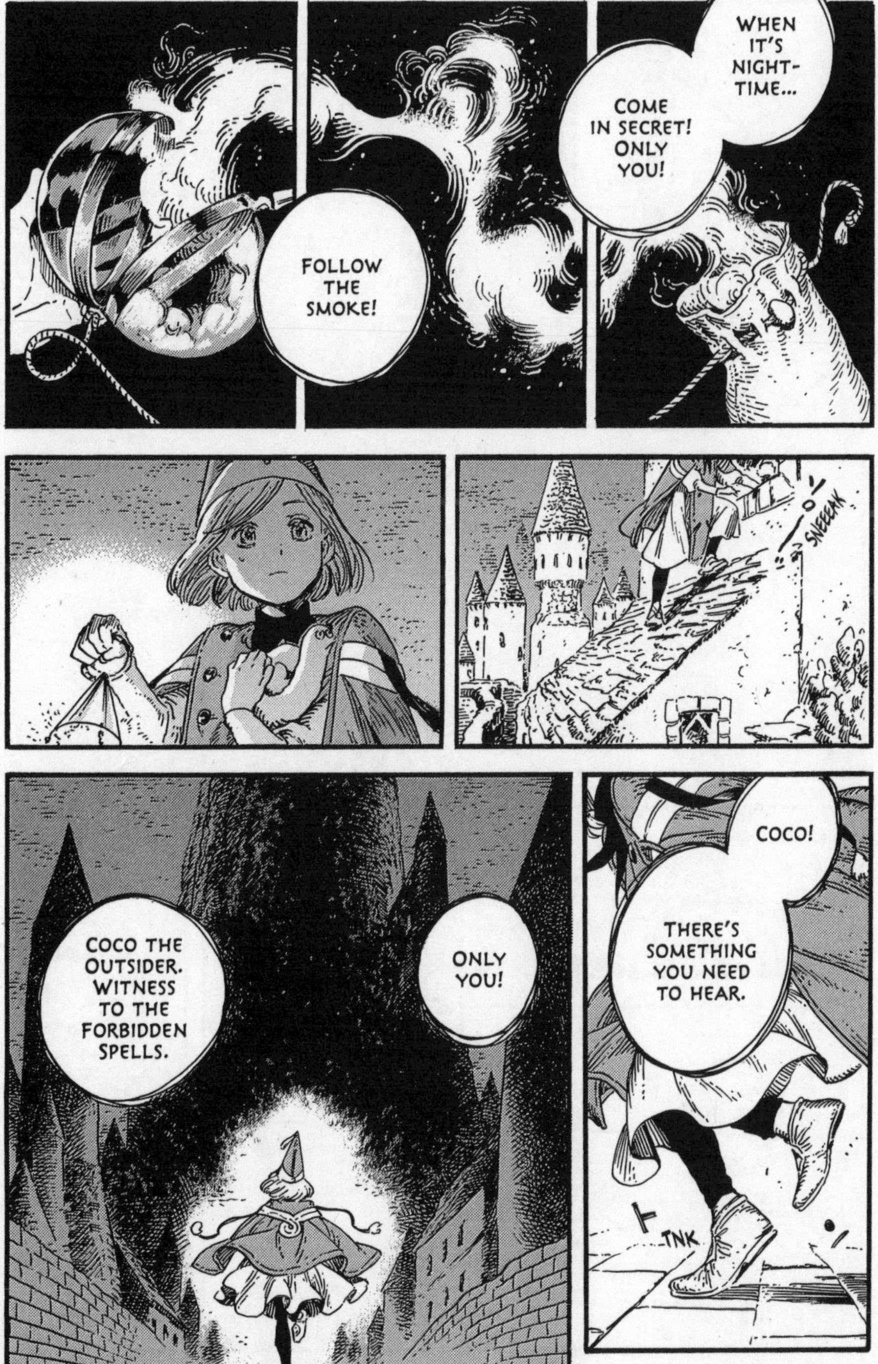
WHEN IT'S NIGHT-TIME...
COME IN SECRET! ONLY YOU!
FOLLOW THE SMOKE!
SNEEEAK
COCO!
THERE'S SOMETHING YOU NEED TO HEAR.
TNK
ONLY YOU!
COCO THE OUTSIDER. WITNESS TO THE FORBIDDEN SPELLS.

Chapter 34 ♦ End

Witch Hat Atelier

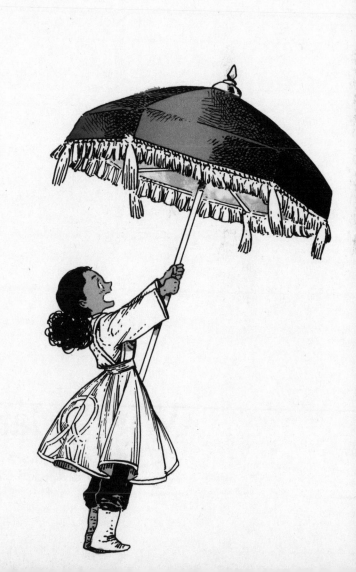

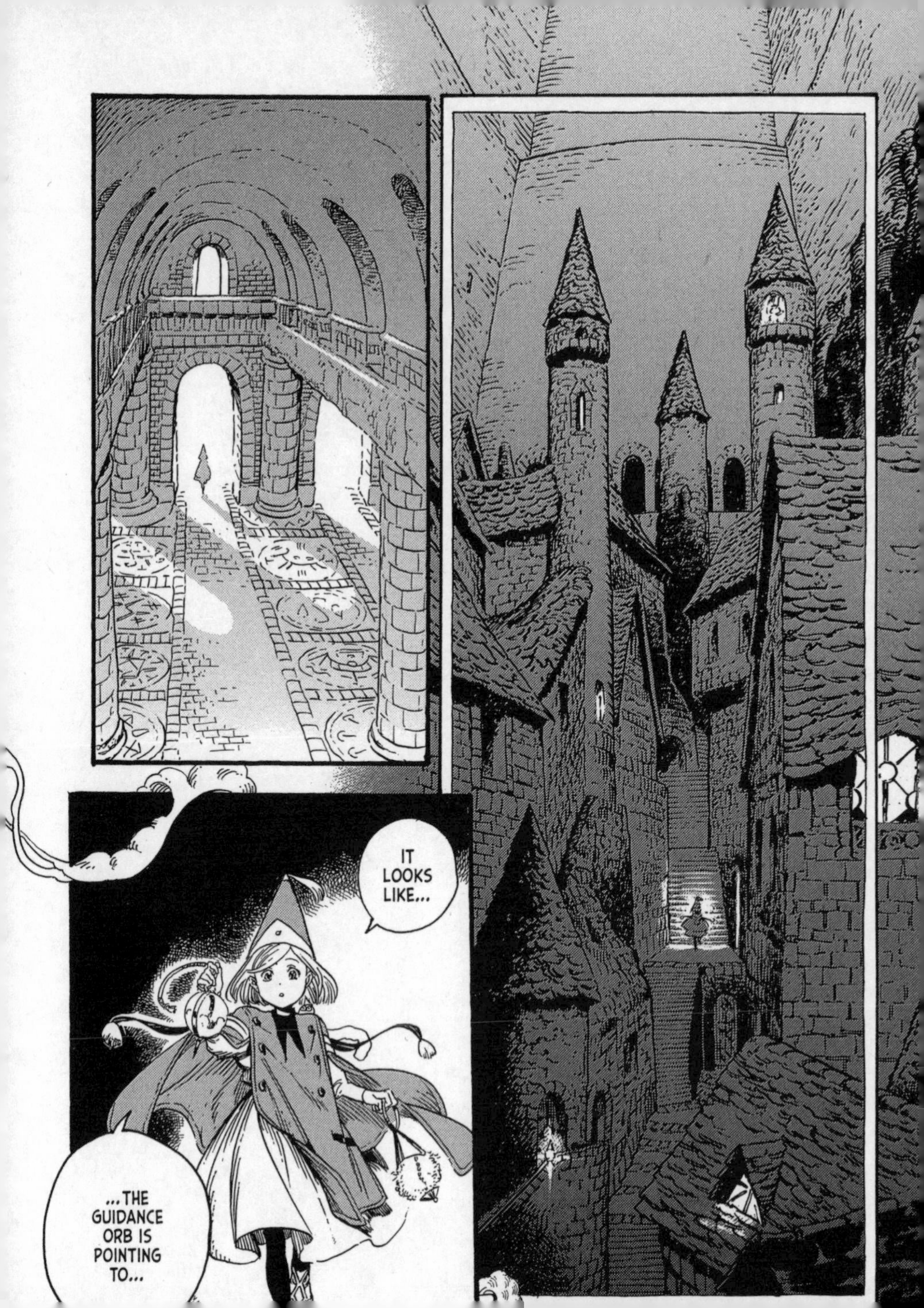
IT LOOKS LIKE...
...THE GUIDANCE ORB IS POINTING TO...

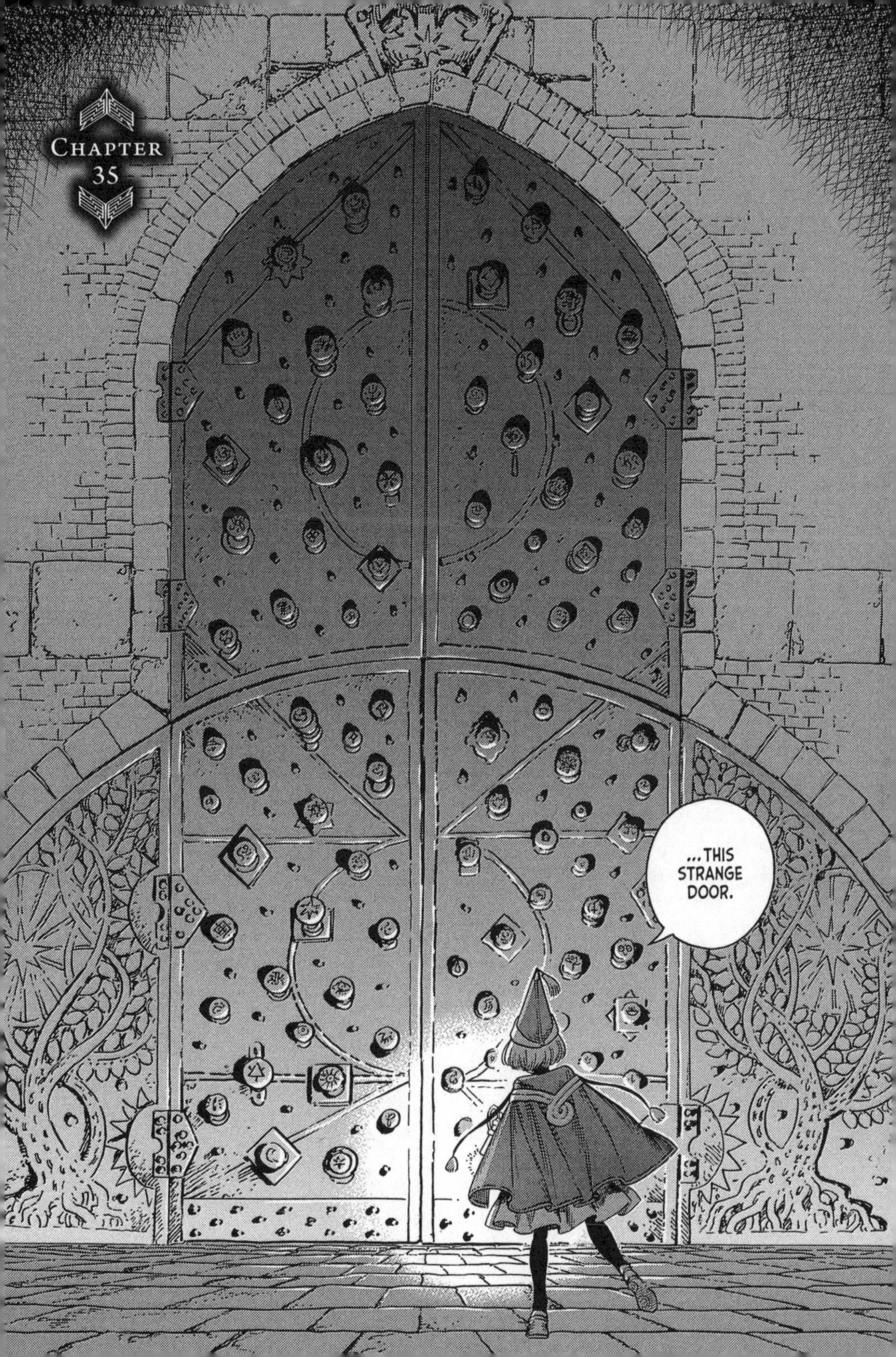

CHAPTER 35
...THIS STRANGE DOOR.

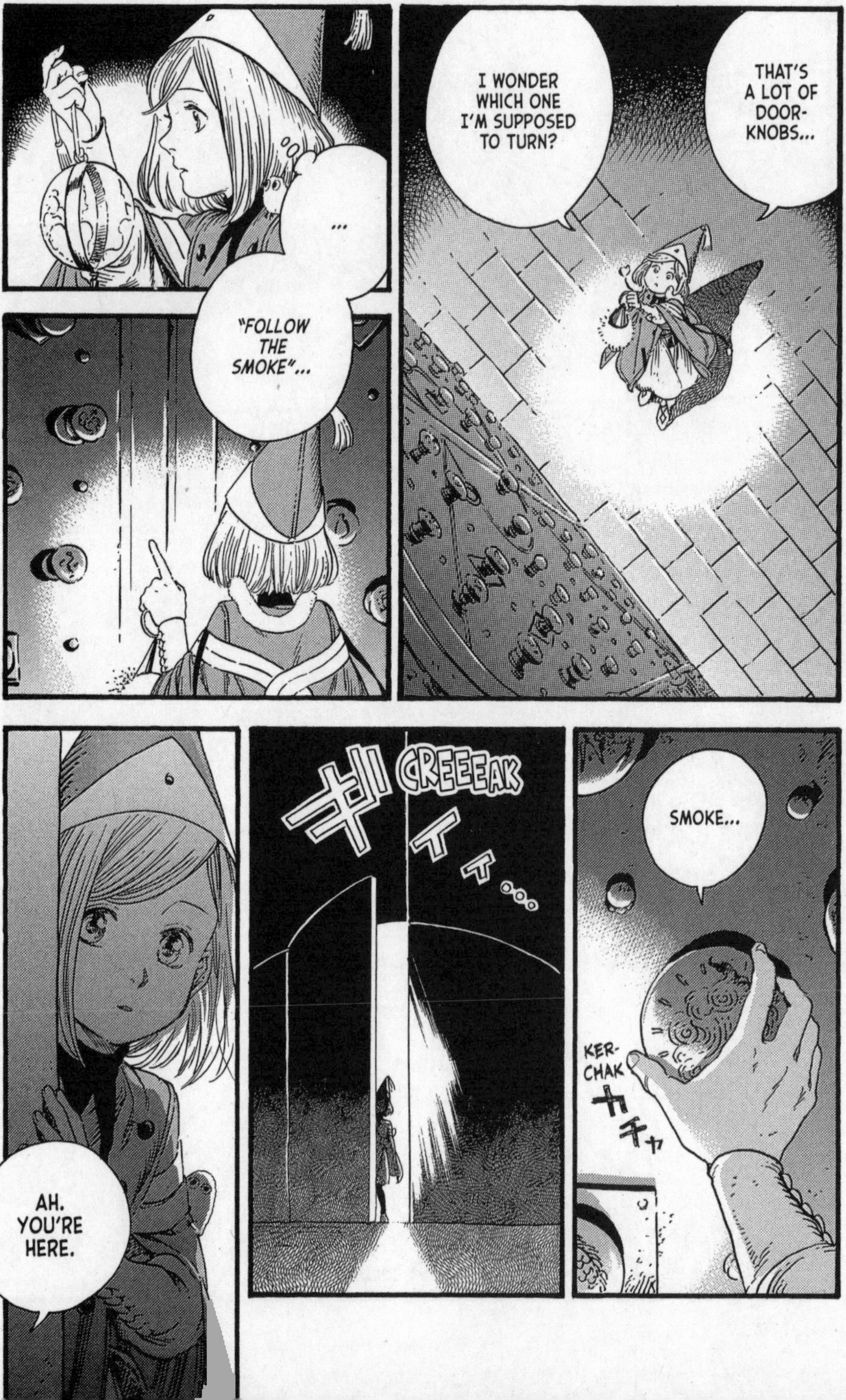

THAT'S A LOT OF DOOR-KNOBS...
I WONDER WHICH ONE I'M SUPPOSED TO TURN?
...
"FOLLOW THE SMOKE"...
SMOKE...
KER-CHAK
カチャ
CREEEAK
ギイィ...
AH. YOU'RE HERE.

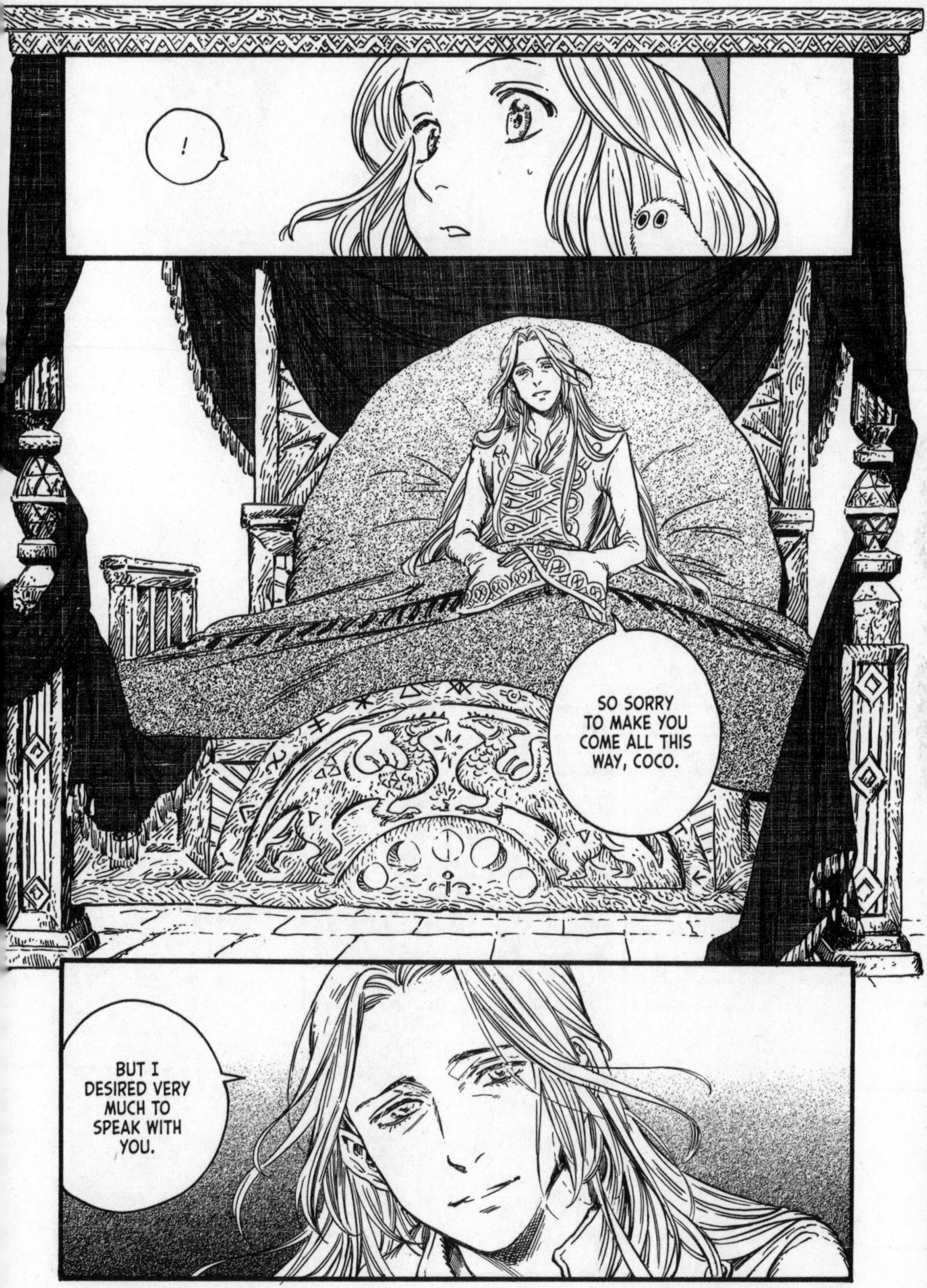
!
SO SORRY TO MAKE YOU COME ALL THIS WAY, COCO.
BUT I DESIRED VERY MUCH TO SPEAK WITH YOU.

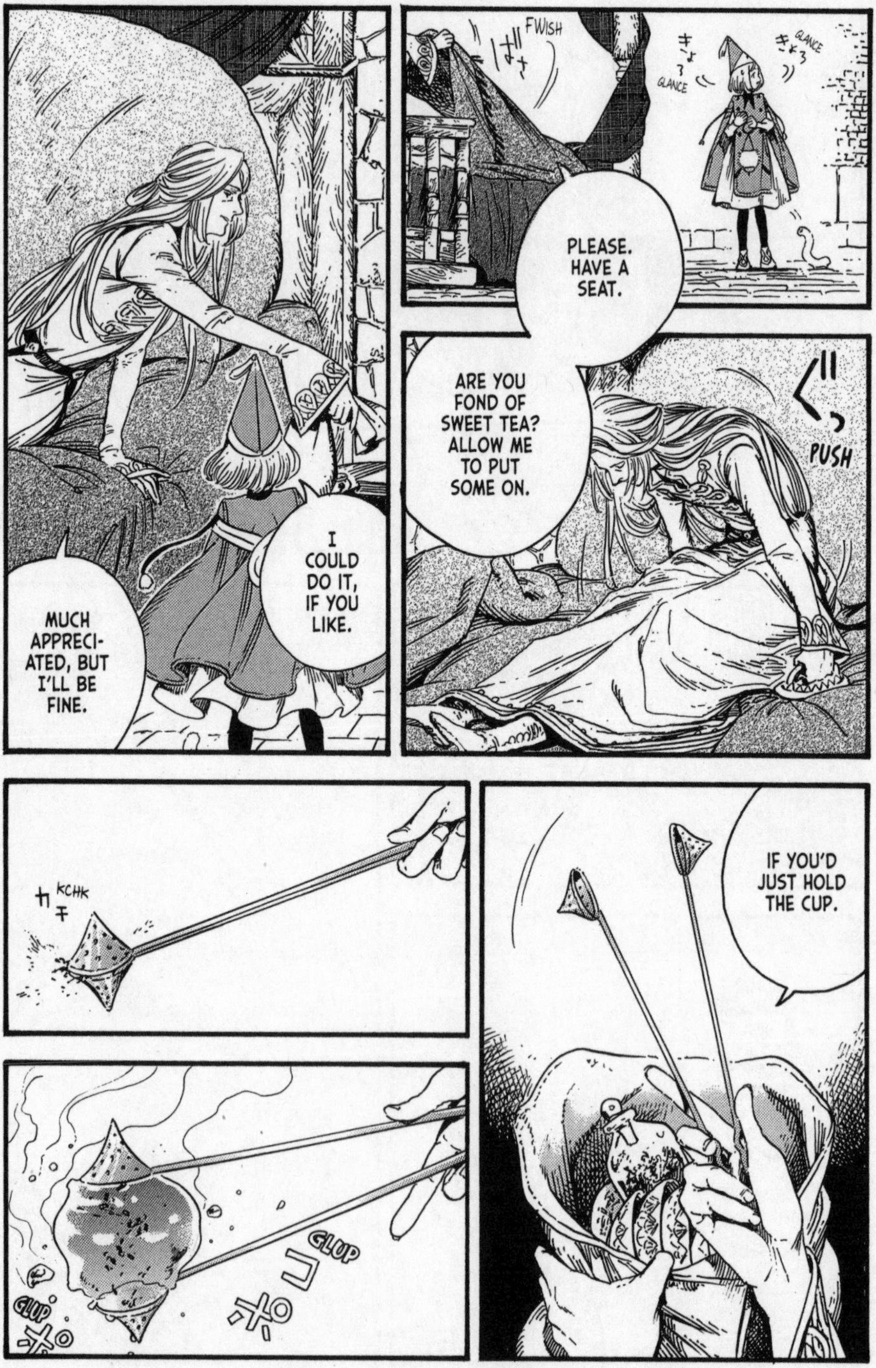
FWISH
ばさ
きょろ
GLANCE
きょろ
GLANCE
PLEASE. HAVE A SEAT.
ぐっ
PUSH
ARE YOU FOND OF SWEET TEA? ALLOW ME TO PUT SOME ON.
I COULD DO IT, IF YOU LIKE.
MUCH APPRECIATED, BUT I'LL BE FINE.
IF YOU'D JUST HOLD THE CUP.
カチ
KCHK
GLUP
GLUP

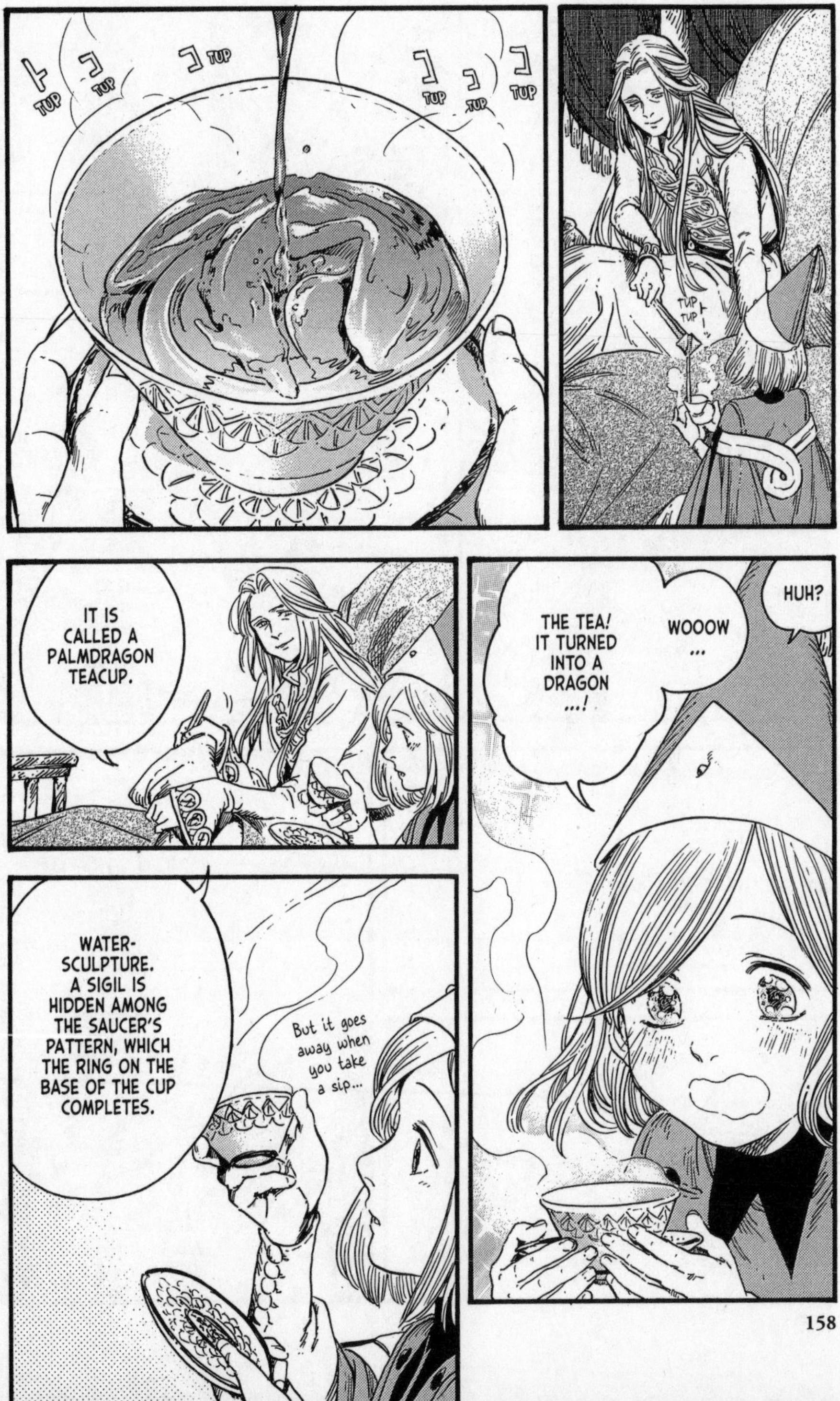

TUP TUP
TUP
TUP
TUP
TUP
TUP
TUP
HUH?
WOOOW ...
THE TEA! IT TURNED INTO A DRAGON ...!
IT IS CALLED A PALMDRAGON TEACUP.
WATER-SCULPTURE. A SIGIL IS HIDDEN AMONG THE SAUCER'S PATTERN, WHICH THE RING ON THE BASE OF THE CUP COMPLETES.
But it goes away when you take a sip...

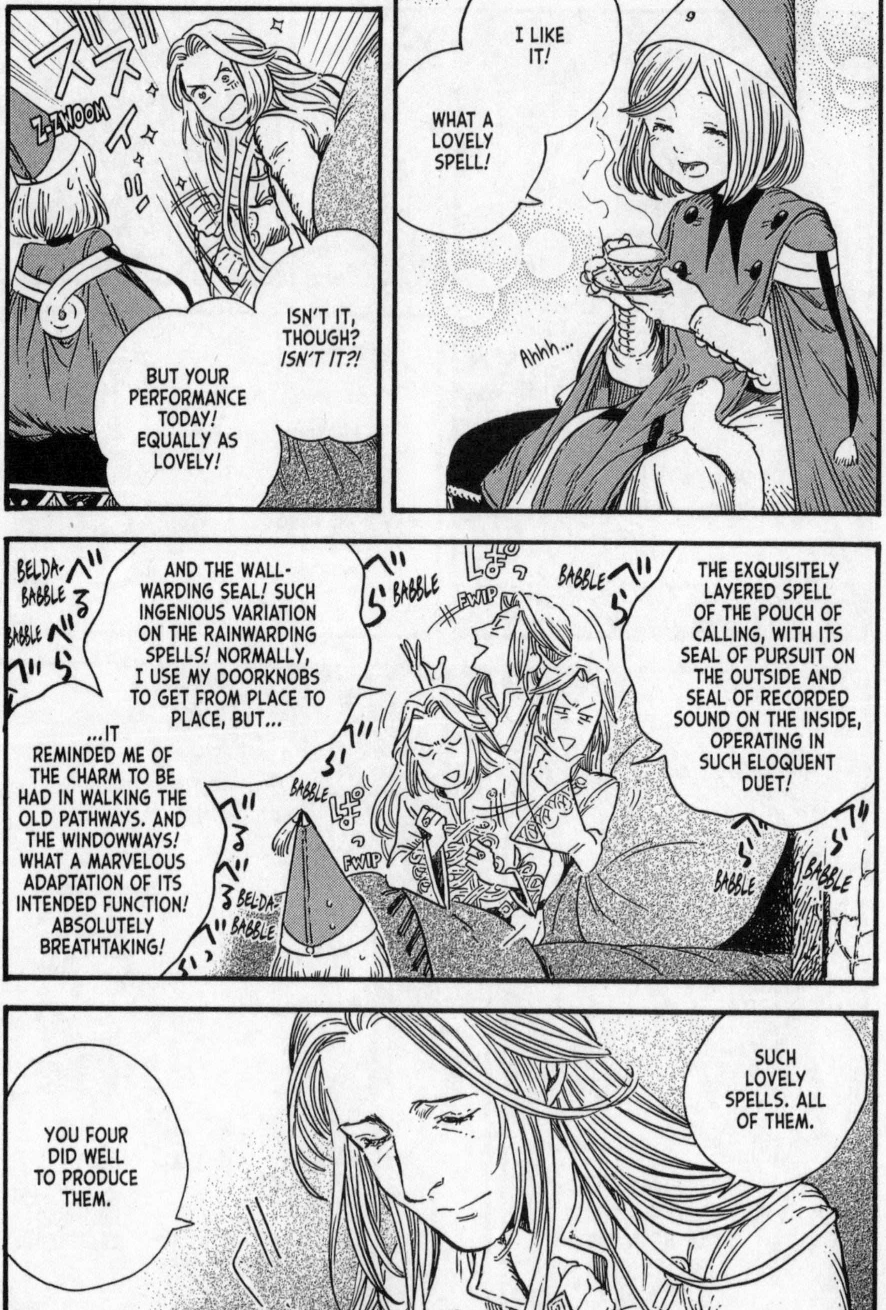
I LIKE IT!
WHAT A LOVELY SPELL!
Ahhh...
Z-ZWOOM
ISN'T IT, THOUGH? *ISN'T IT?!*
BUT YOUR PERFORMANCE TODAY! EQUALLY AS LOVELY!
THE EXQUISITELY LAYERED SPELL OF THE POUCH OF CALLING, WITH ITS SEAL OF PURSUIT ON THE OUTSIDE AND SEAL OF RECORDED SOUND ON THE INSIDE, OPERATING IN SUCH ELOQUENT DUET!
BABBLE
BABBLE
BABBLE
FWIP
BABBLE
AND THE WALL-WARDING SEAL! SUCH INGENIOUS VARIATION ON THE RAINWARDING SPELLS! NORMALLY, I USE MY DOORKNOBS TO GET FROM PLACE TO PLACE, BUT...
BABBLE
FWIP
...IT REMINDED ME OF THE CHARM TO BE HAD IN WALKING THE OLD PATHWAYS. AND THE WINDOWWAYS! WHAT A MARVELOUS ADAPTATION OF ITS INTENDED FUNCTION! ABSOLUTELY BREATHTAKING!
BELDA-BABBLE
BELDA-BABBLE
BABBLE
SUCH LOVELY SPELLS. ALL OF THEM.
YOU FOUR DID WELL TO PRODUCE THEM.
GWIP

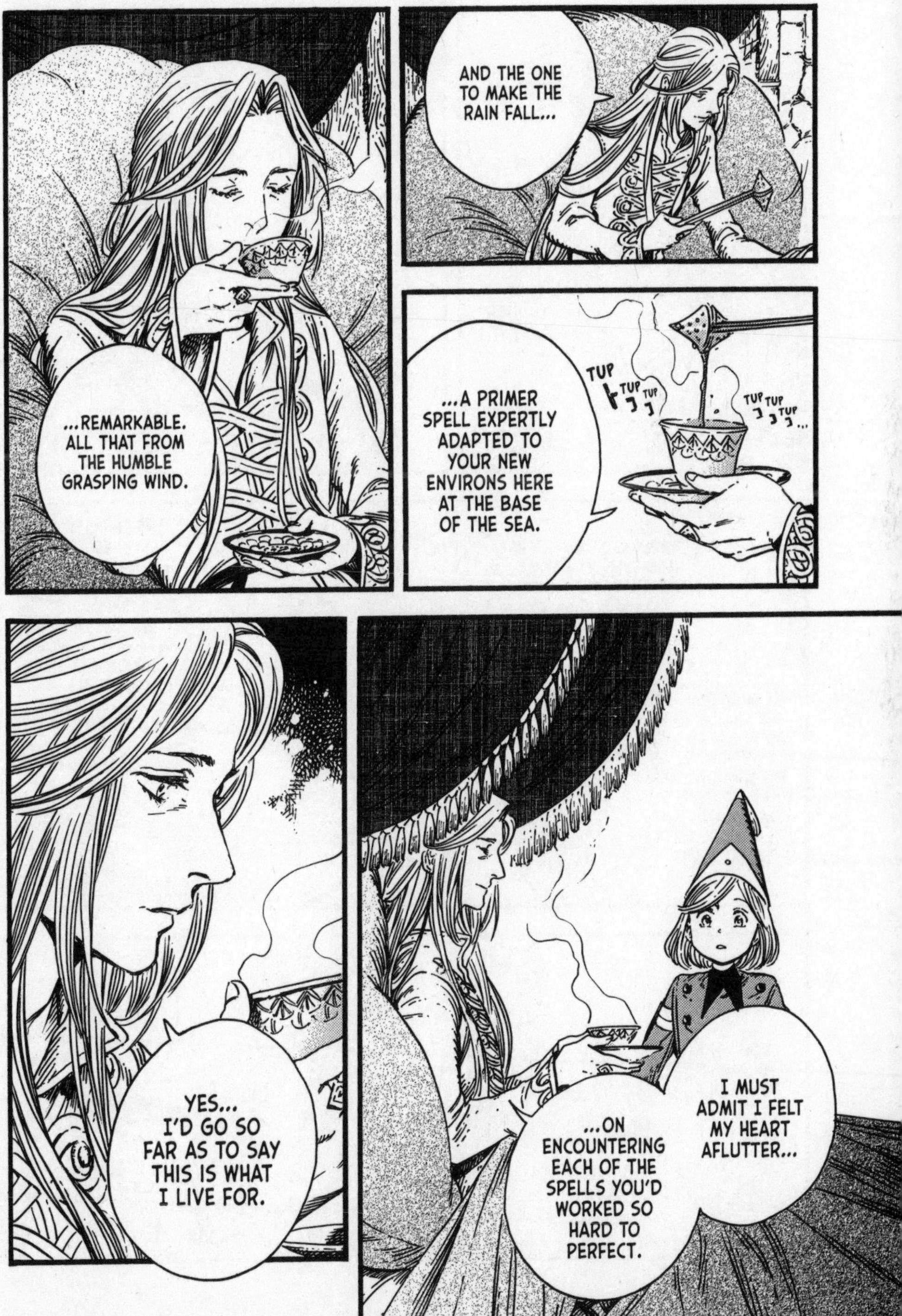

AND THE ONE TO MAKE THE RAIN FALL...
TUP TUP TUP TUP...
TUP TUP TUP
...A PRIMER SPELL EXPERTLY ADAPTED TO YOUR NEW ENVIRONS HERE AT THE BASE OF THE SEA.
...REMARKABLE. ALL THAT FROM THE HUMBLE GRASPING WIND.
I MUST ADMIT I FELT MY HEART AFLUTTER...
...ON ENCOUNTERING EACH OF THE SPELLS YOU'D WORKED SO HARD TO PERFECT.
YES... I'D GO SO FAR AS TO SAY THIS IS WHAT I LIVE FOR.

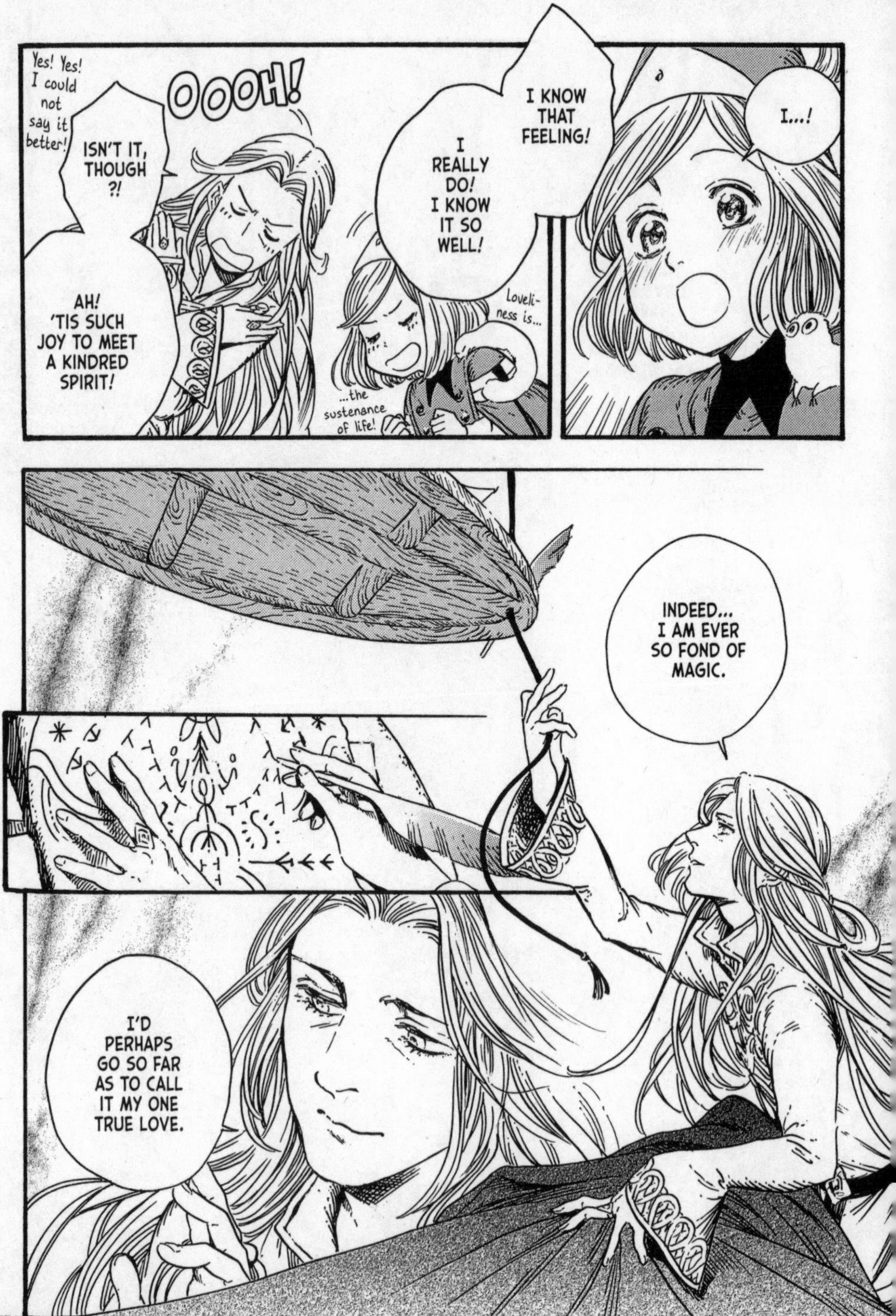
I...!
I KNOW THAT FEELING!
I REALLY DO! I KNOW IT SO WELL!
Loveliness is...
...the sustenance of life!
OOOH!
ISN'T IT, THOUGH?!
Yes! Yes! I could not say it better!
AH! 'TIS SUCH JOY TO MEET A KINDRED SPIRIT!
INDEED... I AM EVER SO FOND OF MAGIC.
I'D PERHAPS GO SO FAR AS TO CALL IT MY ONE TRUE LOVE.

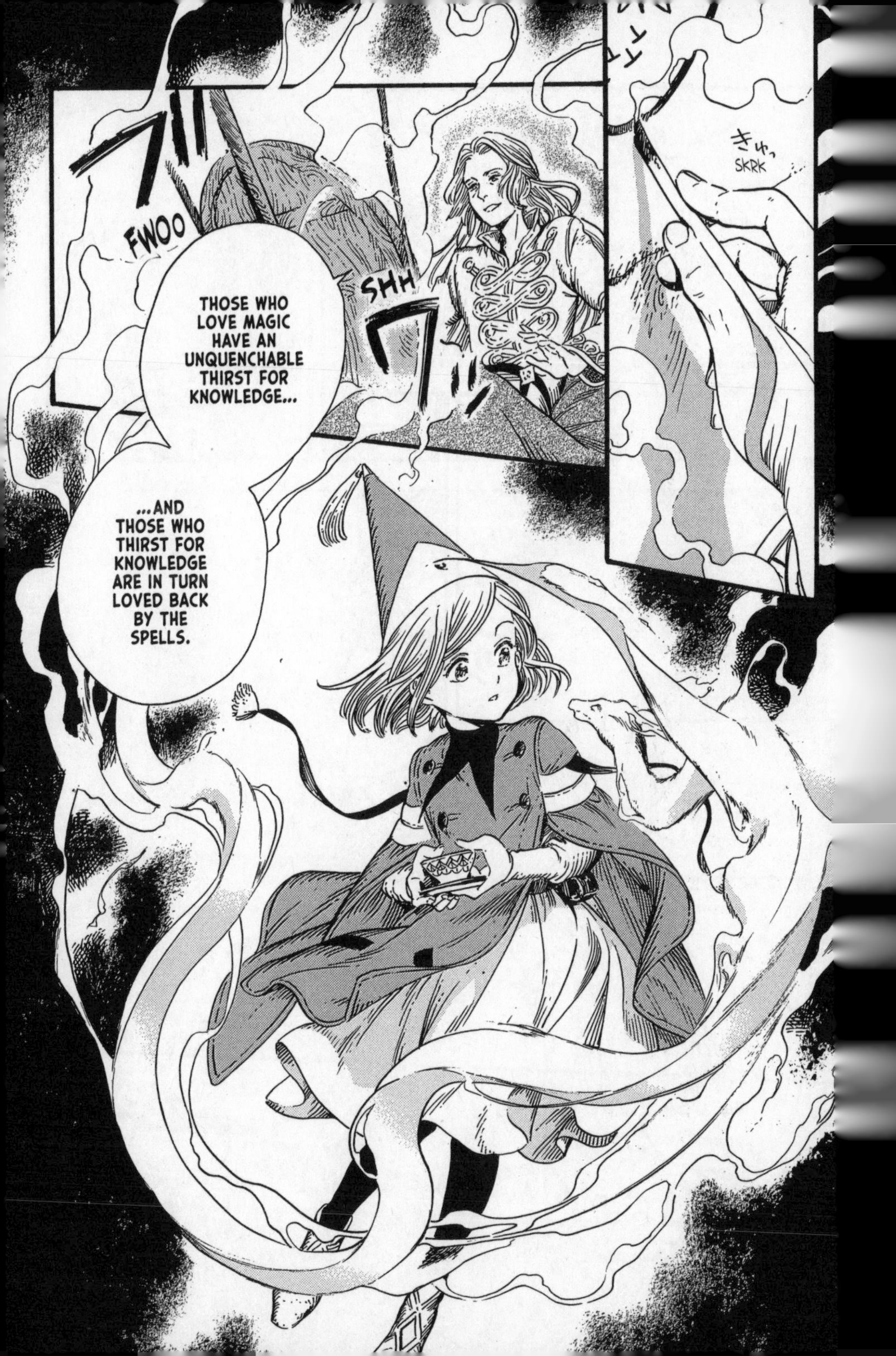
きゅっ
SKRK
FWOO
SHH
THOSE WHO LOVE MAGIC HAVE AN UNQUENCHABLE THIRST FOR KNOWLEDGE...
...AND THOSE WHO THIRST FOR KNOWLEDGE ARE IN TURN LOVED BACK BY THE SPELLS.

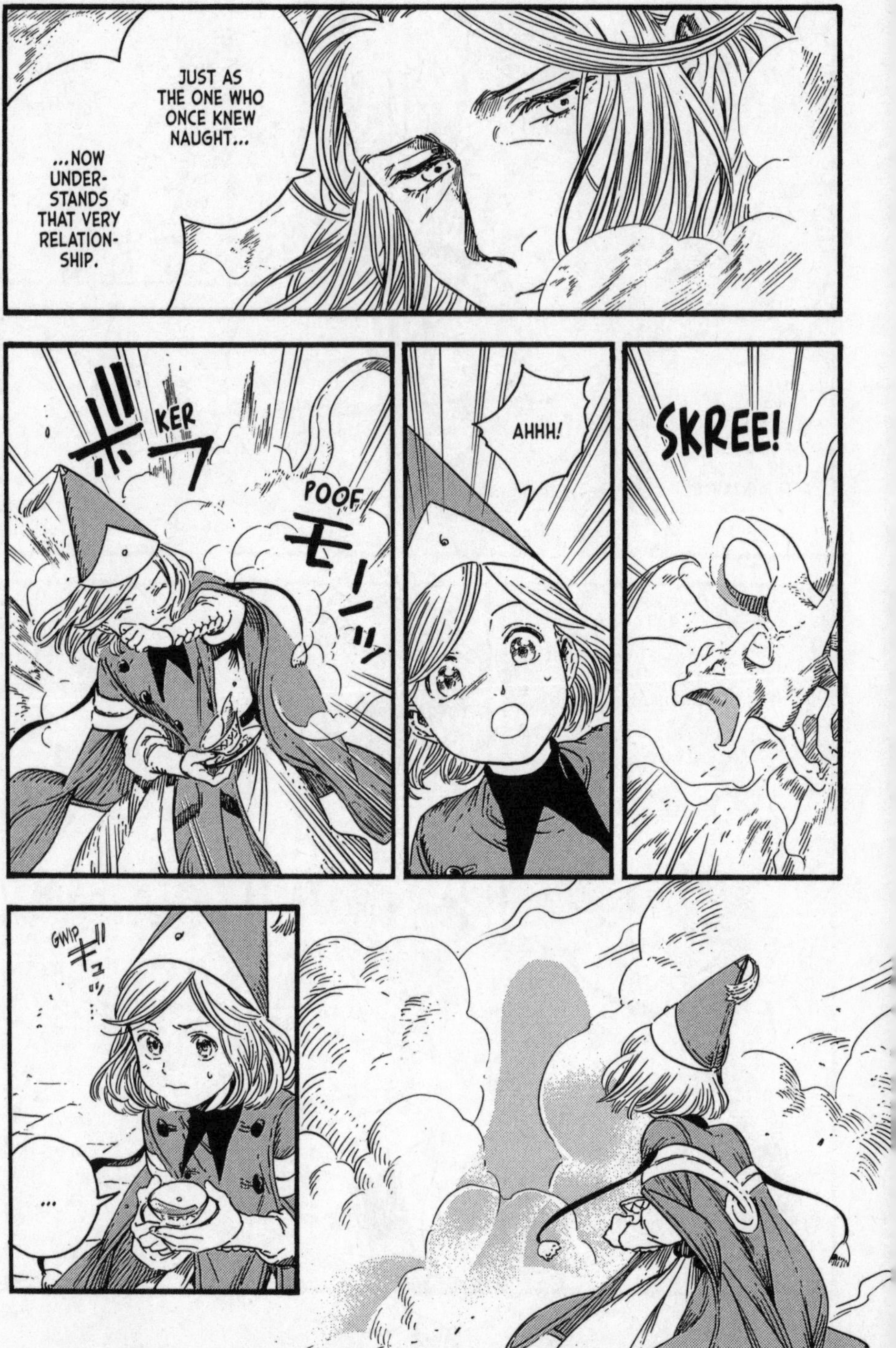
JUST AS THE ONE WHO ONCE KNEW NAUGHT...
...NOW UNDERSTANDS THAT VERY RELATIONSHIP.
SKREE!
AHHH!
KER
POOF
GWIP
...

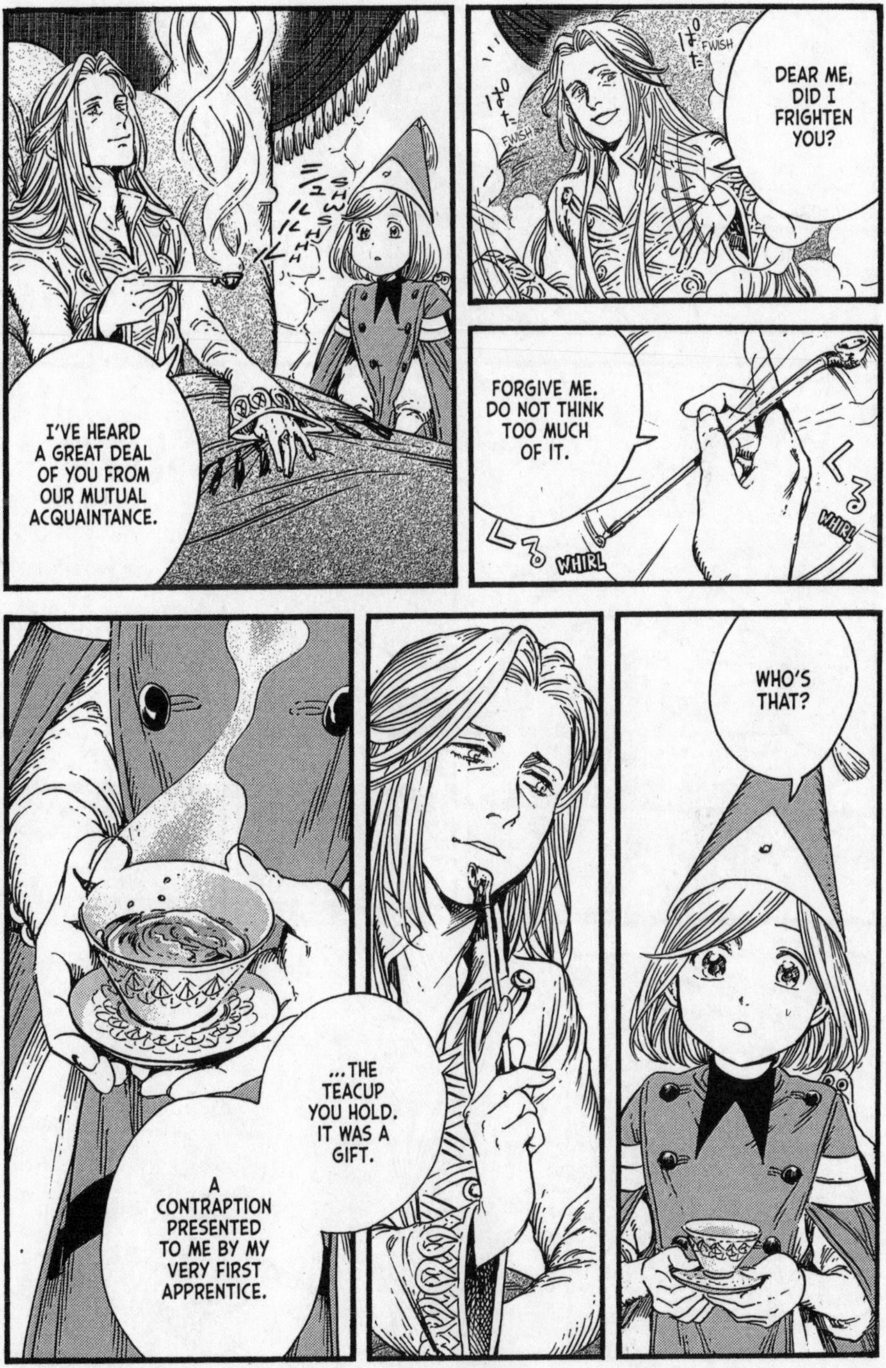
ぱた FWISH
ぱた FWISH
DEAR ME, DID I FRIGHTEN YOU?
FORGIVE ME. DO NOT THINK TOO MUCH OF IT.
くる WHIRL
くる WHIRL
シュルル SHWISH
シュルル SHWISH
I'VE HEARD A GREAT DEAL OF YOU FROM OUR MUTUAL ACQUAINTANCE.
WHO'S THAT?
...THE TEACUP YOU HOLD. IT WAS A GIFT.
A CONTRAPTION PRESENTED TO ME BY MY VERY FIRST APPRENTICE.

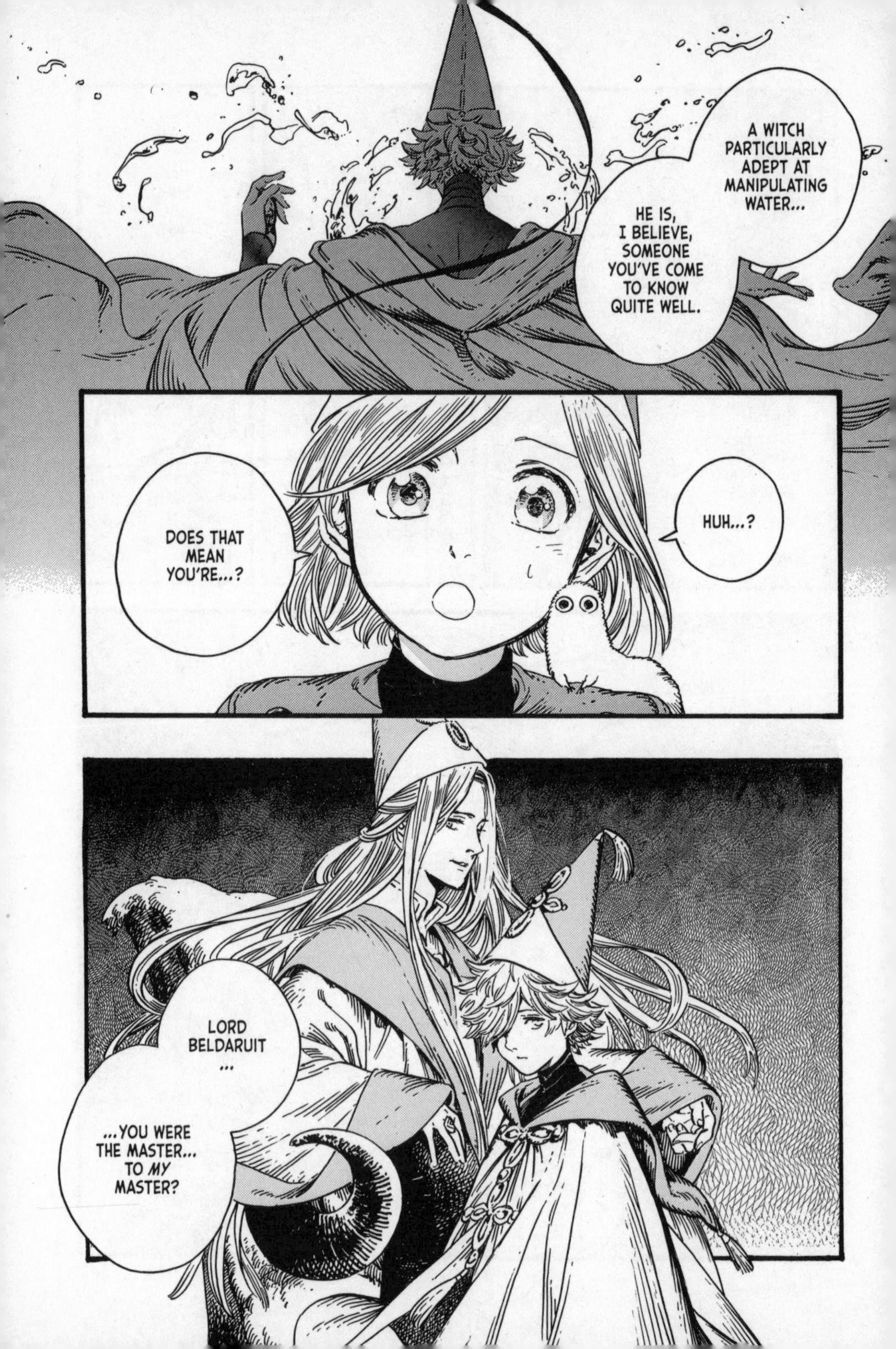
A WITCH PARTICULARLY ADEPT AT MANIPULATING WATER...
HE IS, I BELIEVE, SOMEONE YOU'VE COME TO KNOW QUITE WELL.
HUH...?
DOES THAT MEAN YOU'RE...?
LORD BELDARUIT ...
...YOU WERE THE MASTER... TO *MY* MASTER?

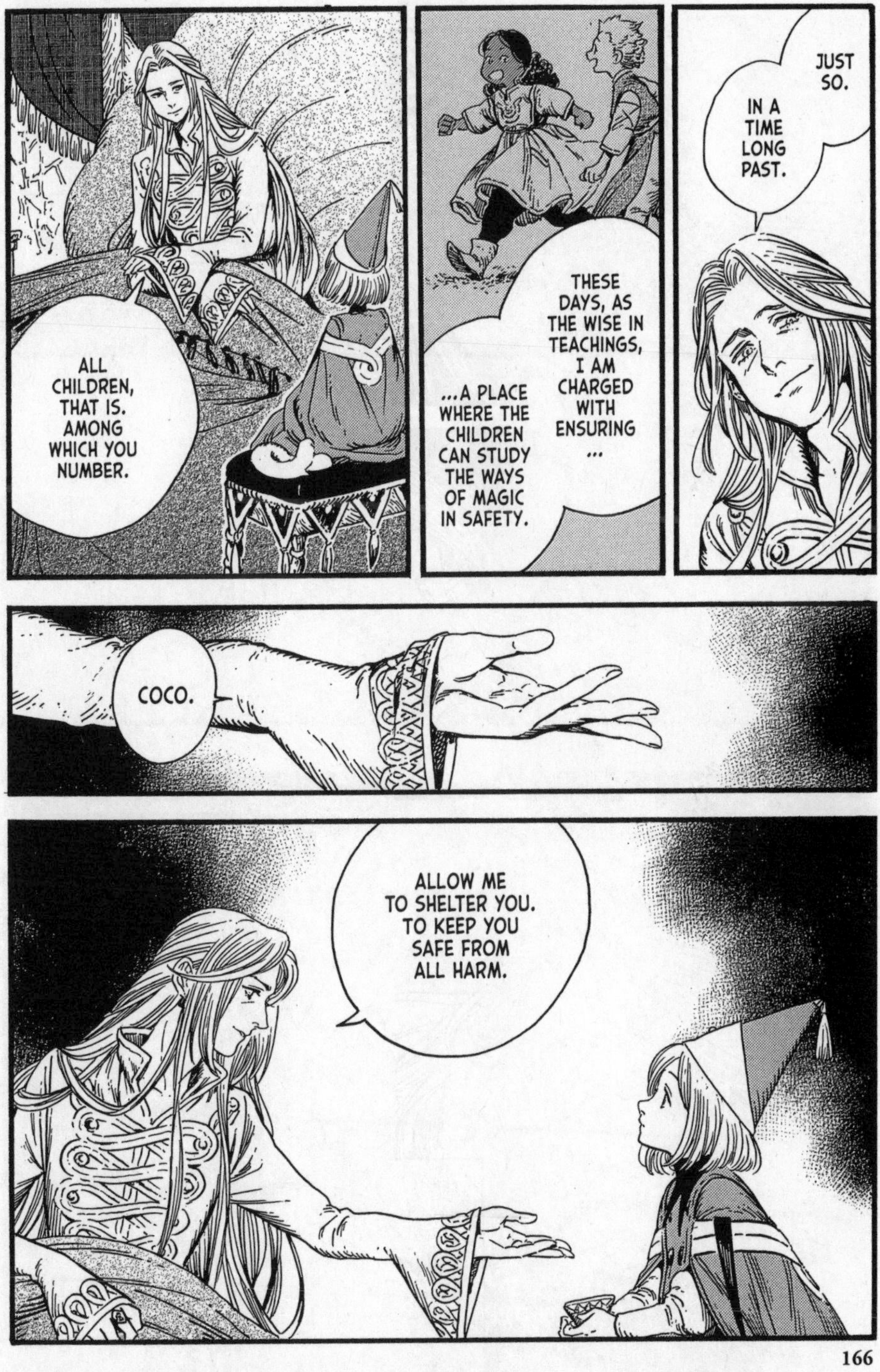
JUST SO.
IN A TIME LONG PAST.
THESE DAYS, AS THE WISE IN TEACHINGS, I AM CHARGED WITH ENSURING ...
...A PLACE WHERE THE CHILDREN CAN STUDY THE WAYS OF MAGIC IN SAFETY.
ALL CHILDREN, THAT IS. AMONG WHICH YOU NUMBER.
COCO.
ALLOW ME TO SHELTER YOU. TO KEEP YOU SAFE FROM ALL HARM.

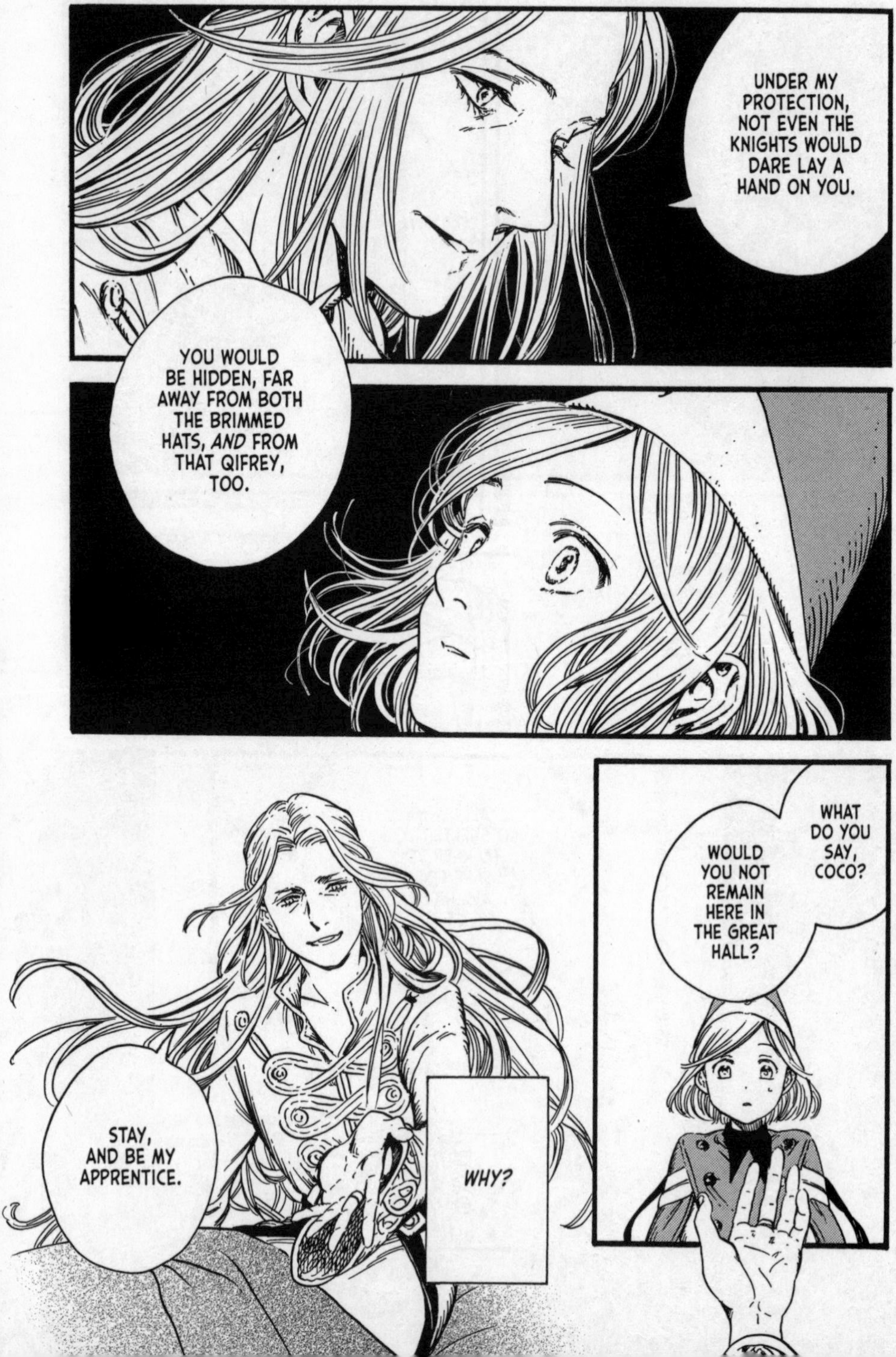
UNDER MY PROTECTION, NOT EVEN THE KNIGHTS WOULD DARE LAY A HAND ON YOU.
YOU WOULD BE HIDDEN, FAR AWAY FROM BOTH THE BRIMMED HATS, *AND* FROM THAT QIFREY, TOO.
WHAT DO YOU SAY, COCO?
WOULD YOU NOT REMAIN HERE IN THE GREAT HALL?
WHY?
STAY, AND BE MY APPRENTICE.

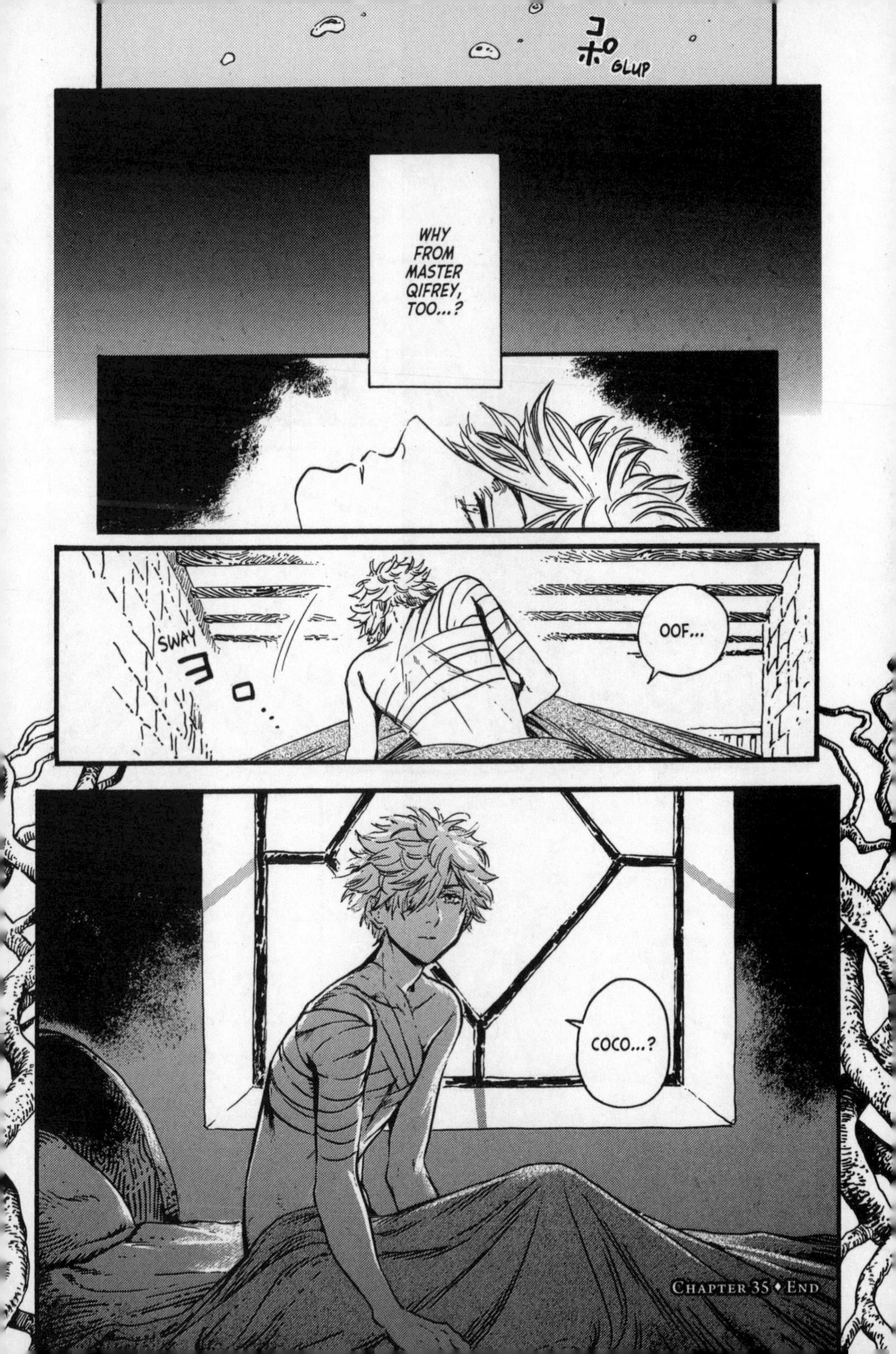
コポ GLUP
WHY FROM MASTER QIFREY, TOO...?
OOF...
SWAY ヨロ...
COCO...?
CHAPTER 35 • END

THE TOOLS OF WITCH HAT

PART 1

TOOLS ENCHANTED WITH MAGIC ARE KNOWN IN THIS WORLD AS CONTRAPTIONS. SUCH ITEMS ARE PRIZED THROUGHOUT THE WORLD, AS THEY CAN BE USED EVEN BY THOSE WHO DO NOT PRACTICE MAGIC. THEY CAN ONLY BE CREATED BY WITCHES AND THEREFORE COMMAND HIGH PRICES. THE CRAFTING OF CONTRAPTIONS BEFORE ONE HAS TAKEN THE TEST AND BECOME AN APPRENTICE IS FORBIDDEN. BELOW IS A SELECTION OF THE VARIOUS CONTRAPTIONS THAT HAVE APPEARED IN THE STORY THUS FAR, AS WELL AS SOME OF THE TOOLS AND COMPONENTS USED TO CAST MAGIC.

SYLPH SHOES

FIRST DESCRIBED IN CHAPTER 4

A CONTRAPTION THAT ENABLES ITS WEARER TO FLOAT. ONE HALF OF A SEAL IS DRAWN ON EACH THE RIGHT AND LEFT SOLE OF A PAIR OF FOOTWEAR. WHEN BROUGHT TOGETHER, THE SEAL ACTIVATES. EXTENDED USE LEADS TO FATIGUED AND QUIVERING THIGH MUSCLES.

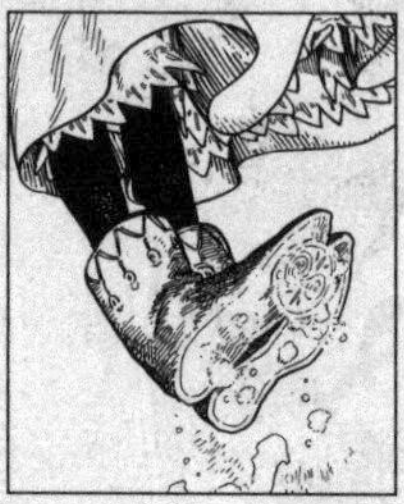

TOILET OF THE VOID

FIRST APPEARS IN CHAPTER 3

A CONTRAPTION THAT LINKS TO OUTER SPACE. DESIGNED SUCH THAT WASTE SIMPLY DISAPPEARS INTO THE VOID. DEVELOPED BY A WITCH WHO MYSTERIOUSLY DISAPPEARED THE VERY NIGHT AFTER COMPLETING THIS INVENTION.

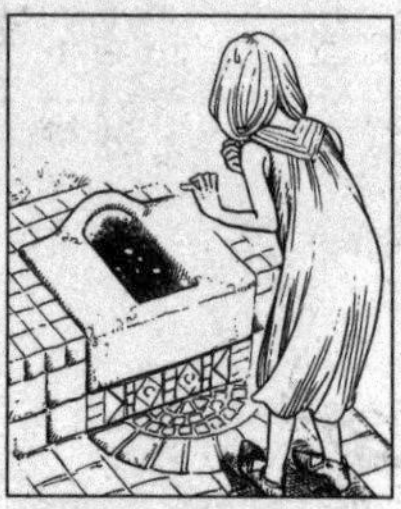

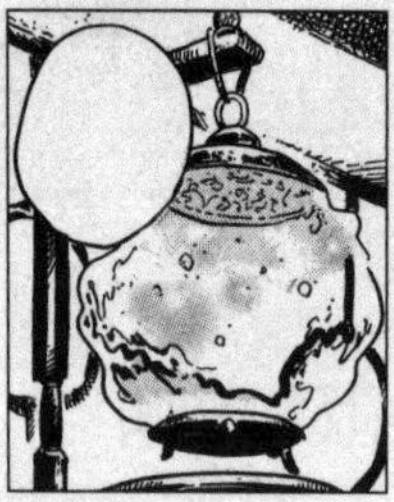

VAPOR BUBBLE

FIRST APPEARS IN CHAPTER 2

A CONTRAPTION THAT COLLECTS MOISTURE FROM THE AIR INTO WATER THAT CAN BE CONVENIENTLY POURED. THE BOTTOM PLATE FORMS A SPOUT WHEN TIPPED. USEFUL AS A SOURCE OF DRINKING WATER.

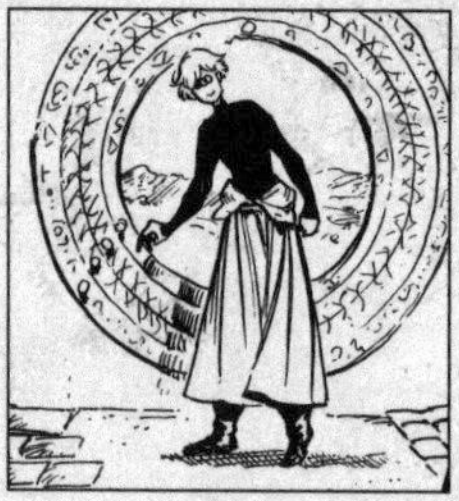

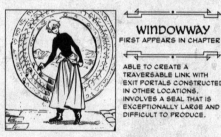

WINDOWWAY

FIRST APPEARS IN CHAPTER 2

ABLE TO CREATE A TRAVERSABLE LINK WITH EXIT PORTALS CONSTRUCTED IN OTHER LOCATIONS. INVOLVES A SEAL THAT IS EXCEPTIONALLY LARGE AND DIFFICULT TO PRODUCE.

COMPONENT PESTLE

FIRST APPEARS IN CHAPTER 3

USED TO GRIND INGREDIENTS TO MIX WITH CONJURING INK IN ORDER TO PERFORM PARTICULAR SPELLS. USES AN EARTHENWARE CONSTRUCTION.

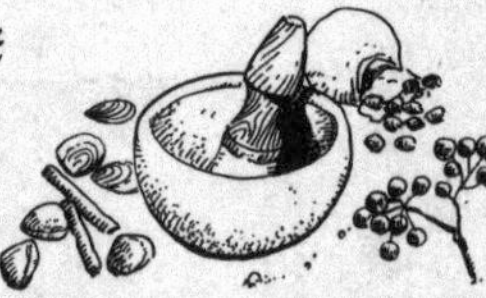

CONJURING INK

FIRST DESCRIBED IN CHAPTER 3

INK MADE FROM A SPECIAL LIQUID CALLED WOODCRUOR, WHICH IS HARVESTED FROM THE SILVERWOOD TREE. ONLY SEALS DRAWN IN THIS SUBSTANCE WILL ACTIVATE.

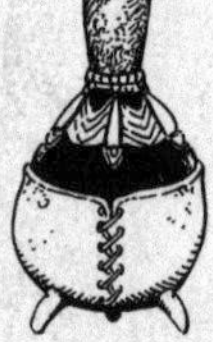

WOODCRUOR WAND

FIRST APPEARS IN CHAPTER 3

A ROD OF HARDENED WOODCRUOR. USEFUL FOR INSCRIBING SEALS UPON SURFACES SUCH AS WOOD OR STONE, BUT ITS MARKINGS RUB AWAY EASILY, AND IT IS THUS SELDOM EMPLOYED.

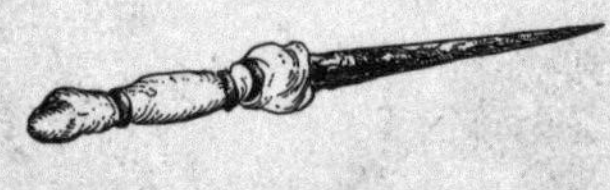

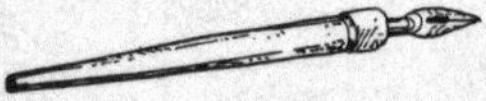

INK WAND

FIRST DESCRIBED IN CHAPTER 3

A WAND USED FOR DRAWING, CONSTRUCTED OF A WOODEN SHAFT FITTED WITH A METAL TIP. THE SHAFT IS COMMONLY WHITTLED AND DECORATED FOR APPEARANCE AND EASE OF USE.

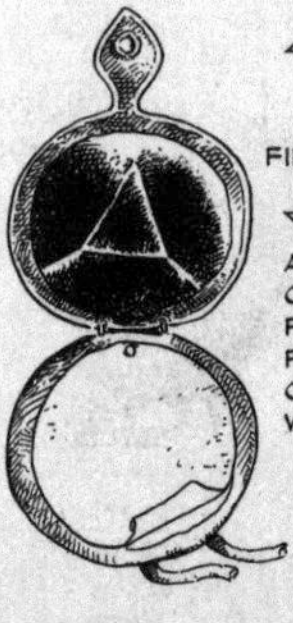

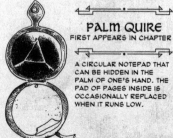

PALM QUIRE

FIRST APPEARS IN CHAPTER 3

A CIRCULAR NOTEPAD THAT CAN BE HIDDEN IN THE PALM OF ONE'S HAND. THE PAD OF PAGES INSIDE IS OCCASIONALLY REPLACED WHEN IT RUNS LOW.

Bonus Chapter
Eating

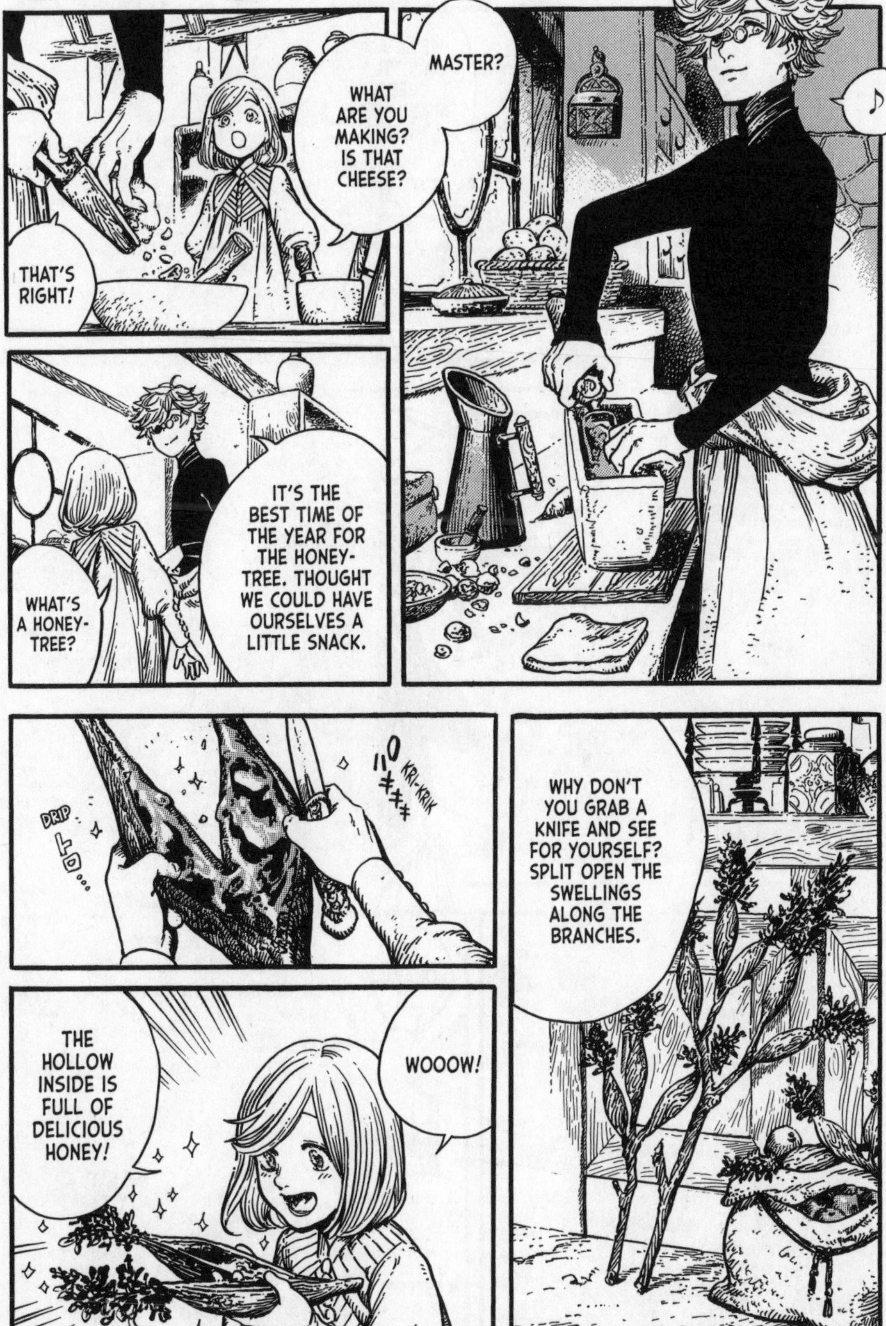
♪
MASTER?
WHAT ARE YOU MAKING? IS THAT CHEESE?
THAT'S RIGHT!
IT'S THE BEST TIME OF THE YEAR FOR THE HONEY-TREE. THOUGHT WE COULD HAVE OURSELVES A LITTLE SNACK.
WHAT'S A HONEY-TREE?
WHY DON'T YOU GRAB A KNIFE AND SEE FOR YOURSELF? SPLIT OPEN THE SWELLINGS ALONG THE BRANCHES.
KRI-KRIK
DRIP
WOOOW!
THE HOLLOW INSIDE IS FULL OF DELICIOUS HONEY!

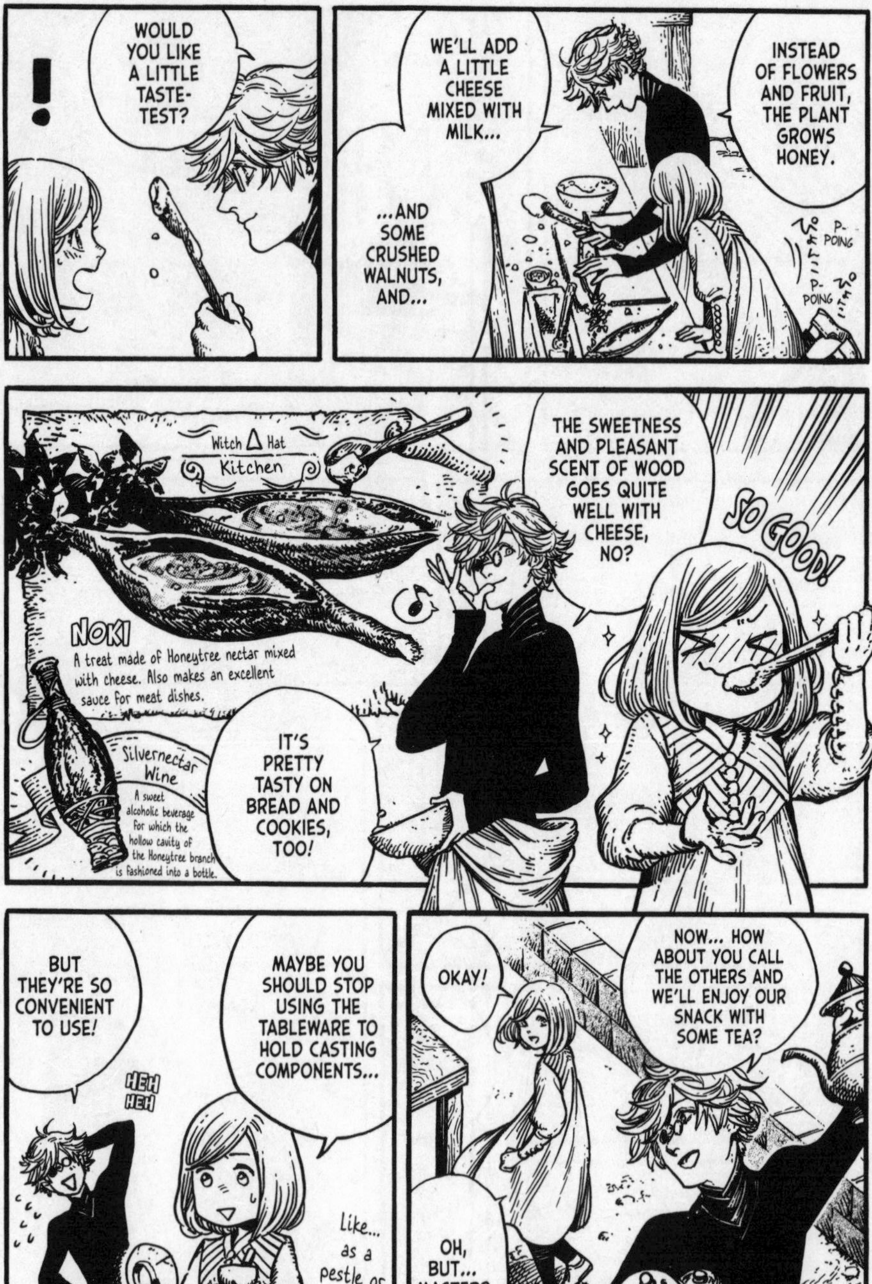
INSTEAD OF FLOWERS AND FRUIT, THE PLANT GROWS HONEY.
P-POING
P-POING
WE'LL ADD A LITTLE CHEESE MIXED WITH MILK...
...AND SOME CRUSHED WALNUTS, AND...
!
WOULD YOU LIKE A LITTLE TASTE-TEST?
SO GOOD!
THE SWEETNESS AND PLEASANT SCENT OF WOOD GOES QUITE WELL WITH CHEESE, NO?
Witch Hat Kitchen
NOKI
A treat made of Honeytree nectar mixed with cheese. Also makes an excellent sauce for meat dishes.
IT'S PRETTY TASTY ON BREAD AND COOKIES, TOO!
Silvernectar Wine
A sweet alcoholic beverage for which the hollow cavity of the Honeytree branch is fashioned into a bottle.
NOW... HOW ABOUT YOU CALL THE OTHERS AND WE'LL ENJOY OUR SNACK WITH SOME TEA?
OKAY!
OH, BUT... MASTER?
MAYBE YOU SHOULD STOP USING THE TABLEWARE TO HOLD CASTING COMPONENTS...
BUT THEY'RE SO CONVENIENT TO USE!
HEH HEH
Like... as a pestle or an ink dish...

Bonus Chapter
Sleeping

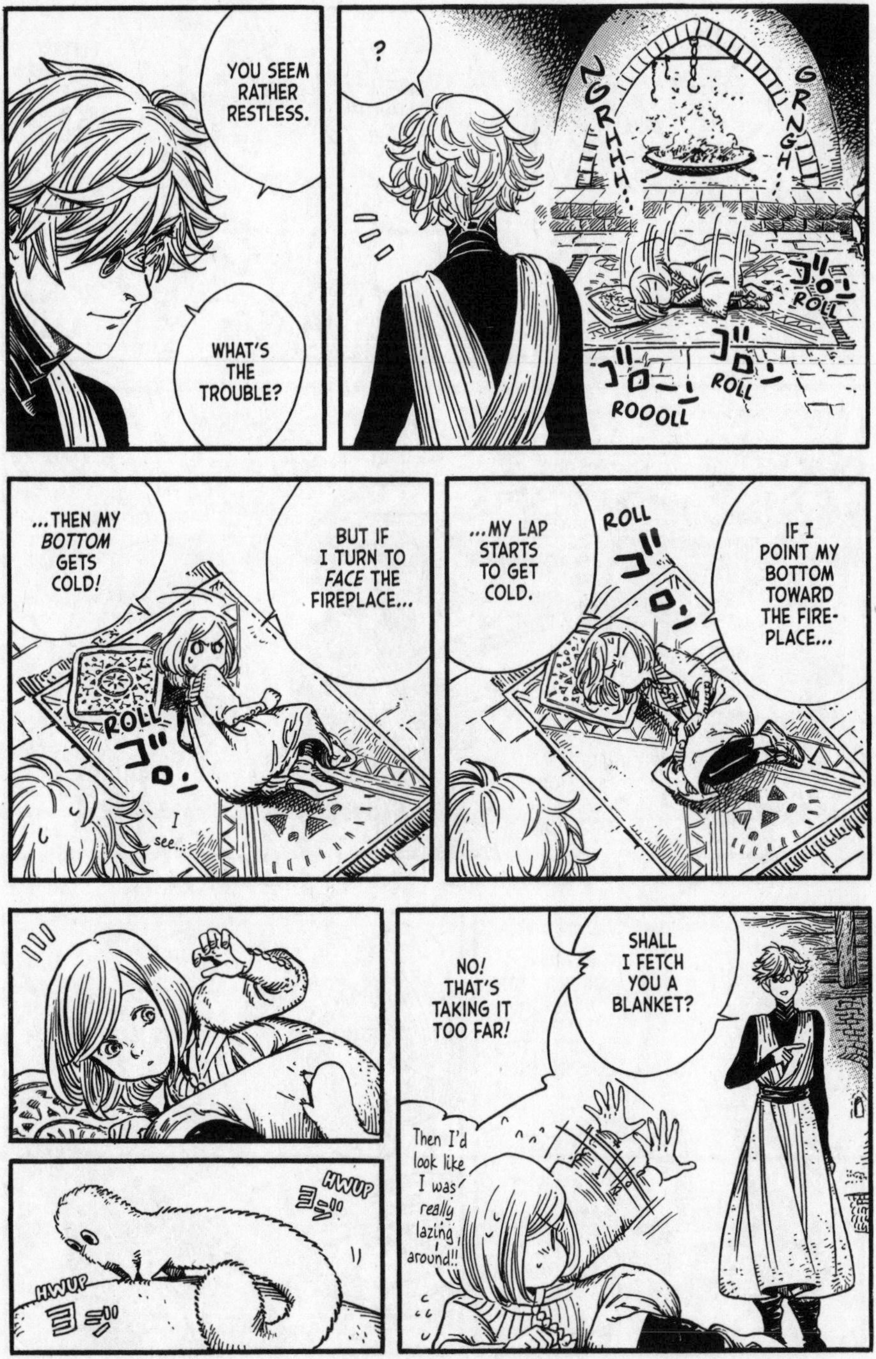
?
NGRHHH...
GRNGH...
ROLL
ROLL
ROOOLL
YOU SEEM RATHER RESTLESS.
WHAT'S THE TROUBLE?
IF I POINT MY BOTTOM TOWARD THE FIRE-PLACE...
...MY LAP STARTS TO GET COLD.
ROLL
BUT IF I TURN TO *FACE* THE FIREPLACE...
...THEN MY *BOTTOM* GETS COLD!
ROLL
I see...
SHALL I FETCH YOU A BLANKET?
NO! THAT'S TAKING IT TOO FAR!
Then I'd look like I was really lazing around!!
HWUP
HWUP

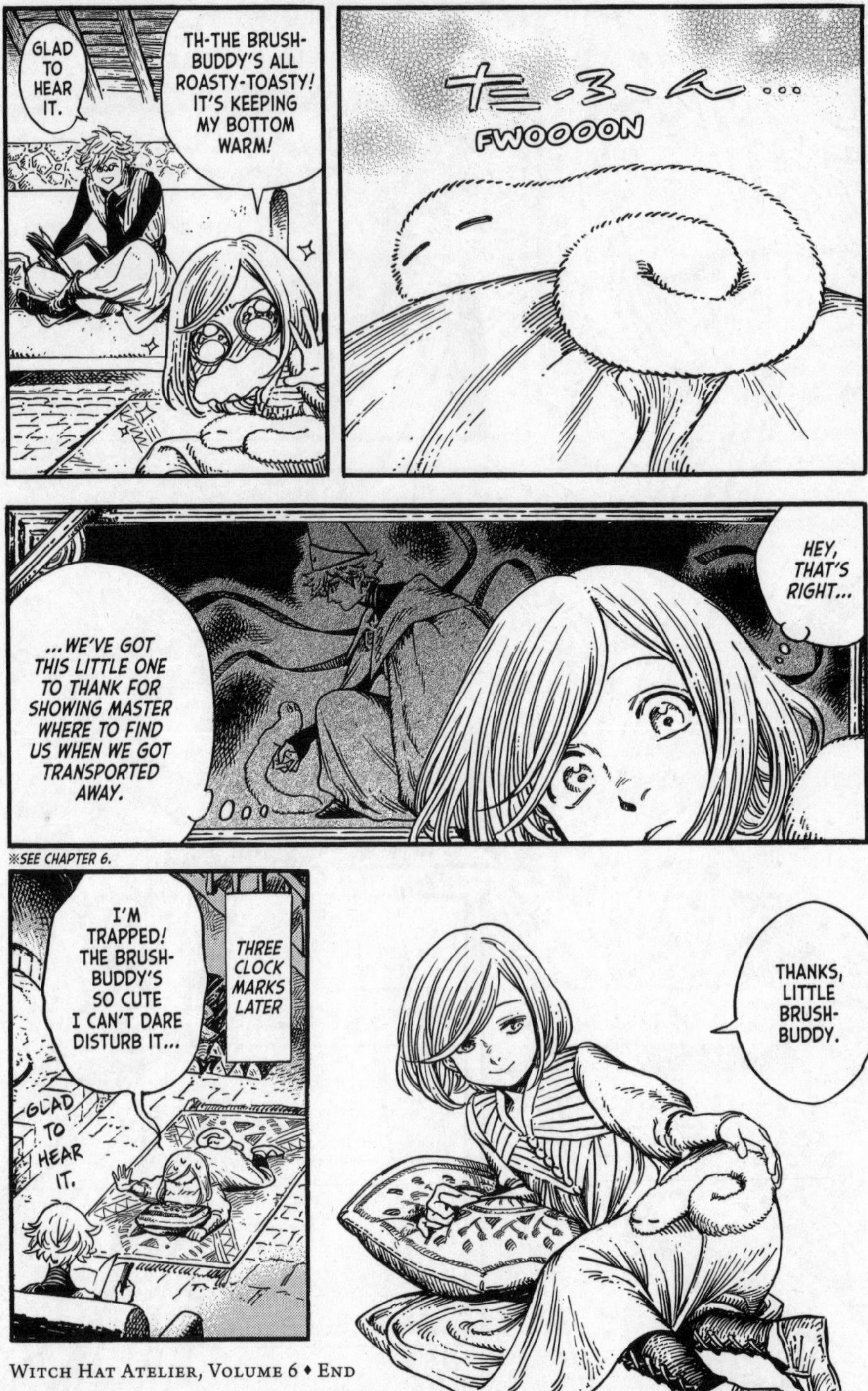
FWOOOOON
TH-THE BRUSH-BUDDY'S ALL ROASTY-TOASTY! IT'S KEEPING MY BOTTOM WARM!
GLAD TO HEAR IT.
HEY, THAT'S RIGHT...
...WE'VE GOT THIS LITTLE ONE TO THANK FOR SHOWING MASTER WHERE TO FIND US WHEN WE GOT TRANSPORTED AWAY.
※SEE CHAPTER 6.
THANKS, LITTLE BRUSH-BUDDY.
THREE CLOCK MARKS LATER
I'M TRAPPED! THE BRUSH-BUDDY'S SO CUTE I CAN'T DARE DISTURB IT...
GLAD TO HEAR IT.

Witch Hat Atelier, Volume 6 ♦ End

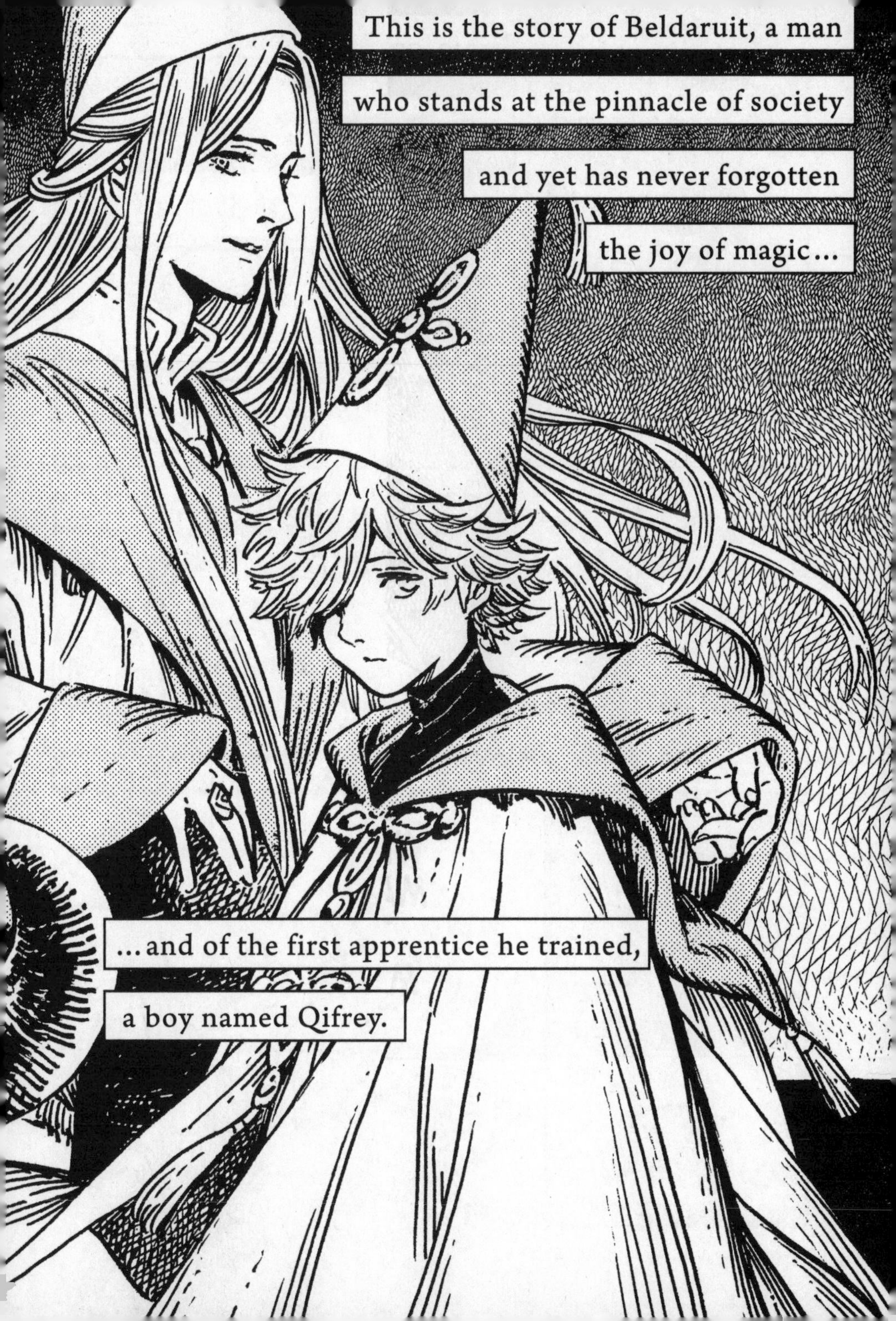
This is the story of Beldaruit, a man
who stands at the pinnacle of society
and yet has never forgotten
the joy of magic...
...and of the first apprentice he trained,
a boy named Qifrey.

What could have caused

these two who love magic so much...

...to grow so distant?

A TRAGIC TALE FINALLY COMES TO LIGHT...

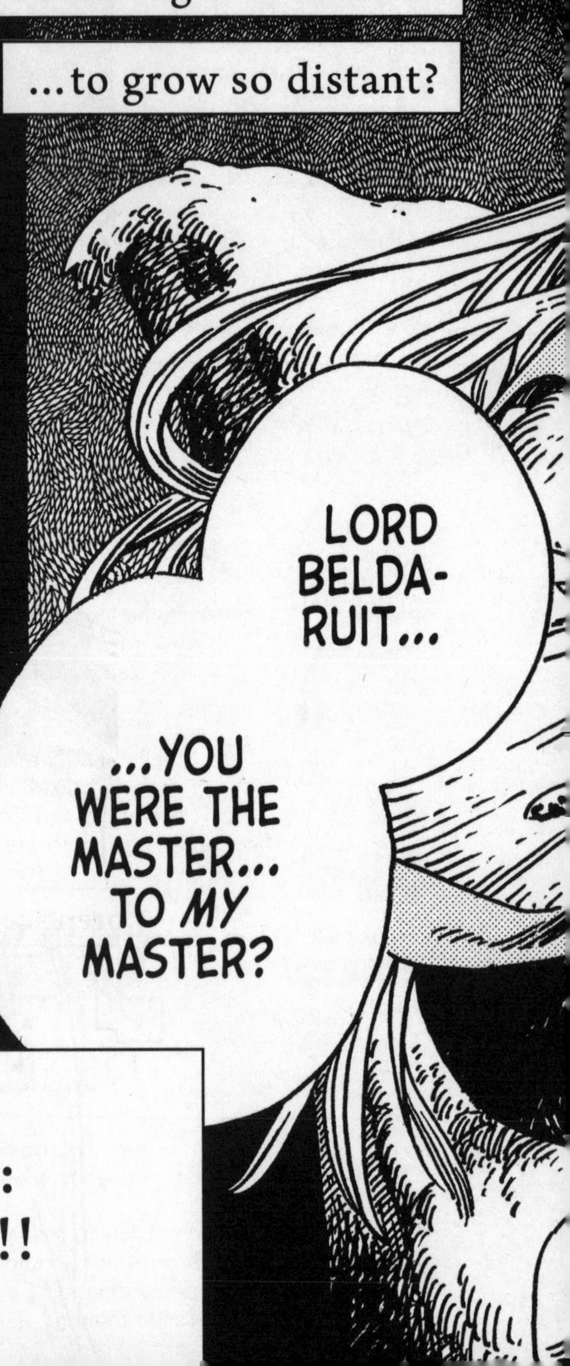
LORD BELDA-RUIT...
...YOU WERE THE MASTER... TO *MY* MASTER?

VOLUME 7:

COMING SOON!!

Witch Hat Atelier 6 is a work of fiction. Names, characters, places, and incidents are the products of the author's imagination or are used fictitiously. Any resemblance to actual events, locales, or persons, living or dead, is entirely coincidental.

A Kodansha Comics Trade Paperback Original
Witch Hat Atelier 6 copyright © 2019 Kamome Shirahama
English translation copyright © 2020 Kamome Shirahama

Published in the United States by Kodansha Comics, an imprint of Kodansha USA Publishing, LLC, New York.

Publication rights for this English edition arranged through Kodansha Ltd., Tokyo.

First published in Japan in 2019 by Kodansha Ltd., Tokyo as *Tongari Boshi no Atorie*, volume 6.

ISBN 978-1-64651-010-8

Original cover design by SAVA DESIGN

Printed in the United States of America.

www.kodanshacomics.com

9 8 7 6 5 4 3 2
Translation: Stephen Kohler
Lettering: Lys Blakeslee
Editing: Haruko Hashimoto
Kodansha Comics edition cover design by Phil Balsman

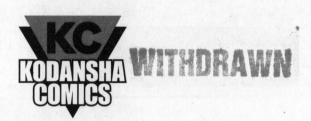

Publisher: Kiichiro Sugawara
Vice president of marketing & publicity: Naho Yamada

Director of publishing services: Ben Applegate
Associate director of operations: Stephen Pakula
Publishing services managing editor: Noelle Webster
Assistant production manager: Emi Lotto, Angela Zurlo